The Secret Journal of Dr Watson

Phil Growick

Paperback ISBN 9781780921327
ePub ISBN 9781780921334
PDF ISBN 9781780921341

Published in the UK by MX Publishing
335 Princess Park Manor, Royal Drive,
London, N11 3GX
www.mxpublishing.com

Cover design by www.staunch.com

For my four: Maiju, Kevin, Matt & Jamie

AUTHOR'S NOTE

Many of the characters in this book are historical personages. In this narrative, as well as in history, all were at their posts as described herein.

The Romanovs, The Imperial Russian Family
George V, King of England
Sidney Reilly, SIS (Secret Intelligence Service) Master Spy
David Lloyd George, Prime Minister of England
Vladmir Illyich Lenin, Head of the Bolsheviks
Arthur Balfour, Foreign Secretary
Father Storozhev, local priest at Ekaterinburg
Sir George Buchanan, British Ambassador to Russia
Admiral Alexander Kolchak, "The Whites" Supreme Leader
Thomas Preston, British Consul at Ekaterinburg
Arthur Thomas, British Vice-Consul at Ekaterinburg
Yakov Yurovsky, Commandant at the Ipatiev House
Alexander Beleborodev, Bolshevik Commissar of the Urals Soviet
Count Otto Von Mirbach, German Ambassador to Russia
Major General Frederick C. Poole, Supreme Commander,
Allied Invasion Force, Archangel

Contents

Preface

My name is Dr. John Watson. The grandson and namesake of the Dr. John H. Watson who wrote the remarkable stories about his adventures with Sherlock Holmes.

My practice is at 43 Dover Street, Kensington. I'm affiliated with St. Bartholomew's Hospital. I was born on December 28, 1954 in London; my wife, Joan, was born here, as well. We have two sons: Jeffrey, age twenty, and James, age nineteen.

I never knew my grandfather as he died before I was born, but in 1993, he spoke to me. Across seventy-five years of history, his voice came through as clear as if he spoke to me directly.

I came into possession of a journal kept secret as per his instructions. What he wrote will irrevocably change a major piece of world history; that is, if you wish to believe him. I, of course, absolutely do.

My grandfather, from everything my family told me, and from everything I've ever heard or read about him, was an extraordinarily decent, loyal, loving and truthful individual. That he cared about people is evident from the fact that he was a physician. And if he wasn't such a damned good one, my father wouldn't have followed in his footsteps.

The whole world knows the care and love that my grandfather put into his stories about Holmes. The love he had for that man is palpable in every word, every syllable and every punctuation mark. Everyone knows the pains my grandfather went to in order to make sure that the truth of each adventure was recounted faithfully.

From every bit of evidence available, it seems that my grandfather was incapable of telling a lie. In fact, the one person in the world who knew that better than anyone else, my grandmother Elizabeth, used to laugh as she told me stories of how grandfather would jumble his words, head down, trying not to lie about some horrible new crime to which Holmes had made him privy. She said she'd purposely ask him about the more grisly details just to see how boyish his discomfort would make him; and that she'd finally release the poor man from his torment with what she called "a private laugh heard only by him."

I still miss her. She's been gone now over thirty years, but she made my grandfather seem as alive as she was. So even though I never knew him, I knew him better than most.

Therefore, what my grandfather wrote to me is no lie. Yet it's so absolutely incredible, that even my solicitor advises against its retelling. Which is why I haven't gone public before today.

However, my grandfather left that decision entirely to me, and I've made it. After a brief description of how I came into possession of my grandfather's secret journal, I'll simply let the words of his journal speak to you as his words have spoken the truth to unimaginable millions since his first published adventure with Sherlock Holmes.

On the afternoon of August 10, 1993, while I was still in my Kensington office, I received a telephone call from Wyatt & Stevens, the solicitors who had handled my grandfather's affairs, and who, like a family heirloom, were passed down to my father, and then to me. I'm personally represented by Christopher Wyatt, the grandson of Alistair Wyatt, the man who directly represented my grandfather. And like our fathers before us, Chris and I have been friends since very early childhood.

In this day and age, that two families should share such continuity, and that two grandsons should maintain the same business relationship is probably without equal. Be that as it may, that tight family bond has served me very well.

After the usual pleasantries, Chris told me to be at his offices at five minutes to midnight, August 12. At first I thought he was playing with me.

"Chris, you're joking. What are you talking about?"

"John, I have a sealed package here from your grandfather. It was sealed in 1920 and my grandfather was told that it was to be opened by Dr. Watson's eldest surviving descendent at one minute after midnight on August 13, 1993. I haven't the faintest idea what's inside because we weren't made privy to its contents. But my father told me he hoped your father had lived long enough to open the package."

"Why didn't my father tell me about this?" I asked.

"Because he didn't know. Had he lived, I would be contacting him now and not you. In fact, from what I know, not even your grandmother was aware of this package. From the day your grandfather passed it into the possession of my grandfather, no one ever spoke of it again. Since your grandfather wasn't the cloak-and-dagger type, whatever's inside must be exceedingly important."

We both laughed at that one because of my grandfather's relationship with Sherlock Holmes. But I knew what Chris meant. My grandfather was not a secretive man.

I thanked Chris, hung up, and though I had patients piling up in my waiting room, I sat in my chair for the longest time trying to puzzle this out.

My wife, of course, expected exotic treasure hidden away from some extravagant Holmes sojourn. But I sensed something else. I didn't know what, but I just didn't think I was going to uncover the Kohinoor's equivalent.

Anyway, I awaited the date as anxiously as the birth of both my boys. Here was a mystery of my grandfather's making. I reported to Chris' offices an hour before time.

Chris was there alone to greet me, laughing at my early arrival, but refusing to let me open my present before my birthday, so to speak.

What he did do, though, after handing me a much needed whiskey and soda, and I'm not sure if he did this to calm me or to torture me further, was to seat me in his private office, in his personal chair, and set the package down on his desk right in front of me.

It wasn't a fancy-wrapped package or any of the sort like that, but rather a fairly flat package, wrapped in thick, plain paper with the texture of burlap, and wax-sealed with my grandfather's personal stamp: a solemn "JHW" in the middle of the Hippocratic insignia. And when I first placed my hands on it to feel it, I knew instantly it was a book or journal of some kind.

Until exactly one minute passed midnight, Chris stood there watching me intently watching my package. Then with a happily taunting, "Good luck, John," he closed the door behind him.

The second he left, I split the seal and slipped the contents from the wrapping. I was thrilled and disappointed. I guess that some part of me did wish for fabulous wealth, which at a glance wasn't there.

But from the moment I opened the journal and read the first words, I knew I had something that paled the wealth of the Punjab. For there, in the unmistakable, erratic scrawl of the physician, was easily the most sensational Dr. Watson and Sherlock Holmes adventure of all.

MY SECRET JOURNAL

My dear descendent, first, please do forgive me for so concise a salutation, but I know not who you are, what you are, or even if you are. For as I write this journal in the midst of a winter less harsh than the Great War it is immediately following, not only are you not as yet born, but my son John is a happy boy of only twelve. Would that the events I shall shortly convey be half so happy.

Secondly, I again beg your forgiveness for the lateness of the hour at which you were asked to appear, but as you read on, you will learn that I desired this information to be yours at the literal moment it could be yours.

What I am about to reveal to you could not be revealed until now. The Official Secrets Act forbids the divulgence of information considered a state secret, or of vital importance to the state, or of detrimental nature to the state for a period of seventy-five years after the fact. And the information I reveal is not only all of those, but considerably more. For what you shall now learn runs contrary to every history book in every country, contradicts everything you have learned as a good subject of the Crown, and would, if made public, bring the wrath and condemnation of the world down upon England's ears. And since I know that you will be seated safely in my solicitor's office as you read this, I have no fear that you will fall over from the shock you are about to receive.

The world has been taught that on the night of July 16, 1918, in the Ipatiev House in Ekaterinburg, Siberian Russia, Tsar Nicholas II, the Tsarina Alexandra, and their children, the Tsarevich Alexei, and the four Grand Duchesses, Olga, Marie, Tatiana and Anastasia, were brutally executed by the local Bolsheviks.

It is a lie. A damnable, perfidious, perversion of the truth. Of paramount importance that it be believed at the time, it became sire to a family of lies so hideous, so twisted, so cynical, that I cursed my heritage as Englishman.

How do I know this? Because it was Mr. Sherlock Holmes, and me, who were sent to effect the Romanovs' rescue. And you shall learn later from this journal the events as they truly transpired.

And though I wrote of Holmes' quiet retirement to Sussex in 1903, he lost his life many years later in the midst of rendering the greatest of services to a beloved Sovereign.

Now then, the truth about that searing, Siberian summer, when the Russian world was Red or White, and millions were dying to decide the fate of seven miserable people. The Romanovs.

June 13, 1918

Early this morning, so early the sun had not yet risen, while my wife and I slept quietly at our home in Queen Anne Street, contentedly unaware of the conscious world, someone pounding against our door awakened us, sending my wife into an extremely anxious state and me into a headlong race down the stairs, shouting as I ran, for the pounder to cease.

You can imagine my utter amazement at opening the door and finding none other than Mr. Sherlock Holmes. Somewhat stunned I opened the door wider and he swept passed me and into my home.

"Watson, Watson, Watson…" was all he could manage while his frenzied dance continued unabated.

From upstairs Elizabeth called down, "John, are you all right? Who was it?"

"Holmes, my dear. It is only Holmes."

"Mr. Holmes? At this hour? What ever is the matter?"

"I don't know yet, my dear. Holmes is behaving rather peculiarly; even for Holmes."

"Are you all right, then?"

"Quite, quite. Please return to bed. Everything will be explained presently, I'm sure."

"All right, John. Give Mr. Holmes my regards."

I conveyed my wife's greeting to Holmes and asked him to sit. He did so, taking a seat by the fire while I took the one opposite.

Holmes' face showed the shared, yet contradictory, emotions of exultation and dread uncertainty. I'd never seen such a look on Holmes, nor on any other human being. It startled and frightened me, and kept me silent until Holmes spoke again.

"Watson, without a word of explanation from me, if I were to ask you to accompany me on a journey so secret that you cannot even confide in Mrs. Watson, and so dangerous that our lives would certainly be imperilled, would you agree?"

I surprised myself at my own answer, for it came like an involuntary reflex, or the at-attention response to the command of a superior officer in the field, "Yes, sir."

Holmes openly laughed, "Sir?"

Though embarrassed, I was full of curiosity, "Holmes, what is this all about? What is so perilous that it requires that you assault my door?"

"My friend, we are about to begin a task that might even have daunted Hercules."

"Hercules did not have your brain, Holmes."

He laughed, "And at my age now, I have not his strength."

It seemed an odd remark for Holmes to make since he had always held brain in much greater regard than brawn. Nor had he ever confided a question of age; though both he and I were no longer the young men of our early adventures. And since I then intently studied his face for signs of physical strain or ill-being, and found none, it was something else that worried me.

For the first time since I'd known him, Holmes seemed to be struggling with a restless doubt.

Then, so quietly as to be almost a whisper, he said, "Watson, we are going into Russia."

"Russia?" I shot upright, "Russia?"

3

Holmes' eyes widened at my response. But again, and with a small nod, he said resignedly, "Russia."

"But why Russia? There's a civil war on that makes our war against Germany look like croquet! They're slaughtering themselves with such gleeful insouciance as to make Attila envious. They're barbarous, Holmes, barbarous! I know that I said I'd follow you, but this is suicidal recklessness."

I was quite agitated now, and Holmes, knowing me as well as I thought I knew him, waited until I calmed down.

"But why, Holmes, why? Why Russia?"

And then, with the most calm, measured and determined of tones, with placid eyes to match, Holmes looked at me and said, "Because that is where we are needed, my friend. That is where we are needed."

Holmes' Astonishing Tale

Holmes then set about recounting the unbelievable events of the previous night. Had this tale been told by any other, I would have immediately sought the man a room in an asylum.

Holmes told me that at precisely twenty-two minutes past nine on the previous night, as he pensively fiddled in the study of his quiet villa that he claimed commanded a great view of the channel, he was shaken to see a rather large man with a deathly serious look on his face suddenly appear in the room. This man was in the company of a man even larger than he, and with equally grey a visage.

Holmes realised that he had no immediate fear of the duo since had they been intent on doing him any degree of harm, they would already have done so. Indeed, Holmes was now utterly intrigued.

"Yes, what do you want?"

"You are to dress, Mr. Holmes, and come with us!"

"I am, am I? Just who are you, and to where am I to accompany you?"

The larger of the two took a step towards Holmes.

"Get dressed, sir. We have our orders."

"I must say, gentlemen, for two such hulking individuals, you caught me quite unawares in my meditations. If I did not suspect your true profession, I might profess the both of you to be involved with ballet, so ginger were your movements."

Holmes said that the remark quite passed over their heads, which was probably just as well, considering the size and sheer density of the two.

Holmes asked the two if they would wait while he dressed in his bedroom, assuring them that he had no intention of making an escape, so keenly had they piqued his curiosity. But it was to no avail. They followed him upstairs and waited as he dressed himself.

As Holmes proceeded, he asked in half-jest if there was a particular manner in which he should dress; formally, for hunting, morning coat, etc. And he was quite surprised when a serious answer came back.

"Dress so as not to embarrass yourself before your betters."

As soon as he had dressed, the two took Holmes bodily, each holding an arm, down the stairs and into a large, black motor car with drawn curtains sides and rear.

The motor car was then driven to Eastbourne Station where a train was waiting. Homes noted just a locomotive and one passenger car with all the curtains drawn.

Holmes turned to the smaller of the two and said "Well, well, what a lovely idea; a train ride in the middle of the night. Charming. But you should have told me, so I could have packed. Will this be a long journey?"

The two men said nothing, physically escorted Holmes aboard, sat him down, one on either side, didn't say a word and stared straight ahead.

"And I don't suppose you would be so good as to tell me where this train might be taking me?"

The larger one then said "Home, Holmes" and laughed. The other just smirked.

"Very humorous, indeed," Holmes said.

The length of the journey was approximately one and one-half hours, and, as he had suspected from the moment he saw the train, he was now at Victoria Station. He and his unwanted companions made their way outside where another black motor car was waiting.

From the direction in which they seemed to be going, and the time quickly elapsing, he was convinced that he was heading towards a rather unexpected destination.

After driving for precisely twelve minutes in the middle of the night, in the middle of the capital of a nation at war, the motor car stopped. And as Holmes alighted, held again by "his nannies," as he later called them, he was happy to find himself in front of perhaps the most celebrated address in all England, save for Buckingham Palace, 10

Downing Street.

Holmes wasn't precisely sure if he was delighted to be at 10 Downing Street because it confirmed his sense of direction or deduction, or because he now knew for certain that he was in no danger.

The door opened before the trio as if triggered by their movements, and Holmes was brought through the hallway and led into the office of no less a personage than the Prime Minister, David Lloyd George, who stood there, obviously awaiting their arrival.

It was now a few minutes past midnight.

The moment Holmes and "his nannies" entered the room, he was released from their grips and the two closed the door behind them.

"Prime Minister."

Lloyd George, all nervous business, did not return the courtesy, and though Holmes was not overly surprised to find the Prime Minister at the end of his midnight journey, the reasons for it still intrigued him, and what happened next most assuredly did surprise Holmes.

Lloyd George, still without a word, opened a door to an adjoining chamber, and with the greatest conservation of gesture, bade Holmes enter that chamber.

In the darkened room, only two objects made themselves immediately discernible to Holmes. The first, a fireplace with intricately carved mahogany gargoyles framing a fire too large even for this uncommonly cool June night.

The second, and the most arresting, was a rather oversized wing chair facing the fire, hiding almost entirely its occupant; except for a perfectly manicured right hand grasping the arm of the chair so rigidly as to turn the tightened appendages almost white.

Holmes noticed the solitary ring on the hand, but before even his lightning mind could grasp its significance, the figure rose awkwardly.

Sherlock Holmes, the king of consulting detectives, now stood face to face with none other than His Imperial Majesty, George V.

7

"Mr. Holmes, so very good of you to come."

"Your Majesty, under the circumstances, I had very little choice."

"Yes, quite so. I do apologize for any inconvenience or disturbance you have been put through. Please sit down."

Holmes waited for His Majesty to seat himself, and when he did not, neither did Holmes, a fact not even noticed by the King, so deep was His Majesty's pondering.

"Mr. Holmes, what I am now about to ask of you must be asked by me and me alone. My government can have no official knowledge of this request, and you should know that it was I personally who asked the Prime Minister to summon you to me. Mr. Holmes, I want you to solve perhaps the greatest riddle of your life, and, quite possibly, prevent the greatest crime in history..."

"I understand perfectly," said Holmes calmly, "you want me to rescue the Tsar and his family!"

King George stared at Holmes in amazement.

"But Mr. Holmes, how did you, how could you..."

"Your Majesty, it is not a feat of Olympian magic, I assure you, but simple logic.

"To be summoned to 10 Downing Street in the middle of the night, I need not have been of significant intelligence to deduce that whatever the government wanted of me, had to be kept in the strictest confidence. And upon meeting with Mr. Lloyd George personally, I, of course, knew that whatever the matter, it was of utmost national importance.

"Upon seeing your fingers so powerfully dug into your chair, I immediately knew that whoever you were, you were deeply disturbed and desperately groping for a seemingly unreachable solution to the matter aforementioned or you would not be here in this room.

"I would have to be an imbecile to be ignorant of your

extremely close, familial and personal relationship with His Imperial Majesty, the Tsar, and an oaf to be unaware of the threat to not only his life, but to that of his family, as well.

"As soon as you mentioned a riddle and the prevention of a monstrous crime, it was not so great a leap to deduce the predicament."

It was at this point that His Majesty broke his tone to whisper to himself, "Alexei, Alexei, poor little Alexei." There was a brief and uncomfortable moment before the King again spoke.

"Mr. Holmes, because of who I am and what England stands for, I cannot officially ask my government to aid the Tsar and his family." Here, the King's anger began to rise with every reason he set forth to Holmes.

"I am reminded, by the Prime Minister, that I am a constitutional monarch, that we are still in the midst of the worst war our nation has ever endured, that the British people are happy at my cousin's misfortune, that there is, and will be more, violent social unrest here at home, and that because of these things, the government cannot be placed in the position of being a tyrant's saviour. That my own first cousin and his family should perish rather than reach safety on English soil. Does my own government not know that I am aware of these things? Do they suspect of me a limited intelligence, happily to limit myself to mere functions of ceremony? By God, Mr. Holmes, no subject ever felt chains as biting as mine at this moment."

The King had now turned to face Holmes directly, his eyes fixed fiercely on Holmes', a look, Holmes later said, "of commanding Majesty."

Perhaps for the only time in his life, Sherlock Holmes was held mesmerized.

"Mr. Holmes, I am fully aware of the great service you rendered unto your country in what your Dr. Watson called 'The Naval Treaty'; and that alone has given you valuable grounding in the delicate and arcane realm of international diplomacy. But you have remained outside of government, retired, untainted, and there would be no reason to suppose another involvement at this time.

"I shall not appeal to your patriotism. I shall not appeal to your loyalty as my subject. But I shall appeal to your sense of humanity and ask you to believe me when I say that in all the Empire, it is you alone who can accomplish this miracle."

His Majesty finished speaking and took a small, gentle step towards Holmes, his eyes still holding Holmes as fixed as a fly in a web. Then he upturned both hands towards Holmes.

"Will you help me, Mr. Holmes?"

The question was a command; quiet and calm, yet a command nonetheless.

"I will, sir."

The Bargain

As Holmes walked back out into Lloyd George's private office, the Prime Minister seemed as nervous as ever. And this time, he spoke.

"Well, Mr. Holmes, quite a lot for one evening, I surmise."

"Indeed, Prime Minister."

"Mr. Holmes, when you helped the government with that nasty naval business, I was not yet Prime Minister, as you know. My philosophy on certain delicate, international matters differs much from that of my predecessor. We've been in this damnable war since 1914 and now we have some end in sight. The Americans are hot and heavy in the breach and they're turning the tide. We need their guns and butter, so to speak, and our people especially need the butter.

"The American President, Mr. Wilson, is still a naif, as far as I'm concerned, and for all his sermonizing, he just doesn't grasp the realities of geography nor the concept of empire."

"Perhaps he does; all too well."

Lloyd George looked at Holmes harshly.

"I don't need your editorializing at this hour, nor at any other, Mr. Holmes..." Holmes cut him off.

"Then with all respect, Prime Minister, I need not a parochial Sunday school lesson on world politics."

The Prime Minister's expression changed to that of one who knows he's in for a battle of wits, and who now fiercely suspects that he may be the loser.

"Quite. Then, Mr. Holmes, I shall come to the point. My government cannot upend the political or martial boat. Yet I, in all good conscience, cannot refuse my Sovereign his request without going to my end heaping calumny upon my soul. And there are others, invisible others, who share my sentiment entirely.

"However, there are those who would use the knowledge of this night to further some ulterior, republican motive. There are enemies who would use this against us in the arena of world and

11

internal politics. And there are those, simply in opposition to my government, who would use this to try to oust me in the middle of this war.

"Mr. Holmes, we already have men in place in Russia; put there before the hostilities commenced in August 1914, put there before the century was born. These and others have supplied life's blood information to our intelligence services, and a special, trusted few have matters in the ready.

"I cannot and will not tell you more at this juncture, only that you will be afforded every aid it is possible to provide. All that will become known to you as you need it.

"Now it is imperative that you leave as soon as possible, because you are going into Russia as an infinitesimal portion of a force of invasion."

"An invasion? Ah, Archangel," and Holmes waited smugly for the inevitable reaction of the Prime Minister.

"Good God, man! How did you know? Are there lips flapping like sails again in the Admiralty?"

"Calm yourself, Prime Minister. I have not obtained this information from some careless officer. On the contrary, all men in service whom I've met have been most circumspect."

"But how then?"

"Sir, it is no geographical conundrum that once the English held Murmansk..." here Lloyd George instantly interrupted.

"At the Bolsheviks' request, mind you. At their request."

"Yes, of course; the logical port large and close enough to hold an invasion force would be Archangel. And since the civil war has been especially heavy in that unfortunate part of Russia, I should naturally suspect that the Allies would want to secure that area for themselves."

"You mean to ensure neutrality, don't you?"

Holmes' eyes narrowed slightly, "Of course, by all means, neutrality."

For the first time, Lloyd George seemed to actually exhale.

"You know, Mr. Holmes, I have often read of your exploits and unique deductive powers, but until this moment, I had no personal appreciation of them."

"Ah, yes, well, this was merely one of the more simple paradoxes."

"Really, well perhaps you might like to predict the outcome of the war, as well. I mean the precise outcome, since it is already evident that we shall win this war at any time now."

"Prime Minister, the day the war began, I wrote the war's virtual history, which I then sealed and placed in the care of Dr. Watson, with specific instructions that it not be opened until the war was over."

"Did you, now? And what had you predicted?"

"Deduced, Prime Minister, deduced. And since I no longer have my history in my possession, and have given such specific instructions to Dr. Watson, I would rather not make mockery of my loyal friend's diligence by despoiling my own dictum."

It was clear to Holmes that he and Lloyd George were not getting on, at all. And as Holmes later said to me in the utmost of confidence, he had the distinct feeling that had he not been needed for this particular task so urgently, Lloyd George could easily have dispensed with him.

I asked Holmes what he meant by that remark, and looking straight and intently into my eyes, as if he were trying to physically send his answer to me through the sheer power of his will, he said, "Fair is foul and foul is fair: Hover through the fog and filthy air."

Based upon the events that were to grimly unfold over the next several months, and furtive hints from Holmes along the way, I could not but help to wonder if Holmes in fact did have some premonition as to an undeserved end. That he had instantly grasped that fact upon speaking with the King: once his necessity was ended, he could, and must, be dispensed with.

The conversation continued between Holmes and Lloyd George.

"Very well, Mr. Holmes, keep your prognostications to yourself. While Rome burns, you fiddle. Have it as you will. But I hope I make myself clear: you and I have never met. You have never been here. The person with whom you spoke in the other room does not exist. Not even this room exists. This all could be nothing more than a cocaine-induced hallucination; something with which, I understand, you are more than familiar."

Holmes bridled, but chose not to give the Prime Minister the satisfaction of a reaction.

The Prime Minister continued to bore into the wound.

"You will pack what you need and leave immediately. The two gentlemen who fetched you to me will see you safely home and then onto your place of embarkation. You will say nothing to anyone you should encounter until you are with those who will accompany you on this task. Do I make myself absolutely clear, Mr. Holmes?"

"As clear as your explanation during The Marconi Scandal," said Holmes, referring to the scandal which led to an investigation in the House of Commons in 1913. A shady matter, indeed.

"But you now understand me. From the moment of illumination as to this task from the gentleman who does not exist, I comprehended completely its implications and I accept all save one: I shall need the assistance of one without whom, I fully believe this undertaking shall lead to failure."

"And who may that be, pray tell?"

"Dr. Watson."

"Dr. Watson? Your chronicler? Out of the question."

Holmes smiled.

"To what does Dr. Watson owe this casual dismissal?"

"From what I have been told, your Dr. Watson is a mere tail of the dog," Holmes' smile faded slightly, "an errand boy with a minor literary talent for turning your aid to Scotland Yard into stories for the masses."

"Given the circulation of The Strand Magazine, Prime Minister, I think it is clear that Dr Watson's literary talent is a little more than that."

Lloyd George was unmoved.

"Dr. Watson, as shall all of your intimates, remain innocent of this evening's events."

"On the contrary, Prime Minister, Dr. Watson shall accompany me or you shall be forced to seek aid elsewhere."

"How dare you say this to me? How dare you?"

Lloyd George's voice raised to such levels that Holmes' two nannies burst into the room. Lloyd George waved them out vigorously.

"Who do you think you are, Mr. Holmes?"

"The man that you need."

"Arrogance as well as disloyalty?"

"Disloyalty! You call me disloyal! Have I not already agreed to undertake this task knowing more than well the many dangers to my very existence? Disloyal, for demanding the aid of the one man whom I believe with all my being to be indispensable to the success of that task? Retract your words, sir, now, or I swear that I shall re-enter that room so that the gentleman who does not exist shall learn of your words."

Lloyd George was in absolute, yet silent, fury. Holmes, ever equitable, reported that not only did Lloyd George fight to contain that fury quite admirably, but that as he did so, his boar's bristle moustache stood so virtually on end that Holmes suspected he had been hiding tusks.

Finally Lloyd George calmed himself, sat in his chair, clasped his hands together on his desk, pointed at Holmes, yet did not look at him, and almost inaudibly asked, "Just why is this Dr. Watson so indispensable to you, Mr. Holmes?"

The smile had returned to Holmes' face.

"Sir, I am a complex individual and take quite a time to be gotten used to. Not only has Dr. Watson succeeded in that unenviable task, but through the years and countless cases in which he has aided me, we have established a symbiosis of sorts that has become second nature to us both.

He has not only chronicled my cases, as you have stated, but he has been part of the very fabric of each and every one. He has provided succour when it was needed, a firm hand upon my psyche when called for, and unending trust through all. No man could ask for a better friend nor brother, for that is what he has become to me. Even my own blood, Mycroft, has not meant to me what Watson has.

"Further, Dr. Watson, as his title states, is a physician. And if memory serves, a particularly important member in this undertaking of mine has constant need of a physician, has he not? I believe he is a haemophiliac?"

"You have made your point, Mr. Holmes."

Lloyd George looked at Holmes with all the bitter vengeance of the supplicant. Holmes sat opposite, his very proximity demanding a response from the P.M.

"Mr. Holmes, the more people who are involved in your task, the more opportunity for mistake. We cannot afford mistakes. We have had too many in recent years."

"There shan't be any on this occasion."

"What guarantee have you?"

"Why I should have thought that quite plain, sir. My life."

"That is no guarantee at all. You can be struck by a hansom cab crossing Piccadilly," Lloyd George spat.

Was this a threat? A warning of some sort?

"Where I am off to, there are no hansom cabs."

Lloyd George unclasped his hands, stood, crossed the room to the door and opened it. As Holmes rose and moved to leave, the Prime Minister took hold of his left arm.

"You shall have your Dr. Watson. But remember this: his fate is in your hands. Should you fail, the consequences will not only crush a certain person, but will most certainly, and quite literally, crush those who failed."

Holmes pulled his arm free.

"And does that not include you, Prime Minister?"

"You forget, Mr. Holmes, this night never happened."

And with that, Lloyd George shut his door and Holmes went back into the black morning; a reluctant charge still, of his two Neanderthal nannies.

At this point, Holmes was brought straight to my home where he proceeded to rouse the household with his pounding on my unfortunate front door.

I now knew all, or thought I did, and understood completely why we had to go into Russia. But what, I thought to myself, what will I ever tell Elizabeth?

And as if he had read my mind, Holmes said, "Leave Mrs. Watson to me, my friend. You shan't have to dissemble on my account."

Holmes suggested that he leave immediately to gather what clothing and equipment he would need from acquaintances in London who could help. This would give me time to begin my own packing. As for my wife, he would attend to her questions upon his return; which he felt, would be no more than a few hours hence.

With that all agreed, I accompanied Holmes to the door, and there, waiting next to the large, black motor car, I saw for the first time, the nannies of whom Holmes spoke. When Holmes walked down the stairs and paused for a moment at the vehicle's side, I saw precisely how large they were.

Holmes got into the vehicle, with the larger of the two right behind. Although, I was not sure, I thought the smaller gave me a tiny,

17

knowing nod, as if to say, "Don't worry." With that, he, too, hopped inside, and the motor car, still with its curtains drawn, sped off into a city receiving its first morning light.

We're Off

In three hours Holmes was back, and he hadn't been so excited or happy since his successful solution of the mystery I came to call "The Adventure of the Second Stain."

Holmes was buoyant, and knowing full well the daunting task that lay ahead, I thought his actions incongruous, to say the least.

"What is it, Holmes," I asked, "that makes you flit about so?

"I am merely smacking my lips at the challenges ahead and of how I shall overcome them."

"But Holmes, our burdens are behemoth. They should weigh one down, not buoy one up."

"No, no, Watson. The burdens, or challenges to which you refer, are quite separate from mine."

I shook my head in absolute puzzlement at this newest, inscrutable Holmes remark. What challenge ahead could be separate from his? And it is only through time that I dare to suppose that what Holmes had been referring to was linked somehow to David Lloyd George. To some hidden, yet mutually understood, contest of the two. But what was it? Did it pertain to the unseemly words spoken at their clandestine meeting? Or was it something more visceral between the two?

You shall learn of this later; because even though I shall have to reveal to you what all this meant, and must do so in utmost sorrow, I have this compulsion to keep its meaning cryptic at this point in my journal, hoping that you shall unravel the meaning yourself, before it is divulged to you.

And should you wonder why this completely illogical compulsion on my part, perhaps it is some deep, inner longing to find in you, strong traces of me. No, that is not it. I long for you to find in yourself, Holmes. Such irrationality on the part of a physician, no doubt, comes as a shock. But I feel that you may need the test. Tests to which I found myself continually subjected by Holmes.

Holmes suggested that perhaps now was the proper time for him to speak with Mrs. Watson. I wholeheartedly agreed as I had, with tremendous difficulty, remained silent through her questioning, more thorough and sustained than any given by Mr. Sherlock Holmes and the whole of Scotland Yard combined.

Elizabeth and I had married in 1903. Holmes was later to complain that my absence had forced him to record his own account of the case he later entitled "The Blanched Soldier". He did however admit that it had demonstrated to him that writing up his cases for a literary audience was harder than he had at first supposed.

Mrs. Watson was seated nervously in our solarium, waiting for Holmes, who repeated to me on our journey, verbatim he claimed, the extent of their conversation; although, I learned later that he had lied.

"Well, Mr. Holmes, after all this time, where are you dragging our John now?"

"Dragging, Mrs. Watson? Do you see a rope around Watson's waist and I pulling maniacally at the other end?"

"Do not play your word games with me, Mr. Holmes, for we both love John, do we not?"

"That is so. And that is why I can tell you, with utmost truth, that I would perish myself rather than cause him even a scratch."

"I know that, too, Mr. Holmes. There is no finer friend to John than you. Yet I feel that there is something very different about this particular matter. Just my feminine feeling if you will, but I am as certain of this as I am of the sun rising tomorrow morning."

"Mrs. Watson, because of what your husband and I have been through together, much of which you have read or heard about, you know full well that there are sensitive things of which we may not speak."

"I am fully aware of that, Mr. Holmes. But this matter, as I have said, seems eerily different and frighteningly dangerous."

"Has Watson communicated to you any hint of danger?"

"Mr. Holmes, don't be foolish. You know as well as I that

John is as a sphinx where you are concerned. No, it is because of what he has not said that I fear so."

"Then listen to this, please, madam. It is true, where Watson and I go there is more danger than he has faced since Afghanistan. But his service to his country in that awful place has been one of the shining points of his life. He bears his scars for England nobly. Remember this as well, young John is much to live for. By the way, where is he? I've not seen him about."

"He is away for a visit with my parents in Yorkshire for the blooming of spring, one of my fondest memories of childhood; and something that John and I wish him to experience likewise each year. But please don't change the subject, Mr. Holmes."

"Mrs. Watson, your husband loves you and your son above all else in this world. But there are other husbands and fathers who are serving their nation at this time of travail who have not been as fortunate. Watson knows this. At the time when fate has finally chosen to ask a favour of him, he knows that he must grant it. He would not be who he is if he stayed behind. He would not be the man you love so devotedly. He would not be the brother I have taken by choice."

"Then take him, Mr. Holmes. I place his soul and his safety in your hands. And I know that you will return him to me. And Mr. Holmes, God bless you. For through John, I have come to cherish you, as well." With that, Elizabeth had embraced Holmes, probably causing him some discomfort, and bidden him send me to her.

I went to her more reluctantly than I had ever done anything before. Facing wild Afghanis seemed infinitely more inviting at the moment, and I approached her with some considerable hesitation.

"You wanted to see me, dear?"

"Yes, John, of course I want to see you. I want to see you every moment of every day. I want to see your eyes laugh when looking at John. I want to see the way they sadden when you cannot help some poor patient. I want to see you sleeping at night, in almost the same repose as your son. I want to see you silently smiling at me

21

when we're alone in the privacy of our night.

"But for a time, and I don't know how long, I am resigned to not seeing you at all. I shall tell John that you and Mr. Holmes are off on another one of your famous adventures; I know that will please him as it always does. I shall tell myself that you are off on nothing more eventful than a carriage ride in the country. I shall lie to myself so that you shall not have to.

"I shall go to bed each night knowing for certain that you shall return to us in the morning. And arise each morning knowing for certain that you shall return to us that night.

"I love you, John. And I pray you return swiftly."

My wife then kissed me more tenderly than I ever remembered, and with tears in our eyes, I turned to join the waiting Holmes, totally unaware that I would not see my wife and son again for over one year.

Harwich

Holmes' nannies put my baggage into the motor car and we were on our way; the nannies in front with the driver, Holmes and I in the rear.

Since the nannies said nothing, I asked Holmes if they still possessed the power of speech, to which he laughed and nodded. Yet throughout our entire ride, for a period of close to three hours, not one word was exchanged between them and us. Indeed, they did not once turn their heads towards us nor towards each other.

Of course at this juncture I had absolutely no idea where we were headed, and after what I thought a reasonable lapse of time, inquired of Holmes just where he believed we were going.

"A most pertinent question, indeed, Watson; and if my bearings hold true, I believe we are headed for Harwich."

Harwich, during the Great War, was a most important naval base, and since Holmes' travel sense was as keen as ever, he gleaned that although Chatham, another naval base, lay closer, it lay southeast. Since we were aimed northeast, the only logical destination was Harwich, a distance of some seventy-nine miles.

I had never been to a naval station during the war, closeted as I was as a civilian in the heart of London, and I was immediately impressed with my first contact, smart sailors in full battle dress barring our entry at the gates.

They reacted sharply to the papers shown by the smaller nanny, and the sailor in charge pointed off towards the right as he and said nanny exchanged words I could not hear.

"It shan't be long now, Watson. In a few moments we shall meet the intelligence officer who is to guide us to our ship and perhaps even impart some new information."

Holmes was quite correct. For no more than four minutes evaporated before the motor car stopped in front of a small and evidently temporary building. The smaller nanny went inside, and after a few moments, reappeared and gestured us to join him.

As we went, I noticed sailors already taking charge of our baggage. The larger nanny stayed inside the vehicle, not glancing at us at all. Yet as Holmes and I passed the smaller one who indicated the room we were to enter, he spoke.

"Mr. Holmes, Dr. Watson, I have seen you both safely to your destination; those are the extent of my instructions. But," and here he hesitated, "good luck, gentlemen, whatever your task."

And with those unexpected words, he let the door close and joined his compatriot in the black vehicle which cautiously moved away from us, sinister no longer.

I looked at Holmes, "What do you make of that, Holmes?"

"Rather more than I expected, Watson," said Holmes as he moved down the hallway and I followed hard behind.

As we walked on I was surprised to see a quite young officer, who, in these surroundings, looked wet behind the years. He advanced with an endearing smile to greet us.

"Why, Mr. Holmes," his hand stiffly outstretched, "this is more than I had hoped for."

"Ah, you give yourself away, Commander. You were told to expect a V.I.P., but you were not sufficiently entrusted with precisely who to expect."

"Sir?" the officer was sandwiched between awe and evaluating a Holmesian deduction, and a coherent response appeared beyond him.

"And that, Watson," Holmes said to me so that only I could hear, "means that we shall be passed between many links on our chain, each link unaware of the strengths or weaknesses of that adjoining; and perhaps not prepared for the chain to break."

I was about to comment on that, but the officer was now holding out his hand to me.

"And this is Dr. Watson, Commander," said Holmes.

"An equal pleasure, doctor, I'm sure."

"Thank you, Commander," I said. After the handshakes and

smiles, our young officer asked us to sit.

"Forgive me, gentlemen, in my excitement it seems that I have omitted to introduce myself. I am Commander William Yardley, and I shall be your liaison at Harwich. I will escort you to your ship just before boarding," he stared at the clock on his desk, "which should be only a very short time now, indeed."

The young commander reminded me greatly of someone, and until Holmes and I exchanged that glance it hadn't come to me. Then, immediately, it did. The commander looked like a young Holmes. I don't know if Holmes noticed this, although there was not much that Holmes did not notice. But when it came to his own appearance and dress, Holmes seemed to be continually lost, or profoundly disinterested. And because of this resemblance, I felt very at ease with the young commander.

"Tell me, Commander," said Holmes, "might you happen to know where Dr. Watson and I are going?"

"I'm afraid not, sir. That information, I suspect, is most secret. In any case, and I do not mean this in an ill way, it has nothing to do with me. My orders are to see to your comfort and security while you are at Harwich, and to see you both safely aboard the ship now making ready."

"Commander, might you at least tell us its name?"

"Uh, I think so, sir. Yes, I do believe that would be within limits. You will be boarding HMS *Attentive*, a light cruiser. The captain is a splendid fellow; in fact, by coincidence, an old friend of the family. His name is David. Captain Joshua David."

"Splendid, Commander," said Holmes, "all those superlative biblical associations reassure me greatly." We all laughed.

"Gentlemen, may I offer you some lunch, or perhaps a drink?" asked the commander.

I spoke up readily, since I had not eaten since a pre-dawn breakfast brought about by Holmes' incessant excitement.

"Lunch would be welcome, Commander, very welcome."

25

"And you, Mr. Holmes?"

"Don't put yourself out on our behalf, Commander."

"Of course he should, Holmes, that is what he is here for, remember?"

"No bother at all, Mr. Holmes. Of course the fare is most assuredly not what you may be used to, but we do nicely here, even with the war on."

"Whatever is convenient, Commander," said Holmes, as he lit a cigarette.

The commander stepped out for a moment and then rather unsettled, returned.

"Gentlemen," said he, most unhappily, "I've just been informed that you are to report aboard the *Attentive* immediately. I'm sorry for the inconvenience and change of plans."

"Nonsense, Commander, plans change, you know," I said, remembering my own days on active service.

"Your bags have already been taken aboard, so if you'll both just follow me." He held open the door, followed us out into the hallway, and led the way towards our vessel.

Holmes' eyes seemed to survey each square inch of the station as Commander Yardley escorted us. I chuckled to myself as multitudes of sailors scurried to every discernible compass point; each attending, no doubt, to a mission that would quickly end the war.

Presently we approached our vessel and the commander made it official with an envious sweep of his arms.

"Here she is, gentlemen, HMS *Attentive*. And I shan't mislead you at all by confirming her as sweet and swift a vessel as I have ever encountered."

The Commander then paused at the gangway and again extended his hand to Holmes.

"I know not what adventure you are off to now, Mr. Holmes, but I wish I was going with you. Good luck, sir."

"Thank you, Commander. I hope we shall meet again when the war is over. But..." Holmes' words trailed off as he began upwards.

"Watch after him, Dr. Watson. We need men like that in England."

"Watch after him: Who'll watch after me? Don't we need men like me in England, as well?" Of course, I was just having sport of the officer, but by the dark look on his face, I instantly saw that I had truly wounded his sensitivities.

"No, Commander, I was only jesting," I said.

"Thank you, sir. I meant nothing untoward, I assure you."

"Nothing of the sort, lad. Good luck, Commander."

We shook hands, and as I stopped for a moment's look back in the midst of my climb, I saw the commander standing at attention, looking in our direction, and saluting. It was one of the most touching sights in my long memory.

Holmes and I were piped aboard in very fine style, shown to our quarters, which seemed cramped even for a small ship of war, found our baggage already there, and were then brought to the captain's cabin where he was waiting to greet us.

"Ah, gentlemen, do come in and sit down. It is a great pleasure, Mr. Holmes," he said, shaking Holmes' hand with both of his own, "a singular honour, Dr. Watson," and he then shook mine; but with only one hand. "I am Captain Joshua David."

The captain was a man in his mid-fifties, I would say, not wanting more girth at this stage of life, with thick dark hair that I suspected he coloured. He moved about as would one walking on eggshells, with his hands clasped behind his back. Other than this entirely unique gait, I saw nothing extraordinary about him.

"Well," said Holmes upon sitting, "I see that you were more informed than your young commander. He didn't know who to expect."

"Really? I wasn't aware that you were not brought directly to me. Which young commander are you speaking of? We have a surfeit of young commanders these days, you know. Were you inconvenienced in any way?"

"Not at all," I said, "it's just that we were about to partake of a light luncheon when we were summoned."

"Oh, I do beg your pardon. I shall see to your comfort post haste." He then ordered his steward to have luncheon brought up to his cabin.

"The Commander's name is Yardley, Captain. William Yardley."

The captain took on the typical "rub the chin, scratch the head" gestures of someone trying to appear in the act of taxing his brain.

"Yardley...Yardley, no, not familiar, at all," said the captain.

"But," and before I could say one syllable more, Holmes had jumped into the conversation.

"It is of no consequence, Captain. Tell me, if you will though," Holmes had risen and walked to a large map on the far wall of the cabin, "where are we bound? This map should show our destination."

"And that it does, Mr. Holmes. But until I receive orders, I'm afraid that I am as much a part of this mystery as are the both of you."

"You mean that you shall receive your final orders at sea?"

"That is exactly what I mean, Mr. Holmes."

"Well, then, can you tell us when we are to sail?"

"I can and I shall. We shall be underway presently. If we are not clear of Harwich within the half-hour, I will be very much surprised."

Lunch was brought to us, tepid in flavour as well as in temperature, but I was happy regardless and ate heartily. Holmes spoke little during the meal, so I regaled our nautical host with tales of the army; perhaps not the most intelligent of subjects to choose while in the power of the navy; but, we were all fighting the same war, were we not?

Once back in our quarters, Holmes checked the corridor to see if there was anyone about. When he was sure there was not, he sat, and I could see his mind adding, subtracting, dividing and sorting information at a furious rate.

"Well, Watson, what make you of all this?"

"Do you mean about David supposedly not knowing Yardley?"

"Or is it Yardley supposedly knowing David? Yes, that's part of it. But even before that, did you find anything curious about Harwich?"

"How do you mean?"

"Remember that we were supposed to be part of an invasion force? To Archangel?"

"Yes, and it seems that we are, with all these ships. Are we not?"

"Not in the slightest, Watson. First of all, if this were the staging point for an important invasion force, tell me this: how many soldiers did you see?"

"Soldiers? Why, of course," embarrassment had no greater offspring at that moment.

"Precisely. There weren't any. It was all naval personnel at Harwich. Not one troop ship. And I don't seem to recall a successful invasion without an army with which to invade. Furthermore, since when in all of British naval history, has its captains set forth on some great undertaking without specific instructions as to where and when? It knots my mind, Watson, to think them so contemptuous of my powers that I would believe this Captain David!"

"I don't understand, Holmes. Lloyd George told you himself of this invasion, did he not?"

"No, I told him. He only play-acted; brilliantly, too. Making me believe that I had deduced some deep military secret."

"I still am not following."

"Watson, you and I both know what our task is in Russia. But what if we are the only two, besides Lloyd George and his minute, inner circle of invisible others, who know it?"

"You've completely lost me now, Holmes."

"I am saying this: what if each of the links I had mentioned to you onshore, is not only unaware of each other, but unaware of what our goal is, as well? If they have been given only enough instructions, as say, to take us from A to B and no more, then who is to say what we are really about? For all intents and purposes, we could be on a secret mission to gather pollen!

"Watson, it is quite obvious by now that Lloyd George has led me as a trainer leads a reluctant thoroughbred into an unwelcome arena. Is it not then also possible that he has obfuscated completely? And if that is the case, then anything is possible - absolutely anything."

"But what about His Majesty, Holmes? Did not the King himself say that he had chosen you for this enterprise?"

"Indeed. And that is one part of this puzzle that does not fit."

"Well, if we are not headed for Russia, Holmes, where are we headed?"

"I still believe that we are being led to attempt the successful completion of our task. And if that is so, then we must still be headed for Russia. Indeed, most certainly then for Kronstadt."

"Kronstadt?"

"Yes, it is the naval base nearest St. Petersburg, approximately forty miles. It guards the way to the capital. If the Bolsheviks were politically practiced enough to invite such unwelcome guests as the English into Murmansk, to guard the capital from flank assault by the Germans and Finns, I am willing to wager there is another game afoot in Petersburg. A much more intricate game than I was led to believe I would be playing.

"I thought it a simple question of Red or White, rather like

30

which wine to choose for dinner, but this is deep, Watson, deep. As yet I cannot fathom the intent, but whatever it may be, I believe that for our direct entry into Kronstadt, the waters will be made calm. And should the German navy act as spoiler, it makes it the more interesting."

With that, Holmes lay himself down in his bunk; and for the first time in what appeared to be two days or more, he slept. I, in no shallow attempt at imitation, did likewise.

When next I awakened, some four hours later, I found that we were long into the North Sea, indeed far from Harwich, but only slightly closer to the solution for which Holmes was searching.

Later that evening at dinner in the officers' mess, we met the ship's elite. The officers had been briefed that we were special envoys to the new government in St. Petersburg, summoned at their request, to help them recover invaluable Romanov jewellery, which, when sold to rich capitalists, would be used to benefit the Russian people.

Throughout the meal Holmes said little, so intently was he dissecting Captain David. After but one sip of brandy at dinner's completion, David rose and began his arresting walk around the table.

"I trust you slept well, Dr. Watson?"

"To be perfectly honest, Captain, I would have napped well even perched atop the Great Pyramid." This brought laughter from all.

"I take it then that you are not fond of our arrangements?"

"Not so. It's just that I am a landlubber, many generations bred, and my body was greatly confused by an unsuspected turmoil, when it is used to terrain remaining stationary and happy to be so." More, and heartier laughter ensued.

The captain waited for the laughter to dissipate, and then, with great earnest, he addressed us all.

"Mr. Holmes, Dr. Watson, men, I understand that many of you have taken to guessing about our destination based upon the headings I ordered. Well, you can stop your calculations as I tell you what that destination is."

With all men, including myself and Holmes, physically bent forward, as you would expect from a crowd at a close horse race, the captain proceeded to pull down a large map of Europe; and then commenced his briefing in the style of a geography tutor.

"Men, as to our direction, Bremerhaven is portside. In about eleven hours time we shall be passing Jutland," at the mention of which, the men tapped the table, "then up and around Skaggerak, down through Kattegat Channel hard by Laesö Island, then down through Oresund, taking us into close enough proximity to Kiel to perhaps have the Huns salivating in wait. However, should we still be afloat, we then proceed northeast through the Baltic to Kronstadt."

Subdued comments from the officers indicated that they expected and hoped for some action.

I looked at Holmes as I always did when one of his theories had been proved true, but Holmes was studying the map.

"Pardon me, captain," I interrupted, "but what, precisely is the importance of Laesö Island?"

"Come Dr. Watson, do you mean that an old military man such as yourself is unfamiliar with that island?"

"Captain," I retorted, "I should like you to find the position of the Isles of Langerhans on your first autopsy!"

"Enough, sir," laughed the captain, "show mercy and I shall haul down my flag."

"Granted, captain," I said, "but in all seriousness, what truly is the significance of Laesö Island?"

The laughter was gone now as Captain David, with the composure of command, slowly looked around the room till he came again to me.

"It means simply this: that we are forced to penetrate the neutral waters of both Denmark and Sweden in an attempt to evade any confrontation with the enemy. And that in waters so narrow, there is no

32

way of knowing if we shall be successful."

"Sir," it was Lt. Leicester, perhaps the youngest of the officers present, "do you think we shall be engaged?"

"Well, Lieutenant, according to Newsome, the enemy should be all over the place. Both on the surface and under. If you ask me, they should be called 'rat packs' instead of 'wolf packs.'"

At this, the men laughed and concurred.

I studied the faces of all the officers, and to a man, they were now sullenly pensive.

Holmes shot up as if propelled by a giant spring.

"Captain, gentlemen, thank you for a meal of such illumination. If we may, I believe that Dr. Watson would like to join me in a stroll around your deck."

"Well, Mr. Holmes, this is not a pleasure ship with decks for promenade, but on a night as beautiful as this, I believe that the rules of war will not be irreparably broken if you have your stroll."

"Thank you, Captain, gentlemen", he gestured for me to rise and do likewise.

"Indeed. Captain, gentlemen."

The officers wished us good evening, Holmes and I left them there, now gathered at the map, and proceeded down to the deck.

"Well, Holmes, what was it that shot you from an invisible cannon?"

"Newsome, Watson, Newsome."

"Yes...?"

"A name thrown out so casually suggests frequent and informal conversations. In other words, a long acquaintance or friendship."

"So what great import does this Newsome hold for us?"

"Not only for us, Watson, but for all of England. For I heavily suspect that the Newsome to whom Captain David so innocently referred, is none other than Sir Randolph Newsome, the Deputy Director of Naval Intelligence.

"And since when does a Deputy Director of Naval Intelligence personally inform a mere captain of a cruiser, and a light one at that, about the chances of hostile encounter; especially when that data is usually laid out by some junior statistical actuary."

"I see. So you suspect that Newsome is in on it."

"Perhaps yes, perhaps no. One thing I do know, this ship is, supposedly, assigned to the singular task of delivering us to Kronstadt in one piece. And not even persons high in government, including prime ministers, can play loose with such a prize as this vessel in time of war.

"No, Watson, it seems as if we are being given every opportunity to rescue the Russian family. But I, like a donkey, must perform with a carrot continuously held in front of my eyes."

With that remark, Holmes turned away from me and disappeared into the black that enveloped the ship's bow.

I succoured myself with sleep, but was so suddenly and violently awakened that I smashed my head into the rear wall of my bunk. After rubbing vigorously, I noticed that Holmes was absent.

I became aware of a bleating sound and immediately understood its meaning. After jumping into trousers and grabbing my coat and life vest, I opened the door to find sailors running right and left as if bereft of direction.

As I stepped out into this madness, a tow-headed sailor came running up to me.

"Dr. Watson, you are to follow me, sir!"

"Lead on," I said and he started off. In fact he did so with so much coltish proficiency that he had to stop briefly twice to be sure I was still behind.

Upon reaching our battle stations, I was told that a periscope had been seen and that we were to stand to. Still no Holmes.

As I waited there virtually motionless, with everyone else in

34

perpetual motion around me, I asked myself, for the first time on this journey, just what was I doing here?

Out of the fog, I heard Holmes saying behind me, "Lovely night for a swim, eh, Watson?"

"Very amusing, I'm sure, Holmes. Why didn't you awaken me when you bolted from our cabin?"

"Come, come, Watson, you should know me better than that. I wasn't even in our cabin when this ruckus began."

"I suspected as much. Where were you?"

"Enjoying this beautiful night, Watson. Enjoying this beautiful night."

"Well, it shan't stay beautiful if we're dumped into the sea."

"I srongly doubt that, my dear fellow. After all, that is what life boats are for. Anyway, all we can do is hold onto this rail and wait."

And wait we did. After a few moments, all seemed as silent as a sepulchre. The sailors were all at their stations, heads moving in every direction, eyes trying desperately in the dark to make out an enemy movement or shape.

I sweated in spite of the crisp North Sea air, and was happy to see the same dew on the foreheads and faces of those in close proximity.

Suddenly the ship lurched up with an awful roll to starboard that rent me free of my grasp of the rail. It was Holmes who grabbed me as I began to fall past.

"I've got you, Watson."

"Thank you. Were we hit?"

"I don't think so, there wasn't any explosion. I think it was just a sharp, evasive move."

We then waited for what seemed some considerable time, but nothing more happened. Finally, the all-clear was sounded and Holmes and I permitted ourselves to exhale. Nervous laughter followed, mixed with quiet verbal exchanges and the omnipresent gesture of crossing the body.

Holmes and I, while making our way back to our cabin, passed young Lt. Leicester.

"Well," he said with a big, boyish smile, "you certainly can't fault us for not providing after-dinner entertainment."

We bade him good night again, fell into our bunks fully clothed, and this time, slept uninterrupted.

June 14, 1918

Upon waking next morning, mid-morning, in reality, I once again found Holmes missing. It never ceased to amaze me how little sleep Holmes required. As a medical man I had read case histories where people required as little as twenty minutes of sleep a night. I required the usual dose in order to function.

I renewed my practice of dressing and shaving with the seductive sway of a ship, and after a few, literally close shaves, my hand and eye became adjusted to the yaw. I believe I performed admirably; as well, perhaps, as if I had a scalpel in hand during an operation, in the midst of a bitter engagement with some wild Afghani hill tribe.

I made my way back up to the officer's mess where I partook of a very late breakfast and was informed that the action of the night preceding had been nothing more than a false alarm, and that we would shortly be passing Jutland.

I went topside and saw Holmes at starboard, looking, I surmised, in the direction of that hallowed place of battle. But before I could walk to him, I again chanced upon Lt. Leicester.

"So, Dr. Watson, I hope things are going well for you?"

"Yes, quite. Thank you."

We had reached Holmes by this time, and after hearty good mornings all around, Lt. Leicester took on a mock, conspiratorial tone.

"Gentlemen, you should feel honoured."

"Honoured?" Holmes asked. "How so?"

"Well, that was quite a show the old man put on for us last night. I guess he was just trying to impress us, him being new to the ship, and all."

"New to the ship, you say?"

"Why yes, Mr. Holmes. Capt. David only joined us about five days ago. Our regular skipper, Capt. Stanley, was promoted to a staff job of some sort at the Admiralty. And you won't blame me for saying that the crew still miss him quite a bit.

"This new captain is an all right sort, I guess, but we can't seem to find out too much about the man. Only that he was supposed to have been in at Jutland commanding another light cruiser, the HMS *Pegasus*. And that's the strange part about this. You see, I have a good friend who was an officer aboard a destroyer there, and he seems to remember that the *Pegasus* had been commanded by a Capt. Bartholomew.

"Oh, well, I guess it's all just some misunderstanding. Anyway, I must be off before the crew mutinies. I hope to see you later."

He saluted smartly and strode briskly away, a young man happy with his calling, proud of his ability, and looking forward to the future.

"Well, Watson, whether or not our good captain commanded the *Pegasus*, he's certainly an old sea dog from his ease of command and demeanour around the ship. But I do not think at this stage we shall accomplish an unmasking. Capt. David is now confirmed as merely the second link, although a much more important and formidable link than the first."

Within the hour, we were passing Jutland, rather larger than I had anticipated, and Holmes and I watched quietly as the officers and men came to a brief attention and then saluted.

Three days later, we were through the Oresund Narrows, and were about to enter decidedly German waters.

Battle

It was exactly eleven-seventeen A.M. when Holmes and I, and the men of *Attentive*, saw that which we secretly wished never to see: an enemy ship. A very large enemy ship.

Battle positions were sounded and we were told later that the German ship was a prowling destroyer; by no means the most potent warship in the enemy's arsenal, but potent enough for a peaceable doctor. Holmes and I were sent below.

I think that Holmes and I both shared the same feeling during the brief engagement: impotence. We could not fight back. We could not contribute martially. But I could contribute as a doctor and Holmes, with his knowledge of human anatomy, could certainly help.

From what we were told after the battle, this is what happened.

Our crew saw them before they saw us. Our captain immediately called all to battle positions and made ready for a run, knowing that we could not possibly out gun a destroyer. Not only did the Germans have ten-inch guns to our sixes, but the *Attentive*, like all her sister light cruisers, was built for speed and scouting, for escort and raid. Therefore, she was more lightly armoured and armed than our larger and more predatory ships of the line. So Capt. David was counting on speed and luck. He received both in moderate measure.

We were about ten miles distant when the Germans fired their first shots. They missed and our men gave a loud cheer.

But some of their second salvo found their mark and we were hit amidships. The two-hundred-pound high-explosive shell landed amongst the ready-use lockers of the rockets, causing those already loaded to explode. And from this one direct hit, all our casualties sprung, for there were no more hits. We managed to outrun the Germans who gave up the shelling only after night; though our ship burned and glowed in that night like a beacon.

There was fire and smoke throughout amidships and scalding debris hailing down thick and fast. As misfortune would have it,

Holmes and I were below the explosion and saw much horror at first hand.

Sailors turned into torches of pitch. Limbs severed or torn by massive steel splinters shooting about like arrows. Terrible cries for help lost amongst even more terrible cries. And the stench of roasting human flesh everywhere.

After the fires had been brought under control and it seemed as if there were no more wounded for us to treat, Holmes and I began a terrible tour around decks. After a short while, we came across young Lt. Leicester.

He was sitting upright against a wall, waiting for his turn to be treated by the doctors. Only his head was bandaged, and I could make out no other injuries. I looked into his eyes to determine pupil dilation when he recognized me.

"You see, Dr. Watson, we always provide entertainment."

And with that, he ceased living. I tried to revive him, but Holmes knew it was hopeless; and after a sufficient time, Holmes gently steered me away, back to our cabin, back from the hell we had just shared with five hundred men.

It was now the stillest part of night. But on that ship, we were part of nature no longer. We had just journeyed through a dimension known only to demons, and many of us would not come back easily.

But HMS *Atttentive* proved, as Commander Yardley had said, sweet and swift, and the crew were British through and through. Damage was controlled and repaired, our speed was maintained, and we sailed quickly on. And as Holmes had said, whoever Capt. David was, he was truly an old sea dog.

Towards evening, all hands turned out for the solemn burial at sea. Sixteen souls sailed downward; and as each released from its Union Jack slipped away, I wondered which was Lt. Leicester.

We were now well into the Baltic, nearer the end of our journey than the beginning, and I pondered mightily on just who and what awaited us in Russia.

June 18, 1918

This day passed, thankfully, with nothing to jar routine. The wounded men rested and healed, but the wounded ship did not rest. It pushed onward.

The captain sent for us this morning and told us to prepare. We would be on the island-base of Kronstadt before the end of day - if all went well.

We made ready, the *Attentive* arrived late afternoon, and by early evening, the captain came on deck to see us off.

"Gentlemen," he said, "your trip has not been a happy one. I wish you better fortune here."

We thanked him and then Holmes said, "Captain David, you have shown us your worth and wits in battle. It is we who wish you good fortune on your journey home."

"Ah, yes. Well, we shall be here for a while for more permanent repair, then we must be home rather quickly. I greatly suspect that Kaiser Willy will try to make our voyage home even more eventful. There is more to this business, you know."

He saluted as we went aboard the packet boat, and as we chugged into Kronstadt, Holmes and I saw what was left of the Russian North Fleet; battered so harshly by German guns and seamanship. Searchlights only served to heighten the damp air of death and doom that clung so tenaciously to that melancholy place.

Since March 3rd, when the treaty of Brest-Litovsk had been signed and took the Russians actively out of the war, a kind of limbo had engulfed all here, men and ships alike. They were thrust into a very personal purgatory.

As we neared the dock, Holmes and I focused on a large, black motor car with what looked like a military escort in front and behind. It was flying red flags of revolution.

As we stepped ashore, a Russian soldier opened a rear door for his officer who emerged and then strolled casually towards us. He stopped quite close, looked intently at both of our faces, took a deep breath and then, in a perfect English accent, said, "Welcome, comrades, I am Colonel Relinsky."

Reilly

Relinsky, as we found out later, was Sidney Reilly, about forty, wiry, with a chiselled face as hard as that of a statue, and eyes of such sharp intelligence, that, as Holmes told me later, he immediately sensed an intellect of the first order.

When Reilly removed his cap in the auto, he revealed coal black hair combed severely straight back; an indication of how this man kept his own persona so rigidly in check. And though, at the time, neither Holmes nor I had any idea of who this man really was, I found out much later how singularly important he was not only to our task and to Britain - but to the entire Allied cause.

In fact, in the complete history of my human contact, Sidney Reilly ranks as the only man who I truly believe was as extraordinary as Sherlock Holmes.

There were, however, many differences: while Holmes was brought up on the inside of society, Reilly was shunted to the outside (he had been born in Russia, the son of an Irish sea captain and a Russian woman of Odessa); Holmes, though born with a superlative mind, cultivated it through learning and books until he had gained more practical experience, while Reilly it seems, almost from the beginning, was thrust into enough practical experiences to last many lifetimes; Holmes used his knowledge and powers solely for good and aid to his fellow man, while Reilly used his, including a startling fluency in seven languages, complete with sub-dialects, not entirely for the betterment of his adopted country of England, but most certainly for the betterment of Sidney Reilly.

Yet he was so important an asset to Britain and the Allies that he could virtually name his price. Permit me to give you just three instances of the powers and incomparable exploits of this man Reilly, as I would learn later.

First, before the war, the Admiralty needed knowledge of Germany's submarine construction plans. It was Reilly who conceived of the method to obtain these plans completely shunning the usual cloak and dagger. He simply secured the post of naval armaments purchasing agent for a very important Russian boat-building firm. As such, he was feted at the Hamburg shipyards by the company of Bluhm and Voss, who, wanting to secure a rich, Russian contract, willingly gave Reilly all the plans England sought.

The second instance found Reilly entering Germany through Switzerland at the height of the war in 1916, gaining entry to the German Imperial Admiralty by posing as a naval officer, and making off with the entire German Naval Intelligence Code.

The third, and most incredible instance, involved Reilly being put into revolutionary Russia by the British. Reilly became Comrade Relinsky of the Cheka, heirs to the Tsar's Okhrana, the secret police, and rose so high so quickly, that an organized plot of his almost put him into supreme power. Lenin would have been dispensed with.

Such were the abilities of the man who now stood before us and continued his address.

"We heard of your near miss. I hope you weren't scathed."

"Only our souls," I said.

"Tell me," said Holmes, "if you may, just how does an officer in the Red Army..."

Reilly cut him off, "Not the Red Army comrade, the Cheka."

Holmes and I both knew of the infamy of that sinister organization, and wondered into what situation we had walked.

"Are we under arrest then?" asked Holmes.

Reilly laughed. "On the contrary, Mr. Holmes, you are under my very special protection."

"And how come we, British subjects, to be under the special protection of the Bolshevik Cheka?"

"By the same humour of the fates that has brought all this madness about."

He was answering in riddles. Was he talking about the task Holmes and I had to perform, about the revolution, or about the Russian

Civil War? Holmes pressed on.

"Well, then, how do you come by such perfect, Etonian English?"

"Ah, your ear is quite practiced, sir, and the answer is simple. I am half English, well Irish, to be exact, and I spent many formative years in the vicinity of very proper Englishmen."

These were clearly half-truths and evasions, so Holmes pressed him further.

"Then perhaps you may tell us this, are you working for us, or for them?"

At this, Reilly really laughed. "I say, Mr. Holmes, you are certainly not a man to lay soft with words, are you?"

"When the lives of two people are at stake, namely mine and Dr. Watson, I have no time for courtesies."

Reilly then looked hard and cold at Holmes. "Only two lives, Mr. Holmes?"

There was a long pause at that, until Holmes again spoke.

"Where are you taking us, Colonel Relinsky?"

Mockingly, I believe, Reilly said, "Comrade, if you please. We are all comrades here. And I am Comrade Relinsky."

"Well, I'm not your comrade," I said huffily.

"Oh yes you are, Dr. Watson. And indeed you will be. Gentlemen, you have nothing to fear from me or my men. They are true Russians and speak no English. But they do speak fluent Relinsky."

"Why I am a high ranking officer of the Cheka, and who exactly I am, is of no concern to you. What is your concern is that I will be your compatriot on every foot of your journey in Russia. There are many still in Russia who feel, as do some of my men, loyalty to the former government of this country. They are Whites. They wish for the return of the old order, or at least some noble to their liking. Privilege and power are hard commodities to accrue, and infinitely more difficult to accept the loss of. That is why a civil war rages in this

44

land. It is barbarism run rampant and is all for power and privilege. The rest is but rhetoric.

"I know why you are here, and I am placated that I will be aiding such men as yourselves in accomplishment of your task.

"Things are not always run as they should be by our comrades in England. But this time, it seems that someone has found some common sense. A marginal attribute of many, I have found.

"Now, to answer your question, Mr. Holmes, I am taking you to a safe place where you will both rest until you're visited by someone who has been instructed to meet with you. He is very important to our mutual endeavour, for he holds much power at this precise time. However, that power, which is implied, may vanish at any instant, based upon the prevailing political winds of the moment. On this topic I shall not say more. You will know as much as needed when the time is right.

Now we must board a small vessel to take us to the mainland, where we have quite comfortable lodgings for you; what in Petrograd is now considered a feast, and you will be as safe as if you sat in Parliament itself. The only other words I can give you at present are these: trust no one who is Russian, trust one tenth those who are British. As for myself then, by law of percentages, you should be able to trust me only one time in twenty." Reilly chuckled to himself on that.

We made the next stage of our journey without incident. Presently, with our guards front and rear, we stopped at what had once been a house of much means. There were discernible scars of battle about the house and its immediate environs, and other guards waited at the ready.

We followed Reilly in and found that the feast to which he referred was potatoes, onions, and some meat. Reilly watched as we ate, asking if the fare was to our liking, and remarking on how the room in which we dined, which I thought must once have been spectacular, but now was greasy and bullet marked, had recently been used as a makeshift morgue.

For all intents and purposes, our meal ceased upon that disclosure. And since it was now rather late, Reilly asked if we might not like a nightcap before retiring. I was amenable, and Holmes needed no coaxing at all, so fascinated was he, as was I, with our new companion.

Though the immediate soldiers about were, and acted, as his junior in rank, we sensed an unspoken compact between them that seemed welded as steel. Holmes said later that for all we knew, they might all be British agents; although, we both doubted that strenuously. We also dismissed the idea of mercenaries. Holmes felt that at times such as these, men with strong beliefs on both sides had, perhaps, even stronger hidden motives for their actions. Whatever they might be, we would have to trust in Reilly's control of his men and of the situation.

After pouring what Reilly assured us was one of the last bottles of Napoleon brandy in all Petrograd, and with some of his guards moving about quite freely, Holmes continued the conversation.

"Tell me, Comrade Relinsky, what is your exact rank?"

"I already told you, a mere Comrade Colonel."

"Come, come, now," prodded Holmes, "there is nothing mere in that, at all."

Reilly laughed again. "True, you are absolutely correct. How I shall enjoy our precious time together, comrades. I have not lately had my wits sharpened verbally by so skilled a rhetorician."

"Well, perhaps it's just the company you keep," said Holmes. We all laughed. The brandy was relaxing us all.

"I tell you, comrades, these are interesting times. My men are completely devoted to the work I do; although none are completely aware of precisely what work it is. Within my cadre of cut-throats, there are those I must trust with my life. And on any number of occasions, I have.

"The rather small man in back of me with the clean-shaven head is Stravitski. I knew I could trust him from the beginning because

46

he had killed his own father."

"What?" I gasped incredulously, almost spitting the precious brandy into oblivion.

"Oh, it was all very political and perfectly acceptable. The only other man who has saved my life, but only once mind you, so he still has a way to go before he's trusted only that much," he held up his index finger and thumb so that the distance between them would not permit paper through, "is the man standing behind the both of you right now with a revolver in his hand."

Holmes moved not a muscle and sat perfectly still watching Reilly. But I quickly turned to see this menace, an imposing brute with prematurely white, curly hair, a typical peasant-type, down-turned moustache, but who gave off not one vibration of malice. He indeed held a revolver, but it was pointed downward. He looked at me looking at him as if I were a naked bushman who had wandered into a royal cotillion.

"His name is Sergei Alexandrovich Obolov."

"And what is his crime?" asked Holmes.

"None that you or I would consider a crime, Mr. Holmes. But when the Bolsheviks, in their turn, overthrew Kerensky, Obolov here, called a comrade major a pig. So his tongue was ripped out."

"You mean?" I spoke no more, yet continued looking at this man.

"He is dumb. But highly intelligent."

"So even though these two fine specimens of Russian manhood have saved your life before, they are in no way to be trusted, even though you jest that you do?" asked Holmes.

"Absolutely not," said Reilly, "after all, what you do today is no guarantee of what you will do tomorrow."

"Life here must be very constricting," I said.

"That is one word. I prefer the term 'magnificently precarious,'" said Reilly.

We were now growing weary from our trip and our sips, and

47

Holmes suggested that we make our way to our chambers. Reilly concurred, and as he personally led us up a magnificent, circular stairwell of marble, with Stravitski and Obolov bringing up the rear, he said to both of us, over his shoulder, "But pray tell, comrades, what do you think of Mother Russia so far?"

"So far?" I said. "So far we have met nothing but soldiers, killers and martyrs."

Reilly stopped, turned, and after a laugh that tilted his head to the rooftops, looked down at me with eyes stretched wide and said, "But Dr. Watson, those are the only manner of beings who inhabit this nation."

Holmes and I had adjacent rooms, and I slept quite well that night in spite of the mid-summer phenomena when the sun refuses to hide itself in night. I also think that at some time the door to my room was opened for an instant while eyes peered to examine the state of affairs within.

June 20, 1918

Upon making my way downstairs in morning, I found Holmes and Reilly in animated conversation over coffee, tea, and some black Russian bread.

Both bid me good morning and I do believe that the omnipresent Obolov nodded. I sat and poured some tea while Reilly explained the day's agenda.

"I was just informing Mr. Holmes that your visitor should be here in approximately," he glanced at a most magnificent watch he kept in his tunic pocket, "one hour. In the interim, whatever questions I am permitted to answer, I will happily do so."

I turned to Holmes, "Well, what have you dug out of our comrade, so far?"

"Not much, I'm afraid. Comrade Relinsky is blessed with occupational lockjaw."

"Now, Mr. Holmes, from what I know of you, your mandible would prove as immobile as mine."

"Touché," said Holmes, "humour aside, you will not tell us more of yourself or your connection with our government, which, of course, Dr. Watson and I are at liberty to surmise. Allow me, from my own humble knowledge of the situation to put our positions to you for your own expert assessment."

"So you wish to attempt an analysis of the current political climate here?" asked Reilly.

"That is easy enough, and difficult enough," said Holmes, "since currents here, I understand, alter course with alarming frequency."

Reilly returned to our table, and Holmes, in a spellbinding mixture of satire, sincerity and suspense, laid out all of Russia on our table for our digestion.

"For Russia at the moment, to paraphrase Dickens, this is the best of times and the worst of times. Russia stands at the epicentre of its destiny. A move to the left, liberty; a move to the right, repression.

"The Supreme Soviet has moved the government to Moscow where it is desperately trying to keep power over, and order in, the whole of the Russian Empire. It is a virtually impossible task. Russia is not England, nor the British Empire.

"On one side, you have the Reds, the revolutionaries; wanting a new world for the people, and telling the people what this new world will be. Make no mistake, they would achieve their new world even if they had to kill every Russian, including themselves, to do it.

"On the other side, you have the Whites, the would-be restorers of the old order, supposedly made up of nobles and those loyal to the Romanovs and Christ; not necessarily in that order. In fact, while there are some of the aforementioned, many more are renegades, soldiers of fortune, and misguided opportunists believing that aristocratic titles lie in the crimson snow, ripe for the snatching.

"Between the two groups, Russia is being ripped to shreds. But there is more. Within the Reds and the Whites there are factions pulling centrifugally. Imagine, if you will, Russia as a giant carousel spinning so wildly out of control, that the Reds and Whites are flying straight outward, fully extended, and are holding on with only one hand; the other being used to flail about at the closest enemy.

"The Supreme Soviet in Moscow issues orders to the regional Soviets thousands of miles away, and if the regional or local Soviet agrees with the order, all well and good. If they do not, the lines go suddenly dead. Communication is cut for a time, until more satisfactory orders may be received. These local Soviets are fiefdoms in themselves.

"The same holds true for the Whites, basically, except that they have all the power and money of the combined Allies behind them. And therein lays the other mortal danger.

"The United States, Great Britain and France would have supported the devil in this war against Germany. So you had the three greatest champions of liberty in the world allied with its single greatest tyrant. The axiom about politics making strange bedfellows found no greater conundrum in all of human history to prove its truth. Although, of course, it really isn't a conundrum, is it? The enemy of my enemy is my friend, and so on.

"But here come along the Bolsheviks and dissolve that alliance. They make peace with the Germans, releasing a hundred hardened divisions to the Western Front to kill the boys of freedom. Even worse, the Bolsheviks are a capitalist's philosophical anti-Christ.

"So suddenly Russia no longer has any allies, which means she no longer has any money. This also means she no longer has any credence with anyone about anything, except, of course, with the people in power, and the people the people in power have their boots upon.

"Now, not only has Russia lost its allies, but those allies may quickly become enemies. Because as I've said, the allies are capitalists, and what could be better to capitalize on than the wealth of the Russian

50

Empire with no hand upon its purse? What self-respecting capitalist could refuse such an opportunity? Certainly not England, the founder of the philosophy; nor America, its most ardent adherent in the world.

"So in summation, the very civil strife that renders this nation prostrate, that starves its population and robs much of its next generation of its very life, is our friend. It shall shield us and hide us in very plain sight. And if luck were a tangible commodity, we should require but a thimble full to complete our endeavour with success."

I sat almost slack-jawed at perhaps the greatest single piece of analytical oratory I had ever heard. While Reilly, whom I suspected to be extremely knowledgeable of politics in the extreme, simply looked at Holmes and quietly said, "Bravo."

Reilly was as good as his word; for within the hour, our visitor arrived. As Holmes and I watched from a window, a Rolls Royce pulled up to the house, ostentatiously flying the Union Flag. The motor car was saluted by the guards and its passenger emerged stiff and formal, and strode in. He was none other than the British Ambassador to Russia, Sir George Buchanan.

Holmes knew of Sir George through one of the many acquaintances one makes in Holmes' line of work, and later confirmed my feelings about the man that I derived solely from our meeting: that he was ramrod Raj, a certain term of disparagement we used in the army to describe martinet officers; that he was cold, calculating and cautious; and that he knew his business hands down.

Of his appearance, it bespoke the man: fair, greying parted hair, a generous, upturned, Edwardian moustache, perpetually pursed lips, eminently formal attire, even for an Ambassador of the Empire, and a slim, hard physique on a moderately tall frame. His eyes were ice grey, the colour of the Arctic.

After a very brief talk with Reilly, Sir George was brought to us.

"Mr. Holmes, Dr. Watson, may I have the honour to introduce,

51

His Excellency, the British Ambassador to Russia, Sir George Buchanan."

We received firm, curt and correct handshakes and then Reilly bade us sit. Sir George spoke immediately and succinctly with not a word wasted.

"Gentlemen, your roles as envoys in this forbidding hour are much needed. Of course I know of your true intent and extend my personal thanks for what must best be termed a great humanitarian mission. I have been in contact with our consul in the Urals capital of Ekaterinburg, Thomas Preston, and he has been informed of your expected arrival between now and July 1, some ten days hence, barring any unforeseen problems.

"Colonel Relinsky and a small cadre of his men will be with you on your undertaking; and you shall be guided by a plan devised by Colonel Relinsky himself. After all, it is the Colonel who knows the Russians better than we do; and he has had some experience in these matters. I have not given him permission to divulge his plan to you, but will shortly do so.

"Upon successful completion of your task and your arrival at Archangel, you shall board a waiting ship which will take you all to safety out of this God-forsaken country."

He then abruptly stopped talking and with the swiftest of turns of the head to Reilly, and then back to us, as a gesture of indication, said, "Your plan."

Reilly nodded an acknowledgement.

"Yes, well it's as simple as a machine with only a few moving parts. The fewer the parts, the less chance of a breakdown.

"The particulars of the plan will be discussed on the train to Ekaterinburg. But the idea is simply this: we arrive as the Supreme Soviet's special detachment of the Cheka. We are to remove the Romanovs from Ekaterinburg because the Whites are coming too close and the Supreme Soviet has decided to put them on trial for the entire world to see. If the local Bolsheviks at Ekaterinburg refuse to turn over the Romanovs, they shall be told that they then will have to deal with a large contingent of regular Red Army troops being sent south to counter the Whites' advance north. It will not seem a happy prospect.

"Since my men and I are already Cheka, we should be convincing. If the locals wish to telegraph the Urals Soviet for affirmation, they will find that the lines have been cut. This will be blamed on White partisans, of course.

"Our information says the men guarding the Romanovs are mere jailers, not first-rate troops or first-rate minds. And, as Mr. Holmes has so eloquently expressed it, with just a thimble full of luck, we shall carry the day.

"As to the chase, should there be one, that is part of the specifics you will be informed of later." After a moment's pause and that unique Reilly grin, he asked, "Any questions?"

Holmes said nothing and I followed suit, suspecting that he had reasons for his silence.

"Good, well, there's more I should impart, gentlemen," said Sir George to Holmes and me. "I am sure that this is the most significant and urgent assignment of your lives. It comes from the highest authority and carries the fullest weight imaginable. It has been kept in the strictest of secrecy and there are but few in the entire Empire who know of its particulars. We are all counting on you and you must count on the Colonel and his men, with your very lives. I trust them implicitly."

Sir George rose. "I shall take my leave of you now. I must return to Vologda before Comrades Lenin and Trotsky. There will be much to do then." He shook hands with us all, and was gone. I looked at Holmes, he looked at me, and then we both looked at Reilly.

"Well, Comrades, so what did you think of the British Ambastardor?"

Holmes needed to think and made his excuses. He headed

53

outside and into the gardens at the rear of the mansion. As he did so he beckoned me to follow,

Once outside I spoke. "Well, Holmes, what do you make of all this? Especially Relinsky's remark about Buchanan?"

Holmes furrowed his brow and said, "Watson, I am now certain that Buchanan is one of Lloyd George's invisible others; as was Captain David. And though, as yet, I have not made the connection between them all, they are all in it."

"Together?" I asked.

"My dear fellow, I am afraid that 'together' may be the domino that sets all the others to fall into place. For while they are all most assuredly in this thing, are they all in it, literally, together? I am convinced that Relinsky knows much, but not all. I feel that he may well be the single most important link in our chain. And that deduction is not the most pleasant, by any means.

"Furthermore, I suspect that Relinsky knows there is something interesting afoot here, and that he will follow his orders, if orders there are, to see if the true meaning of this poison can be extracted."

"Holmes, I still cannot see it. I do not understand how the King is involved in this 'poison,' as you call it, whatever it is."

Holmes froze and smiled.

"That's it, Watson! Why, of course, that's it! The King is not at all in on it! I have foolishly allowed my mind to wander down an alley without an exit. Oh, the time I wasted trying to decrypt the King's direct role, and now the simple answer is there is no direct role. I am absolutely now positive that the King knows nothing of what is unfolding here before us.

"Of course, he cannot know because he should not know, but he does not know! And that is the important thing here."

"Holmes, please explain yourself."

"It's perfectly simple, Watson. The King, being the King, should never know of any arcane government activity that may endanger, or even embarrass, the throne. He is supposed to be above it.

Therefore, since he should not know, it is believed, through constitutional law and tradition that he cannot know; although, in fact, he may indeed know. It is a charade that governments play at and sincerely believe when addressing the public.

"But in our case, he truly is ignorant of events, officially and unofficially."

"Holmes, once again you are being opaque." We both smiled. I was at least assured the King was not involved in any underhand plot.

Holmes too seemed pleased. He produced his old, black pipe, filled and lit it and then resumed his walk around the gardens.

According to Reilly, we were free to tour Petrograd for a few hours, and we would have a small guard with us to be sure there would be no problems. He reminded us, as if he had to, that as yet, there was no great influx of British tourists into Petrograd, and that without the proper protection, we might be taken for something other than what we truly were; which, of course, was backwards since what we would have been taken for, should we have been taken for anything other than Sherlock Holmes and Dr. John Watson, was what we now truly were: British agents.

Reilly informed us further that after our tour that day, there would be one more person for us to meet. He would probably be waiting for us upon our return.

We drew Stravitski as the man in charge of our guards, and for the next several hours, Holmes and I were treated, if that is the right word, to the still-living history of the Tsars; and the signs of torment attesting to the Bolshevik Revolution and the birth of their new world order.

Our first stop was the Winter Palace, the Romanov official residence in the capital, built by Peter the Great. Compared to this incredible edifice, Holmes and I were forced to admit, Buckingham Palace seemed nothing more than a cosy, aristocratic cottage. However we were pleased this was so, because as Englishmen, we felt that such ostentation and indulgent opulence was totally inappropriate. It suited the tastes and requisites of slothful, oriental potentates swathed in silks; not the vigorous dynasty of the Windsors.

It seemed as if gold covered all, including the exterior of that monument to megalomania; the ceilings, the doors, the walls, the very air itself. Where gold was not visible, there were the most precious examples of marble, onyx, gems, and inlaid woods. There were objects of art everywhere, masterpieces covered the ceilings, and the Winter Palace housed the largest collection of Rembrandts in the world; this thanks to Peter, a contemporary of that incomparable Dutch genius, who he had become acquainted with while studying shipbuilding in Holland.

We were later told by Reilly that the gold would be stripped from all surfaces for the good of the people, and anything of any value would be sold or traded to keep the Revolution alive. Yet his words seemed as rote. They lacked spark or conviction, and were recited as perfunctorily as a schoolmaster giving a lesson for the thousandth time. Surely this was not the way of a fiery Red.

The tour continued through what seemed like countless numbers of rooms, until at last we stood in the very heart of the palace itself, the throne room. Here, indeed, was a throne for an emperor - or a god.

Peter had been nearly seven feet tall, and the throne, and room, were as immense as any Roman or Greek temple. I can easily see how the first instinct of any being, not free-born, would have been to fall on one's knees in abject supplication to the Tsar. This place would easily dwarf any to follow Peter who could not make up for want of gargantuan size with will or intellect; the former being no guarantor of the latter.

We knew from pictures that Nicholas II was a man of somewhat less than medium height; indeed, he was about the same height as our Sovereign; and when younger, the two were almost as identical twins. From the history of his rule, he seemed a man with distinct lack of judgment or even basic common sense.

That he was the autocratic Tsar of All the Russias was as undisputed a fact as that of George V of England being a constitutional King-Emperor. But what of the real man and his wife, the Tsarina? Were the stories true? Were the press reports accurate? Was he truly "Bloody Nicholas?" Had she been the dupe, or worse, of that blackguard Rasputin? How did they really fit into this Victoria Station of a throne room? Did they fill it with all the mystical pomp of imperial majesty? Or were they humbled by being void of true majesty from within?

We knew that we must leave these questions unanswered until we met the Tsar and Tsarina. This, of course, depended on whether we lived long enough for that to actually happen.

We slowly made our way back to our guarded motor car, and as we thought of what we had seen, Stravitski watched us intently, as if he were trying to gauge our thoughts. Whether this was for himself or for his master, Reilly, I did not know. But what we had seen deeply affected both Holmes and me. For all that unearthly wealth had been stripped from Tsar Nicholas and his family, and now, like countless millions of Russian peasants, they were reduced to helplessly waiting for their fates; in their case, death.

I thought about the regicides of Louis XVI and Marie Antoinette and the parallels between them and the Romanovs. I recall feeling decidedly pessimistic about their future given such precedents.

We were next shown the cruiser Aurora whose Bolshevik guns had honed in on Kerensky and his government and made them finally realise that their noble democratic experiment was soon to be a victim of infanticide. Holmes indicated to Stravitski he had no desire to stop; indeed, he wished to return to our base. He was no longer in the mood for a tour.

The inactivity coupled with our conundrum was taking its toll on Holmes. He needed to feel physical movement of some sort to replace real progress in our task. Perhaps the train would be ready to take us way from this bacillus of a capital. Holmes would then gain the movement he required. He could feel the velocity and hear the clatter of track. He could feel that he was speeding towards his destiny; whatever that may be.

Stravitski did immediately as indicated and we were shortly back at the mansion, now a virtual armed camp. There were Red Guards and regular Red Army soldiers everywhere. Reilly was waiting for us at the door when we arrived. He came forward to greet us and before Holmes or I could ask anything, Reilly said we had a visitor; and that he was waiting, most anxiously to see us in what had once been the library. I shrugged at Holmes and we both followed Reilly.

The door was blocked by eight armed guards who came to attention upon seeing our Cheka Colonel; one opened the door. Reilly gestured us in, then came after.

As we entered and the door closed behind us, a small, bald man, with a short, pointed beard, and a fringe of red hair about his egg-shaped head, looked up from a book and with a big smile rushed toward us; one hand outstretched to Holmes, the other waving the book. He looked like one of those crazed, star fanciers you avoid at Covent Garden or the more fashionable music halls.

Reilly stepped to one side, and trying to compose himself said, "Mr. Holmes, Dr. Watson, I have the honour to introduce Comrade Lenin."

Lenin

For what seemed for a long time, but was probably no more than an eye-blink, Holmes and I did nothing except perfunctorily extend our hands to Comrade Lenin.

There before us stood the Russian Revolution and none too high, at that. The man was five-foot-four, give or take a little. Not that I am mocking the man, I am a physician and do not make just of another human's stature. Holmes and I were astounded to learn, through Reilly acting as interpreter, that Lenin was a huge admirer of ours.

It appeared that while in exile in Switzerland, he had consumed all of my works on Holmes, and seemed to regard Holmes as a kindred spirit of sorts. He had preached to his wife and to Trotsky that we were the type of men the Revolution needed: Holmes for his logical, unemotional mind, me for the loyal chronicling of Holmes' adventures; a trait Lenin ranked high in his need for a Russian version of myself. That is, someone to chronicle the Revolution for posterity and in Lenin's favour.

He bid us sit, which we did, and through Reilly, began to ask Holmes all sorts of questions about his methods of deduction and his opinion of Scotland Yard. Holmes was forthcoming, and even seemed flattered at Lenin's attention. But I personally got an uncomfortable feeling about Lenin's questions concerning our police methods. I could see, in my mind's eye, a monolith in the middle of Moscow with the attendant sign: Siberia Yard. The whole scene had too strong an air of absurdity.

After about an hour of fawning questions to Holmes and me, Lenin said that he had to leave to meet Trotsky, and then gave us the biggest surprise of all. He held out the book in his hand to Holmes, which turned out to be a Russian edition of my works, and asked both Holmes and me to autograph it; which, of course, we did. Holmes with an audacious flourish I had not seen before.

He looked at the autographed page as I remembered my boy John looking at a bright, red wagon my wife and I had given him for Christmas when he was only five. Then, gently closing the edition, he shook hands, straightened, became the Revolution again, and was gone.

Reilly looked at Holmes and me, drew a paper and pen from his tunic pocket, and asked, "Oh, can I please have your autographs?"

I asked Reilly how he could mock Lenin so if he were one of Lenin's minions. Reilly said that in reality, Lenin was a bourgeois at heart, and for all his rhetoric, was not one tenth the stone wall that Stalin was. Neither Holmes nor I had heard of this Stalin, and were told by Reilly that Stalin was from Georgia, he was not a true Russian. His mind was oriental in its quiet subtlety, and his only thought was of power. We were further told that Stalin had already gauged Reilly's potential as a powerful, future opponent, and that if Reilly didn't eliminate Stalin, Stalin would surely eliminate Reilly.

There were many questions Holmes wanted answered about Lenin, Trotsky, Stalin and the rest, but because now all was at the ready, and we would be leaving shortly, Reilly would only answer one question.

"Very well, then," said Holmes, "what did you tell Comrade Lenin we were doing here?"

"Comrade Lenin is an admirer, as you saw. He was told you were travelling incognito to catch a jewel thief here. He loves the cloak and dagger aspect, you see."

"You mean that he thinks we're on a case?" asked Holmes incredulously.

"Why Mr. Holmes, what else would the two of you be doing in Russia?" countered Reilly.

Events started to now get underway. Reilly said there was a train going out to Perm, and from there we would board another to Ekaterinburg. We would have a private railway car befitting the status of a high-ranking Cheka officer. It would also serve as the Imperial Family's on our return trip. If there was such a trip.

For one thing I was very grateful, we were assured that we would be left entirely alone. We would have time to rest and ruminate.

Yet what I had thought would be adventure, turned almost immediately into overwhelming anxiety for the masses of skeletal Russian children, women and men assailing the Petrograd main station; a place of slovenly Red Guards, debris of battle and debris of humanity; a slum of a place ripped straight from the pages of "Oliver Twist." Decay ate the living, and no battlefield was more horrific, for there are no children in battle.

Though our motor car, with heavily armed guards front and rear, moved as a sabre-toothed saw through this human forest and brought us directly to our train car, Holmes and I looked towards the freight carriages into which humans were being stuffed, locked like livestock, paltry possessions held fast against the dangers of the journey.

The starving children were the worst to see, confused and terrified, holding desperately onto their parents' hands, or carried more tightly than gold by their mothers or fathers when too small or infirm to walk. The Red Guards pushed and kicked and rifle-butted these people into the cars; and when the guards thought the cars full as possible, they slammed the wooden doors shut to prevent more from entering, and any from leaving. Coffins on wheels, I thought.

These were the refugees of the Revolution. Those who could not live longer in a capital of carnage, who could not find food for their families, who refused to watch as their loved ones became strangers and died. They were going to the country, where they thought there was food. Where they could once more literally breathe air not infected by hate or death. They would make their escape to places of quiet nature, where this new world order destroying their souls would take time to reach them again; time they would use to live and wait and choose by whose hand they would find eternal peace.

61

Holmes' eyes collected all evidence of this tragedy, to be filed in his darkest sub-conscious, his face betraying not one speck of emotion. Yet as I turned my eyes away from Holmes' face, I noticed that both his hands were clenched into fists as they grasped his jacket, creating two, crumpled balls on the bottom. No spoken word could have been more telling.

Then, as our guards made way for us to our railway car, Holmes suddenly broke from our ranks and moved as rapidly as he could towards the nearest freight car. It all happened so quickly that I could not even react; but Reilly and Obolov did.

Holmes had been watching as one particularly frail family was pushed onto the train. The youngest had been torn from his father's arms and the Red Guards were shutting the door. Holmes bolted to the guard holding the baby and grabbed it, and in the process, knocking the guard to the ground. Now Holmes was holding the infant up for the father to take before the door was sealed. All this happened as one seamless movement.

The guard on the ground was already retaking his rifle, and some of his comrades closest were running to his aid. But Reilly and Obolov were already there, Obolov pointing his rifle at the running Red Guards, which stopped them instantly, and Reilly pushing his pistol into the mouth of the guard on the ground.

Reilly literally raised that guard to his feet by simply moving his pistol upward; the guard, now crying and terrified, in unison with the movement of Reilly's pistol. By this time, Holmes had handed the infant to its father and turned to witness the events behind.

There was a grin on Reilly's face, but it was as cold as a corpse. He told us later that he had said: "Don't worry, comrade, I shan't shoot you. Your blood and brains, if you have any, would stain my uniform. But I know you now. And I never forget a face - even one as unfortunate as yours."

Reilly took the gun from the guard's mouth and the guard soiled himself, fell to the ground on his knees and shook uncontrollably. Obolov gestured with his rifle to the other Red Guards to lift the man and take him away, which they did immediately and silently; looking back as they retreated.

Reilly turned to Holmes.

"Don't ever play the hero again unless it's what you were sent for. Above all others, you should be able to keep compassion in check. Save it for Ekaterinburg." Reilly holstered his pistol, Obolov behind again, and all three came back to where Stravitski, the other Cheka guards and I had remained.

Finally, as we boarded the train, Holmes said to me, "It is now almost all before me, Watson. Answer this, if you can, for this is the question of questions: while we now begin a most crucial phase of our task, played out against this incomprehension," he made a damning sweep of his arm at the station, "and with Relinsky as saviour, just why, Watson, are you and I even here?"

"What do you mean by 'why are you and I even here?' I should have thought that obvious and basic. It seems so to me."

"But I am not you, Watson. Put aside, if you will, your thoughts and confusion about the King, and let your mind open to these questions. If, as Sir George stated, Relinsky has direct experience in these matters, and whatever he may be, is in a position to take advantage of his rank and power, as he has just given ample demonstration, why am I here? Second, and I mean this as no questioning of your considerable abilities, there are physicians in Russia. Why import one even at my urging? Which leads to the overall question, why take the time and trouble, especially when time is so desperately precious, to send you and me on our task?"

I sat back. Holmes had sired some most savage questions. I had not one hint of explanation. And could only sit there, mute.

"You know that I refuse to come to a conclusion until I have all the facts in a case," continued Holmes, "but this is most certainly not our usual case. It is not a case, at all. And while there may be no new facts, per se, there is certainly an ever-expanding cast of characters. I shan't confide further until I know more. What I see in this miserable country is scraping away at my soul. Layers are being sliced away at regular intervals, with each breath. Were it not for a certain seven lives, I would quit this nation right now."

It was much for me to absorb. Not only any personal postulations on my part about Holmes' questions, but Holmes' remarks on Russia. The sights of the day, and the events we'd now just witnessed had also made marked inroads into my usually happy disposition. Usually it would be I who would be the one to display emotion, so for Holmes to comment as he did upon our surroundings, meant something profound was happening to him.

Holmes and I sat in our private compartment in Reilly's private car, the train painfully moving out of its charnel house. It flew two large red flags, front and rear, with our car positioned where normally rode the caboose. Our compartment was towards the front of the car, with the bulk of Reilly's guards riding the roof and positioned at the only two points of egress and entry. Reilly was to our right, Stravitski and Obolov together to our left. Holmes confined himself to saying something about Scylla and Charybdis.

As we pulled free from the station and started east on the main line of the Trans-Siberian Railway, Holmes and I were given the views of Petrograd we had been too dismayed to see earlier that day, and that I shan't recount now; for they are, even at this distance of time, and upon the scenes I have just described, too despairing and melancholy to relive or impart. Yet there was more of that infamy to lie ahead; always, it seemed, directly on the pathway of our train.

It was quite late now; the white nights, like so many Venus Flytraps, luring us into folly of physical exhaustion. It was only then that I fully noticed our compartment; it was sumptuous in the extreme.

64

In fact, as later related by Reilly, the car had been the private travelling coach of a man who owned a conglomerate of mines. When the Revolution began, Reilly said, "His miners had the courtesy to show the man the bottom of one. And since they believed the man to be enjoying the experience, they agreed to leave him, chained to a beam, amidst his blackened joys."

I looked down at Holmes in his berth, and was surprised to see him already in the embrace of Morpheus. I wondered to what torment his unconscious mind would consign him this night.

Through all the years we had been together, and the years before which Holmes had detailed, I knew that Holmes had rarely experienced anything the likes of which we were now witnessing. Perhaps, luckily for me, I had the experience and shock of war as a point of association. But Holmes had not experienced war. His life had been, at times, nothing more than periods of deduction, broken only by intervals of action. And though that action had involved the most base criminals in England, there had been little to prepare the singular and delicate mind of Holmes for the horrors it was now witnessing.

Yes, Holmes could accept individual crimes of passion as routine, based upon his chosen profession and the profusion of literature on that melodramatic topic. But this was something new and infinitely more sinister. To me it seemed to be a form of genocide; something to which a prodigiously logical mind like Holmes' had absolutely no direct, previous reference.

I cursed the Bolsheviks along with Lenin, Trotsky and Stalin and shut my eyes.

June 21, 1918

As usual, upon awakening, I found Holmes gone.

I dressed to the shaking of the train, looked out the window to find we were well into the country somewhere, then went into the hallway and made my way to the rear, where I found the salon area.

Stravitski and Obolov were seated at a beautiful table of ebony, they raised their heads in recognition, and went about their breakfasts. It was Obolov who gestured with his fork to the door. I walked over, opened it, felt a swift, warm breeze envelope me, then saw Holmes and Reilly in deep discussion.

"Good morning, comrade," said Reilly. Holmes just nodded.

"We have just passed through Volkhov, Dr. Watson. A place of no renown and even less substance," said Reilly.

"Well forgive me for sounding rude," I said, "but I would like to have my breakfast now, after which, your travelogue would be received with greater enthusiasm." Reilly laughed and waved me back in. He and Holmes stayed out on the platform rear.

As I finished breakfast, Reilly came in. He nodded, passed me by, and Stravitski and Obolov followed him back to his compartment. I immediately joined Holmes outside.

"Well, Holmes, what is happening?"

"A fascinating fellow. I envy the ease with which he dissembles and speaks true; marrying the two so that they cannot be put asunder. He is like an eel: fast, fascinating and repellent at the same time. He is also disconcerting. To us he speaks in English, to his men in Russian; how do we know what the man is saying? He could tell them to slit our throats at any moment."

"But Holmes, that seems so far fetched. Why would he want us dead? And if he did, why wait until now?"

"Good questions, Watson, but questions without answers - for now," For a moment Holmes disappeared into thought, "if I did not know better, I might suspect a tight, blood relationship between our good comrade and the late Professor Moriarty."

"What?" I laughed out loudly in spite of myself. "Relinsky and Moriarty! I appreciate the analogy but doubt its veracity."

"Yes, the thought is amusing. But Watson, I tell you this now, I would not be unsettled to learn we are dealing with a mind and a will and a power as formidable as Moriarty's had been." Holmes' half laugh dissipated quickly with these words, and likewise did mine as he added three, small words, "Or even greater." These words, and the implication within them, chilled me right through; even on this warm June morning.

I managed to bring forth further questions.

"And what of his plan? Has he told you of it?"

"No, Watson, nothing. Through all my verbal tricks, he parried and thrust like a fencing master. Finally, as a last resort, I came out straight and asked him for the plan."

"And?"

"He smiled and said there was much time, and perhaps we could make a game of his plan."

"What? A game, you say?"

"Indeed." Holmes' stiff body slackened markedly as he leant against the wall and recounted Reilly's challenge with too casual nonchalance.

"He said that since I was Sherlock Holmes, perhaps I could deduce the details myself. That it would give my restless mind something to do and would keep me out of trouble during, what he expects to be, a long and boring train ride."

"And what did you say?"

"Why, Watson, what would you expect? Have you ever known me to lose at a game?"

June 23, 1918

The next few days were indeed dull, for the train rolled on relentlessly, the countryside and villages little more than blurs and the train stopping infrequently for fuel or water. The freight car doors were opened on those occasions, their human cargo pouring forth as freely as the waste from the slop cauldrons; fresh, unusually warm air for the

67

month, filling filthy lungs and sweetening the stench of railway steerage.

On the second day we passed through the city of Vologda, the cross-junction for the all-important railway running north to Archangel. Holmes said that we must return to Vologda, from whence we would continue up to Archangel for our exit rendezvous with whatever ship our navy would have waiting.

On we travelled, listening to the strangely high-pitched women's singing voices coming from the freight cars up front or Reilly's guards atop our roof; the occasional spell on our rear platform for flowing fresh air and closer study of the landscape and peasant farmers not bothering to look up from their toil.

It was on the last leg of our trip to Perm, that Holmes announced to me the completion of his "Relinsky Theory," as he termed it. This time, it was Holmes with the Cheshire cat grin as he, Reilly, Stravitski. Obolov and I gathered in the salon for Holmes to do what I'd seen him do so many dozens of times before: present all the facts in a case like so many dead fish laid out to dry.

Since Stravitski and Obolov supposedly spoke no English, we thought them there merely as appendages of Reilly; it was to Reilly that Holmes directed most of his speech.

"My dear Comrade Colonel," began Holmes, with the air of master addressing his pupil; although, I knew in my heart this was not the case in this instance, "I believe your plans for our rescue of the Romanovs and our eventual escape, shall proceed as follows:

"As both you and Sir George have already stated, Thomas Preston, your consul in Ekaterinburg, is waiting for us. No, I should clarify that remark, he is not merely waiting, he has all at the ready. Quite frankly, Comrade Relinsky, I believe there is more to this venture than merely 'brazening it out.' Even though the Romanovs' guards may be mere jailers, as you suspect, I have a strong feeling that the Urals Soviet would not leave so delicate a task of indelicate murder to a mere jailer. It would take someone with guile, ferocity, and a keen sense of the politics involved here.

"To continue, whomever that man may be, he will most certainly question your authority, Comrade, he will not be deterred by cut lines, he will order you to wait until he has specific written instructions from his superiors, and if you object or make trouble in any way, he will put you all under arrest or order his men, which, I am sure, will greatly outnumber your tiny band here, to open fire on you.

"Therefore, I am also sure that you have already devised an alternative scheme with Mr. Preston, who, undoubtedly, has a fair amount of men in British pay or with White sympathies. That scheme, however, can take a myriad of shapes and sizes, and since I have not diagrams, nor plans, nor detailed information regarding the Romanovs' place of confinement, nor of Ekaterinburg itself, I shall not venture any further theories.

"This whole exercise has been a game, but one with you sir, holding the advantage."

Now Holmes turned sharply on Reilly, uncompromising grey eyes holding Reilly's as a magnet a piece of metal. Reilly's grin returned while Holmes' grin vanished as he continued.

"You thought this not merely a jest, but a test, comrade. You thought to find me exploring vast deserts of possibilities, my mind inexorably moving towards a non-existent, mental oasis, with the outcome a victory for you in either of three ways.

"The first, that I would lose myself in those burying sands of cerebral solitude, too occupied or disheartened to worry you further. The second, that I would go blithely over the precipice of your challenge, postulating a solution that would be as ludicrous as it would be contemptuous. With either outcome, you would have gained over me the superiority you carry with the derision of a matador flaunting his cape."

"And what about the third victory of which you speak, Mr. Holmes? What would that be?" asked Reilly.

"Why nothing more than you have just witnessed. You now

know, without reservation, that you cannot underestimate me. That I shall not be fooled. You know now that you, as well as I, must be on eternal guard. In short, you now have the true measure of this opponent.

"Perhaps I should have given you wild theories and left you to think of me as a mere fabrication of Dr. Watson's writings. A pleasing product of public relations with no more incisive capacity than your average Scotland Yard functionary.

"But I have no time for such sport now that our time grows truly meagre and the sport for which we came is about to begin. I have only one question to ask, comrade, why are Watson and I here?"

At that question, the grin was gone from Reilly's face and he stood to confront Holmes, almost eye to eye. Stravitski and Obolov were caught off-guard and they looked at me as if to inquire, "What is happening?"

Then, after Reilly and Holmes used their eyes as microscopes to fathom the very atoms of each other, Reilly said, "So, Mr. Holmes, you have divined the true game."

And with that, he turned and walked away.

June 30, 1918

Our train pulled into Perm, the closest real city before the Urals, situated on the Kama River, a Red enclave soon to be beleaguered by Whites. Reilly and Stravitski spent some time at the Cheka headquarters at the crossing of Petropavlovskaya and Obvinskaya Streets.

Upon their return, about one hour later, Reilly bade Holmes and I attend him, as once again, there was someone who would be waiting to meet us. Since Holmes and I had no choice, we accepted the invitation.

We left the station to find two motor cars waiting for us, with

Reilly's men in the first car, and our immediate 'family', including Stravitski and Obolov, in the second.

From what little we saw of Perm, it consisted of double-storied, and squat, uninspired stone buildings hard by the river fanning outward in no logical pattern. The Urals were faintly discernible to the East.

After a brief ride, we stopped at what looked like a building for bureaucrats. Only the five of us entered, and I was immediately aware that the entire building must be empty, so harsh were the echoes of our footsteps.

Reilly led us to the middle office, opened the door, walked in, and we followed. Inside were rows of records sailing off to infinity, with an old, small, wooden desk in the centre; a pack of cigarettes, almost empty, and an ashtray almost full, the only objects on that desk.

Seated at the desk was a man in his mid-forties, with a long, sharp, straight nose, and very short dark hair. He was dressed in drab peasant garb; short, olive green shirt and loose, black trousers. Solely from the intense concentration on his face, I knew this man was no simple peasant. He rose as we walked towards him, but made no move to meet us. I noticed Holmes' eyes looking under the desk.

It was then that Reilly tried to make another of his startling introductions.

"Mr. Holmes, Dr. Watson..." and before he could get in another syllable, Holmes finished the sentence for him.

"Admiral Vaslevich Kolchak, the Supreme Commander of all the White Armies in Russia."

I saw Reilly's head move backward almost imperceptibly, and I am sure that I was the only one to notice it.

The Admiral was angry and expressed that anger immediately to Reilly; surprisingly, in English.

"I thought you said these men were not told who I was."

Reilly looked as if he weren't sure whether to laugh or lie.

"Admiral, they were not told."

"Then how does this man know who I am?"

"Rather simply, Admiral," said Holmes. "First of all, upon entering, you were seated so erectly in your chair that I immediately knew you were someone used to command and power. While your dress is purposely peasant garb, your boots are shined to the gloss of only a very important officer." The admiral, and Reilly, looked downwards in unison. Holmes continued.

"I would suggest you immediately scuff those boots or rub soil onto them.

"Next, the brand of cigarette you are smoking is of Turkish origin, and, please correct me if I am mistaken, but one of your more famous exploits in this war was your routing of the Ottoman fleet in the Black Sea, and your subsequent occupation of large tracts of Ottoman territory, where, no doubt, you acquired your fondness for that particular Turkish tobacco.

"Your fingernails, from constant manicure care, are almost as glossy as your boots; your face bears the ruddiness and attendant white creases around the eyes that come only from long periods, squinting at the sea; and your hair is cut in the sparse, precise manner of the Imperial Russian Navy.

"There is a tiny scar, from the kiss of a badly aimed scimitar, directly under your right ear that I remember reading you received in gallant action while still an ensign, again fighting the Turks.

"As inconceivable as it first seemed to me that you, the Supreme White Commander, could possibly be here in this Red bastion, knowing Comrade Relinsky and all the magic he has managed to conjure for us since our arrival in your country, plus all the facts I have just recounted, I was led to your identity."

I was as amazed as Reilly and Admiral Kolchak. Not only at Holmes' utterly brilliant deductions, but that we were there in harmonious company with a presumably double agent Cheka Colonel and, most assuredly, the Bolsheviks' most wanted man.

Admiral Kolchak was still disturbed. He was no longer angry, that due to Holmes' bravura performance, but he was still uneasy.

Holmes spoke again.

"Admiral, please be at ease. This mundane act of deduction set before you is merely what I do, if you will, for a living. It is nothing about which to be uncomfortable. You have come here, at incredible risk to your life, to speak directly with Dr. Watson and me. Pray, tell us why you've come."

With those remarks, the admiral seemed to calm himself. He sat behind the desk, and we then sat in the chairs before it.

"Gentlemen, I have seen much in my years that would flay the eyes of most ordinary men. But those were things of horror and battle. I am used to military feats. Not mental feats. That is why I have been so taken aback."

He turned to Reilly and said, "This, Mr. Holmes, is even more than I had expected. Our friends shall be in trustworthy hands, I can see that. Yes, I can see that. Mr. Holmes, Dr. Watson, that is why I have really come - to see the two of you for myself. If all goes well, you shall shortly be holding the most precious jewels in the world, and I could trust no one's judgment of you but my own.

"In fact, had I thought the two of you unworthy, I may have even withdrawn my support from this entire venture. However, I am now here specifically to give you our plan and route of escape once you have left Ekaterinburg." Holmes bent his body closer to the desk.

"Even the Colonel here, knows nothing of this plan. Gentlemen, my men are too far to be of use upon your initial stage of rescue; but upon your return through the mountains and back through Perm, we shall make a lightning strike at your train near the village of Viatka using White irregulars comprised of Russians and Czechs. Once Colonel Relinsky has surrendered and his men have been dealt with," he smiled to himself as he said those words, "we shall continue northwest towards our main concentration of forces. Once among them, you will be escorted in the greatest of safety and comfort to Archangel. Until our direct attack at Viatka, I have given orders to all regular units not to advance anywhere near the rail lines. Do you have any questions for me, gentlemen?"

The admiral's tone was almost seductive now. Again, there was such a remarkable dissimilarity between his voice and his face that even to this day I wonder at it. It was at this point that I expected Holmes to ask the same question he had put to me and to Reilly; just why were we there? But Holmes did not ask the question, so, of course, neither did I.

What Holmes did ask, however, was a startling as had been his deductions.

"Sir, what if you fail?"

I saw Reilly wince.

"I do not understand you, Mr. Holmes. Please repeat yourself."

"I mean, sir, just what I asked. What if Relinsky's men revolt? Soldiers in revolt should be no novel notion here. What if our train breaks through? We shall be deep in Red territory, caught red-handed, so to speak."

Reilly remained still, as did I, as Holmes and Kolchak stared at each other.

"Mr. Holmes, my men shall not fail." The admiral's tone was quiet, even, and forceful; a loving father reprimanding his son.

"But if they do?" pressed Holmes.

"Then, Mr. Holmes, look here to Colonel Relinsky; for neither God nor the devil, in that circumstance, shall be able to do more for you than he."

We left Kolchak in his bureaucratic mortuary and joined our waiting guards. Until this point, I had suspected them to be Reilly's men, on our side. But Kolchak's words led me to believe that aside from Stravitski and Obolov, these other men were, in fact, real Red Guards on a mission with their Colonel. They knew nothing of who we just met. They knew nothing of the plans for their death. They were goats to the slaughter, with Reilly, Holmes and I as Judas goats. I shuddered to myself as now familiar men smiled at me as we got into

74

our motor car. For the first time I understood what it meant to be what Reilly was; what it felt like to be friends with men you would knowingly lead to their death.

Upon our quick journey back to the station, we found two of Reilly's men in a high state of agitation. One handed a slip of paper to Reilly that turned out to be a telegram. Reilly came to us.

He looked at Holmes and me and said, "Well, our friend may have given orders to his regulars to stay away from the rail lines, but those orders seem to have eluded some highly motivated soldiers - breakaways from the Czech Brigade."

"What do you mean?" I asked.

"It means, Watson," said Holmes, "that a band of Czech partisans has disrupted the track between here and Ekaterinburg. We are stuck."

"Quite," said Reilly.

We were so near, and yet so far.

We were now only a day or so away from Ekaterinburg when the Czechs did their mischief. With the day getting brighter by the minute, the Urals seemed as if one could touch them with a walking stick. Now, it appeared that some of the very people fighting for the Romanovs were inadvertently preventing their rescue.

Since the day was growing unseasonably warm, Holmes and I, as well as Reilly's men, remained outside, simply waiting for instructions at the station. The refugees were out now, as well. Their ranks thinned by the numbers who had stayed in village stops along the way, and by those who had died en route.

It was then that the family Holmes helped in Petrograd came towards us. Holding their bundles, it was obvious they would be leaving us here in Perm, and the mother dropped to her feet in front of Holmes and grabbed his ankles in fealty. The father was holding the baby. Holmes lifted the mother, looked down into her eyes and said,

"Nyet, Matushka. Charoshe schast", which he later explained was Russian for "No, Mother. Good luck."

The woman kissed Holmes' hands and her husband's eyes said everything that could be said of thanks. They turned, and walked off into the city. I hope to God they survived.

"Since when have you begun speaking Russian?" I asked Holmes.

"Why, Watson, one cannot help but pick up the odd word here and there."

"I haven't," I said.

"Well, you haven't been listening, then."

"I have, but I can't make anything out other than 'da' or 'nyet.' And that infernal alphabet of theirs is confounding."

"No, it isn't, my friend. It is just that you are set in your ways and do not wish to trouble your complacent cranium." Holmes laughed.

"Watson, had I a more profound knowledge of this language, I would, as I have so often done in London, become another and vanish into the multitude, returning when that which I seek has been found."

"But Holmes, that is sheer insanity. Strike it from your thoughts. In this place you are no more powerful than that babe you saved. It is an absurd notion. I shan't permit you to even consider such a foolish act."

I was becoming so agitated that Holmes quieted and assured me he would not go off seeking some solitary adventure. I was about to rest on a barrel when Reilly, Stravitski and Obolov appeared out of the station house and came towards us.

"Well, my friends. It seems that my men and I are about to attend afternoon tea."

Of course, he was referring to a military engagement.

"We're to set out with regular elements of the army, and bless me, a detachment of local Cheka under the command of a Colonel Mikoyan. Virtually all available men and units are to be used. We shall return when we return. Oddly enough, the lines have not been cut, so a message has been put through to Preston that his package will be delayed. How long, who knows? But that track must be repaired. We have no time to lose. Every moment of delay takes our friends nearer death. I'm leaving Obolov with you. I don't think you'll need more than one baby-sitter."

There was nothing Holmes nor I could do but wish him well and wait. Within two hours, the various units were assembled and the cavalry rode out at full gallop. Motorized units of the Red Army followed, Reilly and his group came next with a small contingent of cavalry to the rear.

We watched them all, hundreds in number, evaporate into huge screens of dust.

July 2, 1918

Two days passed. The lines had finally gone dead about two hours after Reilly had set out. We did not receive any word until late on the second day.

Obolov ordered an English teacher he had found in Perm to give us the news, which was read to us in the manner of any good Red automaton: 'A resounding victory for the ever-victorious Red Army. The criminal Whites and their stooges, the Czechs, were easily beaten; some few survivors cowardly escaping into mountain passes. The glorious soldiers of The Revolution will be returning tomorrow. The wounded have been sent ahead.'

July 3, 1918

The next morning the wounded began coming in and by late night most of the remaining forces had returned.

Reilly and his men met us at our railway car around six. Stravitski was not with them.

Obolov was extremely saddened by the loss of Stravitski. Reilly was rather matter-of-fact about it. He sat in our railway car's salon, vodka his refreshment, his uniform bearing the filth and residue of battle.

After a few minutes, he began to tell us what really happened.

"On the second day out, we approached the village of Kungur, right at the foot of the Urals. The Czechs were waiting. And the Czechs had artillery. We did not. They weren't free-booting irregulars, they were highly disciplined troops.

"They waited until the cavalry came in range and opened fire. We had to move up very slowly, but move up we did. The cavalry hit them on the flanks. We had more troops than the Czechs. Why such a small group of men had artillery is beyond me. I am not a military man." He laughed to himself.

"I recount in brief what was, in fact, either a patriotic embellishment or calumny for more idiotic slaughter. But I am not a patriot. I am what I am.

"There were only about a hundred of them but they held on. When we got into Kungur, we learned it had been burning overnight. Most of the people of the village had been killed. Whatever villagers were left alive, our local Red Guards killed as White sympathizers. The Reds lost considerable numbers. That will be good for us on the return. They'll still be regrouping, and their wounded will not, as yet, have been replaced. The losses to my men were slight.

"We left men behind to repair the track and men to guard the men. It should take another day or so."

I interrupted. "What happened to Stravitski?"

"He never made it into Kungur, poor bastard. Oh well, one day you kill your father, the next day it's your turn. Gentlemen, I'm tired. I think I'll sleep for a while."

With that, he stood up, one hand holding his glass, the other his bottle, which he used to salute us, and he slumped his way to his compartment. Obolov sat with his back to us, his head down, his shoulders heaving. Holmes and I went outside.

"What do you make of his reaction, Holmes?"

"Even in such straits he remains sphinx-like. But he is obviously still much fatigued and vexed from the battle. It is not something he expected. Our Comrade Relinsky is quite fallible, after all."

July 4, 1918

In the morning, Holmes waxed philosophical about the day being America's Independence Day while we were in the midst of another revolution.

"But," Holmes said, "I sincerely doubt this country's revolution shall have the same effect on its people." I nodded in affirmation.

The greater part of the day was spent on my own, with Holmes having gone off somewhere alone, in direct negation of his promise to me, and it proved to be the cause of great concern for Reilly once he became aware of Holmes' disappearance.

Reilly sent Obolov with some men into Perm to find him. Obolov returned that evening, and in his special form of communication with Reilly, made it known that Holmes was nowhere to be found. Reilly was clearly annoyed and demonstrated this by glaring at me and everyone else around him.

After more talk with some of his other men, Reilly came towards me, through the ranks of refugees on the platform, his men pushing aside the occasional wretch, male or female, who was in their way. One filthy soul, poor man, just could not seem to find his way safely out of the guards' path. If he was shoved to the right, other guards would shove him to the left, and so forth. I was about to intervene on the man's behalf when he was finally pushed clear of he advancing guards. In fact, he was pushed so forcefully, that he virtually landed at my feet. I would have made a move to help the man up, but he reeked of waste and his clothes were so stained and shredded that my concerns for personal sanitation gained the upper hand.

Reilly's men surrounded me as he put his hands on my shoulders, moved me further from the stench of the peasant on the platform, and very slowly asked, "Dr. Watson, are you quite positive you have no idea where your friend has run off to?"

"I assure you, Comrade Relinsky, I am as puzzled and worried as yourself. Holmes swore he would not do this kind of thing in such a hostile environment."

"Blast the man," said Reilly, "just who the hell does he think he is?"

Suddenly we heard a loud laugh followed immediately by, "That depends on the circumstances."

We all turned towards the words which came from the direction of the stench. The peasant was standing there smiling broadly.

It was Holmes.

Once he had washed and changed back into his own clothing, Holmes joined Reilly, Obolov and me in our railway car's salon. He was still smiling broadly.

"Well," he said, "it is nice to know when one is missed."

Reilly exploded as he leapt to his feet.

"How dare you? Are you totally insane? This is the second time you have done something so foolhardy, and I promise you this: should you try something like this again, I shall have you shot! Shot! I may do it myself! Do you understand me?"

Holmes was not concerned.

"And disappoint all who have given you instructions?"

Reilly advanced on Holmes.

"You are not in London, Mr. Holmes. You are in my territory." Reilly was now shouting at Holmes. "You could not last the day here without me or my men. Nor could Dr. Watson."

At that, Holmes' smile vanished into strong words also.

80

"Is that a threat against Dr. Watson?"

"A threat, yes. A promise, no. My only promise to you is what I have said. You shall not cause me distress again without paying a high price for your entertainment."

And before Holmes could say another word, Reilly turned to Obolov and said, "These men are not to leave this car until I personally give you further orders. Is that understood, Sergei Alexandrovich?" Obolov nodded in the affirmative.

Reilly turned back to us. "Consider yourselves prisoners, consider yourselves what you will, but you shall not leave this car again until we are in Ekaterinburg!" And with that, he strode out of the car.

Holmes turned to me and said, "Do you think I upset him?"

"Good God, Holmes, have you gone completely mad? You swore to me that you would not attempt so rash and ignorant an act."

"Rash? Ignorant? Why, Watson, you astound me! In all the years you have been in my company, have you ever known me to act without first weighing all evidence or facts?"

"Well, no."

"And ignorant? Think on this, who is ignorant here, when you who knows me perhaps better than any living soul cannot even see beyond my mask? And Relinsky, perhaps the only man other than our departed Moriarty who I feel can test me to the fullest, cannot uncover me right before his eyes? And you call me ignorant?"

"All right, all right. Then what was the point of all that?"

"Precisely what I said to you earlier, to find that which I am seeking. And that, I have done."

"How?"

"I now know, with some fair degree of certainty, that as in London, I may go about in disguise unremarked. Furthermore I have learned that my modest Russian vocabulary should be more than sufficient for my purposes."

"Which are?"

"Having to vanish again when the time is right, or circumstance dictates."

"But Holmes, you heard Relinsky. He does not bluff. He will shoot you, and me, if he must."

"Calm yourself, my dear fellow. He said that we are to remain in this car until Ekaterinburg; and so we shall. He has said nothing about that which shall happen afterwards."

"Oh, I say, you are quite right."

"Of course. No, I shan't give our Comrade Colonel any more cause for alarm now. But I now have at least one card up my sleeve to offset Relinsky's stacked deck."

We left it at that and retired for the night after an extremely modest meal meant specially to show Reilly's disfavour.

July 5, 1918

In the morning, we were told the track had been repaired ahead of schedule, and we pulled into Kungur late in the day. Holmes and I, with Obolov beside us, went onto the platform to see the town for ourselves.

It was as Reilly had said. Burnt out buildings, animal and human carcasses already decomposing in the summer sun, burial parties at work - apparently since the earlier hours. It seemed unnaturally quiet until I realized that Kungur was nothing more than a mass graveyard.

As the train started again, the three of us grasped onto the various rails or hand holds fixed on the car's wall. We all knew that barring any more interruptions, our next stop would be Ekaterinburg.

I spent a rather restless night; although, Holmes said he slept rather well. It did not matter, though, we were both anxious.

At fifteen minutes past ten, our train pulled into the station at Ekaterinburg. Our railway car was disconnected and then connected to another locomotive; ours being the only car, except for one more added to the rear for the bulk of Reilly's men, which were down to no more than a dozen since the battle at Kungur.

Before Reilly left to go into the town, he reminded us that if all went per Kolchak's plan, the lines between Kungur and Ekaterinburg would be cut later that day. This, for some reason, produced an uncomfortable sensation in my stomach.

Reilly beckoned Holmes and me out onto the station platform.

"Well, gentlemen, we are here at last. Everything that has gone before means nothing and I can now show you this." Reilly pulled some documents from his tunic, opened one letter, and showed us the signature of none other than Lenin.

"What is it?" I asked.

"It is your paper of safe transport. Comrade Lenin could not bear the thought of two of his favourites travelling without at least his signature to shield them. The other papers are mine. In brief, they tell whomever I give them to, to give me anything, or anyone, I want."

Reilly took great pleasure in the looks on our faces.

Our car was at Station Number 2, only ten minutes northwest of the British Consulate, which, we found, was virtually across the street from the Ipatiev House; the house where the Romanovs were held.

A motor car waited for us, and we went with only Reilly and Obolov down Glavnaya Street, between two lakes. Reilly left specific instructions with his only other officer, Lt. Zimin, that if regular Red Army or local Red Guards showed up, they were to direct them to the British Consulate where they would be told Colonel Relinsky was escorting two important British diplomats.

I now include a map of Ekaterinburg so you will better understand relationships of distance, structures and places of import upon our arrival and after we left.

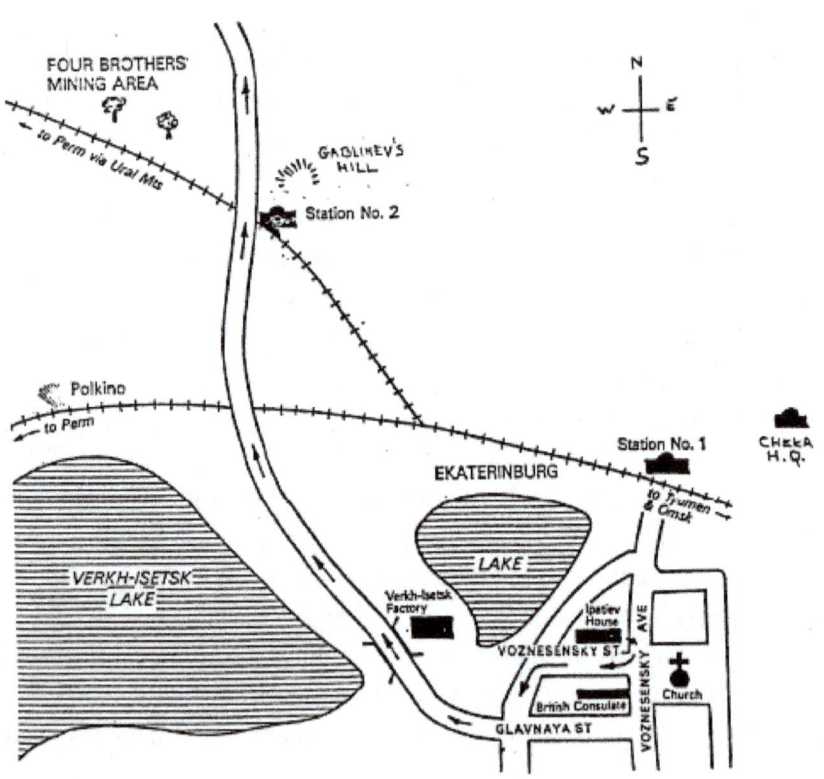

The entrance to the British Consulate was on Voznesensky Avenue, the same as the entrance to the Ipatiev House. Reilly told the driver to go by the Romanovs' place of imprisonment, and as we passed, we saw workers busily constructing what was a wooden palisade in front of another not as high. It seemed about twelve to fifteen feet tall.

Presently, we were at the consulate. As we pulled up, we heard artillery in the distance. The Whites were drawing closer already.

As we alighted from the car, a man in his mid-thirties came out to us. He was slim, had a very warm smile, dark hair, wore wire-rimmed glasses and introduced himself to Reilly as Thomas Preston, the British Consul. A moment later another young man came out, a bit more stout, in his early thirties, with thick, blond hair and large, blue eyes. This was Arthur Thomas, the British Vice-Consul. As the introductions were concluded, and hands shaken vigorously, Preston gestured us inside, and into his personal study.

He bade us all sit, offered us a drink, then questioning began from both sides.

"Tell me," he said, "what is really going on at Kungur and Perm?" Reilly told him everything. Preston sat back in his chair, his hands forming a steeple in front of his face.

"As you hear, the Whites are fairly close. They're getting closer every day, and the Bolsheviks are getting more nervous with every mile. If you do not try an immediate release, all may be for nothing."

"Then tell us," said Reilly, "what's the situation with our friends here? How many guards? Who are they? Who is in charge? Have you seen our friends?" The questions were many and logical, the same that you yourself would ask in like circumstance. Preston answered them all, giving us a chilling account of the Romanovs' lives at the Ipatiev House. He pulled out a more detailed map than my effort, with diagrams showing the interior of the building, as well.

He was animated as he showed us the salient points of the map, and Holmes later confided that he suspected a prior knowledge of the military.

"In case you are not aware, gentlemen, Ekaterinburg was once a very wealthy mining capital. Metals, gems, fortunes were made and lost every day. It was like those American gold-rush and mining towns of their West, one hears so much about. The Ipatiev House, the place of the Romanovs' confinement, was the home of a mining magnate.

"The Romanovs were brought here on April 30th. There are approximately fifty guards, some at various sentry boxes at the entrances, some stationed in the courtyard or garden, some remain inside, near the Romanovs' rooms. There are machine guns at the attic windows and new emplacements downstairs." Reilly and Obolov studied all this with great care, as did Holmes.

"The house is built on a slight hill, so on one side of the house there is a basement, though it is quite small. Beyond that stone archway is a courtyard where the Romanovs exercise. Beyond that is a garden.

"Upstairs, there are six rooms. The four girls share one room, the Tsar, Tsarina, and the boy another, he is quite ill now, but recovering."

"What happened?" I asked.

"One of the guards saw a gold crucifix the boy had and beat him trying to grab it away. The boy's nurse and bodyguard, a sailor named Derevenko hit the guard. It stopped the robbery and beating, but it cost Derevenko his life. Now the Tsar carries the boy personally."

"The blackguards," I said. Preston continued.

"Even with all this heat, the windows have been ordered to remain shut, and they have also been whitewashed so no one can look in or out. There is only one entrance, here, to their rooms, and another sentry as well.

"To get to the lavatory, the family must leave their rooms and pass before the guards on duty. Some of the guards had drawn obscene pictures of the Tsarina and Rasputin on the lavatory walls, and others continuously taunted the girls and the Tsarina whenever they passed by.

"I am constantly besieged by those formerly in the Tsar's party to inquire as to the family's health and safety, and Arthur and I do all we can. We claim to be inquiring on behalf of the British government, which we are, of course, to keep the pressure on the local Bolshies to let up. But I don't believe they do. Yes, they claim all is well, but we know it's not.

"There is a priest here, Russian Orthodox, named Father Storozhev. Back in June the Reds let him in to say mass for the family in the basement. It's the only eye-witness account I have of the family since they were put into captivity here.

"The Father said the Tsar was sombre but warm, wearing a simple khaki tunic and trousers. The girls seemed in good spirits, but their hair had been cut short, and they were all in dark skirts and faded white blouses. The Tsarina looked very much older than her years, she turned forty-six here. Father Storzhev said she had deep lines in her face now and seemed very apathetic. She's always been of a mystic bent, just remember Rasputin, and the Father believes the Tsarina is just waiting to die.

Alexei is another matter altogether. He is almost totally crippled since the beating incident, and he relies on his father for all mobility. But the boy has pluck. He hasn't the strength to lift himself from his cot but his eyes are alive with forgiveness and compassion. The Father cries when he recounts these tales to those who ask.

"But they've been treated worse than they're treated now. When they first arrived, the Red Guard commander was a pig named Avdeyev. He would invite his drunken friends in to gawk at the family and would grab food from the Romanovs' table. One time he even struck the Tsar in the face.

"Things are getting a bit strange. Events are happening of which I have not been informed."

"Like what?" asked Reilly.

"Last month there were all sorts of rumours and stories in the press that the Tsar had already been shot. Somehow, a French intelligence officer got in and out of Ekaterinburg with the truth; the Tsar was still alive. Now how the hell are the French involved in all this?"

"I haven't the faintest idea," said Reilly, "as far as we all know, this is strictly a British operation."

"Perhaps that is the key," said Holmes, "as far as we all know." Reilly, Preston, and Thomas looked at Holmes warily. Preston then continued.

"Anyway, Avdeyev became more drunk, more crude and so did his men. Almost everything of value that belonged to the Romanovs had been stolen. The Chairman of the Urals Soviet, Alexander Beleborodov, once showed up and found Avdeyev passed out cold on the floor.

"Just two days ago, the bastard was arrested. So was his assistant Moshkin. And the guards have already been changed. I'd be surprised if the whole lot hasn't already been shot. Beleborodov and his group are terrified of Moscow. With the Whites so damned close, and the Red Army under Trotsky coming to meet them, Beleborodov and his council members don't know exactly what to do. Everyone wants the Romanovs, it seems. But dead or alive, that's my question?"

At that remark, I noticed a certain look on Holmes' face. It was a look that he only adopted when some profound idea had taken hold. I also noticed his entire body relax. It seemed that whatever idea had captured his imagination, it had freed his body of its terrible tension.

When my concentration returned to Preston, he was in mid-sentence.

"...all new. The commander is Yakov Yurovsky. He's the Regional Commissar for Justice. That's a joke. I met him yesterday for the first time. He's about forty, and you'll appreciate this Dr. Watson, he attended the Imperial Army Medical College during the war. In fact, on a visit to the Ipatiev House before he became commander, he suggested that a swelling on the Tsarevich's leg might go down if the leg were put in plaster. Supposedly, it worked."

Preston continued: "It bothers me that I can't get a handle on the man. He's obviously educated and he's already shown concern for the boy. He told me his hand-picked men were moral and disciplined. In fact, most are not even Russians. They're Letts. Where the hell he dug up those men is something else again. But he also promised that the stealing would stop, although, there's nothing left to steal, and the family would fare much better now that he was in charge. He seems to be truly concerned about British opinion, and if not a charade, it means that he himself is under intense pressure from Moscow to keep the Romanovs in hand and keep them away from the Whites in any way he deems best.

"There are nuns that bring in fresh produce and vegetables for the Romanovs, and he's got security so tight that the nuns have to explain who authorized their visits and where they're from. Furthermore, he's increased the number of guard posts, and put more sentries in the back yard.

"So this Yurovsky is like a goose that's been unevenly cooked: tough and tender at the same time." Preston turned to Reilly.

"Now this will concern you greatly, Colonel Relinsky. Yurovsky and his men are all local Cheka. The big joke is that the Ekaterinburg Cheka headquarters are in the Hotel America, of all places. He meets there with all the big Urals Soviet heavyweights: Beleborodov, his deputy Chutskayev, the man that usually deals with my inquiries, and the Urals Commissar for War, Goloshchokin. That's the group that makes the decisions around here.

"What they can't decide themselves is whether to kill the Romanovs or keep them alive. It appears that Moscow will have to live with whatever they decide. This area is theirs; that is until the Whites take it, or the Red Army moves in in strength."

"So with the Whites getting so close, they can't risk the Romanovs falling into White hands?" asked Holmes.

"I suppose so," said Preston lethargically. He was obviously running out of steam.

"There is one thing that haunts me continuously though, day and night. One note that strikes discordantly."

"And what is that, pray tell?" I asked.

"Once the Romanovs were put into the Ipatiev House, the local Bolsheviks, and even the peasants, began calling it 'The House of Special Purpose.'"

We were interrupted by Preston's housekeeper. She had come to inform us that Comrade Commissar Yurovsky and some men were there to see us. We all looked at each other. Yurovsky, she said, was waiting for us in the consulate's official receiving room. Preston and Thomas made their way to see the unexpected visitors, with Reilly and Obolov accompanying them. Holmes and I were requested by Preston to remain in his study until he determined what Yurovsky wanted.

Only about ten minutes passed before Preston returned.

"It seems that immediately upon your arrival, Yurovsky was informed, sent men to the station, was told you were all here, so here he came.

"He was quite curious about Colonel Relinsky and his men, and about the two British subjects they were guarding. Relinsky gave a cover story about the two of you being on a fact-finding mission for the British government, and Yurovsky seemed to buy it based upon the voluminous inquiries Arthur and I make.

"But he sensed something more, so Relinsky took the upper hand by suggesting that all other Soviet business be discussed at Cheka headquarters where such discussion would be appropriate. Yurovsky cautiously agreed, and that is where I assume them to be headed now."

Holmes looked at me and said, "Well, it shan't be long now, Watson. Knowing Reilly, he will probably get to the heart of the matter forthwith."

90

Again there was an interruption. This time it was Father Storozhev. Since his church was located directly across from the consulate, he had seen our party arrive, and then saw Yurovsky and his men enter and leave with Reilly. He sensed something was happening and he wanted to know what.

Father Storozhev looked like everyone's image of Father Christmas, except that he was thin. His beard was pure white and flowing. His eyes were bright and happy and peaceful, and when you looked into them, even briefly, you believed he was a vessel of the Lord. His walk was erect for a man of his advanced years -- and his voice, despite conveying authority, was soft. He came in and sat down, as did we. Thomas acted as interpreter for us.

"So what does this all mean, Your Excellency?" he asked Preston.

"Father Storozhev, these are the men the Cheka Colonel brought from Petrograd. They are special emissaries from my government, here to see firsthand what is happening. This is Mr. Holmes, this is Dr. Watson."

The Father made an attempt to rise, but Holmes motioned him not to. Father Storozhev smiled and we all shook hands.

"So, my sons," continued the Father, "you are here to possibly help the Imperial Family?"

"Not really, Father," said Holmes. "We are here only to observe and to make it absolutely clear to the local Soviet that the British government's concern for the safety and comfort of the Imperial Family is paramount."

The Father seemed disappointed. "Oh, you are here only to see, not to do." The way he cut to the heart of Holmes' statement left us all feeling ashamed.

"I have prayed, I do not know how many times, every day, for a saviour to appear: a man, or men, who would rescue my unfortunate children. I was hoping you would be those men."

Holmes looked saddened. "I am sorry, Father, but we are not

those for whom you prayed."

Father Storozhev looked carefully at Holmes as he spoke those words and his right hand went to the Russian Orthodox cross hanging from his neck. I got the feeling that the good Father did not believe Holmes.

"It is a pity, Mr. Holmes. It is a pity." With that, he lifted himself from the chair and said to Preston, "Did you know, Your Excellency, that the whole town of Ekaterinburg is built upon now abandoned mines?"

"Well, I really hadn't given it much thought, Father."

"It is just tourist information for you and your friends," he said, bidding us all good day.

"Strange sort of tourist information," I said.

"Yes, isn't it, Watson? A most remarkable presence," said Holmes.

"Yes, indeed," agreed Preston. "The man is a saint, if a man can be a saint in the midst of this hell. However, we must continue our discussion. Shall we go back into my study?" We followed Preston, Arthur Thomas did not come with us.

"Gentlemen, we did not expect Yurovsky to be so punctual. We had planned on a bit more time before Relinsky would present himself. So things are moving more rapidly than we expected. You must prepare yourselves. I know briefly of Relinsky's plan, but I am not sure Yurovsky will so easily go along with it.

"You have all been out of touch for too long. Just the last few days has seen the total change at the Ipatiev House. Were Avdeyev still here, chances are the drunk would go along with Relinsky's orders. But Yurovsky is a cool character. He is by no means a fool.

"As per the plan, he most certainly will try to receive direct orders from above. I only hope the lines will be cut."

"Oh, I believe they will," said Holmes.

"Yes, when we met Kol..." Holmes cut me off in mid-sentence.

"Yes, when we met Kolvotsev in Perm, he seemed most

92

emphatic on that point." I looked at Holmes.

"Kolvotsev? Who is Kolvotsev?" asked Preston. I was curious myself.

"Oh, I thought you knew," said Holmes, "a White agent who met us in Perm."

"I knew nothing of any White agent sent to meet you." He stood, thrust his hands into his pockets and turned angrily to his window. "Damn this, gentlemen, I said something strange was going on. What the hell is it?"

At that moment, Thomas came into the study with a telegram. He handed it to Preston who read it, and then leaned back against his wall.

"Well, gentlemen, something very strange *is* going on. This telegram, which was stopped in mid-transmission, says that earlier today, in Moscow, Count Wilhelm Mirbach, the German Ambassador, was assassinated."

"Assassinated," I repeated. "Why?"

"It does not say. Transmission stopped after the phrase 'by radical, reactionary elements'; which means the Reds are trying to pin it on the Whites. I don't think it'll wash.

"Just what does this all mean? What the hell is going on here? Do any of you have any idea?"

"We wish we did," said Holmes.

Holmes and I went out to the consulate's courtyard for some air and for some confidential conversation.

"This assassination is not some coincidence, Watson. And since it was obvious that Preston and Thomas are not aware of all the players in this game, I did not want you to give the man apoplexy with your Kolchak revelation."

"It's all right, Holmes. I quite understand. But I do not understand what this assassination of the German Ambassador has to do with us."

"Neither do I, Watson, as yet. But it is obvious there is even

93

more happening than I would have ever dreamt. But let me take your mind away from that puzzle for a moment and return it to an off-hand remark made by Father Storozhev."

"Are you referring to his tourist information?"

"Very good, Watson, precisely. What do you make of it?"

"Well, I don't know, actually. I hadn't given it much thought."

"Then permit me to guide you. I believe it was a very crafty order of aid that Preston completely missed."

"How so?"

"Mine shafts, Watson. Tunnels. I believe Father Storozhev was letting us know about some secret tunnel of which he has specific knowledge."

"I say, Holmes, do you think so?"

"I do, Watson. I further believe that the Father suspects our mission here to be more than mere inquiry. How he has divined it is not our concern. But I believe if Relinsky's plan should go awry, Father Storozhev shall prove to be an invaluable ally."

Our calm reverie was soon assaulted by the sounds of Reilly's obvious return.

"Ah," said Holmes, "Yurovsky is with Relinsky."

"How do you know that?" I asked.

"Because there are the sounds of more than one car, and Relinsky and Obolov would not need more than one unless there was an escort in attendance."

Thomas appeared at the entrance to the courtyard and signalled us back in. Reilly and Yurovsky were already with Preston in the receiving room. Preston was very correct in his introductions.

"Mr. Holmes, Dr. Watson, I have the pleasure to introduce the Regional Commissar for Justice of the Urals Soviet, Comrade Yakov Yurovsky."

We shook hands and Yurovsky questioned us through Reilly.

"I understand, gentlemen, that you are here to inquire as to the disposition of Citizen Romanov and his family?"

"That is quite correct," said Holmes.

"Tell me," asked Yurovsky, "doesn't your government take the obviously honest word of their own consul in Ekaterinburg?"

"That they do, Comrade Commissar," said Holmes, "but in a matter of such international delicacy, our superiors supposed our four meagre eyes and ears would bring perhaps fresh, new perspective on Consul Preston's reports."

"I see," said Yurovsky continuing, "and I mean no disrespect in this whatsoever, they have sent new watchdogs to augment the old ones."

"An interesting turn of phrase, Comrade Commissar," said Holmes, "no insult taken. But permit me one question now, the only question in which my government is interested. How is the Imperial Family?'"

"Citizen Romanov and his family are in fine health, except for the boy. He is still recuperating from a most unfortunate event. No doubt, you have already been informed of the incident."

"Then you will not have any objection to our seeing the Imperial Family," Holmes asked.

"I am afraid that I do have an objection. Our Regional Soviet has requested that Citizen Romanov and his family not be unduly disturbed by outside influences. We have provided for their every need, and as I am sure Consul Preston has told you, I am personally responsible for their well being.

"I have already made measurable changes in the way the family is treated, and in a general tightening of security against the reactionary forces in the country who might wish to do harm to the family."

"I am afraid I must insist on my personal interview with the Imperial Family. Those are my instructions," said Holmes.

"And I must deny you that interview for now. Those are my instructions. The Comrade Colonel has already presented his orders to me which seem most striking on the surface. But there is an old Russian saying, 'Our troubles are here, and the Tsar is far away.' In other words, Moscow is far away and I need additional proof that the Comrade Colonel's papers are in order; which, of course, I am sure they are.

"However, we are having a bit of trouble with communications at the moment. It seems that our lines have been cut once again, and I have already dispatched a force to repair them and drive off the bandits who pester us in such manner."

Yurovsky turned and addressed Reilly. For a few moments Reilly said nothing, then translated for us.

"He says he has seen to the comfort of my men at the train. Since he was sure they must be tired after their long journey, and certainly in no mood to guard our train, he has ordered food and drink be brought to them. In addition, so they can be relieved of guard duty, his men have surrounded our train for our protection.'"

"He has done well," said Holmes.

"Quite," said Reilly. Preston shifted in his chair and pulled at his starched collar which seemed to be losing its stiffness with Yurovsky's every utterance. Yurovsky rose. Reilly continued to translate.

"As soon as I have confirmation, gentlemen, I shall be happy to turn over my charges to your care. I assure you, it shall be one responsibility I shall sleep more lightly without. Until then, please feel free to enjoy our lovely town. Consul Preston can show you the high points, I am sure.

"Comrade Colonel Relinsky shall be returning with me to Cheka headquarters, along with his aide, Obolov. There is much more we have to discuss. Renegade White pirates and the like are high on the agenda. I have also never met anyone who has personally spoken with Comrade Lenin. That shall be a treat for me, indeed. I look forward to the time we shall be spending together, Comrade Colonel Relinsky. Of course, he is not under arrest, gentlemen. Good day."

He saluted and left us there with Preston, Reilly making brief eye contact with Holmes and shrugging, before he walked out with

Yurovsky.

"Wonderful," said Preston, "just what we needed."

"But surely you have contingent plans," said Holmes.

"Well, yes and no," said Preston.

"It cannot be both, Mr. Preston. It must be one or the other."

"Not in all cases, Mr. Holmes. Look here: until Yurovsky took over, I had men in place, not many, who would have augmented your small band; disciplined men who would have overcome Avdeyev's lot with no great difficulty.

"But now there are disciplined troops on duty. More machine guns than before, and a commander who is shrewd, intelligent and who will not hesitate to use his local power; as he has just so amply and professionally demonstrated."

"Yes, I see what you mean," said Holmes. "This Yurovsky does deserve respect. In one motion he has even temporarily outwitted Relinsky.

"But I assure you, Mr. Preston, there is still room for manoeuvre. Once those lines are up again, Relinsky and his men are done for. Watson and I have been presented as diplomats, and Yurovsky is far too schooled to do us any harm."

"I believe you may have twenty-four hours at the most," said Preston. "I have been told that a small White task force would be left behind to guard the break in the line and prevent its repair. But I was not told the size or tenacity of that force. For all we know, they might be gone even now."

"It is not a comforting thought," said Holmes.

"So tell me, Mr. Holmes, to where do we turn now?"

"Why to heaven, Mr. Preston. We turn to heaven."

Father Storozhev

Twilight was descending, and I thanked nature for its long, summer days in this clime, as Holmes, Thomas and I went touring. Of course, our first stop was the church of Father Storozhev.

"Welcome, my sons, I have been expecting you."

"Indeed?" said Holmes. Thomas continued to translate.

"My son, I knew you understood my meaning before, and I have just seen your Comrade Colonel and his man go off with Yurovsky. I knew you would be here shortly."

"Perhaps Father Storozhev should take up consulting detective work," Holmes said to me under his breath.

The Father showed us into his tiny office where we all sat and shared a glass of cool water.

"Now, my sons, please tell me, who you truly are?"

"Who we are is not important, Father. But you were correct before in your supposition, we are here to rescue the Imperial Family."

"You have not gotten off to a healthy beginning. However, there is an old Russian saying, 'A day cannot be judged by its morning.' I shall help in every way."

"Then tell us, please, Father, the tunnel or passageway you alluded to before, where is it, precisely?"

"It is beneath you, my sons. As I said earlier, all of Ekaterinburg is built over mine shafts and tunnels. When Professor Ipatiev built his house, some workers, members of my church, informed me that they had discovered an old passageway leading from a half-basement under the Ipatiev House which would connect with various tunnels my church had been built over.

"In fact, Mr. Holmes, should you remove your chair and pull back the rug, you shall find a concealed door. It is masked as boards with bolts."

Holmes immediately did so as Thomas, the Father and I watched. Holmes requested a candle from the Father so he could see down the shaft. He was delighted to find an ancient wooden ladder there, still serviceable, though barely so. He slowly and cautiously disappeared into the hole for a few minutes and was then back. "Well, it's broad enough for four abreast."

"Yes," said Father Storozhev, "and let me give you the diagram the men in my flock gave me. It will show you exactly how to get to the Ipatiev House.

"If you can plan some escape for the Imperial Family using this information, we shall truly be blessed by God."

"I should hope we can, Father, but I'm afraid we'll need more than information. Thomas, are the men Preston mentioned still about?"

"I should think so."

"How many were there, Preston didn't say."

"I think about thirty or so."

"That should be enough, I think. Do you have a signal of some sort to call them together?"

"I believe so; I wasn't privy to particular arrangements."

"That's all right, we can get the particulars from Preston upon our return. What about the leader of the group? Who was he?"

"Unfortunately, I believe Relinsky was to take immediate command. But of course that's impossible now."

"True," said Holmes. "There is no other within your group you can trust for command?"

"Not that I know of. What about yourself, Mr. Holmes?"

"No, I am not a military man. Besides, I shall be busy with other things, as shall Dr. Watson. If only there was another we could trust to take command of your men, our task would be made more hopeful of success."

It was then, from behind us, we heard a hoarse voice with a thick Russian accent ask, "What about me, Comrades?"

Holmes and I turned to see the bald head and smiling face of Stravitski.

Lazarus

I thought I was seeing a phantom and took a step backward.

"But you are dead," I said emphatically.

"Do not tell my family, they worry," said Stravitski with a laugh.

"And you speak English!" I do not know which shocked me more. I also noticed Holmes trying to stifle a smile while Father Storozhev and Thomas looked at us uncomprehendingly.

"Remember what Colonel Relinsky say," said Stravitski as he closed a side door and came towards us, "trust maybe no one. Look at me, I speak English! And I not even dead!"

With that, Holmes let out a laugh, and in the midst of my confusion and sputtering, Stravitski gave me a hug and one of those 'one kiss per cheek' things the Russians like so well, though he had never before been affectionate; nor, for that matter, very civil. Holmes continued to laugh, and I sensed that he was laughing as much from humour as from a sense of relief and broken tension.

After Holmes, between laughs, explained to Thomas and Father Storozhev how we knew Stravitski, Stravitski explained to Holmes and me, with the other two men as bystanders, just how he came to be present.

"So my colonel tell you I no make it to Kungur. Well, that no lie. I do not. When most attack, he tell me wait, take horse, and go. So much confusion, nobody see, nobody mind. He right. I to come here, to see what going on. I to watch trains, Cheka, soldiers.

"It take me two more days get here. I see many White soldiers go southeast. Some go northwest. I think White armies coming like this." He cupped his hands together like two vices closing.

"I get here night. I sleep by dead mine. Nobody come. I see what happen in Ekaterinburg, then I say myself, colonel here with you all soon, where I go nobody look? Is simple! Church! Nobody go church no more!" Since Thomas was translating for the Father, Father

Storozhev said something and Stravitski said something back.

"Father say is no true. I say sorry. Father good man. He take me in at night. I tell him I deserter from Reds. I lie to him. He hide me. I no tell him nothing. He come tell me what happen with my colonel, with you, I listen at door. I hear. Now I help. My colonel smart. He know something bad may happen. He send me here to help. I ace up sleeve."

We all laughed at that one.

"Yes, you are an ace, all right," said Holmes. "And you most certainly will help. You have heard all we said?" Stravitski nodded assent. "Good, then," said Holmes, "this is what I hope to do." And with that, he began outlining his plan.

By the time we got back to the consulate, some four hours later, without Stravitski, of course, the day was coming to an end.

Preston greeted us inside with a man who looked like a peasant labourer. And that was precisely what he turned out to be. Mikail Gablinev had been a human mole who spent most of his life in the mines; until the Great War had lifted him literally from the depths of darkness, only to bore into his body and soul like some nightmarish machine. When everything precious was used, he was abandoned like the mines in which he had slaved.

However, he and many more like him, men who had deserted from the Imperial Army and who had battle experience, had long ago been recruited by Preston to fight for something they could see and understand: their living god, the Tsar.

These men had refused to continue fighting a travesty, a losing war against other men they didn't know, for officers who used them as chattel. They returned to their families; but they were still loyal to their peasant concept of the Tsar. To them, he was a god. They knew he and his family were hostage at the Ipatiev House. They had been told by Preston that men were coming who would help them rescue their Tsar.

101

They had waited and watched the Reds.

Ekaterinburg was their town. They knew it literally from its insides out. The Red Guards and troops in the town were from other places. They were outsiders. Many of the new guards at the Ipatiev House were Letts. There would be no trouble killing these outsiders, though Gablinev and his men knew more outsiders would eventually come to kill them.

Preston had Gablinev waiting just in case. Holmes was right; Preston had more than a bit of the military man in him. When we were safely inside, and Holmes had finished telling Preston his plan, Gablinev left. But not before letting us know that he knew about Stravitski. His men had told him of the bald man on the fringes of town, and they thought him a deserter. It did not matter from which side. Shortly, they would be taking orders from the man.

Holmes' plan was like Holmes: multi-faceted, cunning, straightforward, daring, and, of course, brilliant.

Father Storozhev would go to Yurovsky and get permission for a midnight mass, similar to the one he had conducted the month before. If Yurovsky objected, which, of course, he would at this last-minute petition, the Father would tell him it was at the request of the two British diplomats. To Yurovsky, that would make sense, and he would be grateful for this new and rather unorthodox, or should I say Orthodox, method of keeping the two Englishmen satisfied and away from his affairs.

Once Father Storozhev was in the basement with the Imperial Family for mass, where mass had been held in June, and which the guards would not attend, the Father would hold the service. The guards would be listening to the chants and incantations, and would also understand the long period of silent prayer. It was during this period of silent prayer that the Father would lead them all via the secret tunnel back to the church.

Now even during silent prayer, there is some low murmuring, and most of that murmuring would be from women, in this case, the

Tsarina and the Grand Duchesses. So besides having a number of our men waiting at the entrance to the tunnel by the Ipatiev House, we would also enlist the aid of the nuns. As the Imperial Family would be filing down into the tunnel, the nuns and some of the men would continue the low prayer, hopefully allaying any distrust among the guards. If something went wrong, our men would form a delaying action until the Romanovs could reach the church.

Preston interrupted to say that the nuns were still fairly young and it would be only a minor inconvenience to negotiate the tunnel, but Father Storozhev was into advanced age and Preston doubted his capacity for this sort of thing.

Holmes assured him that the Father would be all right. Our men would carry the Father if they had to, but it was imperative that the Father play his part. Indeed, Father Storozhev demanded it. Yet I felt Holmes' argument lacking. Something was amiss.

In addition, upon return to the church, the Father was to be trussed up, so when the Cheka burst in looking for him, he could believably claim to have been overpowered and that he knew nothing of what was going on. As for the nuns, since no one would see them, they would spend one day in the tunnel, our men would have food and water for them, and they would return to their convent under the cover of the next darkness, guarded by the men.

Furthermore, Holmes said, there would be no suspicion if he and I went to the church to see the Father off on his midnight mass, since we would be expected to be waiting for immediate word of the Imperial Family. Holmes would go along with the men in the tunnel; I would wait at the church for their return. Preston would remain at the consulate. Even Thomas must stay behind. There must be no evidence after-the-fact that Preston and Thomas were involved in this rescue. The Bolsheviks would rant and threaten, but in the end, Holmes felt, they would state, for political reasons, that Preston and Thomas were mere dupes in this nefarious plot by dissident and criminal elements acting without the approval of the British government. Holmes knew

103

the strong Allied force in Murmansk was a potent deterrent to any political confrontation the Soviets might consider.

At precisely midnight, when the mass would begin, Stravitski would lead a commando-type raid on Cheka headquarters to release Reilly and Obolov. Holmes said he thought this to be a fairly easy task.

At that hour, most everyone would be asleep, except, of course the few guards on duty. No one was expecting an attack of any sort. The guards on duty would be quickly and silently eliminated, and Stravitski and only one other man, would make their way to the room where Father Storozhev said the Cheka usually held their suspects for questioning. This room was down a flight of stairs to the immediate right as you entered the Hotel America; it had originally been a large billiard room.

It was imperative that silence be maintained for a number of reasons. The first, obviously, was to gain Reilly and Obolov's immediate release. The second, that any shooting from Cheka headquarters, however faint, might alert the guards at the Ipatiev House. Finally, any disturbance might also alert the guards surrounding Reilly's men at the train.

Once Reilly and Obolov had been freed, they, along with Stravitski and his men, were to make their way as quickly as possible to the church, where they would form our guard from the church to the train.

Holmes was emphatic in his instructions to Stravitski that unless absolutely necessary, Yurovsky was not to be harmed. Whatever future plans Holmes had in mind, Yurovsky, it was evident, would figure prominently.

Now, to Reilly's men at the train.

As you will remember, there were only about a dozen or so left under the command of Lt. Zimin. They were being guarded by Yurovsky's men, perhaps twice that number. Holmes suggested, and Gablinev agreed, there would be more guards awake and on duty at this site.

104

Gablinev had only about a dozen men. But combined with Reilly's men, and the element of surprise, it seemed that all might go well. Gablinev and his men were to attack at precisely twelve-thirty, by which time Reilly and his men would have weapons. Yurovsky's men would suddenly be caught between a hammer and an anvil.

When Gablinev and Reilly's men linked up, they were to hold against any counterattack. Once our party arrived, Gablinev and his men would act as our rear-guard and delaying force.

As to what would happen after we were aboard and running, Holmes felt Reilly had other information from Kolchak. We would have to leave that up to Reilly; for from what we knew, there was now nothing between us and safety except thousands of miles filled with millions of Reds with Kolchak's commando forces somewhere in between.

While those were the plans, there was no guarantee of success. Whatever the course of events, it was destined to be the most compelling night of my life.

At half-past-ten, Holmes and I walked across the street to Father Storozhev's church. We were shown to the Father's study where Stravitski was about to leave with a man sent by Gablinev. He asked us to wait a few moments for the Father, and we wished each other luck.

After a few more moments with no Father Storozhev, Holmes became impatient, excused himself and said he would return by the time Father Storozhev came in.

After about ten minutes the caretaker came in and made gestures indicating that I should wait a little more. It was now about fifteen minutes to eleven. Finally, the door to the study opened and Father Storozhev came in. He motioned me to sit again, and went behind his small, primitive desk.

We looked at our timepieces, the Father made the sign of the cross and we smiled at each other, all the while me wondering where the dickens was Holmes. After a few moments of this, I stood, said, "Mr. Holmes," and made a motion showing I was going to look for him.

I opened the study door, and to my utter astonishment, there stood Father Storozhev. I took two steps backward.

"What? What's this?" This was all I could manage while my head, like a tennis ball, went back and forth between the two Fathers.

Finally, I touched the Father at the doorway and asked quietly, "Holmes, is that you?"

"No, Watson," said the Father at the desk, "that's the Father."

"Blast it man, you have done it to me again. When will you ever stop these tricks you perpetrate on me?" Holmes was laughing. So was the Father.

"I don't have an answer for that one, my friend. But very shortly now, I shall go to say mass."

"I beg your pardon?"

"Was I speaking in a foreign tongue? I said I would shortly be saying mass."

"Well, this is the maddest of your mad ideas. How in blazes are you to be Father Storozhev?"

"I have fooled you already, and the guards do not know the Father that well. Remember, they are new. The Father has already obtained the approval we needed from Yurovsky, that is where he has been, and Yurovsky's men will be waiting for me.

"I knew before, during Preston's objections about Father Storozhev, that the Father could not go. He is too old, and he may waiver. I had Stravitski explain the addition to my plan and the Father reluctantly agreed when he was told he would stay behind to guide the nuns and men into the tunnel, and bless everyone as they entered.

"In the time remaining now, he shall say the prayers in Russian and I shall transliterate them so I may read them. Since the guards will not attend the mass, they will not see me reading; and should they, it would still not arouse suspicion.

"The Father has also given me a note to hand to the Tsar

explaining everything. I tell you Watson, it will work."

"The devil, it will! We have enough to worry about without your charade."

"Watson, it must be this way. Father Storozhev is too old. And while I myself have gotten on, I am most certainly not out. I must take his place.

"I hope you know what you are doing, Holmes," I said.

"But Watson, that is why I am here, am I not?"

Had Holmes finally answered the question of why we were here; or was it merely one of his more tauntingly caustic questions?

The Rescue Begins

It was now fifteen minutes to midnight. We shook hands, looked at each other for consolation and encouragement, and Holmes stepped outside the church.

He had been blessed and kissed by Father Storozhev before, he began walking slow and straight, and if I did not know better, I would have believed him to be the Father. I watched him fade into the night and found myself muttering silent prayers of my own.

I learned later from the various participants all that I shall now recount.

At the rear of Hotel America, the Cheka headquarters, Stravitski and six men had crouched and waited in the area where rubbish was stored. After a few moments, Stravitski and one hand-picked man, Tsukov, had slit the throats of the two guards on duty and had put two of his own men in place. The rest had entered through the main door. At this point, two had stayed at the head of the stairwell leading down, while Stravitski and Tsukov had gone to free Reilly and Obolov.

They knew that if the Cheka slept, all would go well.

At the same time as this was going on, Yuri Gablinev lay flat on his stomach on a hill overlooking Ekaterinburg Station 2, just north of where Reilly's men were under guard. He had five other men with him. South of the station, in a marshy part of the lake near the Verk-Isestsk factory, seven other men waited. At twenty minutes past twelve, they would begin moving towards the station.

Gablinev noted happily that most of the guards who were supposed to be awake, were not. But there were four guards drinking vodka and singing just below his hill. Their rifles were stacked neatly as prescribed by their training, still close enough to be of deadly use.

Holmes approached the Ipatiev House.

The guards had been given their orders, as Yurovsky promised, and as Holmes passed by, he was not even given a second glance.

Once through the main archway, he was met by a corporal of the guard who commented to Holmes that it was a nice night. Holmes understood, nodded agreement and continued following after a perfunctory, "Da."

The corporal led Holmes into the house; there was only one guard semi-awake that he could see, sitting in a large chair, his head falling to his chest. Then Holmes followed the corporal to the rear, and then down a flight of steps. Holmes remembered to walk with arthritic care.

At the foot of the steps were two guards on either side of an open door. They were sitting on wooden stools; and although alert, they did not regard this Father Storozhev as a major hazard to their health.

Holmes said nothing, but I suspected his heart would be beating so loudly he would suspect the guards to hear; not only from the strain of this ordeal, but knowing that within scant seconds, he would be in the presence of the Imperial Family.

The Corporal pointed to the door, mildly saluted Holmes and went back upstairs. Holmes walked in and looked around. The room was bare except for a table and seven chairs set up for the mass. As Holmes covered this table with the sacramental cloth as he was instructed to do, and went about the motions of setting the religious items in their appropriate places, he was really looking for the specific bolts in the wooden flooring which Father Storozhev had told him about. For with the loosening of just two of these bolts, which the Father would have the men in the tunnel do from the underside, the boards could be lifted, giving access to the tunnel.

As he heard many footsteps coming down the stairs outside, Holmes located the bolts to the extreme left rear of the basement. He quickly went to the front of the table and placed his hands in imitation of Father Storozhev.

Then with the footsteps ever closer, the moment he had come these many thousands of miles for, rushed up at him as Tsar Nicholas II entered the room carrying his son, the Tsarevich Alexei. They were followed in quick order by the Tsarina and the four Grand Duchesses, the Grand Duchess Tatiana giving her mother support.

As each filed in, Holmes had to remember to make the sign of the cross, to hold out his cross for each to kiss, and, as he finally admitted, to hold his knees stiff for his own support; so deeply did this moment affect him. Especially at the sight of the Tsar holding the Tsarevich.

Yes, Sherlock Holmes admitted to me, he turned to go to the rear of the table to hide his emotion from the Imperial Family. But when he turned and saw them all sitting there so erect, in defiance of their physical appearance and belying all that had happened to them, Holmes felt emotion once again bestirring itself.

As the guards closed the doors, he took his paper from under his robe and glanced at his timepiece. It was seven minutes past midnight.

July 8, 1918   Escape

At a few seconds past twelve, two guards lay dead at their posts outside Hotel America, two of Stravitski's men had donned their uniforms and taken their places, and four men had entered without being detected.

Two more men were left by the stairs, and as Stravitski started down, he heard a sleepy voice say, "Stop making noise. I am sleeping." His own were the last words the guard heard.

Stravitski and Tsukov walked quietly down the hallway till they came to the corner where it went to the right. Stravitski gave a quick glance and saw one sleeping guard, his rifle against the wall, sitting in front of a door which Stravitski hoped held Reilly and Obolov. Tsukov, as stealthily as a Thugee, came close enough to slit this guard's throat, as well. Stravitski came to him quickly while Tsukov had already pulled keys from the guard's tunic.

Stravitski opened the door slowly to see Reilly and Obolov on their backs, on simple cots. As both men looked up, Stravitski had to put his hand over Obolov's mouth to keep him from screaming; Obolov thought himself in the midst of some horrible nightmare with this ghost in front of him.

You see, Reilly, with all that had happened, had neglected to mention that Stravitski was not dead at all. Or perhaps, even then, he still felt Obolov need not know; for if they were to die, what would it matter? And if they lived, Reilly would have a ready explanation if Obolov found Stravitski alive. However, this proved an emotional trauma Obolov would not forgive.

Reilly smiled as he quickly wakened, Tsukov already handing him a pistol. Reilly told Tsukov to watch the door, Stravitski still clasping Obolov's mouth shut as he quietly explained he was not dead. Reilly went and patted Stravitski on the back. Obolov was now just silent.

Stravitski said he would explain all later, now they must get out. But Reilly said his papers were with Yurovsky in his room. They must go to the second floor and get them; they would be needed. Stravitski explained to Reilly that Holmes needed Yurovsky alive. He then told Tsukov to take Obolov outside with him, while he and Reilly went upstairs. The two men from the stairs followed them to the second floor.

The drunken guards at the foot of the hill near Gablinev were getting more drunk. That was good and that was not, because one of the guards had just loudly announced his imperative need to relieve himself, and that he was going to do so on his fellow comrades from the height of the hill.

The guard, already unbuttoning his fly, began making his way up the hill.

Holmes, now having regained his religious composure completely, solemnly began mass. He noticed it was the Tsarevich who first probably realized that Holmes was not Father Storozhev. As Alexei, sitting next to his father began to try to get his attention, Holmes came around the table, gestured that all should continue their prayers, and handed the Tsar the paper from the Father.

Holmes said the Tsar looked at the paper, looked at Holmes, looked at the paper again, then very carefully looked at Holmes again. The Tsar said nothing, but smiled to Holmes in a way of understanding, humour, and thanks. More importantly, in a whisper, he told his family to do everything Holmes said. The Tsarina and the Grand Duchesses did not seem to understand what was going on, but Alexei knew instantly and gave Holmes the biggest grin Holmes had ever seen on a child.

As Holmes made his way towards the boards to the tunnel, everything seemed to be going well. It was sixteen minutes past midnight.

Snoring could be heard through the closed doors at Cheka headquarters. Reilly knew which room was Yurovsky's because he had listened as Yurovsky had given instructions early for one of his new men to fetch something from his room. There were no guards on this floor, these were officers' quarters. Guards slept in the rear of the first floor and in the downstairs area. The rest were billeted at the Verk-Isestsk factory, and most of those were guarding the train.

Reilly had one of Stravitski's men go the far end of the hall to keep watch around the corner; the other remained at the top stairs.

Reilly cautiously opened the door to find Yurovsky leaning over our papers. Reilly pointed his pistol and Yurovsky simply put his hands in the air. He smiled at Reilly and said, "I must show you my other foot so you can put the shoe on."

Stravitski entered and Reilly told him to bind and gag Yurovsky.

"You mistake this, Comrade Commissar," said Reilly, "my orders come from Cheka headquarters in Moscow. If I fail in my mission, it will mean my head. And if I fail because of the Ekaterinburg Cheka, it will mean my balls. I am sure you can see my predicament.

"However, you were courteous to me, so as you see, I am returning the favour and not having you shot; merely bound." Yurovsky nodded as if to say thank you.

Stravitski finished, and Yurovsky was one with the chair.

"Now, I cannot promise that I shall behave this way again; so please be wise and stay put. Someone will happen along eventually and set you free; just as my friends have done with me." But now Reilly's tone became harsh.

"But know this, Comrade Commissar, the Romanovs are mine now, and I shall bring them to trial in Moscow whether you live or do not." Then he turned charming again as Stravitski left the room and Reilly turned to do likewise.

"Think of me as doing you a favour. By me taking the

responsibility for the Romanovs, I am absolving you of yours. Forgive me if I don't wish you luck."

As Reilly stepped outside, the man at the top step turned to go down, and Stravitski followed hard behind. Stravitski then heard footsteps behind but thought it was the second guard bringing up the rear. It was a fatal mistake.

Suddenly Reilly heard a gasp from Stravitski. He whirled around and saw a Cheka officer had plunged a knife into Stravitski's back, and the second guard with Reilly was doing likewise to the officer. The guard was terrified at what he had permitted to happen, but had the good sense to hold the officer's body as it went limp and quietly laid it on the floor. Reilly was doing likewise with Stravitski.

As Reilly held Stravitski's head, Stravitski smiled at him and said, "This time, Obolov will not believe you."

With that, he died.

Holmes was still conducting the loud portion of the mass as the men in the tunnel undid the bolts from below and slowly pushed the boards up. The Tsarina let out a mild gasp as the board-door rose up, seemingly out of the bowels of hell, and the Grand Duchesses were now completely confounded. But as they looked to the Tsar, and saw his calm expression and heard his quiet words, they understood they were being rescued, and continued to obey the Tsar's whispered commands to do as Holmes said.

Holmes now bid them go down into the tunnel, indicating the Tsar to hand down the Tsarevich first. From the expression on the boy's face, Holmes could tell he was just like other fourteen-year-olds, enjoying a great adventure.

As Alexei was handed down to strong, thankful hands, Holmes gestured the nuns and a man up. As a Grand Duchess went down the stairs, a nun would take up her low incantation.

And so it went until only the Tsar remained. He had already taken a step down when he suddenly stopped and turned to Holmes who had been helping him down. The Tsar smiled at him, and continued after his family.

As soon as he had reached bottom, Holmes bid the nuns start down, and then the last man. Then Holmes himself climbed down the stairs and waited at the foot while the last man retightened the bolts from below.

He then rushed back to the church. It was twelve-thirty.

As the drunken guard reached the top of the hill, one of Gablinev's men grabbed him from behind while another stabbed him in the heart. Gablinev, trying to imitate the dead man's voice, then yelled down that he was sick and needed help. Two more guards ventured up the hill never to come down. The last guard was still drinking from his bottle, his face turned towards the station, when one of Gablinev's men stabbed him, as well.

Then Gablinev and his men got close enough to the guards and opened fire just as his other men from the lake did likewise.

As hoped, Reilly's men, thinking themselves under attack, grabbed their weapons and opened fire at Yurovsky's men. Gablinev shouted to Reilly's men, as did others, that they were there to effect their freedom. In a few minutes, the four other Cheka guards surrendered. Gablinev had their throats slit.

The two small forces shook hands as Gablinev explained what they were to do next, and relayed Holmes' orders about getting the locomotive fired up. Lt. Zimin obeyed, and all waited for the Imperial Family, Holmes, Watson, Reilly, and the others to arrive.

When Holmes got to the foot of the stairs leading to the church, the nuns were already seated on chairs in the tunnel, candles lighting their way, their prayer books at the ready. Two of Gablinev's men would stay with the nuns until they were safely out the next night.

Holmes thanked them all, and as he climbed the stairs, the

Ladies blessed him.

When he climbed into Father Storozhev's study, Holmes saw me holding the Tsarevich. He had been lifted up to me, and I could not but think of my son, John, just about the same age as this helpless and weak poor boy.

The Father was busily explaining everything to the Imperial Family, and Holmes did not even have time to begin pulling off his false beard when Reilly burst in. The others with him remained outside, guarding the church.

At the sight of a Cheka Colonel, the Tsarina gave out a scream, but Father Storozhev calmed her and reminded her that this was the supposed Bolshevik he had told them about. The Tsarina quieted herself. Reilly, upon seeing the Grand Duchess Tatiana, stopped himself for ever the briefest of moments just staring at her, then saw Holmes in the Father's hassock, shook his head in disbelief, and motioned Holmes to quicken the pace. He looked back at Tatiana, and she at him, as he ran out.

As Holmes changed his clothing, one of Gablinev's men was already tying up Father Storozhev. The Tsarina and the Grand Duchesses began to cry as this was done and tried to stop the man from hitting the Father across the face; an act of necessity to further convince the Bolsheviks of his innocence when they found him.

The Father was gently laid on the floor, the bolts to the tunnel had already been tightened, and the Imperial Family, with Alexei now given to one of the younger and stronger men, was being hustled out of the study. The Tsarina was weeping as she fled, the Grand Duchesses, as well, their heads craning backwards for one last look at the Father.

Holmes was the last to leave the study, and told me later that in act of sheer role reversal, he blessed the Father; Holmes claimed he still had the cross around his neck, which he then laid carefully on Father Storozhev's desk; along with some papers.

As Holmes left, he heard the Father's faint prayers.

As we passed the British Consulate, we saw Preston and Thomas wave to us for good luck. I waved back. But things seemed to be going too well, I thought. And I was proved correct almost immediately; for as our motor cars approached the Verk-Isestsk factory cum barracks, there were soldiers waiting in ambush.

The lead car with Tsukov and his men was machine gunned. I believe Tsukov was killed instantly. The car with Reilly and Obolov was next and stopped immediately. The next auto bore the Imperial Family, which also immediately stopped, while Holmes and I were in the rear car with the last few of Gablinev's men.

Reilly, Obolov and all the available guards fanned out and returned fire, but there were no machine guns. Reilly had Obolov lead some men to catch the Reds on their right flank, and after some harsh and intense moments, the shooting ceased.

I saw Reilly running back to the Imperial Family. He said something, ran back to his motor car, and we started up again.

Within a very few minutes we were at the station. The locomotive was ready, Gablinev and his men knelt upon seeing the Imperial Family, and Reilly and Obolov helped them into what had previously been our compartments.

Holmes and I thanked Gablinev, and as we shook hands, Reilly called to forget the pleasantries and get aboard. This we did quickly.

As the train pulled out, headed due west towards Perm, Holmes waved to Gablinev and his men as long as he could see them in the night.

It was only much later that I would learn the fates of Father Storozhev, the nuns, Gablinev, and his men.

The Romanovs

I must now pause in this narrative, for a moment, to convey to you my impressions of the Imperial Family as I came to know them: physically, medically, personally.

However, one thing I must relate in general, the Imperial Family truly loved each other dearly. And this in particular, the Tsar and Tsarina were devotedly still in love, even after more than twenty years of marriage, the turmoil of a monstrous revolution, the loss of their crowns and continuous threats to their lives and those of their children. In fact, the Tsar still referred to the Tsarina by his nickname for her, 'Sonny.'

Please also note this, that before the revolution, and to the best of knowledge even to this date, there had been no hard words spoken or written about the Grand Duchesses, so kind and beloved were they.

Tsar Nicholas II, though only fifty, had aged considerably from his last, published photographs. His beard had gone prematurely grey, as had his temples. His soft, grey eyes, even when happy, still showed great pain.

Though only about five-feet-six, while his father, Alexander III had been six-foot-six, and his uncle, the Grand Duke Nicolai was close to seven feet tall, the Tsar gave the impression of additional height with a 'Maypole posture,' which means moving with a very erect carriage. To see this small, powerless man, once a god on earth, carrying his beloved son in his arms in the summer sun, was quite touching, indeed.

As it turned out, the Tsar loved the outdoors. He told us once that his favourite comment to his wife when she would gently reprimand him about his strenuous outdoor exercises, was this: "Sonny, scratch any Russian, and there's a peasant beneath." So perhaps because of his regular exercise, the Tsar was in excellent health, considering all he had been through.

Because he spoke English perfectly, as did all the Imperial Family, Holmes and I were able to converse with him at great length.

We were both charmed by his adroit sense of humour, and a basic innate kindness that we could not help noting was so at odds with how the press had always portrayed him.

The Tsar had been trained from childhood to be aloof and reserved. Yet from all his misfortune had sprung a gentle, fairly open inquisitiveness; and when conditions were safe, we saw him on many occasions speaking even to Reilly's men, who had been instructed to treat the Imperial Family with the utmost of deference still. I even noticed one or two of the men hold their caps when speaking to members of the family; one even called the Tsarina 'Matushka.'

The Tsarina Alexandra had recently become forty-six, and she, even more than the Tsar, had aged tremendously.

When she married the Tsar, she had been one of the great beauties of Europe. She was the daughter of Queen Victoria's daughter, Alice, making her first cousin to both King George and Kaiser Wilhelm. Indeed, she grew up as the Grand Duchess of Hesse-Darmstadt.

Now her once thick, chestnut hair, had harsh lines of grey coursing through, and her complexion, once perfect, was pallid and heavily lined. Though she suffered from irregular heartbeat, migraine headaches and long bouts of melancholia, I diagnosed her state to be more of mind than of body. Her melancholic nature had finally completely taken hold, and even though she was deeply immersed in her adopted religion of Russian Orthodoxy, or perhaps because of it, the more mystical side of her nature reinforced her melancholia, and she simply wished to die. It was as simple as that.

I also believe strongly another contributing factor here was that the Tsarina blamed herself for Alexei's haemophilia; and this retreat from life was her way of taking revenge on herself for the suffering she had brought to her boy.

Because of this, she was especially close to Alexei, looking after him as would a nurse. Among the girls, however, the Grand Duchess Tatiana seemed her pet.

Though Holmes and I tried, in the few days we could, the Tsarina would not permit us into her ever-shrinking world; though she thanked me profusely for treating Alexei so successfully.

Alexei was a high-spirited fourteen-year-old boy in the diseased body of a boy much younger. He was exceptionally thin, this a combination of his most recent encounter with his disease, the constant torment he and his family had been under, and a mild case of malnutrition.

Alexei, like his mother, seemed to be finally giving up. He had not been taking food well recently. One can only guess at what the emotions of such a sensitive boy could be, based upon all that had happened, especially to his father who he absolutely revered.

His large, dark eyes, though at times lively, were also old. They seemed to bear unfathomable secrets of the ages.

I grew quite close to Alexei, since it was he I was especially there for, and because I came to look upon him as the son I missed so terribly, and would come to miss even more as events forced me to stay away.

The Grand Duchess Olga was the eldest of the children. She was beautiful, as were all the Grand Duchesses, but at twenty-two, she was already a woman with a strong will of her own; and a deep suspicion because of all that had happened, that she would never share with a man the love and tenderness akin to her parents'. This distressed her greatly, although she never spoke of it outwardly.

She was tall, about five-foot-six, with what my mother would have called 'sunlight-brown' hair, and large, expressive, blue eyes. Although her royal temperament flared at times, showing she might be more like her mother than her father, it appeared that she showed her love for the Tsar more than the other Grand Duchesses did.

She was generally thoughtful and unaffected and in as good health as could be expected under the circumstances; although, she was still quite thin from her bout with measles which all the Grand Duchesses had come down with shortly before the family was shipped out of Petrograd.

The Grand Duchess Marie was as close to the Tsar's peasant adage as you could get in the Imperial Family. She was quite robust and strongly-built, and I was told that in her healthier days, she could lift her tutor. Now, she, too, was still abnormally thin from the measles.

At eighteen, Marie was the most simple of the Grand Duchesses in her tastes and quite surprisingly middle class in her attitude about family. I suspect she got that from observing how content her mother and father had been with each other and with the children.

The youngest of the girls, the Grand Duchess Anastasia, was sixteen, and the soul of the party, so to speak. Anastasia loved to make her family laugh, especially her brother, and would go to extreme lengths to send her loved ones into fits. She once stuffed napkins in her nose, swung her arm like a pachyderm's trunk, and galumphed around claiming she was a gift from her dear cousin, George, the Emperor of India.

Anastasia was still at that awkward, ungainly stage, small and squat, and telling me that soon she would be as tall and slim and beautiful and elegant as her sisters. She absolutely idolized them all. And she was especially proud of the colour of her hair, which was very near spun gold, so beautifully did it shine in the sun.

I have saved my description of the Grand Duchess Tatiana for last because she will play such a prominent part in the rest of this journal. Tatiana was one of the most beautiful women I have ever seen, excepting Mary and Elizabeth. At twenty, she was the tallest of the Grand Duchesses, five-feet-seven, the most elegant, and the thinnest, also, from the measles. She had magnificent dark hair, obviously inherited from her mother, a darker complexion than any in her family, and the most magnificent, gently slanted, blue eyes you could ever hope to look into.

She had also inherited her mother's reserved manner, and kept to herself more than the other Grand Duchesses, always seemingly lost in some deep thought. Yet who knows what truly stirs the depths beneath a tranquil ocean's surface? And without a doubt, she was her mother's pet.

I loved to look at Tatiana because she was so beautiful, and because I missed my wife so. But Tatiana was a human work of art, so graceful in her locomotion, so perfect of proportion. And like all the Grand Duchesses, so innocent of many things.

Thus ends my very brief, general description of the Imperial Family. Much more of substance shall be related as my journal continues.

Our locomotive was moving quickly, Reilly's men with captured machine guns on the roofs of the cars, the last car in use as a barracks.

The Imperial Family had been put into the various compartments of our railway car; the curtains drawn and their doors shut. The Tsar, Tsarina and Alexei were in Holmes' and my old compartment, Marie and Tatiana in Reilly's, Olga and Anastasia in another. Holmes and I would be sharing what used to be the compartment of Stravitski and Obolov. Reilly and Obolov were to stay in the barracks car.

By now we'd all been told about Stravitski, but Obolov just could not believe that his dear friend had been taken from him twice like this. Obolov would not be the same as before and since Reilly saw this, he began to distance himself from Obolov and draw closer to Lt. Zimin.

We were all tense and nervous, except Holmes, fearing an attack at any moment, not knowing if around the next turn the tracks would be blown and the Reds would be waiting.

But amazingly, nothing happened that night. In fact, by four A.M., all except the Imperial Family were dozing in the salon.

July 19, 1918

I awoke about eight to find Anastasia standing in the salon looking from man to man. Since I was the first to open his eyes, she smiled at me and asked, "What are we to do about breakfast?"

With those words all others awakened, and Reilly asked her to return to her compartment; it was dangerous for her to be out, and food would be brought into the salon shortly for her family.

I am not sure, but I think she flirted with Reilly as she thanked him and rushed back to her compartment. As she closed her door, I heard her excited voice saying something to Olga. If she was like any other sixteen-year-old girl, I can guess at the conversation she had with her sister.

Reilly said something to Obolov and he left the car. Then he turned to Holmes and me.

"There is much we must discuss."

"Indeed," said Holmes.

"First, now that there is time, I thank you both for helping save my life." Holmes waved his hand dismissively.

Reilly continued. "Nevertheless, I'm told you're both responsible for the Imperial Family's rescue from Ekaterinburg. I don't know yet how you accomplished their rescue in unison with mine and my men, and I'm sure Preston and Thomas had something to do with it, but what you did was nothing short of miraculous."

"I'm sure there are many people who would agree with you," answered Holmes. We all smiled.

"Yes, well, I've sent Obolov for food. I'll have to watch him now. Anyway, this is the last time he'll be permitted in this car. I will come and go, and you shall be free to do likewise when it's safe, but the Imperial Family will remain in this car for all our sakes."

Then he said to himself, but really to us, "I wonder why Yurovsky has not come after us?"

"He may do so or not," said Holmes, "and if not, it is thanks to

123

some papers I left on Father Storozhev's desk."

"Papers? What papers?" I asked.

Holmes was about to answer when the Tsar appeared at the edge of the salon. We were startled.

"I hope I have not disturbed you, gentlemen."

"No, no, not at all, your Imperial Majesty," we embarrassedly mumbled, or words to that effect.

"It is just that I first would like to thank you all, though I still do not know who you are, for saving the lives of my family. They are more precious to me than my crown. I am sure I shall know in time who is behind this, but it is you directly to whom I owe my undying gratitude. I only pray that I may someday be in a position of repaying in part the insurmountable debt I owe you all."

By the time the Tsar had finished his thanks, his eyes were filled with tears. He dabbed at them and made light of his discomfort with the following:

"On a more mundane note, my son and wife are getting quite hungry, and they have sent me to you in hopes of procuring something to eat."

It was Reilly who spoke, and it suddenly dawned on us as we saw it dawn on Reilly's face, that he was not sure how to address the Tsar. Would it be Your Imperial Majesty, or would it be Citizen Romanov? His decision would shape the Imperial Family's journey.

"Your Imperial Majesty," said Reilly, "The Grand Duchess Anastasia, not more than two minutes ago, asked the same question; and upon receiving an answer vanished back into her compartment." Holmes and I could see the Tsar seemingly gain inches upon being addressed so deferentially. He became more erect, while a small, grateful smile took hold on his lips. The smile, in turn, gave way to a small laugh. "And what was the answer?"

"Forgive me, Your Imperial Majesty, breakfast is being brought to us as we speak. When it arrives I shall inform you and your family so that you can come to the salon, if that is all right with you."

"I believe it will be, yes. I shall go and speak with the Tsarina about it."

I stopped him from leaving.

"Your Imperial Majesty, if your son is awake, I should like to examine him and see how he is doing. I am a doctor."

The Tsar remembered and was most apologetic.

"Oh, yes, yes, of course. Thank you doctor for your care of my son. Just give me a moment to speak with the Tsarina and I shall call you in."

His handshake was firm and tender at the same time. "Thank you again," said he. He then made his way back to his compartment.

"Bravo," said Holmes to Reilly, "you have put heart in a man who has had his ripped out. You have done well, comrade."

Reilly looked embarrassed.

"Yes, well, it couldn't hurt, after all. Anyway, I must..." Reilly stopped in mid-sentence and looked to our rear. Holmes and I turned to see what caused this interruption and found, standing there, the Grand Duchess Tatiana. She was staring intently at Reilly as he at her. Now it was I who felt embarrassed, as if I was somewhere I should not be. Or that I had walked in on two lovers.

By Jove, that was it! I could not believe it. I would have been willing to wager a year of my life, and would win that bet as you shall see, that Reilly had fallen in love, at first sight, mind you, with the Grand Duchess Tatiana. With truth being stranger than fiction, she was likewise fascinated by Reilly.

Holmes, being Holmes, and not having much interest in such matters, interrupted their reverie with a gracious, "Your Imperial Highness, may we help you?"

Tatiana kept her eyes on Reilly as she likewise inquired about breakfast, and it was Holmes who told her, with Reilly and Tatiana still looking at each other, what had just been told to her father.

She finally took her eyes to Holmes, thanked him and left, halting for a split second, but not turning.

I looked at Reilly. "I think I had better speak with you," I said.

"Not now, Dr. Watson," said Reilly absentmindedly, and left Holmes and me alone in the salon.

I smiled, put my hand on Holmes' shoulder and said, "Holmes, my friend, that hard-hearted, cold, calculating, murderous rogue named Relinsky, has just had his entire character changed in the flash of an eyelash."

Holmes looked at me.

"Holmes," I was laughing now, "he has fallen in love with Tatiana."

"Furthermore, I am positive that she has fallen in love with him."

With that revelation and a roll of his eyes, Holmes sat down.

I examined Alexei with both the Tsar and Tsarina looking on, and saw that the swelling on his right arm where the guard had hit him was continuing to go down. This was excellent. What was imperative, however, was that Alexei take food. I said this to him in a mock form of admonishment, and maybe because I was new, or had helped rescue his family, Alexei promised to try.

We left the Imperial Family alone to eat, with two of Reilly's men attending them. Holmes, Reilly, Obolov and I ate in the last car. As we partook of breakfast, still thrilled with our luck, we began passing through Kungur.

Reilly had told the soldier-engineer to slow down while going through Kungur but not to stop. We held our breath in fear of Red barricades. There were none.

It was at this point Reilly inquired about all that had happened the night before, which Holmes told him; and that Holmes inquired about the events at Cheka headquarters, which Reilly told us.

Then Reilly asked Holmes about our 'luck,' and what the papers Holmes left for Yurovsky had to do with it. I myself was about to ask that question, and was absolutely astounded, as was Reilly, with Holmes' answer.

"Well, gentlemen, my idea came when Preston said something about everyone wanting the Romanovs, but he wasn't sure if it was dead or alive. Then Yurovsky went on about how the Romanovs were his responsibility and how he could not afford to let them fall into the hands of the Whites.

"So I left a little note for our friend, Yurovsky, telling him that he was absolutely correct in his mistrust of us and that we were, in fact, White agents."

Reilly practically knocked over the table, so quick was he to sit bolt upright. "You said what?"

"Sit down, comrade, and listen further."

"My ears won't tolerate madness, comrade," spat Reilly.

"Well, I have not bayed at the moon lately," said Holmes. "I told him we represented powerful international forces that knew the Whites were eventually doomed, and all they wanted was the safe exit of the Romanovs from Russia. For that, they would keep the true fate of the Romanovs an eternal secret, because they also knew the Reds would stop at nothing anywhere in the world to have them killed if it was known they were alive.

"I reminded him that the Whites would, in fact, be in Ekaterinburg any time now, as we all knew, and that other White forces were heading down from the northwest, which they are, in a pincer movement. This would undoubtedly force Yurovsky to consider one of four possibilities.

"The first being that he and Beleborodov, the Chairman of the Urals Regional Soviet, and all the local Bolsheviks, surrender to the Whites; who, of course, will most certainly put them to death immediately.

"The second being that they try to break through the overwhelming White forces, which they most probably will not be able to do. Once captured and found to be the jailers of the Romanovs, they will be lucky if they are merely executed.

"The third, that if they do break through and make it into Bolshevik territory again, they will be arrested by either the Red Army or the Cheka for letting the Romanovs fall into White hands without a struggle; and they will most certainly be executed.

"Finally the fourth possibility, and one of my own devising. What if they leave evidence proving they have killed the Romanovs? Moscow will be pleased that the decision of what to do with the Romanovs has been taken out of their hands, and they can show their hands as clean to humanity. It will show how strongly committed the common people are. How their revolution has now finally and completely swept the old order away and enabled a new order to emerge supreme.

"The news of such an event will halt the onrush of the Whites since they have only been converging on Ekaterinburg with the intention of freeing the Romanovs. It may even throw the entire White counter-revolution into disarray because the symbol of what they had been fighting for has now been removed. Even if they hold up their advance ever so slightly, it will give better odds that Yurovsky and his men can slither out of the vice before it is too late.

"I reminded him about the deserted mines called 'The Four Brothers,' just outside of town, and suggested that this is where they claim the bodies were disposed of. Since it is a mining town, there are plentiful supplies of acids and chemicals which may be used to destroy as much false evidence as possible; including bones they should disinter from the local graveyard. Since Ekaterinburg is the epicentre of the fighting at the moment, no one should question in minutiae the evidence of the Romanovs' deaths, if it is handled wisely and adroitly. How they choose to portray their method of execution I left to Yurovsky.

"In case he felt like a gambler and decided to follow us or wire ahead once the lines were back up, I also reminded him about the orders signed by Lenin himself. How would other Red forces behave?

Especially the Cheka in Perm, from whence we had just come and who knew of Lenin's safe order of passage; they of course did not, but Yurovsky did not know this. How indeed would they react after Colonel Relinsky's account of the offhand dismissal of Comrade Lenin's orders, and the counter-revolutionary actions on the part of a Regional Commissar of Justice who is obviously now terrified of losing his life because of his irrational actions in the face of advancing White Armies? Oh, I laid it on with a thick brush, all right.

"Of course, I could not write Russian, so I had Thomas do it. That was why he was not with us for a time. He was busy translating my notes into Russian.

"I also suggested they bring Preston and Thomas into this affair in the following fashion, for they most certainly shall not be able to keep them out of it: Yurovsky, when asked about the shooting of the previous night, shall tell Preston that Relinsky escaped, and with the aid of myself and Watson, made a foolish, and ultimately unsuccessful attempt at freeing the Imperial Family. He will state, of course, that he knows Preston and Thomas had nothing to do with this; because even if he would like to murder them for the sake of murdering someone, he needs them as credible witnesses and as contacts to London.

"He shall insist that Preston let London know, through his ambassador in Moscow, of course, of this latest White outrage, and that there can no longer be a guarantee of Romanov safety. Since no one except the guards has access to the Ipatiev House, no one will know that they are no longer there. As usual, Preston shall demand to see the Imperial Family, Yurovsky can, as usual, refuse. It shall seem like business as usual and buy Yurovsky time to fake the executions."

Reilly and I just sat there staring at Holmes. Finally it was Reilly who spoke.

"That is the most fantastic scheme I have ever heard. It is either the work of a true genius or the demented imaginings of a raving lunatic."

Holmes looked at him and asked, "Which do you favour?"

"I am not yet sure," said Reilly quietly, "I am not yet sure."

"Well, whilst you decide, I am certain that Yurovsky has already secretly met with Beleborodov and Yermakov on my proposals, and perhaps even with key leaders of the guards to explain to the rank and file their imminent peril should the truth be known; and this blissful quietude to which we are heir is the result of their direct inaction.

"Now, if you don't mind, whatever this is that I was trying to eat has grown quite cold."

Holmes and I decided not to return to the Imperial Family's car. We would give them complete privacy. Of course I would attend Alexei a few times a day but we would not enter the car unless summoned by a member of the family.

Just as night came, well past Kungur and in the middle of the eternal emptiness that is the vast body of Russia, Reilly halted the train because he felt the Imperial Family, and his men as well, needed a half-hour's relaxation after the previous night's exertions; and here, quite in the middle of nothing, it seemed safe to do so. Furthermore, he confided, given all that was happening on this gigantic field of play, he was not sure when we would again have this opportunity.

I also think it might have been something more.

Reilly asked me to inform the Imperial Family of his orders, and to stress the importance of their partaking of the freedom of the night with its moon and soothing air. I did.

I stayed in the salon while the Tsar spoke with the Tsarina and the Grand Duchesses, and after a few moments, all, except the Tsarina, appeared with wide smiles on their faces; Alexei, of course, in the arms of his father.

They followed me outside, where some guards had already taken defensive positions, and began to stroll the countryside, the girls picking a few wildflowers for themselves and their mother; Marie kissing her father on the cheek and presenting him with a bouquet.

130

I watched the guards watching them, and saw the smiles on these men's faces, obviously thinking of their own families, and, I believe, wishing our charges well.

Then I saw Reilly was moving back and forth quite strangely, as if he could not make up his mind about something. I did not have to strain my intellectual powers to guess on what he was thinking, and had my suspicions confirmed when the Imperial Family broke up into smaller groups, Tatiana and Olga going off together. Reilly walked over to them.

He saluted them quite correctly and they acknowledged his salute in the best Imperial manner. Then the three walked slowly in circles talking, Tatiana and Olga sometimes laughing.

Reilly was working his magic once more.

After no more than fifteen minutes or so, Reilly and the Grand Duchesses began coming back, and Reilly signalled to the others in the Imperial Family to do likewise.

They all re-boarded the train, Reilly helping the Grand Duchesses up with the gentle strength of his hand, and I watched as Reilly's and Tatiana's hands remained as one for just a touch longer than the rest.

July 9, 1918

This evening, the guard at the door of the Imperial Family's car told us the Tsar wished Holmes, Reilly and me to join his family. This we did with alacrity.

It was at this session, again with the Tsarina absent, that we explained as much as we could to the Tsar of the true events of the world outside his confinement, which deeply distressed the family. We also explained who we were and the dangers that could well lie ahead.

At the sound of our names, the Tsar became wonderfully

excited, as did Alexei. It seems that many were the times the Tsar had read to Alexei my accounts of the adventures of Sherlock Holmes, and even the Grand Duchesses had a vague understanding of who we were.

Holmes and I were absolutely surprised to learn that on one of the Tsar's holidays with King George, he had even said that when he could bring Alexei to England, he would love to have his cousin arrange an audience for us.

Alexei became something of a grand inquisitor, firing rapid and numerous questions at us. These were not idle questions, but specific questions about specific cases and they were all intelligent questions. It was a joy to behold, and I saw the happiness on the Tsar's face as he watched his boy come alive.

The Grand Duchesses talked among themselves, and to Reilly, with the bulk of Reilly's attention being paid to Tatiana. At one point, I am positive I saw the Tsar notice this mutual interest, and then turn back to Holmes with an understanding in his eyes and in his smile of precisely what was happening between his daughter and Reilly. If I was correct, I thought to myself, then this man was truly a very unique man and father, indeed. Given our circumstances, and the extreme tenuousness of our very existence, the Tsar was tacitly giving his daughter permission to love for perhaps the only time in her life she might do so.

July 10, 1918

This morning we arrived in Perm. Even though the Imperial Family knew to stay closeted inside, Reilly thought it best to impart a gentle reminder. Then, with Lt. Zimin, and leaving Obolov with the guards at the train, Reilly left to go to Cheka headquarters and Colonel Mikoyan.

He returned in an hour. Yes, the lines to Ekaterinburg were finally restored and no, there had been no unusual messages. Either luck, or Holmes, or a combination of the two, was working overtime.

Reilly also informed us that he thought it best for us to leave as soon as fresh water, food and fuel could be put aboard. He said he finally did show the Lenin papers to Colonel Mikoyan, in command in Perm, who was very correct and, Reilly laughed, seemed to regard the papers he touched as sacred articles once he realized who had signed them. There would be no trouble in Perm.

Though the colonel would have liked to know who or what was aboard the train, Reilly simply asked to be alone with the colonel, as if to take him into his utmost, deepest confidence, and then told him that the train was carrying something so secret, that even Comrade Trotsky did not know. This was a private, and highly personal mission that he, Colonel Relinsky was undertaking for Lenin. Relinsky then leered and laughed to the colonel to give him the impression this mission involved women. The colonel understood immediately and laughed and leered in response.

Now Mikoyan, his chest puffed out, could regale his comrades about the highly personal affairs he was privy to about Comrade Lenin. Reilly had done a masterful job. Holmes and I shook our heads in amusement, and Reilly, after asking if everything was in order in the Imperial Family's car, went about seeing to his men.

We left Perm three hours later, and had a very good laugh to see, as we pulled out, our Cheka colonel waving us off at the station, complete with what appeared to be a small guard of honour.

The day concluded without further incident, the only matter of note being Reilly's increasing sense of "not finding a place for myself," as he put it. Plain and simple, the man wanted to see Tatiana and he could not just go barging in on her. He was ridiculously restless, and for the two seconds I saw him stop his movements, which resembled a June bug racing from flower to flower, plus the look on his face, an uneasy feeling that took hold that he was actually wishing for something untoward to happen so he could again rescue his maiden fair.

133

He did not have too much longer to wait.

July 11, 1918

By seven A.M., our train had come to a slight pass between Glazov and Kirov. Reilly, Holmes, Obolov and I had risen about an hour earlier and this was just as well as a shell landed near enough to shake us almost off our feet. It appeared that our journey was no longer going to be without incident. Before Holmes and I could even gather our thoughts, Reilly was on his way to Tatiana's car.

In an effort to elude further shells, the train gathered speed as it continued through the pass. Then, just as a decent speed had been reached, the emergency brake was pulled. The track in front of us had been blown and everyone in our car was sent careening to the floor or smashing against the walls as the train screeched to a halt.

My first concern was for Alexei. I began to run to his car as Holmes and the men scrambled outside for cover. The guards on the roof were already returning fire with our captured machine guns.

The ladies of the Imperial Family were being directed by Reilly to exit the car as quickly as possible, and I was relieved to see Alexei being carried out by the Tsar, who gave me a quick nod that the boy was all right.

Reilly helped the Tsarina down to a waiting guard, and everyone was directed to seek shelter behind a small incline on the obverse side of the direction from where the shelling originated.

Reilly told me he was off to organise his men, and also said that if the shelling continued, we were finished. We could not stand up to a sustained artillery bombardment. Then, before I could say anything, he glanced at Tatiana and rushed off.

The shelling continued with me thanking the Lord mightily that our enemy's aim was so poor. Anastasia was crying, as was the Tsarina, Marie trying to comfort her sister. The Tsar was holding Alexei's head down despite his son's best efforts to get a better view of the battle. Tatiana held her mother tightly and Olga was flat on the ground, her hands covering her head in the instinctive, protective position.

A shell hit the rear of the soldiers' car, only blowing apart the rear platform. Our guards on the roof were trying to fire towards the artillery to keep them from shelling our positions, but without much success. I saw some of our guards fall, either wounded or killed. I could not go to their aid.

While all this was going on I was also wondering if Holmes was safe, but knew, of course, he would be. It was then I heard bugles coming from our rear. When I turned to see from where, and from whom, the sound came, I was astonished to see another train stopping behind us; a train, like ours, flying the red flags of revolution.

We were the ones caught in the vice. The Reds had us trapped and now my only thought was that I would never again see Elizabeth or John.

Then, much to my surprise and relief, I saw that the Red troops pouring out of the train were firing not on us, but at the direction from which the shelling came. For whatever reason, they were there to help us, not attack us. While thanking the Lord for this bizarre deliverance, and wondering heavily at what God hath wrought, I received the answer to my question. Colonel Mikoyan appeared from the train, directing his troops against the ridges in front of us.

It was at that moment I realized I must get the Imperial Family back into their compartments. If they were seen by any of these new troops, our game would be up. Since I was the only man now with them, I screamed at them to get back into the train and to be quick about it. They did not know why, but they obeyed immediately, I personally lifting the Tsarina aboard.

I got them all back into their compartments, grabbed a rifle from the hand of a dead guard on the coupling, closed the door from the outside, and felt, but just for an instant, that I was a young surgeon again at Maiwand.

135

My brief reverie was interrupted by one of the new troops. He was trying to climb aboard the car. I pushed him back with the side of my rifle and he began calling to some of the other troops to come help him. I was certain that he had seen the Imperial Family and he wanted to claim his prize. Now he was holding my rifle and pushing in, and I was holding and pushing out. Just as I got into position to kick him down, he let go and fell backwards. Reilly was standing there, his pistol now aiming down at the dead soldier.

I moved aside and let him up.

"Are they all right?" he asked as he opened the door.

"Yes, she is," I answered.

Reilly smiled for a brief second and dashed in.

Meanwhile the new troops seemed to be pushing back the forces on the ridge. The shelling had stopped and Reilly's men had joined the Perm Reds in a counter-attack up the ridge. I lowered my rifle and fell back against the wall of the car.

Reilly came out and as he jumped down and ran towards his men I heard him yell over his shoulder, "Yes, she is." And as I stood watching him run off, I also heard, "Well, that was unexpected." I looked down to see a quite dishevelled Holmes, also with rifle in hand, looking up at me.

After about thirty minutes, the Perm Reds, and some of our men, began plodding back to their respective trains. Only sporadic firing was heard and I knew from my own battle experience that enemy stragglers were being hunted.

By the time we saw Reilly returning, walking closely with Colonel Mikoyan, I had told Holmes that the Romanovs were safe, and how I had so undiplomatically bundled them back into the car for protection. He agreed wholeheartedly with my actions.

Then Holmes and I went down to meet Reilly and Mikoyan. They were both laughing.

Reilly introduced us as British diplomats, all the while

Mikoyan still laughing and chattering away at Reilly. Reilly, we could see, was forcing a laugh, as he began telling us what had happened.

"It's quite all right, he doesn't understand English. It seems that Yurovsky decided to try a gamble. He finally telegraphed to Mikoyan here that we were White agents who kidnapped the Imperial Family and killed many of his men in the process. Our train was to be stopped by every means available.

"After Mikoyan argued telegraphically with Yurovsky, he cursed him and said he would go after us. But he made it clear that if this was a wild goose chase, he would see to it personally that Yurovsky and his men would be arrested and shot. So bizarre did Mikoyan feel the message to be that to avoid any embarrassment he took the only copy of the telegram from the operator, ordered the man, on pain of death, to remain silent about it and brought him along on this expedition.

"Then, he came after us."

"But they joined in our fighting," said Holmes, "why didn't they join in those Reds up ahead and annihilate us all?"

"Because, Mr. Holmes, the troops up ahead weren't Reds. They were Whites."

Before we could take that in, Mikoyan, still laughing, Reilly later told us, said he had better take a look inside for himself anyway. With arched eyebrow, he said he just had to see who was causing this fuss. Some of his men were only a few paces away.

As he began to pull himself up, Holmes and I looked at each other to see if the other could stop him. Before we could think, there was a shot from behind and the back of Mikoyan's head exploded. He fell backwards and landed at our feet. In that fraction of a second, Holmes and I spun around to see from where the shot came. There was Reilly, his arm still straight out, with the pistol pointed at Mikoyan. As Mikoyan's men came towards us, their weapons at the ready, Reilly whirled around and emptied his pistol into the already dead body of one of his own men. He then began screaming in Russian at the corpse as the men led by an officer came running up.

Reilly continued screaming at the body as he began kicking it. Mikoyan's men began a frenzy of stabbing the body with their bayonets. It was like a feeding frenzy of sharks. Holmes and I stepped back for safety amidst this senseless brutality.

Quickly spending themselves, they turned towards us as Reilly stepped between us as barrier and talked with the officer. Whatever Reilly said, it worked. The officer had his men carry Mikoyan's body back to their train. The officer turned and saluted us all, and his train began backing up to Perm.

Holmes was about to demand an explanation when, after just a few hundred feet, the train stopped, and the soldiers began coming towards us once more.

"Holmes, it looks like we're in for it again."

"Calm yourself, Dr. Watson, please just watch," said Reilly. And as we did, we saw the Perm Reds begin digging up the track between their train and ours. They were going to lay it into the spaces in our path blown by the Whites.

The cold sweat into which I had once again broken, evaporated at this, and I told Holmes and Reilly I could use a spot of whiskey. To which Reilly replied, "Will vodka do?"

Before Reilly could turn from killer to host, he hoisted himself aboard the car. Holmes and I followed closely. Reilly went straight to Tatiana's car and pounded. Tatiana opened the door, and when she saw Reilly standing there, she simply threw the door wide as he pulled her to him and began kissing her. Marie literally sat there with her mouth open. I pushed them both inside the compartment and closed the door so I could get past them to Alexei; and so they would not be seen.

I knocked at the Tsar's compartment and announced myself. The Tsar opened the door as I saw Alexei huddled in his mother's arms, she rocking back and forth, chanting something in German.

138

The Tsar and I looked at each other, he with great concern, I with fear from the look, or lack of it, I saw in the Tsarina's eyes.

The Tsar gently separated Alexei from his mother, the body seemed all right, and I bent down to the Tsarina.

"Your Imperial Majesty?" Nothing but the chanting. I tried again. "Your Imperial Majesty?" The chanting continued as she looked blankly into the drawn window shades.

I looked up at the Tsar with question in my eyes.

"It is a German lullaby her father sang to her when she was a little girl," said the Tsar. "She had always been afraid of the dark, and this was the only thing that would comfort her. She began it when we got back into the compartment, just after she grabbed Alexei from me."

I noticed the look of great fear and incomprehension on Alexei's face and asked the Tsar if it would be acceptable for Holmes to carry Alexei into the salon while we stayed with the Tsarina.

"Of course, doctor, yes." He handed Alexei to Holmes, and as Holmes started towards the salon, Alexei said, "Don't worry, papa, Dr. Watson is a good man, a good doctor, he will help mamma, I promise you."

The Tsar looked at me and I went back to further examine the Tsarina. Her heartbeat was fairly regular, her pupils were not dilated, but it was grievously obvious, the Tsarina was no longer with us.

Dr. Freud of Vienna has treated cases like this, and I shall paraphrase what he has said. Sometimes, a final, sudden shock may send a more delicate or troubled psyche running for lasting, emotional cover; at last free from fear and harm. It is the only true protection the mind can create and deal with on its own terms. There have been cases where a patient has returned to what can be called normal, but, unfortunately, the majority of such cases remain locked in their self-forged fortress. I explained all of this to the Tsar.

"She has always been frail of spirit, Doctor," he said, fighting to maintain an imperial composure. "Even when we were first married, she had much to endure. People called her cold and aloof, but she was just too sensitive. How could anyone who is cold and aloof raise such warm, loving children? Because she was German she felt no one accepted her. When the war came, no matter how much she did for the soldiers with her nursing and her immense donations, people said because she was German she was secretly helping the enemy.

"Then revolution, imprisonment, and barbaric treatment at the hands of our enemies. I have been amazed she has not slipped into a comforting, protective world of her own before this. I believe it was only because of Alexei and the girls that she did not.

"Tell me, Dr. Watson, perhaps with rest, and kindness, and love, she might..." He broke off in mid-sentence, fell to his knees by her side, grabbed her hands in his and kissed them repeatedly as he kept sobbing, "Sonny, Sonny..."

I left him alone with her.

When I got back to the salon, Alexei was seated on Holmes' lap, of all places, a not completely incongruous sight since Holmes has performed the same function for John when he was just a baby. Anastasia, Olga, and Marie were seated by the table. Tatiana was not there. Reilly was absent also. I thought it best not to inquire of Tatiana's whereabouts, and decided to let all know the condition of the Tsarina. I also felt Tatiana's absence to be a blessing since she was the closest to her mother, and I thought it better that she be told later by her sisters or father.

Alexei began to cry, as did Anastasia. Marie and Olga just looked at each other, their eyes damp. Then Olga moved next to Holmes and took Alexei to her, comforting him as had her mother, rocking him back and forth, her lips on his forehead, her hands holding him tightly.

Holmes and I went outside; and though the news of the Tsarina had disturbed him, he went to the heart of our problem.

"Watson, this is the first chance we've had to speak since the battle. What make you of the attack by the Whites?"

"Holmes, it is an absolute puzzle to me. I thought, from what Kolchak said, that they would simply surround the train at Viatka, Relinsky would tell his men to surrender, and we would be safe. I have not the vaguest notion of what is going on."

"Nor do I, Watson. However I am sure our friend Relinsky does." Holmes looked around. "By the way, where is he? For that matter, where is Tatiana?"

"Holmes, are you so removed from everyday passions that you still cannot comprehend the most normal events unfolding before you?"

"I'm sure I don't understand what you're getting at, Watson."

"Then let me give you an elementary lesson." I had been waiting for years to reverse the direction of that word.

It was several hours before the Perm Reds had finished their task. Reilly had returned to us a short time after Holmes had wandered off, and as he walked towards the construction, he gave me a look that showed great inner turmoil. I simply thought it had to do with his liaison-de-coeur. I was to be proven monumentally mistaken.

Reilly heartily thanked the Perm officer, saluted him majestically and waved him and his men back to their train. Holmes appeared from nowhere and the three of us watched as the Perm train finally backed away for good.

Holmes immediately turned on Reilly.

"Before you begin to explain what is happening here, what was that business with Mikoyan and your dead soldier? What were you screaming? What did you say to that officer?"

Reilly asked us both to step away from the train, away from his men, and especially Obolov who was now standing on the roof of the soldiers' car, staring down at us. He directed us to a flat area at the top of one of the ridges our train had been passing through.

"Gentlemen, with all I have to tell you now, I am not sure if I should suggest you seat yourselves on the ground or chance a reaction from you both I do not wish. Before we find out, I'm going to hand you my pistol, Mr. Holmes.

"Mr. Holmes, Dr. Watson, I'm surrendering my weapon, because it's the only way I know of trying to prove to you my good faith.

"First, so you will understand why I am perhaps better suited to deal with certain indelicate situations than yourselves, I am going to tell you exactly who I am and a very brief account of my peregrinations during this war."

Reilly then gave us most of the information I have already imparted to you about his past.

"Now, to answer your immediate question about Mikoyan, it was obvious to me that both of you could do nothing. And in that situation the only possible course of action was to shoot him instantly. Remember, he had taken the only telegram, which I have removed from his tunic, and given orders to this telegraph operator, upon death, not to reveal what the message was. Through his laughter, he recounted the death of that poor man in the battle. Therefore, Mikoyan's death would obliterate any trace of who is in our railway car.

"Secondly, I obviously could not be seen as the man shooting Mikoyan, so I merely shifted the blame to one who would not mind. What I was yelling was, 'traitor, traitor'. Mikoyan's men then believed that man to have been a White traitor in our midst. It was that simple."

"Simple to you, perhaps," I said. "That is the finest example of quick thinking and action I believe I have ever seen." I noticed Holmes did not appreciate my remark.

"Now, gentlemen, I am going to relate to you something very painful. What we are all truly here for." Holmes and I took a step closer to Reilly.

"Mr. Holmes, Dr. Watson, in Petrograd I had told you to

believe nothing of what any Russian said, and only one tenth of what any Englishman said. By that yardstick, you could measure my credibility in a percentage of mere fractions. I have never spoken truer words than those.

"I was not sent to aid you in your task of rescue, I was sent to make sure you failed. Not only that you failed, but that you and the Imperial Family all died in the attempt."

I just stood there, almost not even able to breathe.

Holmes, however, just shook his head in revelation and said to me, "So, Watson, we finally know why we were here. *We* were to be the scapegoats."

Revelation

This revelation was frightening and infuriating. Holmes began walking around Reilly as a hawk would circle its prey. It was as if he was kicking himself internally for not unravelling the one mystery that may have cost all of us our lives. He said nothing, stopped for a moment and then returned the pistol to Reilly as he looked him in the eye. It was clear to me that an unspoken truce had been reached. He then resumed his circling while listening to the rest of Reilly's story.

"Why you were to be killed, I don't know. Those few in my field who are like me, only follow orders; or, at least, the orders we want to follow.

"I was seconded from SIS to naval intelligence, and was given specific and direct orders by the deputy director of that branch."

"Sir Randolph Newsome," Holmes interrupted.

Reilly seemed surprised. "Do you know him?"

"Let us just say that we know of him. This is not the first time we have come upon the name of Sir Randolph Newsome."

"We met quite clandestinely months ago at a safe house near Harwich, and I was told that Sherlock Holmes and Dr. John Watson were going to try to rescue the Imperial Family. I was told there was the strongest resistance to this in the highest circles of government; and while there were those who wanted you to succeed, I was taking orders from those who did not.

"Further, these same people wished the Imperial Family dead, but under no circumstances did they wish the blame for their death attached to the Bolsheviks. This he emphasized quite strenuously.

"The methods I chose to carry out the assignment were left entirely to my discretion. I would be given as much money as needed for whatever I required.

"Sir George Buchanan, I am almost sure, was told another story. His superior is, of course, the British Foreign Secretary whose name every Englishman knows, Arthur Balfour. From what I could gather, Sir George believed what you believed; that you were sent to rescue the Romanovs, and that I was sent secretly by the British government to help. He told me also that special arrangements had been made with the White leader, Admiral Kolchak, to help me in my task.

"Usually, an ambassador would not know of my true identity or what my true assignment would be; unless he has a direct need to know, which Sir George did not. So I am still not sure if Sir George knows exactly who I am, or what my main function was before I was seconded. That, by the way, is something I promise to disclose to you at another time.

"Stravitski and Obolov I had known many years before in Russia, and they were of the greatest assistance to me thirteen years ago at Port Arthur during the Russo-Japanese War."

"Do you mean you were already working with SIS back then?" I asked.

"Yes. That is where Stravitski saved my life. Obolov was with me only because Stravitski was with me; if you understand." Holmes and I both nodded quietly.

"As for my men, they are Cheka through and through. But they think I am as well. They, too, believe this to be a very special and personal request by Lenin to bring the Imperial Family back to Moscow for trial. A trial designed to show the world why the Reds were forced into their revolution and to lay the blame solely at the feet of the Tsar. They believe it will absolve them and their Comrade Leader Lenin of any blame.

"I don't know how much Lenin knows. He, too, is a wild card here. Yes, he knows your identities; but what else? Can Lenin be in collusion with the British? Anything is possible; and for a multitude of reasons we can't even guess at.

"My men also knew how dangerous this mission would be because we were heading right into the middle of the civil war. In addition, even the regional Soviets, like the one in the Urals with which

145

you have become so familiar, were in virtual rebellion against Moscow. Many of the commissars want to set themselves up as autonomous leaders in their own area. So my men were ready for trouble. In fact, they almost wished it.

"However, one thing bothered me greatly. It was a direct order from Balfour to Buchanan to have me work with Kolchak. Why bring Kolchak into this? If Kolchak was privy to my task, Newsome had not said so. It felt wrong on many levels. So I decided to use Kolchak for my own purposes.

"When I met Kolchak, before you did, he told me exactly what you heard yourselves with me. During our return trip, our train would be surrounded, I would order my men to surrender, they would be shot by Kolchak's men as traitors, and you and I along with the Imperial Family would be in the safe hands of the Whites, who would then see us safely to Archangel. There, after an invasion by the Allies scheduled for the middle to end of July, you would all be taken out of the country.

"It was now very evident the Admiral knew absolutely nothing of my orders from Sir Randolph. In fact, it now seems that no one I have met knew."

Holmes interrupted again. "Does that sound familiar to you, Watson? One link not being aware of the other link's function?"

"Oh, yes, quite," I said.

"Links?" asked Reilly.

"Yes, I shall tell you more of it later. Please continue."

"I was going to use the White attack as my cover for yours, and the Imperial Family's deaths."

"How?" asked I.

"I would not have my men surrender so easily. During the battle, Stravitski and Obolov would have shot you all. I could then claim to Kolchak, when I finally surrendered, that some hard line troops under my command had taken it upon themselves to kill you all rather than have the Romanovs rescued by the Whites. After a brief struggle between men loyal to me, we prevailed and managed to kill the fanatics

146

in turn.

"We could then claim, and I could almost see the propaganda, that the Imperial Family, in the midst of an unfortunate rescue attempt by private British citizens in the pay of unknown forces, were killed when they were caught in a clash between Red and White forces at Viatka. The two British subjects killed along with the Imperial Family were the internationally known consulting detective, Mr. Sherlock Homes, and his celebrated chronicler, Dr. John Watson."

"Absolutely brilliant, Reilly," said Holmes, "you satisfy everyone and you not only remain alive, but prosper from your exertions."

"Perhaps, but something went amiss. The Whites attacked full out and with artillery and in the wrong place. It was supposed to be Viatka. They themselves were out to kill us all. That wasn't part of the plan. Kolchak double-crossed me."

At that, we all realized the humour in the remark and laughed. Reilly then appeared to have a revelation.

"Of course, that's it! That's why the bastard met with us in Perm. He put himself in danger to personally gauge our mettle. To see just exactly how large a force would be needed. What a cynical son-of-a-bitch. And I now think I also see why."

"I believe I do, as well," said Holmes.

"Right now," said Reilly, "Kolchak is merely the military head of the Whites. But with the Imperial Family dead, and others of the blood executed or in Red captivity, Kolchak can set himself up as the new Tsar. If the counter-revolution succeeds he becomes master of all Russia. The new question then becomes are the British behind this or not? If 'yes', he's recognized immediately by the Allies, and with their unlimited funds might even bribe Russia back into the war. But if 'no...'"

Reilly then trailed off in thought. Holmes already had.

"The pieces begin to fall into place," said Holmes, "but I fear only Lloyd George and his invisible others know all the pieces and all

147

the places."

While these two sterling minds turned into themselves for solutions to the questions they sought, I had one very pertinent question to which I felt I already had the answer; but I had to ask to see what Reilly would say.

"Forgive me, Reilly for interrupting your thoughts, but now that you have confessed all this to us, I have a question to which I would like an answer, if you don't mind"

"Please."

"If the Whites had attacked in the method agreed upon, what would you have done?"

Reilly instantly gave a small smile.

"Well, Dr. Watson, I didn't know you were also adept at arcane deduction."

"Not at all. It is simply there for anyone with eyes to see."

"Not necessarily," and he nodded towards Holmes who remained lost in his own thoughts.

"Anyway, to answer your question, I would not, of course, have kept my part of the bargain. I would have simply surrendered as planned. Then everyone would've lived happily ever after." Holmes looked at us as if we had taken leave of our senses.

"It is strange, is it not, Dr. Watson, how something like this can completely change one's life? It's like the silly tale of the sinner becoming a saint; although, I don't think we have to go that far." We both laughed.

The track was sufficiently repaired for us to continue. Reilly's remaining men, only about eight in number, excluding Obolov, Zimin and the engineer, were aboard, as were Holmes and I; it was Reilly who gave the order to move.

148

With all that Reilly had told us, I had completely forgotten about Tatiana learning of her mother's condition. Her sisters, knowing she was her mother's pet were very gentle with her; but she did not take it well.

When I went in to check on her, she was asleep, as was the entire family. They, like all on this train, needed that sleep.

Night could not come quickly enough for me.

July 12, 1918

Upon waking in the morning, I found myself alone in the railway car, the train swaying back and forth like a drunken sailor, its speed quicker than I had remembered.

I went out to the platform of the soldiers' car to find Holmes staring off into the numbing flatness of the terrain. The day was even hotter than yesterday, and I was already perspiring profusely.

"Good morning, Holmes."

"Good morning, Watson."

"Where is Reilly?"

"Here!" The voice came from above and I looked up to see Reilly beginning to climb down from the roof of the car. He had been up checking on his men. Two were on machine guns, two had rifles, as did the engineer and stoker, Obolov and Zimin had pistols.

"We shall be nearing Viatka shortly where we'll stop for water and food. Doctor, I'm going to the Imperial Family's car now to see how they are."

"Good. Just wait one moment and I shall come with you. I must check on Alexei."

Holmes seemed uncommunicative, and I had very long since learned to leave him to his thoughts at such times

I got my bag and after attempting to tidy myself up, went to find Reilly who was already waiting at the door to the Imperial Family's car. The man was having trouble not knocking.

149

"All right, go ahead," I said.

He knocked and heard the Tsar say, "Enter."

Upon entering the salon we saw all, except for the Tsarina and Tatiana. Reilly's face registered his disappointment.

The courtesies of the morning finished, I asked to have a look at Alexei who was sitting in a chair next to his father. The swelling was almost completely gone now and the Tsar told me that Alexei had, of his own volition, eaten some fruit. I applauded the Tsarevich and he laughed and applauded back. The Tsar and the Grand Duchesses also joined in the mock celebration.

I then asked the Tsar if I might attend to the Tsarina. He agreed and asked me to follow him. Reilly was awkwardly smiling at Marie who was knowingly smiling back.

The Tsar gently rapped at his compartment door and Tatiana bade him enter.

Upon seeing me, Tatiana stood up and moved to leave, sensing that Reilly was waiting in the salon. She kissed her father gently on the cheek as she nodded good morning to me and I watched the Tsar look at her as she left. I am positive it was the look a parent displays only once per child: that being when the parent first realizes their child is no longer one.

I turned to the Tsarina. She was as before.

"Has she given any indication of who she is, who you are or where she is?" I asked.

"None, Dr. Watson. She has remained as you saw her yesterday. I fear I have lost my Sonny forever."

I could not truthfully tell him otherwise, so I was forced to dissemble.

"But Your Imperial Majesty, that is not necessarily so. The science of psychiatry, although still a new science, is making giant leaps every day. New treatments are found for illnesses that yesterday were nameless. Please, sir, do not give up hope."

"Thank you, Dr. Watson. You are a good and kind man,

besides being a true healer."

Odd, I had never been called a healer before. Always doctor or physician. That simple word was suddenly heavy with meaning for me. I felt a primal sensation in my body, akin, I believe, to a first remembered pleasure of childhood. It was a happiness of spirit if you will. I could not help the Tsarina, I knew that, but I could and would help Alexei; and any other who needed me. I suddenly felt my wife and John there with me.

The refuelling went without event in Viatka, as did the next few days before we reached the all-important junction at Vologda.

In summary of those days, the Tsarina grew worse, the Tsarevich grew better, almost as if one was directly affecting the other; the Tsar grew more to accept what had happened to his wife, and grew even closer to his children. Olga, Marie and Anastasia struck up a friendship of sorts with Holmes. They begged to hear of his adventures with humanity's villains, as if they had not had enough of their own. Holmes seemed to relax as he recounted those adventures. Tatiana and Reilly spent time alone together, either on the platform of the train as it raced on, or on private walks away from the train when Reilly felt it safe enough, and the rest of mankind separated enough, to do so. Reilly's men eased and opened; only Obolov remaining sullen and reclusive.

Yet even with our inner tensions about the terrors surrounding us, I truly believed these few days to be a quiet, much needed time of personal rediscovery for us all.

The only thing that kept pulling me back from immersing myself in this wonderful sense of peace and near-innocence, was the summer sun of Russia that each morning and each evening turned the crimson colour of the Red star of revolution.

151

July 18, 1918

We arrived in Vologda amidst mass confusion and snakes of vehicular traffic stretching to what seemed infinity. In this case, infinity was in the direction of Archangel. Whatever was happening, it seemed, at first sight, cataclysmic. The noise was monumental if your window was rolled down, and only unbearable when rolled up. Since the heat was worse than the noise, windows were down. The Imperial Family, naturally, kept their shades drawn.

It was towards dusk and Reilly asked Holmes and I to stay with the Romanovs in their car. His men remained on guard on our roof, with Obolov in command, while Reilly took Zimin into Vologda to see what was happening. This was new territory for Reilly just as much as it was for us. Had he concluded his original business, he would have been travelling in a different uniform, and with quite different companions.

His sole concern now was for the safety of Tatiana and her family. Holmes and I were merely appendages which, if frost-bitten, could be severed when threatening the health of the body. Being a disposable appendage is not an enviable position.

In the salon, the Grand Duchesses, except Tatiana, who was with her mother, talked amongst themselves about the madness outside. Holmes and I made small talk with the Tsar who had become expansive with curiosity about the surging chaos. At one point, he even asked "Do you think the counter-revolution has succeeded?" It was Holmes who shook his head and quietly said, "No, Your Imperial Majesty. It could not happen so quickly."

I watched the Tsar's face show only the slightest twinge of emotion then he shrugged his shoulders and said brightly, "I do hope Colonel Relinsky returns to us in one piece."

"Knowing Relinsky," said Holmes, "he would return to us even if he were in two pieces." We laughed at that and the Tsar turned to Alexei, who, I must say, was now doing very well. They began speaking to each other in Russian.

Within the two hours that passed until Reilly returned, Obolov knocked, an odd event since Reilly had banned him from the car's vicinity; and some rather well-dressed men and women in their middle-ages pounded on the sides of our car, jabbering in Russian, until forcefully pushed away by two of our guards.

The Tsar looked puzzled as he translated for us.

"They were asking of whoever was inside if they could come in. They said all were killed, there was no way out, and the Germans were coming. I do not know what they meant by 'all were killed,' but about the Germans, could this be?"

"Your Imperial Majesty," said Holmes, "we have been out of touch with the real world for some time now and knowing how fluid is the situation within the borders of your country, anything at all seems possible."

The Tsar thought about that for a moment. "Yes, anything is possible."

Hard upon that, Reilly returned. Zimin was sent to check on the men. All in the salon waited on Reilly's words, with which he was more than forthcoming as soon as I had given him a look confirming for him that all was well with Tatiana.

"No, gentlemen, the Germans aren't coming. That insane rumour seems to have taken hold and has spread as quickly as a rash."

"Well, something must have started this mass of humanity on its rampage of flight," said Holmes.

"Yes, something did. Remember that the entire diplomatic corps was precipitously moved here back in February when they thought the Germans were going to threaten Petrograd? Well, here they've sat, quiet and happy, until early yesterday.

"It seems that SIS got hold of the American Ambassador, David Francis, and warned him of the coming Allied invasion. Why SIS told the American Ambassador is beyond me. I would've thought his own people would tell him; or at the very least, his brother ambassador, Sir George.

"Francis was the head of the diplomatic corps here, and he went to all the other Allied Ambassadors, then to the Italian, the Chinese, the Japanese, and the bloody Brazilian Ambassadors, for God's sake, and told them likewise. So all those ambassadors then went and told all their families, and all their dependents, and all their employees, that very shortly, as soon as the British and Americans landed at Archangel, they would not be smiled upon by the local Reds.

"Somehow, that warning about the British and the Americans transmogrified into an impending attack by the Germans, even though the Russians aren't even in the God-damned war any more. What you see is the result."

"Where are all the diplomats?" asked Holmes.

"Gone. Francis commandeered a train for them and they headed north last night. Once everyone woke up and found all the diplomats gone, the terror took hold like a snapping turtle."

"Incredible," said the Tsar.

"Quite," said Reilly.

"But why did Francis and the others leave so quickly? Surely they still had ample time?" asked Holmes.

"True enough," said Reilly, "but the other news coming at the heels of the German rumor really tore it. Since no one knew how the Reds or Whites or anyone would take the news, Francis and his friends decided flight was the better part of valour."

"What other news?" asked the Tsar.

"Forgive me, Your Imperial Majesty, in the excitement of the moment it seems I've forgotten to convey it. Quite simply, you and your entire family have been executed by the Bolsheviks at Ekaterinburg. You're all dead."

Playing Dead

After the shock of this statement and sufficient time had elapsed for its full meaning to register, the entire Imperial Family, Holmes and I, broke into spontaneous, extended, tension-breaking laughter. Each time any of us would look at Reilly, standing there with his studied nonchalance, the laughter would begin anew.

Of course Holmes had, by now, told the Tsar as much of our tale as we were able to tell. Reilly's identity remained Colonel Relinsky to the Tsar; Holmes just saying he was with the British, and the Tsar understanding that certain questions could not only not be answered, they could also not even be asked.

When I regained sufficient composure, I was the first to congratulate Holmes on his coup. Holmes soon became the recipient of mild back-slapping from Reilly and me, and imperial handshakes of gratitude.

The Tsar then said, still laughing, that he must go to the Tsarina and Tatiana to tell them the good news: they were dead! The Grand Duchesses and Alexei nudged each other playfully and continued to laugh while Anastasia suddenly fell on the sofa, straight on her back with her hands folded across her chest.

"Oh me," she said, "do I make a pretty corpse?"

The laughter began anew, but then I suddenly stopped when it occurred to me that if not for Holmes and me, it was very possible that Anastasia may have indeed, by now, been a pretty corpse. It was a horrifying thought and I swiftly shook it off.

Finally, after we had truly calmed down, and Tatiana had come to join in the merriment, and to see her Reilly, he told us how he and Zimin virtually fought their way to the British Embassy; Reilly hoping to find some word or order from Buchanan. This he did in the form of a young naval commander who said he was left there specifically to wait for "two British VIPs who may be showing up any time now, if luck has been with them." So said Sir George Buchanan.

155

Furthermore, in case we "two British VIPs" did show up, the officer had specific instructions as to where in Archangel we were to be brought.

It was at this point Holmes interrupted.

"Reilly, Watson, please let me speak with you for a moment." Holmes led us to the corner, the three of us forming a triangle closed in upon itself for privacy.

"Reilly, if the news of the Romanovs' death has reached here, it has surely, by now, reached London. Which means some great distress at 10 Downing Street and at Buckingham Palace, where, I am afraid, an even more despairing reception has been the result." At those words, I myself felt the pangs of pain for what our sovereign and his family would be feeling.

"But of even greater concern to me," continued Holmes, "is the fear that Lloyd George has had the Navy recall the vessel or vessels meant for us, no matter what that officer may have conveyed. While I am most anxious for the Prime Minister and the King to learn the truth of our situation, it is more for our direct health than to soothe their immediate emotions."

"In that respect, Mr. Holmes," said Reilly, "I told the commander at the Embassy to try to send through an urgent message to London. In fact, it was the message I was to send in any event, upon reaching our embassy on return. It was this: 'Augustus alive.' But I added, 'Proceed as planned.'"

"Augustus?" I asked.

"Yes, Dr. Watson. Augustus was the premier Roman emperor, was he not?" He underscored the word 'Roman' in so strong a stage whisper than even a person without ears would hear.

"One more question," said Holmes, but Reilly answered before the question was asked.

"There were no messages from Preston. He is keeping mum as planned, hoping not to interfere with our safe exit."

"Good man! Well, I suppose if he were to learn of our true

demise, Preston would get the salient facts to London of his own volition. Now, then," continued Holmes, rubbing his hands together as if chilled, "let us keep our fingers crossed that the message has been received."

"I have every reason to hope so," said Reilly, "the commander raced back to the code room to put it through immediately. No dust settled on his tracks.

"In fact, he has completed all arrangements to take us north to Archangel. We should be leaving shortly; as soon as he gives orders at the station to have our cars hooked up to a new locomotive -- one flying British colours."

Just hearing that we would be travelling under the Union Flag buoyed me immensely.

After about thirty minutes, there was a knock at the door of the Imperial Family's car. Reilly went out briefly, then returned to tell us all was now ready and we would be leaving in just a few minutes.

As he left to join the commander, Holmes and I followed. As we took the few steps down, the young man came to full attention and saluted us.

It was 'the young Holmes' from Harwich, Commander William Yardley.

"Commander Yardley," said Holmes in greeting.

"Mr. Holmes, Dr. Watson. I am terribly happy to see the two of you alive, and, it seems, in good health?"

"You know each other?" asked Reilly.

"Only in passing," answered Holmes. Then he whispered, "I shall tell you more later when we are alone."

"But why didn't you tell me you knew these gentlemen?" inquired Reilly of Yardley.

"Well, I wanted it to be a surprise," answered Yardley, a bit sheepishly. "I hope I haven't done anything wrong?"

157

"On the contrary," said Holmes, "a more agreeable surprise I could not imagine. Isn't that so, Dr. Watson?"

"Yes, quite so. Splendid surprise, Commander. Good to see you again. Glad you're aboard once more. And this time, quite literally."

"Thank you, gentlemen. Well, as soon as Colonel Relinsky tells me so, we're off."

"That I will do in a moment," said Reilly, "but one of my men is coming towards me and I think I'd better speak with him. It's someone who needs attending to." The words were spat out like bile. Holmes and I turned to see Obolov. Reilly went to him, they both walked back towards the rear of the train and disappeared around the other side.

After a delay of twenty minutes, Reilly returned, angered.

"Commander, I shall address myself to Mr. Holmes and Dr. Watson because they are already privy to the history of that man and me. You must not be offended." Without waiting for a response, Reilly turned to us.

"Obolov indicated the men feel funny travelling on a train without the red flag; especially a train with the British flag. He said Lt. Zimin felt the same way; so I went with him to speak with the men. He wasn't lying. The men did feel extremely uncomfortable and for the first time, I got the distinct impression that Obolov, although it's laboriously time-consuming for him to communicate with signs and the written word, had been stirring things up.

"Zimin still controls the men, but he was wavering. So I told him that if he would feel better, he and the men could stay here. I would get men from the local Cheka. But I swore that when I returned with those men, I would use them not only as my new troops of escort, but also as all his men's firing squad. And that included him and Obolov.

"This show of bravado put them off. I then took Zimin aside and spoke to him as an older brother, ordering Obolov to keep his distance. I told Zimin that there are certain things he has no business knowing because he was an officer under my direct orders and he had to obey me absolutely. I then tried the ploy that usually works well with men who need to feel let in on big things.

"I told him that Obolov must be watched carefully as since Ekaterinburg, his conduct had concerned me. I said that I feared for his revolutionary conviction, but stopped short of accusing him of anything counter-revolutionary. Zimin got the message. He told me he would personally watch Obolov and not to worry. He would handle the men and Obolov as well.

"I thanked him for his understanding and then promised something men like him covet perhaps above all else. I said that when we returned from Archangel, not only would I put him in for a promotion, but that I would personally mention him to Comrade Lenin.

"Now, Commander Yardley, we can go."

With that, Yardley saluted briefly, and ran towards the locomotive as we boarded the barracks car. In just a few moments, we would be heading north to Archangel. We had all just relaxed with our backs resting against the sides of the carriage, when Obolov appeared at the doorway with a ghoulish smile on his face and a pistol in his hand pointed at Reilly. His other hand was behind his back, as if he was holding something.

It was Zimin's head.

Obolov rolled the bloody head across the floor towards Reilly who didn't even flinch. The head stopped when it hit his leg. Holmes and I could do nothing, so close were we to Reilly.

Obolov began advancing, pistol straight at Reilly, while he reached to his belt in back and pulled free the bloody sword with which he had just committed murder.

Obolov was making animal sounds at Reilly. They were harsh, low, guttural sounds. As he came close, I could see he was frothing at the mouth; I knew he had gone quite mad. He was nothing more now than a lunatic, governed only by blood-lust.

In those horrible seconds, as this monster came so close I could count the pock marks in his face, it seemed to me as if Obolov was not walking, but slithering towards us; the sword raised higher with each reptilian move.

Then, just as he raised the sword to its apex and was in the act of bringing it down, Reilly rolled to one side as he pulled his pistol from its holster, and shot every single bullet into the madman.

Obolov tottered for a second, then fell heavily onto Reilly, right across his legs, pinning him to the ground. Reilly began kicking him away as Holmes and I swiftly rose and went to help throw off the body.

My heart was beating so fast it felt as if it was attacking me, but I knew it was just the adrenaline and coarse excitement.

Reilly kicked away Zimin's head as three of his men came running into the car. They stopped short at what they saw, one man retching mightily upon seeing Zimin's severed head.

Reilly gave them orders loudly and led them outside. In no more than a moment's time, two of the men came back to retrieve the body and the head, and to clean up the mess made by the third. While they performed their task, they refused to look into our eyes. We could not tell if it was shame or loathing that made them act so.

The stench, being horrendous in that heat, drove Holmes and me to the platform of the car where we saw Reilly approaching us once again. He had a terrible look on his face: anger mixed with disgust.

"The first chance I have, I'm going to have them all shot - every last one of them. I'll do it myself if I have to. So look at them now if you wish, gentlemen, and behold the countenance of dead men."

With that he went into the car and virtually at the same instant, the train started moving.

After the two soldiers had made our car clean, and we were well on our way north, Holmes and I re-entered the car to find Reilly sitting where he had been before, quite calm again.

160

"I fear, gentlemen, that this episode has been quite unsettling for you."

"For us?" I asked incredulously. "Good God, man, what drugs are you taking to calm you so? Were I you, I am not sure if I would still be in control of my bowels!"

Reilly laughed, slightly. "I had been warning you for some time that evil would happen where Obolov was concerned. It took longer than I had suspected. But in truth, gentlemen, had not this horrible incident occurred here, it would have been somewhere else, and perhaps without so pleasant an outcome."

"You say pleasant, do you?" I asked.

"Why yes, Dr. Watson. Any time you are alive and your adversary is not, that is pleasant. Look gentlemen, I don't lead a quiet life but it's the life I have chosen. I make no complaints, I make no apologies. Mr. Holmes, what of your experiences? Surely you must come across an insane murderer or two in your line of work?"

"Yes, I do," said Holmes with a mild laugh, "only I usually have time to prepare myself for proper introductions."

We all laughed at that and some of the collective tension was released.

"But tell me, Mr. Holmes, this Commander Yardley, how do you come to be of his acquaintance?"

"He was the liaison officer waiting for us at Harwich and he may have given away too much in his brief conversation with us. But I see that he has either been redeemed, or forgiven, or his faux pas was considered inconsequential enough to return him to us."

"Do you have any idea why he's here?" asked Reilly.

"In truth, I suspect he is here for exactly the reason he has given you. I believe our Commander Yardley is completely on the square and has only the best of intentions where we are concerned.

"He professes no knowledge of what our task has been nor who our charges are. This strikes me as odd, but he may simply be obeying orders given him, as any young English commander would in time of war.

"He can be trusted to do everything within his power to guard our lives and see that we arrive where we are supposed to, when we are supposed to."

"Well, Mr. Holmes, if that's the way you truly feel, I bid you and Dr. Watson good night."

With that, he turned to go to sleep. Holmes and I looked at each other with a shrug before following his lead

.

July 19, 1918

In the morning, I looked in on our charges. Alexei and Tatiana were both doing nicely, although I could not say as much for the Tsarina. Later, Yardley joined us in the barrack's car. We would be at Archangel that very night, if all went well.

On our approach, late that afternoon, to the River Dvina, across which was Archangel, the train was halted before the railway bridge. We were stopped by, of all people, apple-cheeked American sailors.

It seems the invasion had begun at precisely 8:00 P.M. of the night before. The first ashore were twenty-five of these men who had come from the HMS *Olympia* and had engaged a Bolshevik unit fleeing south. The sailors had commandeered some flat cars, mounted a machine gun on the one forward, and were off on their joy ride after the first group of Reds, like the famed American cavalry and cowboys, when they ran into us.

The Americans saw the British flag, but they also saw the Red Guards at their machine guns. At the sight of these evidently well armed strangers, our men, who were outnumbered and tired, surrendered.

We were now prisoners of the United States of America.

Of course, this bizarre state of affairs did not last long.

Commander Yardley, along with Reilly, went to talk with the ensign commanding. Yardley convinced him of the urgency of his mission to bring his party into Archangel, there to rendezvous with a ship of the invasion.

The American wanted to know why a British commander was travelling with a group of Red Guards, and Yardley answered quite elegantly that it was none of his business. He furthered added that if the ensign and his men did not, at once, reverse the direction of the flat cars and serve as his escort and guard into Archangel, there were going to be some very angry senior British and American officers who would just love to have roast ensign for dinner.

The American got the message, but in an effort to avoid complete humiliation, he did demand that our guards relinquish their weapons. This was something Yardley completely understood. After all, with England and America now both fighting the Reds in this part of Russia, we couldn't very well have our men, now the enemy, running around loose and armed. Either they would be shot, or they would shoot someone else.

Furthermore, the American explained that there was a much larger force of invasion troops behind him, and he would just love to take our guards in as trophies. It was Reilly's choice.

It was then Reilly worked out his compromise. He told Yardley to tell the ensign this: since these Red Guards were under British protection, and the ensign obviously had no wish to blemish Allied relations, Reilly would give his men their unconditional release from service. They would be discharged on the spot, Reilly writing the discharge papers and signing the things there and then. The ensign grudgingly agreed.

Reilly went to his men, explained that they were now free, they could go back home, their duty was over. But they had better move quickly as a much larger body of troops was moving this way and would be looking to capture any Red soldiers. Russia had been invaded, he told them, and he was going into captivity in return for their release; such was his love for his men.

He reminded them of their oath of secrecy and that should any one of them break that sacred oath, they would all be hunted down and killed as would every member of their family. They all swore on the Revolution that they would remain silent.

Then, under the watchful eyes of the American sailors, as Reilly wrote out their formal discharges, on pieces of paper bags, his men suddenly began jumping up and down and hugging and kissing each other with joyful abandon; one even dancing a kazatski.

The Americans watched this and obviously thought the group had gone quite mad. Some sailors were laughing so hard they could hardly keep their weapons trained on the Reds.

Soon, however, our men began to drift away in small groups, heading back the way they had come, their rifles still with them. A few looked back at the train, one or two saluted Reilly, but they all could not get away quickly enough.

When all this had been completed, and Yardley had joined the American ensign on the front flat car, we started up again. Reilly hoisted himself aboard and headed in the direction of the Imperial Family. He would inform them of what had just happened. He later told me that he was approached by one of the Americans who had asked him who we were guarding in our first car. Reilly said he gave the American quite a good laugh when he answered, "Why, the Tsar and his family. They're taking tea with President Wilson!"

Reilly elicited the same resounding response from the Imperial Family upon recounting his tale, and I had not seen the Tsar laugh so hard. When he finally ceased, he said he was going in to the Tsarina to tell her the story, too. He hoped she might enjoy it. The Grand

164

Duchesses all looked at each other in embarrassment. But who knows, maybe the Tsarina could comprehend what was said to her; and somewhere, deep inside, she would smile.

The confusion engulfing Archangel made the chaos at Vologda seem as neat and tidy as a London librarian's desk. We were truly in the middle of a great Allied invasion force. And this time there were troops. Thousands of them all around. We picked out men from America, Britain, Canada, France and Italy. A group we could not identify, later turned out to be Serbs. It was certainly a different sort of invasion force.

Night had now fallen and Yardley and the American ensign had departed, leaving the American sailors to guard our train until their return. About an hour later, they were back with us, accompanied by a platoon of Royal Scots Guards and three large limousine cars still flying the red flags of their previous owners. The red pieces of cloth were swiftly exchanged for appropriate British flags.

Holmes, Reilly and I went out and watched as the ensign and Yardley shook hands and saluted each other. The American ensign assembled his men in good order, and just before he led away, he turned to Reilly and said, "Do me a favour, will you? Tell President Wilson and the Tsar that I make my tea with two sugars." With all of us giving a mighty laugh, he marched his men away; eyes right at the Union Flag.

Reilly and I went in to the Imperial Family to have them begin packing the few things they still had with them. We would now be transferring to the motor cars which would take us to a waiting ship.

Yardley told us the ship had just served as the vessel of the invasion's commanding officer, Major General Frederick C. Poole, one of the army's most respected and vigorous officers. The ship, HMS *Salvator*, was a recently converted yacht; fate having certainly supplied her with a more than appropriate name.

It was then Holmes broached an interesting question to me on the sly: "Why has not Yardley, after all this time, inquired as to who is in the train car?" I shrugged.

We asked the ladies to cover their faces with scarves or handkerchiefs, and the same for Alexei. Since the Tsar wanted to carry Alexei, it was agreed he could just keep his head down for the few seconds of exchange.

When the Imperial Family was ready, the soldiers were given the order to about-face away from the train and motor cars, and to come to attention. This they did smartly.

The Imperial Family got into the motor cars without incident; Holmes, Reilly and I into the last, and the soldiers moved out with us; they marching in front, on the sides, and two at the rear.

We were at the water in about thirty minutes, the war material mounting around us as our motor cars stood waiting. Suddenly all activity around us ceased, it was obvious that orders had been given to clear our immediate area.

Reilly and Holmes got out of the motor car; I simply looked out and saw the gangplank leading up to the *Salvator*. After just a minute or so, Yardley came to ask us to bring the group aboard. He would go back aboard first, all hands were already quartered, only the captain would greet our charges, and the captain would personally bring us to our cabins.

I thought this over cautious, but I was thankful for it in no small measure. Once Yardley was back on the ship and out of our sight, we began to board in this manner: first the Tsar and Alexei, then the Tsarina and Tatiana with Reilly, then the other Grand Duchesses with Holmes and me.

Although Holmes and I were at the very tail of this Imperial train, as we got closer to the *Salvator*'s deck, we became extremely confused because the British voice greeting the Imperial Family sounded all-too familiar.

It was. It belonged to Commander Yardley.

166

Reilly Departs

"Gentlemen, you'll pardon me for now; an explanation will be yours once I've seen to the Imperial Family's needs."

Holmes, Reilly and I just looked at each other in complete surprise. In fact, I felt a part of history, in which I had the honour of being on the spot when Mr. Sherlock Holmes and Mr. Sidney Reilly both stood quietly, seemingly at a loss for words. The company I was in was high, indeed.

After the Imperial Family was shown to their quarters by Yardley, and Holmes and me to ours, Holmes asked Reilly, "But where are you to be?"

When Reilly just looked at Holmes, we both knew what this meant.

"Mr. Holmes, Dr. Watson, please permit me," said Reilly as he indicated his desire for us to go into our cabin. He closed the door behind as Yardley said, "When you're finished, please join me on the bridge." Reilly signalled his agreement and turned to us.

"Gentlemen, I shan't go with you any farther. This is the end of my assignment. When my work with you was completed I was to return to Petrograd. I shall come to that shortly.

"There's much I've wanted to say, much that I should've said these weeks we've been together. I shan't say they've been uneventful. You've saved my life, you've saved their lives, you've become a major part of the history of this adolescent century. I thank you now for all you've done for me, for them and for her.

"I promised you I'd eventually speak of what I'm supposed to do in Petrograd. It's as bizarre as my task was with you. With you, I was to eliminate the Romanovs. In Petrograd, I'm to eliminate Lenin."

Holmes and I looked at Reilly in amazement. We were always looking at this man in such manner because he always gave us cause to. He continued.

"I am to foment my own counter-revolution with quite strong

forces within the Cheka loyal to me; and with the collusion of important factions within the Red Army. The timetable is my own, but it must be within the next month or so. That's all I can tell you now. The newspapers will tell you more."

"Is Lloyd George completely mad?" asked Holmes. "Is everyone in power in England devoid of reason? What is happening there at Downing Street?"

"Mr. Holmes," Reilly was speaking very quietly, "I'm not even sure Mr. Lloyd George knows of my directive in Petrograd. Just as we don't know who wanted you all dead. But this I will say, and I say it to you both from hard, piercing experience. In fact, I have said it to you before. Trust only one tenth anyone who is English. And perhaps not even that. A perfect example is your Commander Yardley. Although he does seem to be here solely for the benefit for the Imperial Family and yourselves, he is obviously not the callow youth you thought him to be. Who knows who he's really working for? To which ministry is he really attached? That riddle is for you to solve and I have absolutely no doubt that you shall.

"Let me try to give you some more advice. Mr. Holmes, in your work, the criminals you deal with are outcasts of society. In my work, however, the criminals I deal with are the vanguard of that society. It is only a difference of accent and class.

"You once said something about 'links' Mr. Holmes" said Reilly. "I understand what you meant by that and while you may be correct, I have my doubts.

"For instance," said Reilly, "your Captain David. He claimed he didn't know anything about Yardley, yet Yardley claimed David was an old family friend. Only one can be telling the truth. Furthermore, Sir George knew of your mission in Russia, as did Kolchak, Preston and Thomas.

"No, Mr. Holmes, though it seemed so at the time, I don't believe your link theory holds true."

"Thank you, Reilly," said Holmes, "for you have just proved

that my link theory is, indeed, true; but in the opposite way. I shall elaborate.

"Originally, I had thought each link oblivious of the other, and that Watson and I had to then fear the weakest link. But as you have just said, it is now obvious that while the links may not have known about all other links, it seems all knew of our mission. Therefore, a strong chain, indeed, had been forged by our Prime Minister. The question is now whether he is he blacksmith or blackguard?"

"You shall learn that, as well," said Reilly, "but it shall be one class you cannot afford to fail."

"I still have uneasy suspicions of Lloyd George," said Holmes. "I just cannot fix on them. As for Yardley, we do not, as yet, know if he knows."

"That's true; he's a missing piece to the puzzle, all right," said Reilly, "but you'll slot him in shortly, I'm sure; now that he may be flying some true colours."

"Be ever on your guard, Mr. Holmes, Dr. Watson, and keep this one last thought paramount until you're both safely home. However strongly Lloyd George and his invisible others wanted the Romanovs rescued, it is frighteningly obvious that there are those who wish them dead just as much if not more so. These people are just as invisible. The only one I dealt with was Newsome. He is the key to everything. He is so high up I doubt a buffer would exist between him and whoever is behind this. You'll probably find answers with your Captain David, as well. Although it seems he's only a link on the chain. Not the blacksmith, himself.

"Remember, this was only Act I. You may never know the finale.

"I know I don't have to ask you to be especially on guard for her," his head moving in the direction of Tatiana's cabin. Reilly then extended his hand to us.

"Mr. Holmes, Dr. Watson, I wish you both a safe journey home, and I promise you this: if I should survive my adventures here in Russia, I'll make myself known upon my return to England.

"Now, if you'll excuse me, there's someone of whom my leave-taking shall be infinitely more difficult." He smiled, opened the door, and left us there.

Were his words true? Would we, or more importantly, Tatiana, ever see him again?

A Gentle Secret

What I am about to convey is what Tatiana told me one evening, many months later, of her relationship with Reilly.

"Dr. Watson, Sidney was the first and only man I have ever loved. Yet until we parted that night in Archangel, I didn't even know his true name.

"I had been shielded to a degree you wouldn't believe. Matters of male and female were not seemly for a Russian Grand Duchess. Yet my sisters and I talked of little else.

"From the moment I saw him, and he me, it was as if the north and south poles had been pulled together and had exploded and melted from the turbulent heat of the equator.

"Ah, yes, my Sidney. What a mass of riddles and spots of north moss he is," and she laughed as she explained what she meant by that.

When she was very young, her father had told her, that there were magic secrets hidden "'beneath the spots of north moss.'"

"But papa," she inquired, "what is north moss?"

"Tatiana," said the Tsar, "that is the moss you find growing on rocks and trees, and it always grows only on the north side."

"But why, papa?" she asked.

"Because a long, long time ago, a beautiful little girl, just like you, in fact her name was Tatiana also, was lost in this very same forest. She cried because she was hungry and was afraid she'd never see her family again. So she prayed to the Lord and he came and said he would show her the way out.

"He said he would put spots of moss only on the north side of rocks and trees, and that forever after, when she came into this forest, she would always know which direction her home was just by looking at the spots of north moss.

"But how will you do such a thing?" asked the little girl.

"Well, every time a little girl or little boy is good, another spot of moss will grow. As there are so many good little girls like you, and so many good little boys like your brother, all the forests of all the world will soon be filled with spots of north moss. Beneath each spot, in secret letters, will be the name of the little girl or boy who was so good."

"So you see, Dr. Watson, my Sidney was really all spots of north moss, was he not?"

"Yes, Tatiana, you made him so."

This particular day, which I shall get to in the proper course of this journal, had been of great emotion for us all, and when Tatiana told me the little fairy tale and her connecting of it to Reilly, I understood completely.

"Dr. Watson, do you think I shall see Sidney again?"

"Of course, you will. After the adventure that man has been through in his life, after all he has done to bring you and your family safely to this place, do you think there is any power strong enough to stop him?"

"I suppose you're correct, Dr. Watson. Which means I must go as soon as possible to a forest here and count the spots of north moss. The new ones, I am positive, shall all be his."

With a kiss to my cheek and a 'thank you', she took herself off to bed.

July 20, 1918

This day was beautiful, clear and cool from the breezes of the North Sea. Once again we were upon that dangerous body of water, now heading towards England.

Holmes was gone, as usual, so I surmised he had gone to the bridge, something neither of us had the stomach for the night previous. I cleaned myself, blissfully cleaned myself, I should say; the first real shower in such a long while. I then went to check upon Alexei, who was begging his father to go topside, and the Tsarina, who was resting peacefully in her bed. After being asked by the Tsar to find out if we were being taken to the Crimea, to his family's beloved Livadia Palace, I pointed myself upwards.

Once on deck, I could appreciate the true resilience with which the North Sea air infused one. Then I saw our escort; one looking quite familiar. My initial suspicions were confirmed when I arrived at the bridge and was told, "Yes, that's the *Attentive*."

Holmes was speaking with Yardley when I arrived, and Yardley gave me a warm greeting.

"Good morning, I trust you slept well?"

"That I did. And I should sleep even better tonight with some food inside me." He laughed, but had gotten the point, and suggested Holmes and I accompany him to his cabin, which had been General Poole's just the day before. He told the steward, who also looked vaguely familiar, to bring our breakfasts.

On the way down, I found that Holmes had only just gotten to the bridge himself; so exhausted had he proven to be. Nothing had really been discussed, and all that Commander Yardley would now impart was news to both Holmes and me.

We sat at the captain's table.

"Tell me, Commander," said Holmes, "oh, I beg your pardon, it is Captain, here, is it not?"

"I'm afraid it is, Mr. Holmes. On ship, I'm the captain."

"Very well. Why the elaborate charade? Surely, this was not going to be another of your little surprises?"

"It most certainly was. Tell me, Mr. Holmes, weren't you surprised?"

The sheer baldness of the logic and honesty of the question caught us off-guard.

"Well, yes," said Holmes, "but you know perfectly well to what I refer."

"That I do, Mr. Holmes, and I still cannot divulge more information on that score."

"Then tell me, if you can, for which branch of our government do you truly work?"

Yardley looked down at his uniform and stretched out his arms. "Well, unless I'm wrong, this uniform doesn't in the faintest resemble that of a Grenadier Guardsman." He laughed.

"So you are truly a navy man, then?"

"Through and through, Mr. Holmes. Many generations bred. My great, great, great grandfather, I believe, although that may be one 'great' too many, was at Trafalgar with Nelson."

"And your father, perhaps, with Sir Randolph Newsome?" Holmes had sprung his surprise.

The commander's eyes opened wide and his smile broadened.

"Very good, Mr. Holmes," said Yardley, applauding mildly. "How came you by that information?"

At the confirmation of Holmes' outrageous theory, a method of 'educated guesswork', as Holmes called it, I felt every hair on my body stand on end. Here was blithe corroboration of Newsome's machinations; more links in his chain, pulling in the opposite direction of Lloyd George's, with Yardley's father firmly tethered to this opposite chain. Yet, since Yardley did not seem to see anything wrong with this information, indeed, he seemed proud of it, it appeared that he was oblivious to Newsome's real intentions. Yardley thought he was really trying to rescue the Imperial Family, Holmes and me. He probably thought he was going to be a hero.

The scion seemed innocent bait of the sire. Since Yardley was obviously unaware of the damning evidence he had just provided Holmes, Holmes went on as casually as before.

"I, too, am not at liberty to divulge certain things. Tell me, Captain, what are your duties when not employed thusly?"

"Well, I suppose it's all right. Usually, Mr. Holmes, you would find me at sea somewhere. I've been at sea, in one role or another, since

174

I was a boy. About three months ago, however, I was seconded to naval intelligence at the specific request of Sir Randolph."

"My father told me to expect the move, and I'm not afraid to say I didn't like the idea much, at the time. After all, Mr. Holmes, I'm a sailor. Sailors belong at sea, in the thick of things, especially during war."

"I take it then you've seen action?"

"Oh, my, yes. I was at Gallipoli, and have done quite a bit of U-boat hunting; where I might add, I've been reasonably successful."

"Then why did Sir Randolph have this burning desire to tear you away from what you loved doing?"

"It was father, really. He's an admiral, too, you know. He told me Sir Randolph needed me for something he felt he could only entrust to me. It was evidently something very hush-hush between them. When an old friend of the family like Sir Randolph asks for something, he gets it. It's as simple as that. Whatever he and my father had up their sleeves, I knew it had to be big."

"When did you finally learn all this?"

"Well, as you yourself saw at Harwich, I was still rather new to this intelligence thing, and I said a bit more than I suppose I should've. Although it was nothing, really."

"You've learned your lesson well, Captain. You have been a veritable clam this entire go-round."

"Why, thank you very much. But I still didn't know what this was about back then. It was about a week after you left that orders came through for me to report to Scapa Flow. That's where this invasion force originally began, though we've been sitting for a time at Murmansk. Now there's a story for you."

"If you don't mind, Captain, please just continue ours."

"Certainly. At Scapa Flow I reported to this ship and was attached to the staff of General Poole. He met me personally and simply told me to enjoy the ride over, because as soon as we got to Archangel, I would be coming back. He said that upon landing at

Archangel, which, of course, our men would secure with absolutely no problem at all, I was going to be escorted down to Vologda to meet with a Sir George Buchanan, our ambassador to Russia. He wished me well and that, basically, was that."

Holmes and I looked at each other again. Now General Poole was brought into this. But from where? And from who? All we knew was that he had instructions to send young Yardley down to meet Buchanan. Poole may have just been following orders. But with this insidious chrysalis being woven around us, how could we be sure?

"Well," continued Yardley, "as you saw, events quite got ahead of themselves and it was Sir George who came up to meet me. It was at that meeting, which involved Sir George and me, and one other, that this entire plan was revealed."

"Excuse me, Captain, but let me guess at the other person who was present at your meeting. Could it have been Captain Joshua David of the *Attentive*?"

"I say, very good, indeed, Mr. Holmes. Only in truth, he's not a captain, and his name isn't Joshua David."

"Well, well," said Holmes, triumphantly looking at me, "then who and what is he?"

"He's an admiral and the second son of Lord Devon. His name is Richard Yardley and he is my father."

As Holmes had said before to Reilly and me, "the pieces begin to fall into place, but only Lloyd George knows all the pieces and all the places." However, now it seemed that Lloyd George most certainly did not know all the pieces and all the places.

This last revelation by Yardley positively confirmed Reilly's warnings about the secret, powerful group that most assuredly still wanted the Imperial Family dead, and us with them. It left us more uneasy than ever.

In addition to our growing lists of who and who not to trust, Holmes could not divest himself of his "compulsive, illogical mistrust of Lloyd George," as he phrased it. It upset him greatly that this

176

mistrust manifested itself as "a hunch, a mindless, primitive, primeval feeling that has no business being in my mind at this stage."

It also bothered Holmes that he had not deduced the true identity of Yardley, Senior. I reminded him that his mind was working on the larger puzzle of solving who was behind the "Black Faction", as I dubbed our adversaries. As we had just come from a nation filled with Reds and Whites, it seemed only fair that I nominate a colour for this latest group. Holmes nodded consent, and so they became the "Black Faction".

In any event, as soon as young Yardley had told us of his father's identity, Holmes asked if he was still in command of the *Attentive*, now our escort.

"Naturally, Mr. Holmes. My father loves a good scrap as much as the next man. I was quite proud of him in that battle of yours. I hear he was quite the bulldog."

"That he was, Captain. There's no wanting of seamanship or pluck where your father is concerned."

We could see how proud Yardley was of his father, and Holmes just let the matter drop. He turned the conversation to the Romanovs.

"Oh, my, yes," said Yardley, "what a group of beautiful girls. That Marie is really something," said Yardley.

From out of nowhere deep within me, came, "Now you keep your mind to the sea and avoiding the Germans, Captain. The Grand Duchesses are to be left quite alone."

Both Holmes and Yardley were as startled at my outburst as was I.

"I assure you, Dr. Watson, I certainly know my duty. It's just that, I mean, well, she's quite the most beautiful girl I've ever seen. I just don't see what's wrong with stating the unadorned truth."

With much chagrin, I apologised. "Forgive me, Captain. I have become an uncle to the Grand Duchesses. I have full confidence in your chivalry. The Grand Duchess Marie is quite beautiful, as are all the

Grand Duchesses. I commend you on your judgment of true beauty."

"Thank you for your apology and your compliments, doctor. I am here only to tend to their needs. Trays shall be set out for them at meal times by my personal steward; he's been handed down, so to speak, to me from my father."

Holmes shot up from his seat. I immediately understood why.

"From your father, you say?"

"Why, yes. He was in my father's service for years. He absolutely worships my father, and he seemed to always have been in the background, watching over me as I grew up. What prompts this violent reaction?"

"I cannot tell you at this moment, Captain, you will have to trust me. Could you please summon your steward here for some questions?"

"Questions? What sort of questions?"

"You can hear for yourself. You are free to remain. But please, summon him now."

"Mr. Holmes, may I remind you that I am the captain of this vessel. And while you are responsible in general for the well-being of the Imperial Family, they are my direct responsibility on board this ship, as are you and Dr. Watson. I haven't the faintest idea why you behave in this manner, but if you must question him, he's bringing in your trays at this very moment."

Holmes and I turned to see the same man who had served us aboard the *Attentive*. He was in his late fifties, with the air of an important man's servant; yet with a touch of the furtive. It was quite obvious this man had been aboard ships for many years, and while he moved with the sure foot of a seasoned sailor, for a man of his years and his comparatively low station in life, his gait was rather too proud and erect.

He was a tall man, as tall as Holmes, with quite a strong physique for a man of his years. Before I could even begin to examine this man with my cursory medical eye, Holmes was already at him.

178

"Please sit down," said Holmes, motioning the man to the seat I had just vacated.

The man looked at Yardley.

"It's all right, Peters, do as the gentleman asks."

Peters sat after first setting our trays down, with a practiced nonchalance, on the table. He sat there glowering up at Holmes, his eyes as wary as a sparrow's in the middle of a flight of falcons.

"So Peters, how are you, this fine, summer morning?"

His voice became land-tenant coarse.

"Righ' enuff, suh."

"Tell me, Peters, where were you in prison?"

The man jumped out of his chair, his fists raised at Holmes. Yardley was mortified.

"Prison?" asked Yardley. "Mr. Holmes, what are you talking about?"

"Don't ask *me*, ask your steward, here."

Yardley turned to Peters. "Is this true, Peters? Were you in prison? My father never said anything about that."

"'Cawz he wudn'. He swore nevuh to. He's kep' his word, he has. Yaw fathuh wudn' break his word. How'd *he* know?" gesturing towards Holmes.

"Never mind that, where?" insisted Holmes.

Peters sat back down, facing away from Yardley. It was obvious he was greatly embarrassed.

"Newg't."

"Newgate. For how long?"

"Three yeers.

"Now let me guess, you murdered someone with your bare hands, am I right?"

Peters put his head down and mumbled to himself.

"How'd ya know?"

"It was a studied test. A man with your musculature at your age must have been at truly magnificent specimen when you were very young. Though you've learned to serve meals delicately, your hands are as rough and strong as they were when you committed your murder."

Yardley interrupted. "I don't understand, what's this all about, Mr. Holmes?" He was as embarrassed as Peters.

"You shall know presently, I think. Now, Peters, you said you were in prison for only three years. I deal with murder all the time. A charge of murder, in most cases, would have you away for the better part of your life. Or even see you hanged. Now, how did you manage to get out in the time usually reserved for nothing more serious than a minor case of embezzlement?"

"'Twas his fathuh wot dun it. Got me out, he did. I had worked on his land. I grew up on it. I played with the admiral when we wuz boys. He wuz my frend. He got me out. He took me t' sea."

"I understand. And you looked after Captain Yardley, here, when he was a young boy?"

"Sometimes, when we wuzn' at sea. I owes my life t' the admiral."

"Would you commit murder again for him?"

This time Peters flew up at Holmes and grabbed him by the throat. Holmes had managed to hit him soundly when Yardley simply ordered Peters to cease. This he did immediately, obeying his orders as a disciplined sailor.

"Mr. Holmes, I demand to know what this has been all about. You accuse a family servant of murdering for my father, and tell me secrets I was not supposed to know. Now, either you tell immediately what this is all about, or I shall have to think seriously of confining you to quarters."

Peters had come to attention to Captain Yardley's right, and the captain left him that way until Holmes asked if Peters could now be dismissed.

"Very well. But as soon as he leaves my cabin, you had better start explaining yourself, Mr. Holmes. And it had better be a thoroughly relevant explanation."

This was the controlled tirade of someone used to power and command; or, rather, brought up with it. He was showing himself to be the antithesis of what Holmes and I first thought him to be. What Reilly had suspected.

"Captain, you asked for my explanation, and you shall have it. But before I give it to you, I also caution you. I cannot say under whose direct orders I am operating. But should anything untoward happen to Dr. Watson or myself aboard your vessel; or even one strand of hair be moved from its rightful place on the heads of any of the Imperial Family, there are those in London who shall make you and your father pay for it personally."

"What are you talking about? What has my father got to do with this?"

"Captain Yardley, what if I were to tell you that your faithful steward, Peters, may have been put here not to serve your needs, but your father's?"

"You are talking in riddles, sir. I shall not stand for it. Be straight and be brief or this interview will end."

"If that is what you wish," said Holmes quietly. "Very well, I have strong suspicions that Peters was sent by your father to kill not only Watson and me, but the entire Imperial Family. Is that straight and brief enough for you?"

Yardley did not know whether to laugh or have Holmes clapped in irons immediately, so dumbfounded was he by what Holmes said.

"Have you gone completely mad, Mr. Holmes? Do you know what you are saying? Dr. Watson, have you no medicines to calm this lunatic?"

"Captain Yardley," I said, "I think you should sit down and listen to what Holmes has to say. For if you do not, it is certain that you may become accomplice to the very crime Holmes and I were dispatched to prevent."

He sat at his chair, holding the arm to quash his anger, burrowing into his deepest self. Then, after perhaps two minutes had passed, he looked up at both of us, gestured to us to sit, and said to Holmes, "Mr. Holmes, tell me all that you're able; everything that's led to such a base accusation."

Holmes, though reluctant to distress young Yardley further, quickly complied.

Captain Yardley sat there unbelieving.

Sherlock Holmes, while not pulling down his house, had certainly damaged its foundations. All Yardley had been taught, all he had faith in, all he had been nurtured by had just been made perfidious. One of his family's dearest friends had been made into a traitorous villain; and his father, a man he obviously idolized, had been turned into a conspiratorial monster.

Finally, Yardley became the captain of our vessel again, the sworn servant of his King and country, and not the individual whose family honour had just been so trampled. He spoke.

"Mr. Holmes, what you've now recounted is damnable; if it be true. But how am I to know if it's true, and not some insidious flight of fancy of a fractured mind?"

"It is true, Captain," I said quietly.

"I am a serving officer of His Majesty; do you know what this information shall do to me if it be true?"

"We are only too well aware," said Holmes "and we deeply wish you did not have to be burdened with such a dilemma."

"Mr. Holmes, if this story is true, it's not a dilemma. As I said, I'm a serving officer in war of His Majesty. My life has been pledged for protection of crown and country. Any traitor must be rooted out and destroyed. Any traitor. But in ten minutes you expect me to disavow family, friends, and faith with no corroboration of your story. I'm sorry, but I need much more proof than merely your word. Even though your word is gospel to some segments of society.

"In truth, Mr. Holmes, Dr. Watson, all you have given me is a story by Colonel Relinsky, of whom all we know is that we don't know all. Given the man's dubious history, I believe the only way he could tell the truth is if he thought he was lying. And with that supposition, let me pose a question to you, Mr. Holmes. What if it was he who was lying? What if his instructions didn't come from Sir Randolph, but from someone else? Have you thought about that, Mr. Holmes?"

Holmes had not. Nor had I. Because of the circumstance in which Reilly had told his story, and the previous and subsequent events, we had no further reason to doubt Reilly's veracity. But now, this question asked by a son trying to salvage the honour of a beloved father, ripped through Holmes' contemplations and left wide one of Holmes' most sacred dictums: "when you have eliminated the impossible, whatever remains, however improbable, must be the truth."

Under those circumstances, the permutations seemed insurmountable. Holmes was now mired in a maze of magnificent proportions; and at this time, there was no further hint in which direction to travel.

Yardley recalled Peters as Holmes and I, hungry no longer, slowly left Yardley's cabin.

Holmes seemed anguished. There was too much happening and too little evidence to which Holmes could respond. Only tales and suppositions now, since Reilly's story had been thrown open to question. Holmes asked to walk alone on deck, and I let him do so.

It had only taken one, simple question to knock over the steady table on which had lain the carefully pieced-together jigsaw puzzle. Now the pieces lay on a filthy floor, in total disarray. And even I did not know how Holmes would deal with this conundrum.

In all the current distress, I had not even the chance to ask Yardley our final destination. I slowly, and with monumental reluctance, began a walk back to the captain's cabin.

As I arrived, though, I heard Yardley's voice loudly through his closed door.

"...you will."

"Bu' I can't, suh. I promised yaw fathuh."

"Damn you, Peters, either you answer me now or I'll have you court-martialled as soon as we get to base. In the meantime, you'll suffocate down in the brig. Now, answer me or be damned."

"I nevuh though' I'd live t' see the day you'd treat me so, Cap'n. But I understan' an' I'll tell you all I know.

"When yaw fathuh an' his friend, Sir Reginal' wuz young'uns they wuz wild. Sir Reginal' took a'vantge of a girl on yaw family's property. She wuz gonnna have his baby when she came t' me. She said it wuz mine, but I knew it wuzn't. I strangled 'er fer bein' unfaithful.

"That took away the fright from Sir Reginal' an' yaw fathuh got 'im to help me out a prison. It took 'im three years, but out I got. It wuz really yaw fathuh who done it. He pushed that bleedin' Sir Reginal' to do the right thing by me.

"Yaw fathuh enlisted me an' took me t' sea with 'im. An' t' this day, I tell ya, Sir Reginal' is no friend of yaw fathuh. He's awways been a blighter, an' he still is. He likes the ladies and he likes the money, and there's no tellin' what he'd do for the both.

"I don' know wot yaw want from me, but that's all there is to it. Yaw fathuh wanted me here to watch over ya, is all. Somethin' wuz trublin' him fierce since he come back from that trip t' Russia last month."

"What do you mean, Peters?"

"Well, I don' rightly know, Cap'n. When we come back from Russia t' Scapa Flow, yaw fathuh met a Mr. Preston one day. I remember 'im from a few times before. Yaw fathuh wuz a navy aide in Paris when he was young, this Preston was the assistan' to the ambassador or somethin' like that. They'd been friends all these years. You remember him, suh, the man wot give you that big, red book on Nelson an' Trafalgar when you wuz still a boy?"

184

"Of course, now I remember him. Preston, Preston, that name was brought up by Holmes before. I wonder if there's a connection there? Anyway, go on, Peters."

"Lik I wuz sayin, aftuh yaw fathuh met with Mr. Preston, he seemed worried t' me. He wudn' say nothin', but I could tell. That's when he said he wuz goin' t' transfer me t' you, and fer me t' look aftuh you. And that's every single thin' I know, Cap'n. Everythin'."

"All right, Peters, you can go now."

I took my ear from the door and made like I was about to knock when Peter opened the door.

"Oh," I said. I received the same facial reaction from Peters.

Yardley was excited now. He called me back in enthusiastically.

"Dr. Watson, Dr. Watson, yes, yes, come in. Peters, run and find Mr. Holmes..."

"Uh, Peters, he is on the main deck," I said.

"Thank you, doctor. Peters, bring Mr. Holmes back to me."

"Yes, suh," said Peters with visible apprehension.

"Well, Dr. Watson, I've just learned some things I think you and Mr. Holmes should know about immediately. It may shed more light on everything we've discussed. And since I can't confront my father with all this until land, I'll feel much better about it. As soon as Mr. Holmes arrives, I'll tell you both everything.

"Look, Dr. Watson, your trays are still here. Perhaps the food is not too cold for you to partake?"

It was, but I did. When Holmes arrived, Yardley was as good as his word and recounted everything I had heard while eavesdropping. Just the mere fact that he held nothing back and reported all so accurately, buoyed my spirits; and did likewise for Holmes when later I recounted my own bit of sleuthing.

Upon completion of Yardley's news, Holmes became electric.

"My word, Captain Yardley, if this is true, and I do believe it is, much may be explained."

185

"What?" asked Yardley.

"Well, obviously, the Mr. Preston to whom Peters referred, is probably none other than Thomas Preston's father; or at very least, his uncle. As do the families in the army and navy, those of the Foreign Service look likewise to their own for continuity, trust and tradition.

"It is also obvious that Preston, Sr. had come upon some greatly disturbing information which he imparted directly to your father; trusting not telegram, nor telephone, nor post. Would it not seem odd for a senior member of the foreign service to show up at a major port of invasion just for afternoon tea?

"My guess is that whatever information Preston had, it directly affected your father. That is why he could only trust himself for relay of that information. And once your father learned this news, his immediate concern was only for his son's safety. By God, there is a man for you."

Holmes was absolutely jovial now as was Yardley; although, he didn't quite understand all Holmes was laying out for him. And I too, now, was happy; I had Holmes back and it seemed that he was now sailing ahead as swiftly and true as the *Salvator* and the *Attentive*.

186

To Someplace Safe

Yardley had gone to the bridge upon completion of our meeting. I decided to follow him and ask to where we were headed. I told Holmes I would carry back this information and he responded with indifference.

"The Crimea? Livadia Palace? No, Dr. Watson, I'm afraid not. But we're heading to a like climate. We're heading towards the Bahamian out-island of Eleuthera," said Yardley.

"I have not heard of it."

"I suppose that is precisely why we're heading there. From what I've heard about the place from salts who have been there, and from what I've read about it, it sounds a veritable paradise.

"Sun most of the year, a median temperature in the upper seventies, turquoise blue waters bountiful with fish, and natives, what there are of them, friendly and disposed to labour. It is a difficult place to get to, Dr. Watson, if you are a mere tourist. So it fulfils the prerequisites on many counts: security, serenity, comfort, and privacy. It seems the perfect amalgam of British pragmatism and Romanov desire."

"That it does. From your description, Captain, should you ever find the need to leave the navy, you should do quite well, I believe, as a travel agent."

We both laughed at that, and then Yardley suggested he personally impart the news to the Imperial Family. After all, he said, he was the captain and it was only fitting that he pay his respects this day and offer such good news. I sensed his slight, ulterior motive, but concurred with his suggestion. He was as a child at the moment of unwrapping a present. He preened in the mirror for a moment, set his cap just so, and then indicated that I lead the way.

I knocked at the Tsar's cabin door.

"It is I, Dr. Watson, Your Imperial Majesty. I have Captain Yardley with me. He wishes to pay his respects and bring you some glad tidings."

"Then come in, please, doctor."

We did so and found the Tsar standing in the salon part of his cabin. Alexei was seated on a sofa. The Tsarina was obviously in the bedroom. When she heard the voices, Tatiana came out.

"Your Imperial Highness," I said; Yardley followed suit.

"Your Imperial Majesty," said Yardley to the Tsar, "I think I have wonderful news for you." He proceeded to relay to the Tsar, the Tsarevich and Tatiana, with even more embellishment, the home to which they were now headed.

All three seemed very pleased, and the Tsar, after excusing himself, went to tell the Tsarina.

"With Your Imperial Highnesses' permission," said Yardley, I'll now go tell your sister, the Grand Duchess, Marie." He paused, his expression revealing that he was conscious of what he had just revealed. "I will tell your others sisters, as well."

Tatiana smiled. When Yardley was gone, she turned to me.

"Dr. Watson, is that what I think it is?"

"Your Imperial Highness, I could not begin to suppose nor judge such a thing." I smiled. "But since you have plainly asked me for my modest opinion, yes, I do believe it is."

She began to laugh freely and Alexei looked at her with what I suspect is the universal expression of the younger brother when confronted with something he cannot quite grasp.

Respite

With the tension lifted, the next few days were rather calm. Since the *Salvator* was a medium-sized yacht, the crew were only a dozen or so, and I was assured by Yardley they were hand-picked by his father.

The Imperial Family was given free time on deck for sun and invigoration; and Tatiana and I would nod to each other knowingly when Capt. Yardley managed, with convenient regularity, to find some reason to be on deck at the same time as Marie.

The Tsarina always remained in her cabin, and on the third day out, the Tsar called Holmes and me to the deck, along with all the Grand Duchesses, save Tatiana who would stay with her mother when the Tsar was out.

Holmes and I had no idea what the Tsar wanted, but an Imperial Command is an Imperial Command. We went on deck and found the Grand Duchesses in a row, with the Tsar, holding Alexei, at the centre.

Then, gently, the Tsar put Alexei down, and the boy, ever so slowly, began an unsteady walk toward me. Alexei had made a wonderful recovery, and I credit the removal of impending murder as the most significant, contributing factor.

I also believe his spirit had been restored by the news of where he and his family were going; with the fresh sea air and good, English food doing their part as well. The only thing that still disturbed the lad was the condition of his mother.

The Tsarina was not improving at all. Her needs were tended to by her daughters, and it could break your heart the way the Tsar would spend hour upon hour just speaking to her. He spoke of things long past, of things to come, of things only shared by the two. Secret and loving things that did as much for the Tsar in his recalling them from his submerged memory, as he hoped they would do for his Sonny.

The man's adoring attention was something to marvel at and

admire. Here was a man, only recently still one of the most powerful men on earth, personally tending to the unknown needs of a damaged wife. Yet even with that, the Tsar's disposition improved each day. I could almost swear his beard had lost some of its grey, but that was only a trick of the wind and the sun.

There was one other tension of which no one would speak, but which Holmes and I had the misfortune to experience on our trip in, the Germans.

At one point, as we were approaching Kiel, Holmes, holding some book he had been intently studying, approached Yardley about this and asked if we could speak off the bridge. Yardley consented.

"Oh, I don't suspect we'll have too much trouble from the Huns on this trip."

"What do you mean?" asked Holmes.

"It was something my father said in Scapa Flow; just about the time the repairs were complete on the *Attentive*. I had said I wouldn't mind a visit by the Germans, and my father said, 'Don't bet on it.'

"When I asked him to elaborate, he said, 'It's all been arranged. No one will come near us.' I tried to pry more from him, but I had no need to know any more, and that was that."

"Now, what do you make of this, Holmes?" I asked. "What could he have possibly meant? What had been arranged? And with the Germans?"

"Wait a minute, Watson. Captain Yardley, were you aware that on July 6, the German Ambassador to Russia, Count Von Mirbach, was assassinated in Moscow?"

"I remember something about it, vaguely."

"At the time, the Reds tried to fix blame on the Whites. They said it was the work of White renegades. Perhaps their propaganda, in this instance, was not far off the mark."

"What do you mean, Holmes?" I asked.

"Yes, indeed, what?" asked Yardley.

"A small theory, for now, if you will. Watson and I know for a fact who is behind the rescue of the Romanovs, which we cannot divulge at this time, but we do not know who is behind the attempt at their murder.

"Now, please also keep in mind that while the Tsarina is a first cousin of the King, she is also first cousin to the Kaiser. Wilhelm's mother and the Tsarina's mother were sisters; the King's father was their brother. So besides having a possible regicide looming over the horizon, which would frighten any sovereign to the depths of his throne, this regicide would become 'a family affair,' as well. All sovereigns address each other as brother or sister, but in this case, the sovereigns involved literally do share the same close blood.

"Therefore, might not have a representative from our sovereign met secretly with a representative of the German sovereign on neutral ground; most probably, Switzerland? And might not these two officials, with direct instructions from these sovereigns, have agreed that if this rescue attempt succeeded, the rescue vessels would not be hampered in any way?"

Before Yardley or I could even fully contemplate what Holmes was putting before us, he continued.

"There is more. Let us say those in England who wish the Romanovs dead, the 'Black Faction,' as Watson has dubbed them, found out about this agreement. By assassinating Von Mirbach, a man who most certainly was aware of events, would they not give to the Kaiser a message of British duplicity, therefore voiding the agreement?

"Or better still, let us say Von Mirbach found out about them. Before he could inform the Kaiser of the direct threat to the Romanovs' lives, Whites in the pay of the 'Black Faction' assassinate Von Mirbach to insure continuing ignorance of the conspiracy.

"Whichever is the case, Von Mirbach is dead, the Romanovs are alive, and based upon what Admiral Yardley has said, the wolf packs are off prowling elsewhere."

"Incredible," said Captain Yardley. "How did you come up with such a theory?"

"The facts were there, bones that they were. My theory is simply the flesh on those bones. Although there is still too much missing to perform an accurate autopsy."

"You are beginning to speak like me, Holmes. Have you been sneaking a peek at my medical books?" Holmes smiled.

"No, Watson, I have been studying 'Colville's Peerage' and a copy of Wexton's 'Our Parliament: A Guide to Who Sits, and to the Specific Ministries and their Attendant Bureaucracies.' These are part of the bounty each ship of the line reaps from our government."

"Pardon me?" said Yardley.

"There are copies of these books in each ship's library, Captain, to edify the men. I see you are well conversant with both." We all laughed.

"But why were you examining those two tomes?" I asked.

"Why, Watson," said Holmes as he snapped shut one and strode off to the main deck, "to uncover the members of the 'Black Faction,' naturally."

During the voyage messages were sent back and forth in the usual manner. Of course, code names were used when the admiral inquired about the state of the Imperial Family. Our captain enjoyed sending happy messages of greetings to the admiral, and receiving them in return; but in the guise of two officers being merely courteous.

We retraced our inward voyage; passed Laesö and Kattegat, back past Jutland, then down through the Channel and out to the Atlantic. As we began our passage near England, I understood fully the words of poets when speaking of heart-break.

There, so near across the Channel, past my family to starboard, unaware of my proximity. I pictured my wife and John, about to turn in for the night; for it was about that time we began our passage through the Channel. Being a medical man, a man of science, I held no truck with so-called telepathy and extra-sensory powers; but as our ship sailed along our coast, I admit to trying to 'will' my Elizabeth and John

192

a message of love and comfort.

A tending vessel came out to meet our ship, to provide us with more fuel and food so our ship would not actually touch in on English soil.

July 31, 1918

In the morning, Captain Yardley told us that with luck, we would be at Eleuthera in three days time. All passengers, including Holmes and I, rejoiced at the thought of our journey finally coming to end.

On deck, with the summer sun and winds whipping us all gently, Holmes regaled the Grand Duchesses, Alexei and Yardley with some of his unpublished exploits; making it seem as if he inducted them as true members of his closed, inner circle; members privy to only the most confidential information. It was in the midst of one of these sessions that something triggered some recondite mechanism in Holmes' powers and he suddenly ceased in mid-sentence.

"Inner-circle," he muttered to himself.

At first I thought he had been hit by a sudden fever, so quickly did Holmes turn from spell-binding orator to incommunicative zombie; the Grand Duchesses all making a huge fuss over him. I begged their permission and walked Holmes away from the group, noticing how close to each other stood the Grand Duchess Marie and Captain Yardley.

"What is it, Holmes? Tell me, is this physical?"

"Watson, this may be too great, now. Remember, when at the beginning of this odyssey, you saw this as a Herculean task and I said I may not have the strength to see it through?"

"Yes, but..."

"If what I now suspect is true, at this very moment I do not see a way out. It is not physical strength I meant, but intellectual prowess."

"You? Why, Holmes, there are few in the entire world with

your gifts."

"That may be, Watson, but if one with analogous gifts should also have real power, I would be reduced to ineffectuality."

He was quite away from me now, waving me off to be alone to think. I returned to where our group waited worriedly for news of Holmes' state. I reported that Holmes had just formulated another theory which now had taken hold so strongly, he would be lost to us for quite some time while he put it all in order, and was content it complete in his mind.

We then broke into smaller groups, Yardley and Marie walking off towards the bow.

Holmes remained at the stern; his hands on the railing, his head down on his chest, his shoulders hunched in the manner of a man of much greater age. He had never appeared so, so small.

The day was finally here. It was mid-morning and we were now off the coast of Eleuthera. I knew the Imperial Family would be in their cabins, joyously peeking through their portholes at the beauty now revealed before all.

Yardley's description had not done the place justice. There were magnificently tall palms waving in the breeze, as if to beckon us ashore. I could see coconuts falling hesitantly from their homes even as we came closer to shore. There was a wonderful sensation of green-ness to everything around, except the sky and sea which would shame any sapphire or turquoise. I understood fully why the Imperial Family would love such a spot.

The past three days had been a pleasure cruise for us all; all except Holmes, who refused our concourse as he groped for answers and permutations to whatever it was that so vexed him.

Of course the *Attentive* stood to, hovering and watching like a worried mother as the *Salvator* pulled in to her slip.

There were horse-drawn carriages waiting, and motor cars, and a very correct British official in dress whites.

As the official came aboard, only Yardley, Holmes and I were on deck. All hands, even Peters, had been told to lay below, as they had been doing, at specific intervals, the entire voyage.

Yardley saluted smartly, the other man acknowledged the salute and stuck out his hand.

"Captain, this gives me pleasure above and beyond my official duties, here, today. I have not seen you since you were a young man."

Yardley was trying to recall who this man was.

"I'm terribly sorry, sir, but I..."

"Oh, there's no need, Captain. It was quite long ago. But your father and I have seen each other over the years."

"I've been a friend of your father's since we were young men together in Paris. Perhaps you've heard him speak of me. I'm Michael

Preston."

Webs, webs, and more webs. This had become the most delicate and diabolically fused strands that Holmes and I had ever encountered. There was a supremely deft hand weaving events so intricately, so seamlessly, so apparently flawlessly. Now that this latest strand had come into view, Holmes hoped to see the entire pattern.

Michael Preston was a large man in his mid-fifties. He had a benign smile that belied his imposing size, and was one of the most pleasant and diplomatic of men. Yes, diplomacy was his occupation, but it was also natural with this man. He seemed to genuinely care for all with whom he came in contact; and this genuine concern was felt by all. He had a slight Scots accent, and we found out later he had been an officer in the Black Watch when extremely young. Indeed, his grandfather had been with Wellington at Waterloo.

So here, with Yardley and Preston, we had a friendship of descendants of men whose martial exploits stretched back to the Napoleonic Wars.

After our introductions, Yardley showed Preston down to the Imperial Family, and within a very short time, the Imperial Family began making their way up on deck; in the usual groupings.

Once on deck, in the magnificent sunlight and cool trade breeze, Anastasia literally clapped her hands, so excited and taken as she with the island.

Preston then explained that a very special compound had been secured for the Imperial Family; a former estate of Lord Braiborne. It was on a verdant hill overlooking an area called Winding Bay. The water was majestic and while the compound itself extended for a tad shy of one hundred acres, there were charming guest cottages and a manor house magnificent in its colonial architecture.

Alexei said he couldn't wait to see it, and had to be restrained by Olga, so intent was he on running down the dock to his awaiting transport.

Preston gestured the ladies down, the Tsar helping the Tsarina, Alexei and Olga going last. Holmes and I brought up the rear. Yardley had to see to the ship and informed us that he would be along at a later hour; with the baggage, he joked.

Preston and the Imperial Family rode in the carriages. Holmes and I were relegated to the motor cars. We learned later that Preston had given the Romanovs a choice and they chose the carriages immediately. He said the Tsar thought the Tsarina would especially enjoy the carriage ride; just like at Livadia.

The ride was not long, about twenty minutes; though of quite stifling heat since we were separated from the direct Caribbean breezes. Holmes and I removed our jackets, I loosened my collar, and began fanning myself vigorously with my hand.

Then, through nature's wizardry, we rounded a curve and saw Winding Bay; the house as well as the water. It was straight from one's vision of a tropical, colonial plantation, so pure and graceful were the lines of the house and the poetically tended landscapes.

I thought I saw Alexei bobbing up and down from glee, then likewise Anastasia. And the breezes were back. I stopped waving at myself like a lover saying farewell, and just enjoyed the seductive view.

Holmes commented on how he wouldn't mind being banished to such a spot, then thought better of it when he realized there was probably not sufficient murder, mayhem and mystery to keep his mind suitably occupied.

But for now, whether it be this one day or more, Holmes suggested we enjoy this Olympus while we were able. This was one matter for which I needed no coaxing, and was pleased to see Preston coming towards us as we reached the house.

"Gentlemen, the Imperial Family will be settling themselves in now, since there is much for them to become acclimatised to. In the meantime, I suggest that the three of us enjoy a late luncheon, which," he paused and looked at his pocket watch, "I believe is being prepared for us as we speak. Please follow me."

As we walked to the cottage where luncheon was to be served, Holmes asked if the fine, young gentleman who had been of such invaluable help to us in Ekaterinburg was indeed Preston's son.

"Why, yes, Mr. Holmes. What an admirable piece of deduction."

"Not at all, Mr. Preston. It is just a matter of putting two and two together so they tally four." Preston laughed.

"Gentlemen, I hope you enjoy your accommodations; I was given very specific instructions to care for your every need."

"Well, so far, the cottage is charming, the sea is magnificent, and the estate is beguiling," said Holmes. I concurred.

"Then I am doing my job adequately. Here we are." He opened the door and led us through the cottage to a terrace also overlooking the bay, where we found two surprises awaiting us. The first, Captain William Yardley. The second, Admiral Richard Yardley.

"Wonderful!" said Holmes; and he went to shake hands with the admiral. I followed suit.

Then, after Captain Yardley had said his hellos, Preston suggested he go up to the main house; the Grand Duchess Marie had specifically requested his presence at luncheon.

The admiral looked at his son and the son looked back with a huge smile on his face.

"Go to it, William," said the admiral. And with his more shallow of apologies, young Yardley was happily off to Marie.

Preston then said Marie had inquired about the captain's availability, and since Preston desired Yardley not be at this meeting, he suggested a formal invitation through him.

"Well, whatever is going on there," said the admiral, "I may wind up back in Russia as the grandpa of a Tsar or prince or something."

We all laughed, then sat the table which was laid out impeccably. While we consumed a tantalizing luncheon of exotic native dishes, we were also digesting information along with the meal.

"Well," said Holmes, "I trust all masks have been removed?" And when he received laughter of recognition, he went on.

"Admiral, what information had you received from Sir Michael?"

"Mr. Holmes," said the admiral, "I think it might be better if Michael gave you his information himself. It shall save time and avoid inaccuracies in second-telling."

"Would you mind then, Sir Michael?" asked Holmes.

"Not at all, Mr. Holmes. This is a matter of the utmost urgency and secrecy." Here was a man concerned with not only what he believed to be deception and duplicity at the highest levels of his government; but a man also concerned with how this duplicity might threaten the life of a dear friend, and that of his son.

"As I imagine you've already learned, Richard and I have known each other for about thirty years. We've been friends even though our professions have kept us apart much of the time. But there is no one I have more fondness and respect for than that old sea dog over there.

"At the beginning of April, not long after the Bolsheviks and the Germans signed the Treaty of Brest-Litovsk that took the Russians out of the war, I was summoned to the office of the Foreign Secretary, Arthur Balfour. I've known him almost as long as I've known Richard. At times, he still thinks he's Prime Minister.

"When I inquired as to the nature of his summons, Balfour said he had a special assignment for me. You see, there are only very few people in life that you can trust. There are certain families, aristocratic families, 'ruling' families, for lack of a better term, who have intermarried or been friends for hundreds of years.

"The members of these families trust each other and because of their holdings and wealth, they do effectively rule England.

199

"There are also men such as myself, not of the aristocracy as are William and Richard, who have become involved at specific levels of government which greatly concern these people. There are a few, like myself, who have made our careers by being of use to these parties.

"We are called upon, from time to time, to perform certain delicate tasks that our superiors in government would prefer the public and, for that matter, even other members of their own party to remain in ignorance of.

"Arthur Balfour is the nephew of Lord Salisbury; and as I am sure you remember, when Salisbury retired in 1902, Balfour became Prime Minister till 1905. Between the two, vast tracts were added to the Empire.

"So when Balfour told me of this plot to rescue the Romanovs, coming as it did from the highest person in the land, I was both flattered and excited.

"I was to be the personal liaison between the Prime Minister and our charges, here on Eleuthera, until they became accustomed to their new surroundings and were truly at home. I was told about your pivotal roles in the rescue, and since I have long been an admirer of you both, this was another bonus, if you will, in this particular assignment.

"Barlour further told me Sir Randolph Newsome, Deputy Director of Naval Intelligence, would assign the positions, and that's when I suggested that Balfour could not pick a better man for this than Richard. He said he had come to that same conclusion, and that he had already given his advice to Newsome. Of course, Balfour has known the Yardley family for decades.

"Anyway, Richard soon told me of what his specific involvement would be in this mission, and I did likewise. It was then that Richard also told me he would be utilizing the services of his son directly for the first time. He hoped, when this was over, that William and Thomas might become friends as we had.

"You were already off into Russia, and Richard was coming back to Scotland for repairs to the *Attentive* from your battle in the

North Sea, when I happened to bump into an old friend I hadn't seen in years; a captain in naval intelligence.

"We went out to talk about old times over drinks and he mentioned this very strange order he had come across, and wanted to know my opinion. He said he had found a document seconding an SIS man named Reilly, personally to Newsome. He had scratched his head for awhile over this because it was such an odd thing to happen. Usually the two branches wouldn't cooperate in bailing water from a sinking rowboat they were in together; and here, one of their top men, this Sidney Reilly, was being given directly to Newsome.

"I told him it was nothing, to forget about it and go on to meatier things. But now I was intrigued. Anything amiss with Newsome, as far as I'm concerned, smacks of something sour. So I inquired, of a friend in SIS, about this Sidney Reilly and was told just how remarkable a character he was. I decided to broach the matter to Newsome in passing.

"At first, he was surprised that I knew about Reilly and wanted to know how I'd found out. I said I was not at liberty to say. This annoyed him and he said it was no concern of mine, that I should keep this information to myself, and that in any case, Reilly was going to be the personal guardian of the two of you.

"Shortly after my meeting with Newsome, Balfour asked if I'd heard recently from my son Thomas, and said he would shortly be giving him a very plum assignment. An assignment that could make his name. I was assured that Thomas would be 'our man' on the spot in Russia. I could not imagine a more desirable place for a man of Thomas' temperament and intellect. He had always craved excitement, that is why he followed my example and went into the army, then also into the foreign service.

"But when Thomas wound up as our consul at Ekaterinburg right after the Romanovs, I wondered if there had been a connection between that and my meeting with Newsome.

"Since I've been in government, in one way or another, for my

201

entire life, I began to contemplate Thomas' position. I could interpret it in two ways. The first, perhaps a bribe for me to remain silent. The second, perhaps a threat to remain silent.

"Either way, neither bribe nor threat would have been made had something not been amiss. It was then I went to Scapa Flow to tell Richard what I have just told you. It was I who nominated him for his assignment. And then, when he told me Newsome had brought William into this, I had a very ill feeling of a shroud being thrown tight around all our shoulders.

"If this had been the other way round, with Richard being the man in charge, picking who he wanted for that post, I would've seen nothing wrong, at all. But with Newsome's hand, I find the mix of ingredients unhealthy.

"Richard knew nothing of Reilly or anything else that did not concern him. His instructions, plain and simple, were to convey you to Kronstadt and head home. He did not even know what your task was to be; nor from where your directions had originated. He thought you were under orders from Newsome, as was he. When Newsome told him of the other singular assignment, the one for captain of 'a very special rescue vessel,' and asked if his son William might do, Richard leapt at the chance for him.

"And that, Mr. Holmes, is everything I know."

"Admiral, is this all?" asked Holmes.

"I should like to add something to that which Michael has just told you, and to what William has told me," said Admiral Yardley.

"William told me of the events aboard the *Salvator* with my mess man, Peters. He's blameless. As William said, I transferred him personally to watch over William after Michael had spoken with me.

"Due to the way Michael had put things, I too, began to feel uneasy. My wife has been gone these many years, and William is all I have.

"I know the way Newsome is. I've known him all my life. But I've accepted the man, warts and all, because that's the way he is.

202

"Now, I suppose, if you stretch things, you can lay blame back to Newsome for what happened to that poor girl. But Newsome did help me get Peters out. His family was ready to throw Newsome into the rubbish bin, so disgusted were they with him. The gambling debts, the outstanding accounts with all manner of tradesmen and then this business with the girl had driven them to distraction.

"Newsome's father went to his friend, Balfour, and asked if he could arrange a position for him somewhere at the other end of the Empire. But Balfour himself was reticent; he had known Newsome all his life, too. Instead, he suggested Newsome join the military. It might just turn him around, and all the usual cliches of what the spartan life would do for a disagreeable young man were mentioned.

"Newsome chose the navy because he'd look better in the uniform, and I'd already gone in. But oddly enough, while it didn't necessarily change him, it brought out that latent talent of his for duplicity and quick-thinking that he'd used for ill in civilian life. And you see where it's gotten him: deputy head of Naval Intelligence.

"With all his quirks, Newsome has done an excellent job in his post. But this business now, this is something else. I, like Michael, feel that our boys may be glorified hostages in some way. Thomas still in Russia where anything can happen; and William on active duty at sea where anything can happen.

"Mr. Holmes, I haven't the faintest idea of who in England would want the Romanovs dead, or why. I am only following orders in the middle of a war. And, I might add, I have done well by the two of you.

"I was never in on anything dark. I don't know what Newsome is up to nor who has put him up to it. But as soon as I get back to England, Newsome is going to have much to answer for. Especially now that William has told me of your experiences in Russia."

"What experiences?" asked Sir Michael.

"Sir Michael," said Holmes, "I shall now tell you of our experiences in Russia, and of the man Reilly who so intrigued you.

Then, if you please, I would like to hear what you and Admiral Yardley make of it." Holmes then went about recounting all that had happened in Russia, especially dwelling on Thomas Preston's aid and fortitude, with ample praise mixed in for Captain Yardley.

"Well, then, gentlemen." he said as he concluded, "Now that you know as much as we, what do you make of all this?"

"Mr. Holmes," said Admiral Yardley, "if I had been you, I would've thought the same about me. In fact, I would've had me keel-hauled."

"But I just can't see it. All I do see is that Michael's suspicions were more than accurate if this Reilly was telling the truth. On the other hand, if William is right about Reilly, we're back to square one, aren't we?

"And you, Sir Michael? Do you see anything we might have missed?"

"I can't say that I do, Mr. Holmes. But if Reilly was telling the truth, which would then substantiate my worst suspicions, I would advise utmost caution in dealing with Newsome. As much as I would love to see Newsome rewarded for his actions in the manner prescribed by my naval colleague here, I must, being a diplomat, temper immediate action with patient observation."

"Precisely," said Holmes. "To paraphrase your very words, Sir Michael, I suspect Newsome is merely the tail being wagged by a cunning dog. There is no telling who, or how many, or what sort of power is behind him."

"Mr. Holmes," said Admiral Yardley, "why don't I just stick a pistol into his mouth and threaten to blow his brains all over his perfectly fitted dress whites. That might loosen his tongue. Then, if he does talk, I may still pull the trigger."

"An enviable idea, admiral, but as Sir Michael has cautioned, once we are back in England, I should like you to behave towards Newsome as dictated by an ancient, and proven, Italian proverb: Hold your friends close, and your enemies closer."

204

The admiral sat back, not liking this advice, but seeing its merits; and all at the table agreed this would be the method of choice in dealing with Sir Randolph Newsome.

Once all were back in England, that is.

August 4, 1918

In the morning, Admiral Yardley informed us new orders had come through. The *Attentive* would be leaving that very day for the North Atlantic. The mother hen was being taken from her chicks.

Father and son said their good-byes in private; William later informing us that while his father had not told him everything discussed the preceding day, he had held him long and tight before leaving, warned him to be especially careful on the return voyage; and to look to both Holmes and I as if we were family.

Admiral Yardley met with the Imperial Family, with William in attendance, and the Tsar gave him a small token of thanks for all he had done: a coin that had belonged to his father.

"Admiral," said the Tsar, "do not worry yourself about William, Marie seems to be looking after him very well."

These words were so unexpected, that Marie went red, the Grand Duchesses all laughed out loud, and the admiral and William both stood mute, as the Tsar smiled.

Sir Michael, Holmes and I all went down to the ship to send the admiral off in right manner. He saluted us, including Michael, we wished him good fortune, and then he was gone; his launch growing progressively smaller as it came nearer the *Attentive*. Then she steamed up and disappeared. But only William stayed behind to watch her dissolve fully into the horizon.

Further orders had come through that Michael's return trip would be delayed. Not only would he be carrying to England Holmes and me, but Sir Michael would also be passenger. However, the trip would only begin when the Imperial Family felt comfortable enough to dispense with Sir Michael's ministrations; and I felt Alexei well enough, which I did already, to have another doctor sent over. In fact, the orders said replacements were being sent out to Eleuthera even now. Of course all messages were in code, and the Romanovs were still referred to as "Augustus."

At first, Holmes and I were testy that we would be so delayed; but upon the beneficence of continuous, perfect weather and the knowledge that we would be sharing Sir Michael's company to England, Holmes and I relaxed, adopted the requisite stiff, upper lips, and agreed we would do as required.

The Imperial Family was doing wonderfully in their new surroundings. The happy Caribbean sun contributing mightily to their own increasingly sunny selves. All but the Tsarina, fully enjoying everything their cousin George had provided them.

Alexei, though restrained by his sisters from running off and hurting himself, enjoyed the warm water as well as any fish, and spent a good portion of the time rebuilding the strength in his arms and legs in this manner. The boy even seemed to be growing. And he no longer needed the leg brace.

The Grand Duchesses loved the island and would spend many hours in quiet tours of their compound and the island beyond. It was quite safe.

Tatiana thought often, and expressed those thoughts to me, of Reilly. And Marie and young Yardley spent as much time together as duty, family demands, and protocol, would allow.

The most touching sights, again, though, were the hours the Tsar spent with the Tsarina, just sitting on their hill overlooking Winding Bay. He would tell her stories of the Crimea and point out the similarities; and even how much better things were here in their new home because they had no worries of government or state to mar their bliss. And although the Tsar would swear it at end of each day, saying things like, "You see, Dr. Watson, the Tsarina smiled, just a tad, today. She hears and understands. She loves it here," I did not believe she was improving at all.

August 11, 1918

This morning, Sir Michael summoned Holmes and me to the main house. He had news for us.

Upon our arrival, we found the Imperial Family on their terrace with a strange man. He looked familiar, but I could not place him. It was Holmes who let out a laugh.

"Your Imperial Majesty, I did not recognize you, at first, without your beard."

"Mr. Holmes, with this heat, I believed it prudent to do away with the thing. While it may have kept me warm in Russia in winter, and it was a truly magnificent set of whiskers I had cultivated all these years, the idea of continuous scratching did not recommend itself to me. On any level." Everyone laughed.

The Grand Duchesses all commented on how much younger their father looked, and Marie said if her mother wasn't careful, some native girl would steal her "Papa" away. While we laughed again at that, the Tsar went over to his "Sonny," took her hand and rubbed it up and down his now smooth cheeks, and said, "Now, don't you worry, Sonny, your Nicky would never leave you. Even if I am so much younger now." It was funny, touching, and sad simultaneously, and we all remained quiet while the Tsar continued to run the Tsarina's hand lovingly against his cheeks.

August 12, 1918

This morning, Sir Michael came personally to our cottage, and after hearty good-days, he coyly asked, "Gentlemen, do you think it would take you much time to pack and be ready to leave?"

I was overjoyed by the question as, I believe, was Holmes and we agreed that we could be ready at any time.

"Good," said Sir Michael, "last night the Tsar gave us permission to leave whenever we were ready. I had Yardley send out the message, and we received the all clear to sail early this morning. When proper goodbyes are said, and I am sure all is well here, I see no reason why we should not be able to leave tomorrow morning."

"Oh, well," said Holmes, "one cannot have everything."

Sir Michael told us the Tsar would host a special dinner in our, and Yardley's, honour that night; formal attire not required. We laughed.

Finally, we were going home. Every lovely vision of Elizabeth and John standing at my front door with arms open wide rushed through my mind and gave me giddy joy. I was as an adolescent, so happy was I. Holmes, of course, was very pleased to be going home.

That night all was beautiful. The Grand Duchesses, all in splendid, native cottons, the Tsarina being fed by Tatiana as the Tsar did the toasts and held court, so to speak. It was a wonderful night, a truly memorable night between, I wish to believe, warm friends.

William sat next to Marie, as if it could have been otherwise, Tatiana on my left, Alexei to my right, Holmes across from me between Olga and Anastasia. Sir Michael sat at the other end of the table.

After the Tsar's toasts and good wishes, and a remarkable feast of native-spiced suckling pig with attendant island delicacies, the Tsar, Holmes, Sir Michael and I repaired to the salon, while Alexei went outside with William and Marie.

The Tsar sat regaling us with funny stories of how King George had barked like a dog, nipping at his relatives' heels, when the two were boys at an elderly Queen Victoria's birthday party; and we were in the middle of a healthy laugh when Marie came running in to us.

"Dr. Watson, quickly, Alexei has had a fall."

"Oh, my God," said the Tsar. We all ran after Marie.

The Tsarevich had gone out to take the calm night air with William and Marie, who, it seemed, had been paying more attention to each other than to Alexei. Even though Marie had warned him to be careful, Alexei had managed to climb a nearby trellis and pull it from its housings. He had landed hard on the earth from midway between the first and second stories; and had he not fallen in a very soft, freshly planted flower bed, I believe the boy would not have survived the damage.

He had already been carried upstairs by William and by the time we got to his bedside, Anastasia and Olga were there also. The Tsarevich was screaming from pain. The internal bleeding had begun almost immediately, and with it, the swelling. The haemorrhaging was occurring in the areas of Alexei's shoulder joints, where he had taken the fall; the joints being where the blood would collect in cases such as this. So we had to lay the boy on his stomach.

Sir Michael sent a servant to fetch my bag from our cottage, but I knew there was little I could do. The episode would have to run its course as I would try to make Alexei as comfortable as possible. However, at first, and as I found out later has always been the case, the Tsar forbade me to use morphine to ease the boy's intense pain. The Tsar and Tsarina knew of the drug's addictive effects, and for that, they had long ago agreed not to administer anything that might make a slave of their son. The only relief for Alexei from his torment would be unconsciousness.

Holmes took everyone out except the Tsar, who kept kissing Alexei's hands over and over, saying, "My boy, Alexei, my boy." When I told the Tsar I would have to get close to Alexei to examine him further, he moved away saying, "Thank God his mother cannot see this. Thank God." I said the same to myself.

As I feared, and knew, there was nothing I could do to stop the bleeding; but the moment my bag arrived, I begged the Tsar for permission to administer at least a mild dose of morphine, just this one time. It would put the boy to sleep and alleviate him of the torture sure to follow. It would also relieve everyone else of the pain of hearing the boy in agony.

The Tsar at first held firm, but without his wife there to influence him against the drug, and with me saying the boy had suffered enough in the past year to last a lifetime, he finally consented.

The blood vessels inside had been more than merely torn, the severe fall had virtually shredded them. As the blood seeped into the tissue in Alexei's back, it formed so bulbous a hematoma, that if you did not know differently, you would think this boy was a hunchback.

I felt it better if the Tsar leave too, and he did so reluctantly. I had a native woman who lived on the compound as my nurse, her name was Sarah, and from what I saw of the woman that night, she was a natural. She had the compassion and she had the touch. She said nursing was what she did on the island, ministering to the sick. She had been taught by doctors on Grand Bahama Island when she was young; and while they would return every few months to examine the people of Eleuthera, she was there to aid while they were gone. She did splendidly.

Alexei was having a very tough time of it. His fever shot up immediately, which was, in truth, a good sign; but it made him delirious.

By the second day, all colour was gone from Alexei's face. He resembled a wax doll. His eyes had sunken significantly and his breathing was horribly laboured. I begged the Tsar to permit the use of a mild dose of morphine again, but he absolutely refused this time. Alexei plunged into horrific agony, screaming for his mother to help, "Mama, Mama, why don't you help me?"

Everyone who heard these cries were themselves stricken.

Then, as Alexei writhed in the alternating throes of delirium and agony, as if we had not enough afflictions inside the safe confines of the main house, a large storm bestirred itself early that season, and began to do its monstrous work on the island.

It was in the middle of the terror raging outside, and the horror before our eyes inside, that Sarah proved her worth a million times over.

210

"You know," she said, "the doctors on the main island teased me about my witch doctoring, but my people were being helped by our herbs and secrets long before white men brought us here. Perhaps I can help you."

"My God, woman, if you are talking of some native potion that will have a calming effect and no more, then of course you can help. But it is the boy, not me, you will be helping."

And she did. While this hurricane, or whatever it was, crashed down trees and banged on windows all around us, Sarah fought her way out into Hades' brew. She was gone for three hours, but when she returned, she held a small bowl with a white pasty glue of a mix to spoon-feed to Alexei. She swore it would take away the pain.

I spoke with the Tsar, who was concerned about Alexei, the Tsarina, and the storm, and he gave me permission because he said he trusted me. He would stay with the Tsarina and pray to God. I thought it a good place for him to be.

I told Sarah I had decided to try her mixture and she I said must be part native, because white people's heads are too hard to have soft hearts. I think I laughed at her remark, but I cannot remember now.

Whether coincidence or not, not only did her paste alleviate Alexei's pain within fifteen minutes, but his fever broke not long after. And though it would shoot up and down again haphazardly, the paste would always work its magic.

I became something of a believer in natural medicines then, but when I asked Sarah what was inside her concoction, she laughed and said old island secrets not fit for a white man to know; even for me. She simply said, "This boy should not suffer; he is a 'mahtooba.'" When I inquired as to the precise meaning of the word, Sarah said it meant a soul who had suffered much, but did not deserve it." In our lifetimes, we all know 'mahtoobas.'

211

August 13, 1918

In the morning, the Tsar was told of the level of destruction in our vicinity. Two of the guest cottages had been virtually destroyed, and many of the windows and doors of the main house likewise. Trees had been felled and it would be long before the manicure was restored to all cultivated areas. But the heaviest toll was human: two natives had been killed; unfortunately, this included Sarah's nephew.

Sarah would later speak of how Alexei had been helped not by her medicine, but by the spirit of her nephew, Oliver. She firmly believed Alexei and Oliver to be now one, and she begged the Tsar for permission to watch over Alexei as his nurse for the rest of her life. After I told the Tsar this would be more than an excellent idea, especially as he would require a full-time nurse for Alexei, he accepted Sarah's offer and she moved into the servants' quarters of the main house to always be near the Tsarevich. She loved the boy as her own.

August 14, 1918   Holmes Departs

Captain Yardley's orders were to sail that very next day, and that very next day he did sail. And while there was a replacement for Sir Michael, who I shall get to later, there was no physician to take my place. Yardley said the captain of the vessel bringing the new man never had instructions to carry a doctor or any other passenger; only the one. Not that I would have left little Alexei in any case, but that no other physician was aboard distressed me greatly. And I did not need more distress at this time.

To lessen everyone's distress over the seeming solitude of our circumstances, Yardley had set up a wireless in a cottage at the far end of the compound. This would be manned, on and off, by three previously discharged Bahamian locals who had been in the Colonial forces; and were trained wireless operators. They had just been induced to re-enlist to bring them again under strict military rule. As their inducement, they were given a raise in rank to sergeants, and had their pay increased even above that rank.

The Grand Duchesses bid Holmes, Preston, and Yardley goodbye with heavy hearts for two reasons: their departure and Alexei's illness. For Marie, it was worse. She was experiencing what her sister, Tatiana, had silently suffered almost a month before.

I was told by Tatiana later that love vows had been exchanged between William and Marie, and he swore that once the war was over, "which should be any day now," he would be back to ask for her hand. He assured her that all would be well with her brother, and then he had to board his ship.

The Tsar took a few minutes away from Alexei to go to Holmes and Preston. He told me later that he had thanked Sir Michael profusely and begged him to return for visits; which Sir Michael promised, but which, the Tsar knew, would have very little likelihood of happening.

When it came to Holmes, the Tsar embraced him, and with

213

tears running down his cheeks unashamedly, he held Holmes' hands in his own as he thanked him for rescuing him and his family, and for everything he had done.

The Tsar gave Holmes his last item of value that he had: a wrist chain he wore, given to him by his mother at the time of his first communion. Holmes immediately put in on his own wrist and told the Tsar they would meet again. This, the Tsar believed with all his heart.

Then the Tsar came back in and told me to go out to my friend. I saw Alexei resting, and knowing the Tsar would be with him, I went out to Holmes.

"Well, my friend," said Holmes, "do not worry for anything. I shall go to Mrs. Watson immediately upon my return and tell her of your health and good spirits, and when I am able, I shall tell her and John of how heroic you have been and how you have become one with history."

I shook his hand and held it in mine. "No, Holmes, do not tell them that. Just tell them how much I love and miss them, and that as soon as I am able, I shall be with them again."

"I shall do as you say, Doctor Watson."

Holmes turned and left with Sir Michael. As they pulled away down to the slip, I felt like the young Ebeneezer Scrooge, seeing all of his friends going home for Christmas, and he being left behind in tormenting solitude, terribly alone.

September 16, 1918

Now that Alexei had actually walked by himself and I had been assured by William and Holmes and Sir Michael that I would be getting a doctor to replace me, how could I, or anyone, guess that the smallest remark made in passing would change my life for approximately another eight months.

One morning, while the Grand Duchesses, Alexei and I were having breakfast on their terrace, the Tsar being with the Tsarina, Tatiana mentioned something about an unsettling feeling in her stomach. She excused herself from table and did not return. I thought nothing much of it at the time, but a few days later there was a knock at my cottage door; and when I opened it, I was happily surprised to find Tatiana.

"Why, Your Imperial Highness, what a wonderful surprise. Please, do come in." We went out to my little terrace where I sat her down and gave her some cool lemonade my newly assigned man, Lawrence, had just made for me. Tatiana waved it away.

"Dr. Watson, I have come to look upon you these past months almost as an uncle. Not only because of your help in helping Alexei regain his health, but mostly because of your silent understanding of my relationship with Sidney."

"Your Imperial Highness, I believe your brother came around more from his own healing than mine. As for Reilly, that is your matter; there is nothing for me to say about it."

"Well, doctor, it is just because of that attitude that I appreciate you so. And that is why I am here. For the past few days my stomach has been extremely unsettled, and I believe I must've contracted an island illness of some sort. I can't keep food down at times, and I feel positively awful."

"Do you find this nausea at particular times of the day, or all day?"

"Only in the morning, Dr. Watson, though, sometimes later on. But usually in the morning."

"And do you void your stomach at these times?"

"Yes, I do, doctor. Quite often."

"Your Imperial Highness, I think I may have to examine you."

"Doctor, you have been tending to my family now for two months or more. You are a highly skilled physician. Don't be put off because of my station."

"Thank you, Your Imperial Highness."

I then proceeded to give Tatiana the usual examination I would for any woman claiming these symptoms and was given an emphatic answer. After Tatiana dressed herself, she came back to me on the terrace. I sat her down again.

"Your Imperial Highness, I have the happy news to inform you that you are pregnant."

Tatiana's immediate reaction was one of sheer joy.

"Oh, Dr. Watson. How wonderful this is. I am carrying another Sidney," and she kissed me on the cheek.

"Well, Your Imperial Highness, to be perfectly honest, the world is not ready for two Reillys. It is not even ready for one." She laughed.

"Oh, don't be so silly. Of course the world is ready for another spot of north moss." Now it was my turn to laugh.

Then she grew serious. "Dr. Watson, I sincerely believe my father will understand, and I know my sisters will. As for my mother, well... But, my dear Dr. Watson, will you come with me when I tell my father this rapturous news?"

"Are you sure you want me there at such a private time?"

"Absolutely. I cannot want for a stronger ally, nor a finer friend. Will you? Please?"

She had me wrapped around her beautiful, little finger.

"Yes, of course."

"Doctor, you couldn't be mistaken, could you?"

"Your Imperial Highness, the only illness you have picked up is known in scientific circles as 'Bacillus Reillyus.'" We both laughed.

Now all Tatiana had to do was plan when to tell her father for maximum, beneficial reaction. She decided to do it as soon as possible for her own mind's well being. She felt that night, after dinner, would be a good time. Her father would have relaxed with a brandy, and he

216

would be receptive to what Tatiana would tell him. And if I should be needed, he might listen to my council because of my recent restoration to him of his son; whole and vigorous once more.

I consented, and that night just Tatiana, the Tsar and I repaired to the gardens for a stroll after dinner; Tatiana having told her sisters not to intrude.

The Tsar was a happy man as we walked, his arm around his daughter's waist. If it were not for his wife's illness, there was nothing he would want for. Sir Michael had once told us that while, of course, he could not divulge the allowance nor specific arrangements made for the Imperial Family, the Prime Minister was seeing to it that they were treated in reminiscent manner of the style they had become accustomed.

"Papa, there is something I must speak with you about, and Dr. Watson has been good enough to be with us."

"Ah, a conspiracy. But since it is from two of my more favourite people in the world, I see this is one conspiracy from which I have nothing to fear." He laughed.

"Oh, no, Papa. This is something that shall make me the most happy woman on earth, and I hope you will be happy for me, as well."

The Tsar stopped and looked at his daughter. He sensed the serious nature of what was now to come.

"What is it, child?"

"Father, I know you were aware of the very tender affections I held for Colonel Relinsky," until now, I had no idea she had not told her father who Reilly was, "and I believe that because of our circumstances, you understood and approved."

"You are wise, Tatiana and sensitive as a flower." He kissed her on the forehead.

"Father, the colonel and I had fallen in love. Truly in love. Not knowing, literally, what tomorrow held for our family, my time with the colonel became even more precious. And intimate. And though there was no clergy to bind us, we believed that we were wed in the eyes of God."

217

I thought I saw the Tsar's eyes show recognition of what his daughter had not yet told him.

"Papa, today, this morning, Dr. Watson was good enough to confirm what I have suspected for a few days now. Papa, I am going to have a baby." She looked deep into his eyes for his true answer, but she needn't have worried.

"Tatiana, Tatiana. Yes, I knew. I have tried to understand. And since your mother has left us and would not know, this becomes easier. Your baby will be my first grandchild. That is important. And you have a man who loves you. That is also important. It is interesting how one can change when he does not know if he or his family is to live or die. And what becomes truly important. I have learned."

He then began talking tenderly to Tatiana in Russian, and I left the two there in the yellow moonlight.

The joy I felt for Tatiana and the Tsar, indeed the entire family now, was tempered the next morning when Tatiana again came to call. She asked me to accompany her to the main house once more. This time it was her father who wanted to speak with me.

When we arrived on the terrace, the Tsar wished me good day and bade me sit opposite him. Tatiana sat between us.

"This is some news, is it not, Dr. Watson?"

"Wonderful news, Your Imperial Majesty."

The Tsar took Tatiana's hand in his own.

"The other Grand Duchesses and Alexei are as excited as we, and I cannot thank you enough for your help in this matter."

"I assure you, Your Imperial Majesty, I had nothing at all to do with it." It came out not the way I had wanted, and the Tsar and Tatiana looked at each other and began laughing full steam. I did then, myself.

"Dr. Watson," continued the Tsar, the laugh abating, "there is something, though, I must ask of you."

218

"If I am able to provide what you need, it shall be done."

"Dr. Watson," he hesitated, then said, "Tatiana, as do my entire family, wish you would stay here and tend to Tatiana during this most important time of her life."

I was hit as hard as if I were struck in the face with a cannon ball. I quickly saw my homeward journey delayed at least another eight months, and my family began slipping away into the distance without me being able to hold onto them.

"But, Your Imperial Majesty, Your Imperial Highness, surely you know of my wife and son in England. It has been months since I have seen them. And until Holmes speaks with them, they know not if I am alive or dead.

"There are other doctors, specialists, who could tend to Her Imperial Highness much better than I. You do not need me here, but my family does need me there. Please, Your Imperial Majesty, Your Imperial Highness, do not ask me to do this. Anything else I would gladly grant, but I want desperately to be home."

"Dr. Watson," said the Tsar, "we fully understand and you know how we sympathize with your desires. You have meant much to us all, especially Alexei and Tatiana. But this is something we feel should be left to the privacy of our family, for reasons you yourself know only too well. And, quite truly, we have come to regard you as such; a lost, loving cousin we were fortunate enough to discover.

"But it is not rational. There are those better..." he cut me off.

"Dr. Watson, you yourself went through the miracle of your wife giving birth. Tell me, doctor, was there anything rational in her actions for months previous? Or has anything rational come from our shared circumstances?

"No, doctor, you are right; there is nothing rational in our request. And while it may be selfish, you are truly wanted, needed, and loved. I shall implore our new friend, when he arrives, to have you be in contact with your family."

"Please, Dr. Watson," said Tatiana, "I cannot even comprehend another doctor with me now at this time."

I was beaten. And since the Tsar did promise to put me in direct contact with Elizabeth, I consented.

The Tsar and Tatiana thanked me so enthusiastically I cannot even begin to convey the overwhelming feelings of warmth I received from them. The Tsar then asked Lawrence to go immediately and fetch their new liaison to him so he could forcefully put in his request about my familial communications.

The Imperial Family's new liaison arrived presently and I went out to speak with him before the Tsar did so. After all, it was not as if we were strangers.

For the man sent to replace Sir Michael was none other than our ally in Ekaterinburg, Arthur Thomas.

A Friend Returns

Arthur filled in all the gaps, answering all our questions about what happened after we escaped. The most humorous tale being his description of the Bolshies' arguments pro and con on following Holmes' advice about the Romanovs' execution. But before that, let me recount what happened to our comrades left behind.

First and foremost, Father Storozhev: as Holmes foresaw, directly after finding the basement empty, a large detachment of guards from the Impatiev House made a hasty attack on the church. Upon finding the poor old man beaten and tied so, and listening to his cries of anguish and tale of sorrow, many of the guards who had come for blood, were softened and vied with each other in helping the Father. Some brought him water while others made him comfortable on his bed. They completely believed him.

As for Yurovsky, after he had been freed, which happened when his sleeping men heard the battle at the train station, he led his men to that destination. We had all fled, but Gablinev and his men fought on. Eventually they were surrounded by the combined forces of Impatiev House guards, Cheka, and some of the provisional troops in the area. Arthur said Yurovsky told him Gablinev was the last man alive, and rather than fall into the Cheka's hands, he took his own life.

When Yurovsky was told the Imperial Family had escaped, he went back to the church, had his men drag Father Storozhev from his bed, and was only stopped from torturing the poor man by Preston and Thomas who so vigorously protested that Yurovsky released him into their charge. He much later confided to Preston that though he could not prove it, he knew the Father was involved, and he should kill the man just as a lesson to any other White sympathizers. But he never moved against Father Storozhev.

The nuns, as anticipated, were not missed, and the two men left to guard and guide them did as planned and took the nuns back to their convent in the dark of the next night.

As for Preston, when Thomas had been recalled, about one week after we fled, Preston was still there and still very much involved in playing the game. Each day he would demand to see the Imperial Family, and each day Yurovsky proved as much of an actor when he refused to permit such a visit.

After Yurovksy's gamble had failed at Perm, he and Beleborodov and Yermakov struggled with the decision on what to do. Thomas had heard the bickering from the simple expedient of bending down as if to tie his shoes while the three men screamed back and forth in the open air, right outside Hotel America.

The day was finally won by Yurovsky who convinced the others to go along by literally acting out what it would feel like to first have their testes severed, he made a grab at Beleborodov's and pantomimed a quick slice, then to have them stuffed in their mouths, here he puffed out his cheeks and held his breath until he had turned borscht red, then to be hung, and here he pulled on a mock rope, stood on his tip-toes, thrust out his tongue, and held his breath until he was purple. He won his point. They would "execute" the Romanovs.

Thomas said this 'Bolshie Ballet,' as he called it, was hysterically funny, and he had Preston in stitches with its retelling.

So our friend Arthur Thomas was back, and when the Imperial Family learned of his importance to their escape, they could not thank him enough, or show him enough courtesy.

That is what happened to those we left in Russia. Only Thomas Preston's whereabouts now remained a mystery.

November 11, 1918   The War Is Over!

It was on this magnificent day, that Lawrence came running to the main house holding a paper in his hands. He had just been given it by one of the wireless men who was, quite literally, jumping for joy.

It was handed to the Tsar who stood bolt upright, slapped his knee and exclaimed, "It is over, thank the Lord! The war is over!"

I too jumped up, quite forgot myself and virtually ripped the paper from the Tsar's hands. But everyone was now screaming for joy and everyone kissed everyone else. The Tsar ran in to tell the Tsarina. I then saw Thomas coming up the hill.

Even though he was still too far distant for me to hear, I could tell he was shouting the news at us.

"What a glorious day, Dr. Watson." He bowed at the Imperial Family and offered his congratulations.

"Oh, no," said Anastasia, "we should be offering you the congratulations. It was your country that won the war. You, the Americans and the French.

Thomas went on to tell us the Kaiser had been toppled, and that was all the word he had. While this news was being given, Alexei was strutting around in imitation of his cousin, the Kaiser, using his fingers to indicate the Kaiser's upturned, stiletto moustaches and singing,

> "Silly Billy,
> Silly Billy,
> What will happen
> To Cousin Willy?"

And as he said that, he stopped still and his sisters quickly stopped laughing. For it had suddenly dawned on these members of the Imperial Family that their cousin, even though the enemy, was a blood relative; and what, indeed, would happen to him and his throne? Would he be carted off as had they? Or would he not be so lucky? It gave them good for thought, and again it was Olga who spoke.

"No matter what, no sovereign should have to go through what we did."

Thomas and I said nothing, this mood putting a severe damper on our spirits, since we were English and did not give one fig for the Kaiser or his blasted throne. But to see these people that we cared so much about so saddened, Thomas and I decided to just go off by ourselves and perhaps celebrate a little less strongly, and with more homage to introspection.

December 14, 1918

The months were coming and going quickly now. Tatiana was happy and healthy, the baby seemed to be coming along nicely, but I was not happy.

No matter how hard Thomas tried to get permission for me to communicate with Elizabeth, every request was turned down. Even when London knew this was at the direct request of 'Augustus', we received a forceful 'no'.

"Don't be so glum, Dr. Watson," Tatiana would say, "I'm sure Mr. Holmes, in his unique way, has discerned what has happened and is in constant contact with your wife." Of course, I knew she was right, but something still nagged at me. And I spoke of it with Thomas.

"Arthur, you said that when you were ordered to come over by Balfour, no mention was made of a replacement doctor for me?"

"Absolutely not one syllable."

I had not told Thomas of everything that had happened with us since our escape from Russia, only what he needed to know; because even though he appeared to be my friend, and had proved that back in Ekaterinburg, Holmes had left me thoroughly sceptical of all but our immediate group. And I was not about to let Holmes, nor the Imperial

Family, let alone myself, down in any manner.

I will say this for Thomas, though, he was a diplomat all right. Because anyone seeing Tatiana growing larger day by day without saying one word, was either a true man of diplomacy or a blind dolt. I tended to think the former of Arthur Thomas.

More months passed, and we learned of the Kaiser's banishment, of King George's grief over the death of his dear Romanov relatives; although, this last, I knew was not more than official obfuscation.

March 2, 1919

This is my first notation in this new year. Tatiana was due and I would be leaving this blessed and cursed island in a month or so. I literally began counting the days; and before I knew it, as the sun jumped up, as morning suns do in the Caribbean, I was awakened by Sarah. It was time. The baby was coming.

The Tsar was already waiting for me at the doorway to Tatiana's room.

"She will be all right, won't she, Dr. Watson?"

"Your Imperial Majesty, she and the baby are more than healthy. Now please, she needs me more than you do this moment." And with that, Sarah and I went in and closed the door.

Sarah was my nurse and companion during the delivery and when a boy emerged, all bloody and strong and howling wildly, Sarah called this boy a gift of the gods.

Tatiana had not suffered much during the delivery, and only the heat of the island caused her discomfort during the time she carried. She immediately demanded to hold her baby and Sarah happily complied with a smile.

Tatiana was crying, the baby was screaming, and I went out to the Tsar. The whole family was there, except the Tsarina, of course.

"Your Imperial Majesty, Your Imperial Highnesses, it is a

boy."

The screaming from this group was now louder than that from the baby.

"Can we go in?" asked Alexei.

"Yes, but I suggest one at a time. Your Imperial Majesty, you shall be the first." Before I could finish, he was in the room at Tatiana's bedside.

"Look, look at my grandson. Look how big and strong he is. Doctor, look, look here. I bet he grows to be as tall as my father was." At that, he broke down and wept, his hand holding one hand of the baby, Tatiana's hand on that of her father.

When he had regained his composure, the Tsar asked if it would be all right if he brought the baby in to the Tsarina. At first I was going to ask him to wait, but when I saw the look in his eyes, I could not refuse. But for safety, I asked if I might go with them. He readily agreed.

So, after showing the throng outside their new nephew, and they, en masse, running in to Tatiana, the Tsar, the new Prince and I, went in to the Tsarina.

The Tsarina was seated in one of those wicker peacock chairs, the windows wide open, she just staring out at the sea. The Tsar came up to her and turned her face to us.

"Sonny. Sonny. Look, my dearest. This is your grandson. Tatiana has just become a mother. And you and I are now rickety, old grandparents. How does that sound, 'Grandmama, Granpapa?' Here, Sonny, hold your grandson. He is a piece of your blessed goodness."

He took the Tsarina's hands and put the baby, who now was crying again, into them carefully, still holding the baby with his own hands.

And as the baby cried, the Tsarina's head tilted down at him ever so slowly; but with still no expression on her face. It was then I saw it at the same time as did the Tsar. A tear was falling from the Tsarina's eye, slowly making a brook on her cheek. There was no other

226

recognition. No smile, no movement of her eyes of any sort, no physical manifestation at all; just that one tear.

"You see, you see," said the Tsar weeping as did the baby in his wife's hands, "she *does* know, she does know."

That one tear falling so delicately, so comprehendingly, if you will, from the eye of the Tsarina, was even more touching to me than the birth of her first grandchild.

Of course, Tatiana named the baby after his father, and I again chastised her about having two Sidney Reillys in this world. But the deed was done, and the baby could certainly not return from whence he had come.

My work here was now truly nearing its end.

The baby and Tatiana progressed better than well. The bond between the two was that between every mother and babe, pure and loving and hopeful of the future. The Tsar was now spending more time with little Sidney, almost, than he was with the Tsarina; and as often as possible, he combined the two. Amazingly, the Tsarina seemed to be responding. I do not mean that she recognized her surroundings, nor the people who loved her, but she seemed to be holding the baby, now, with her own hands whenever he was placed into them. There seemed to be something beginning to stir within her.

We all saw this, and Olga, who was now spending more time with the Tsarina, mentioned that once when the Tsar tried to take Sidney away, it seemed that the Tsarina actually tried to hold on to the baby. The Tsar was overjoyed at this, and he also claimed that once when the baby was crying in the nursery, the Tsarina did move her head in that direction; as if she understood.

Alexei, though, perhaps, was the proudest of all the Imperial Family. He would spend hours having Sidney hold onto his fingers, and could be heard telling the baby, "You will run and climb and wrestle and play and you never will have to worry about hurting yourself. I promise you that. I will look after you, Sidney."

At those times, as Sarah sat nearby, she would look at these new adopted members of her blood and laugh and cry at the same time. She would tell me, "Dr. Watson, those children will do something special when they grow. They are meant for big things. I know it. I feel it. I promise it."

April 4, 1919

Another month passed, and I, through Thomas, had finally been given permission to come home because I simply threatened to book passage myself to Grand Bahama Island, and from there take a ship home. There was absolutely nothing now here to hold me.

June 20, 1919

It was more than a year since I had bid good-bye to Elizabeth. But now I was going home. Home. What a simple yet deep word that is. I pray to God you are never forced to contemplate fully its true meanings under any like circumstances.

A ship would be here in another two weeks or so, and on it would be my replacement. Thomas said it would most likely be naval doctor, under strict secrecy orders. He would be proved correct.

The Imperial Family now knew I would be leaving, and though they tried to keep me on the island, knowing my duty to them was more than fulfilled, they accepted my impending departure with imperial grace.

July 4, 1919

My 'rescue ship' arrived on July 4, a fitting independence date for me as well as the Americans, and as Thomas had supposed, a naval doctor under heavy orders was to be my replacement. We spent

228

suitable time in the give and take of questions, answers, procedures, foibles, habits, preferences, etc., and I knew that this young physician, a Commander Bernard Harrow, was more than capable to discharge the duties now assigned him. I could leave with no guilt on that score.

The night before I left, much as had happened on the night before my friends' departure last year, the Imperial Family gave me a send-off dinner with Thomas as guest.

There were toasts and tears and times recalled, but emotion was kept to a minimum. The true outpourings would come on the morrow.

But that night, since Olga would be staying behind with her mother at the house in the morning, I gave her my goodbyes, and then went in to say likewise to the Tsarina. The Tsar was with me.

The Tsarina was sitting up in bed, seemingly not comprehending as I bid farewell. I then took her hand to kiss it, and was surprised when I felt her fingers grip my hand as if she did not want to let me go. I was so taken aback at this reaction that I called the Tsar closer to witness it for himself. Of course this made him further convinced that his wife was returning, albeit slowly. From the Tsarina's actions since the birth of Sidney, I too was becoming a subscriber to this way of thinking. I promised to do all I could to have a specialist sent to her.

On my final morning, I said my personal good-byes to Lawrence, and had a special, quiet time of talking with Sarah who gave me an amulet for John, 'to ward off the big evils of big white devils', and a hug and kiss to me until I was safe with my wife. The Imperial Family, accompanied by Thomas, came down to the slip to say their proper goodbyes.

I received warm hugs and kisses from Anastasia and Marie, who admonished me to 'box Captain Yardley about the ears' because he had never communicated with her all these months, and an especially long and strong hug from Alexei who said, "You have been one of my truest friends in all my life, Dr. Watson. I shall miss you terribly, but I shall never, never forget you. And I pray you return to us when you are able."

Tatiana then came up to me, she was holding little Sidney who she placed into my hands.

"You are his true godfather, Dr. Watson. You always shall be so. I pray and promise you this: that for all you have done for me and my family and my baby, some day my baby shall find a way to return even a portion of your deeds. I love you, Dr. Watson, and I hope you find the means and the power to return to us someday. If, by some miracle, my big Sidney should arrive, I shall tell him of all you have done, and take him deep into the forest and show him your so very many spots of north moss." She kissed me, I kissed Sidney, and gave the baby back to her.

The Tsar was the last of the family to say good-bye. There were already tears in his eyes. And though he tried to speak, he could not bring forth the words, so filled was he with emotion. He seemed to be desperately trying to say something or do something to show what he could not say, and then his face suddenly brightened and he raised both his hands to his chest level and slowly pulled from his finger perhaps his most precious possession of all, his wedding ring.

This he put into my hands.

When I tried to decline, he closed my fist around the ring and I could see the joy in his eyes that he had found a gift he felt worthy of his esteem and thanks. Now *I* could not speak. I turned to the launch as Thomas helped me in, shook my hand, told me not to worry about anything, and that he would see me in London when he got back.

As the launch distanced itself from the slip and drew closer to my vessel of passage, the figures so near for so long, were now so far in so short a time.

July 9, 1919   Home

I was back in London in five days, my 'rescue vessel' being an old, light cruiser whose captain and crew seemed to be as lethargic as the ship. This was merely an errand ship, plying special passengers and packets back and forth to places as diverse as was the Empire.

To those aboard I was a Mr. Wilson, and the captain knew not Captain Yardley nor much news of any import to me.

There was no one but a sailor to meet me back at Harwich, and as he drove me back down to London, my adrenalin coursed quicker with every mile.

It was 8:00 P.M. when the sailor dropped me and my bags in front of my house, my knees and legs literally shaking from anticipation and fear. I went up to my front door and was petrified to ring my own bell. Then quickly, I did. I heard the familiar voice from inside.

"Yes? Who is it?"

My throat suddenly went as dry as the Sahara. I croaked out an answer.

"Who is it?"

"Elizabeth, Elizabeth!"

For the tiniest second the door remained shut against me, and then, with a mighty burst inward, it was open and Elizabeth had flung herself into my arms.

"John, John, John," was all she could say between tears. I moved us inside as one, so tightly was she clinging to my neck. After innumerable kisses and tears and screams of delight, we finally let go of each other and fell laughing, onto our parlour sofa.

She had so many questions, so many questions, but my first question now, after seeing that Elizabeth was as perfect as ever, was about John. He was asleep in his room and up we went so I could see him. He lay there, his sheet wrapped tightly around him like a sari. My, he had grown. I looked down at my son and began sobbing uncontrollably. Elizabeth led me back downstairs so I did not disturb John.

She took me back to the sofa, where she held me as all the tears, frustrations, hardship and anguish of the last year erupted to the surface. There was nothing I could do to stop, and Elizabeth, as always, understood; and let these emotions run their course.

Finally, when I stopped weeping due to the exhaustion that took hold, I was able to ask Elizabeth about Holmes. I noticed a very confused and concerned look in her eyes.

"Elizabeth, what is it? What about Holmes? How is he?"

She continued to look at me, her eyes filled with pity and question, and she now began to cry.

"Elizabeth, what is it? What's the matter?"

"Oh, John..."

"Elizabeth, what is it? What about Holmes? How is he?"

"John, Mr. Holmes is dead. He has been dead these many months now."

I sat there as if someone had just kicked me in the solar plexus. All the wind was knocked out of me.

I was still in shock as Elizabeth led me to our room and helped me change from my clothes. Finally, I was able to begin asking rational questions.

"How? Where?"

"The papers said only that Holmes was on a ship in the Atlantic somewhere, on a return trip from a highly secret mission to help shorten the war. They said his ship was sunk by German U-boats. All hands were lost. I saved the papers so you could read them for yourself."

"Elizabeth, please tell me, no one from the government contacted you about this?"

"Yes, they did, John. On the night before the stories came out, I was visited by a man who said he was from the government, but could not tell me who he was or what branch he was from. He claimed war security and the like. But he was a very nice man, John; he was truly concerned. His first words to me, to calm my initial fears that ill had befallen you and Mr. Holmes, was that you were completely safe.

Then he told me about Mr. Holmes. He said the papers would have stories in the morning, but they would be vague and not completely true. He told me that war security still was tight and the true story would probably never be told.

"He said he was here on his own; that he wasn't sent by anyone. He personally wanted to allay my fears and to let me know that you were perfectly all right. He told me you were not with Mr. Holmes, that you had to remain behind, wherever you were, he would not tell me, to tend to a particular medical matter.

"When I asked him if he knew when you would be home, he said that information he did not yet have and he doubted if he would be able to contact me again. But three months later I received this in the post." Elizabeth fetched a letter she had kept locked in my desk. It said only this: HOME IN ABOUT SIX MONTHS. Nothing more.

"Elizabeth, did this man give you his name, or any indication of why he took this personal interest?"

"No, John. From what you've told me of all your dealings with Mr. Holmes, I simply believed this to part of the fabric past. And I believe, after all of my years, that I have become fairly adept at feeling who is a good man, or a bad man. This was a good man."

All this was too much. I had not even been home thirty minutes when this black news was given me. I had not even begun to contemplate on the fates of Yardley and Preston and what Yardley's father had done upon hearing this news. And coming hard upon my reunion with Elizabeth and John, it literally pushed me over the edge of tension and exhaustion, and I fell asleep still holding the letter the man had sent to Elizabeth, and wondering who, in heaven's name, could this man be?

July 10, 1919

I awakened in very late morning to the sight of John, standing over my bed and staring down intently at me. When I turned and opened my eyes and saw him, a huge smile came to his face and with a matured sense of humour he said, in a surprisingly deep voice:

"Well, well, father. You're home." And the next few minutes were spent in hugging and kissing and telling my son how big he had grown, which he truly had, and in commending him on the way in which he had watched over his mother while I was away.

"I'm very sorry about Mr. Holmes," he said later; then immediately followed that sensitivity with, "did you and Mr. Holmes kill many Germans before they got him?" He had read the papers and expected some fabulous war-torn tale.

Elizabeth entered the room at this moment.

"Now, John, don't ask such questions. Your father is quite upset about Mr. Holmes and doesn't need such foolishness."

"No, Elizabeth, it is quite all right. John is just asking the normal sort of thing." I took the time to explain that Mr. Holmes had died a hero. I said he had died helping England with the war. That simple explanation seemed to satisfy John, for now, and he gave me another welcome hug.

Later that day, Elizabeth and I discussed what had become of Holmes' effects and his home near Eastboune. Even though Mycroft had taken charge of everything, he had been in touch with Elizabeth, and had made her promise to have me contact him immediately upon my return.

Elizabeth said Mycroft had disposed of most of the property, had kept some things for himself, and, in time, would sell others to the growing throng of insatiable collectors who now seemed to hound him. Before this, he needed to know which items were of special value to me as he wished me to have them.

My main concern was to now find the truth about what had really happened to Holmes, Yardley and Preston. Mycroft could wait. I felt my first stop must be to where this terrible adventure had begun.

I wanted to go to 10 Downing Street. I needed answers. But I then thought better of it and went to the Admiralty. I needed to speak with Admiral Yardley before I spoke with anyone else. I was sure it would be the thing Holmes would do.

The officer on duty at first felt he could not divulge the admiral's whereabouts, but upon finding out who I was, "*The* Dr. Watson?" he asked, he told me the admiral was not on sea duty, and that he was, again, up at Scapa Flow. I could ring him there.

Then, although Elizabeth had said the newspapers claimed all hands were lost when Holmes' ship was sunk, I inquired about Captain Yardley. After checking through his files, he simply said, "Deceased."

Deceased. Young Yardley, as well. I couldn't absorb it. I needed to obtain more substantial information, and rather quickly. I realized I might know where.

Before going home to call the admiral, I decided to make a stab at checking on Preston. I went to the Foreign Office and was told by a clerk who had known Sir Michael that "he had been killed on that ship with Mr. Holmes."

Since this clerk had known Sir Michael, I asked if she had known Sir Michael's son.

"Oh, Thomas Preston. Well, I don't know him personally, but from what I remember, he was in Russia when they shot the Tsar and his family, I think. Yes, I recall that."

"Well, could you please tell me where he is now?"

"Now? You mean at this very minute?"

"I suppose so," I said testily.

"Why, upstairs," she said.

"What?" I said it so loudly I believe the ceiling shook from the reverberation. "What do you mean upstairs?"

She was looking at me as if I was a lunatic.

"Exactly what I said. Sir Thomas is probably up in his office.

It's Room 2407."

I believe I was up the stairs before the 'thank you' was completely free of my mouth.

I opened the door, told his secretary who I was and after she went in to check, she returned and held open the door to his inner office. I walked in to find a man standing there I had never before seen in my life; a total stranger who came forward to greet me.

"Hello, Dr. Watson; this is quite an honour, sir. But to what do I owe the pleasure? Why have you come to see me?"

"I'm sorry, sir, I don't understand. I am here to see Sir Thomas Preston."

"I am he."

After he had sat me down, and I regained my composure, he assured me that he was, in fact, who he claimed to be, and even showed me a picture of himself with Sir Michael and his mother. When I said that picture could be of friends together, he said he now understood how my mind had been influenced by Holmes and how I must have been of significant help to the great man.

I was in no mood for chit-chat and I told him as much. But since I did not know what he knew, I could not tell him why I had such a bizarre reaction. So I asked him to bear with me as I asked a few questions.

"Sir Thomas, did you know where your father had been or on what purpose, when he was killed?"

"No, Dr. Watson; not at all. I only know it was important. When my father was killed along with Mr. Holmes, I was told by the Ministry that he had been on secret war business, and that I could be proud of what he had done for his country."

"Who told you this, Sir Thomas?"

"Why, the Foreign Secretary, Mr. Balfour."

"One more thing, please, how come you never got to Ekaterinburg?"

"But how did you know that? No one was supposed to know that."

"Please, trust me, what happened? Who or what detained you?"

"Dr. Watson, I'm not sure I should be talking to you about my whereabouts in Russia. At the time, it was most secret."

"Sir Thomas, I was an intimate of your father during the last weeks of his life. I myself cannot tell you where he was or what he was doing for the same secrets of State, but you know from the newspapers and Mr. Balfour that he was doing something very special for the nation. You also know that since Mr. Holmes died with your father,

238

they were working together. Had it not been for a turn of fate, I too, would have been killed along with them.

"Please, Sir Thomas, why did you never get through to Ekaterinburg?"

He thought heavily for a few more minutes while pacing about, then sat opposite me.

"Dr. Watson, it is obvious you know a great deal more than you or anyone not directly involved is supposed to. Furthermore, you are the only person who has claimed to have direct knowledge of my father before he died. Yes, I'll trust you. But I require one guarantee."

"Ask it."

"That as soon as you are able, you shall tell me everything about this business; everything about my father."

"Done.

"Good. Dr. Watson, I had been sent into Russia in early June, into Petrograd. I was waiting for transportation to Vologda, and from there to Ekaterinburg, when I was kidnapped."

"Kidnapped, you say? By whom? For what?"

"The 'whom' I know: Whites. The 'for what', I still don't know."

"This makes absolutely no sense whatsoever," I said. Then it struck me. "Sir Thomas, why were you being sent into Russia?"

"Another good question, Dr. Watson. I was told I would be informed once there. But I never met Sir George Buchanan, he was already in Vologda, and the only person I had direct contact with was a Cheka Colonel..."

"By the name of Relinsky. I know."

"But, my God, how do you know that?"

"That is all part of what I cannot, as yet, tell you. But please, how did you finally succeed in being released?"

"They just let me go. I was released about a week later with the admonition to say nothing to anyone or they would find me wherever I was and see to it that I was killed.

"I don't mind telling you, Dr. Watson, that this whole experience was like nothing I had ever encountered before. It was what I would expect from some clandestine operation thick with spies; or something like you and Mr. Holmes were involved in, I suppose.

"I'm a diplomat. I never had training or classes in kidnapping behaviour."

"But you said these abductors were Whites. How did you know that?"

"They, themselves, basically told me so. They said they were working against the Bolshevik Revolution, and that since I was British, I was a tool of the Reds.

"When I explained the British were practically funding the counter-revolution single-handedly, they would just laugh and demand to see the millions in pounds sterling that I had for them. They would personally turn it over to Admiral Kolchak, they laughed.

"Anyway, I got the impression the whole thing was a sham of some kind. That maybe they weren't really Whites. I don't know anymore. I was treated all right and released, and upon my return to our consulate in Petrograd, I was told to use the name 'Stanley', and I would be taken back to England shortly on a British ship of the line."

"Now, don't tell me," I said, "Let me really play the mind reader here. You were taken back aboard a wounded cruiser, the *Attentive*, correct?"

I have never seen such a look of pure disbelief and astonishment on anyone's face. Had I told him sand would become the most precious commodity in the world on the morrow, I am absolutely convinced he would not have been more stunned. He slowly regained his composure and responded.

Also, Admiral Yardley had been his host on the return trip, and neither knew of the other's connection to Sir Michael. What a pity that was.

"When I returned, I was kept in seclusion for 'debriefing' and rest, I was told, and was permitted my freedom again towards the latter part of July. In August I was made a knight for my services to the crown. I thought it a bit odd, but who am I to look a gift horse in the mouth, as they say."

There was no more he could tell me, and there was no more I could tell him. I said to him I would be speaking with him in the very near future, and I headed home; it now being late in the afternoon.

By the time I arrived, I was exhausted from the day's labours, and was thrilled to see Elizabeth racing towards me as I took a step in through the door. However, this joy turned to concern when I noticed Elizabeth's face.

"John, there is someone here to see you. Knowing how tired you'd be, I tried, but I really couldn't keep him out. I didn't know what to do, so I just let him in."

"What? Elizabeth, you and John are all right, then?"

"Oh, quite, quite. He has been a perfect gentleman."

"Who, Elizabeth? Who is here to see me?"

"John, it is a Mr. John Clay."

John Clay? Here in my own house? I had not actually seen the criminal since 1890, when Holmes solved the mystery of "The Red-Headed League". But he had troubled us much after his escape. Especially after Moriarty died and he had become one of England's most sinister criminals. I rushed into the parlour.

There sat the spider. I could almost see the strands of web emitting from his person, a criminal and crime at the end of each sticky string.

"How dare you come to my home?" I shouted.

"Why, Dr. Watson, I have always known you to be such a civil and courteous man. I would not expect this from you."

"What else could you expect from me?"

"My, my, Dr. Watson, such venom from one usually so pacific. To have listened to Mr. Holmes and yourself over the years, it should

241

be *I* spitting forth venom."

"I do not find you amusing, and I have no wish to find you again. Anywhere. Now what is it that you want? Why are you here?"

"May I sit, again, Dr. Watson?"

"You may not. Just state your business and get out!"

He looked at me through almost closed eyes. I knew I was not the intellectual equal of this man, yet I felt I had the upper hand in my own home.

"Dr. Watson, what I am here to say, you will probably not believe, but I shall say it anyway."

He reminded me of nothing more than a doppelganger of his former mentor as he stood there with dark suit and cloak, even though the weather was mild and agreeable. His head shook from side to side in imitation of the late professor. Holmes regarded Moriarty as a cold-blooded reptile and Clay now appeared to be no different.

"Dr. Watson, whatever you and Mr. Holmes thought of me is of no consequence now, as are you of no consequence now that Mr. Holmes is no longer with us. But whatever you and he made of me, whatever mould you cast me in, however dangerous you portrayed me to the world, remember that I am of royal blood and the one epithet neither of you ever darkened my reputation with was that of 'traitor'."

"Traitor? What are you talking about?"

"I am talking about this, Dr. Watson: that for the many years before Mr. Holmes retired, he had proved my one constant. He was the one man in England, in the entire Empire, who I could count on to be a proper intellectual challenge. While you thought Holmes to be keeping his bees serenely down in Sussex, without your knowledge, we had challenged each other on a semi-regular basis. Now that challenge is gone. I shall miss the parry and thrust, the superlative anticipation of turning a shadowed corner to wonder if Holmes had already divined my thoughts and would be there waiting.

"Dr. Watson, I am trying to say that whatever I may be, I do love England."

242

"This is absurd, Clay. You suddenly claim patriotism."

"I do so because it is true. I am an Englishman. My grandfather, as you will recall, was a royal duke. I, too, in my own way, aided our war effort. Have you not stopped to think why there were never any significant amounts of German sabotage at our shipyards? Have you never wondered why our rail systems and communications networks never experienced major turmoil? Have you never prognosticated on why even the Royal Family slept serenely in their beds unencumbered by the various enemy threats made upon their persons?

"Of course you haven't, nor has anyone else. The only time anyone would have thought on these things was if disaster had struck. If our ships had been blown up like firecrackers in their berths; if our trains ran off the tracks; if our telephones and telegraphs came to a silent halt; if shots had been fired at the King, or Queen, or their offspring.

"It is because of me and my underlings that these things did not happen."

"What are you implying, Clay?"

"Holmes himself said countless times how after Moriarty died I had donned his mantle. I sat at the epicentre of a giant web; and each strand was connected to some nefarious deed or group of criminals. He accused me of power at the shipyards, power at the stations and depots, and he assumed that every pickpocket in the city of London was tied in to me stronger than had been the Artful Dodger with Fagin.

"Well, he was absolutely correct, Dr. Watson. My men were, and are, virtually everywhere. They watch the shipyards and docks; by the way, how do you think I knew you were back the moment your foot touched British soil? They survey the railway stations and railway lines thus preventing any evil act before it can occur. Around Buckingham Palace, the very cutthroat pickpockets your Mr. Holmes railed to heaven about, those very same criminals were the ones whose eyes watched the palace day and night to spot anyone suspicious.

243

"And when they did, whoever it was they saw, saw no more. We do not have to abide by the rules of trial by jury. It is better to step on a bug before it can produce its filth."

"Are you saying that you and your criminals have guarded England during the Great War?"

"Yes, Dr. Watson. By no means alone; but, yes. There was even a tacit compact between certain government agencies and myself to that effect. Since my men would not do well in the army or navy, they did their best to aid our victory in the only way they knew how.

"I have merely come to pay my respects to a fallen hero; for I know that antagonist that he was, Sherlock Holmes was a patriotic Englishman through and through, and much more likely than I to be called upon to do his part for his King and Country."

At those words, a bell rang in my mind. My tone suddenly changed and Clay noticed immediately.

"Please forgive me. I thought you came on some heinous mission to threaten my wife and son and very home."

"Dr. Watson, I am not a monster. I do not harass women and children." He said this warily, like he was expecting something new to arise form our conversation; and he was quite correct.

"Clay, you are right about Holmes. He and I were on very important business to aid the war effort. That is why he met his end."

"I understood it to be those cowardly German U-boats."

"Perhaps." As I said that, he gave an audible grunt. He knew instantly something was amiss.

"What do you mean, 'Perhaps'?"

"Clay, what I am now going to ask you is beyond even my belief. Even one year ago, should anyone have told me I would be asking this of you, I would have thought them quite mad. But if I ever came to you and asked for your help in discovering the full truth behind the murder of Holmes, would you grant it?"

Now it was Clay who was taken aback. He eyed me as would a beggar whose hand held out was greeted by someone dangling a twenty pound note at his palm. He could not believe it, but he did not wish to chase the fortune away.

"Dr. Watson, are you saying that Holmes was not killed by a U-boat?"

"I am not. I am saying that in service to his country, he was killed. As yet, however, I am not sure I believe how."

"This is bordering on absurd, doctor. I am now being asked by the compatriot of my late, great adversary, to help unravel the mystery of his demise." He stopped for a moment and turned coy. "Should I grant you this favour, Dr. Watson, what recompense could I expect?"

"My tone was harsh, I am sorry. But you have come to pay your respects, you say, to a fallen hero of the Empire, even though the man was your sworn enemy. That shows a special chivalry. Something I never thought you possessed. Yet now you want to know how aiding me would benefit you? How quickly we lose our altruism."

"That is not so, Dr. Watson. I would grant you a request to help in such manner. But this is so bizarre, so unexpected, I would not feel comfortable without some small token of your chivalry in return."

"Very well, though I cannot tell you how I shall repay this kindness, will you accept my word of honour as a physician?"

"There are no words of honour from physicians. But I shall accept your word as Englishman."

"Consider it given, Mr. Clay."

"Very well."

And then, though I never thought this could ever happen, and I prayed to the spirit of Holmes to forgive me, I shook hands with the Devil.

I rang Scapa Flow after Clay had gone. I was told Admiral Yardley had left for London the previous day and no, they did not know his destination.

I need not have worried; for a few minutes past ten, Yardley

245

appeared at our front door. After a very hardy handshake, I introduced him to Elizabeth, who with a knowing look, excused herself for the evening.

"Admiral, how did you know I was back?"

"I may not be in naval intelligence, but we old sea dogs have our own methods." I offered him a drink but he settled for some cool tea, the night being so warm. After discussing some trivia, we came to our business.

"Admiral, please tell me all you know about the deaths of your son and friend, and my friend; for on that island we knew nothing."

"You mean you just learned about the tragedy when you got back home?"

"That is precisely what I mean."

"Damn! Close to a year and you didn't even know what happened. I learned about it patrolling the North Atlantic. They said a U-boat had torpedoed the ship and Holmes, Michael, Peters and the rest, were all drowned or killed in the explosion.

"But I did some checking. They said it happened at a certain place and time; I did some calculations and found that travelling at the *Salvator*'s usual rate of speed, and taking into account the time which they left Eleuthera, they could not have been anywhere near their supposed site of sinking.

"My calculations put them closer to Bermuda."

"Bermuda?"

"Yes, and listen to this, doctor. A captain friend of mine who was on duty in those waters, remembers some natives who claimed there was an explosion on the water one night, not too far from the island, at the time my calculations would have the *Salvator* there. It was around one in the morning.

"Which means that the *Salvator* was not sunk when it was supposed to have been, nor where it was supposed to have been. It means the reports were false and I wanted to know where the reports originated."

"Let me guess, with intelligence?"

"Correct. I went to Newsome to see why. He told me that his radio people had picked up the Germans, in their code, talking about this spy ship coming from the Bahamas."

"Spy ship? Where the devil would the Germans have gotten that from?"

"Newsome said the Germans thought the ship to be carrying important British agents and that it had been identified as previously being part of the British invasion force of Archangel. The U-Boat had orders to sink it immediately. Since this ship was nowhere in the logs, remember, it was a most secret mission, the intelligence people had absolutely no idea of what the Germans were jabbering about, and the matter was dropped. They thought it to be just so much mis-information."

"So you are satisfied that the Germans sunk the *Salvator*?"

"That I am, but I am positive it was not sunk where our reports claimed it to be."

"Then do you have any idea then what we should do?"

"No, absolutely none. I only know that my son is gone, along with Mr. Holmes and Michael."

"My God, I have quite forgotten to tell you." And I recounted my meeting with the real Sir Thomas Preston that day. The admiral just sat there more confused and disheartened than ever.

"My God, Michael's boy with me on my very ship; and me in complete ignorance. Dr. Watson, this is too diabolical for me. I lack both the subtle mind of Mr. Holmes and the diplomatic mien of Michael. I am a bluff sailor trained for battle and I believe that tomorrow, I shall go full speed into Newsome."

He left after about an hour later and I bid him farewell.

I had put out all the downstairs lights and was about to retire when the bell rang again. At first I thought it was Yardley returning for something but when I opened the door, I found two large men standing there, not too dissimilar to the ones Holmes had been 'abducted' by at the beginning of this nightmare.

"Dr. Watson," said the first man, with the thick, red beard and anvil body, "excuse us, we know the hour, but we must speak with you." They pushed past me and went into the parlour. They knew where to go and this gave me a chill.

"Who are you?" I asked as I restored light to the room.

"That is unimportant right now. But we are from those who sent you and Mr. Holmes on your task. We have a special request to make of you based upon some information we know you'll find most invaluable."

"What request? What information?"

"First, the information. Dr. Watson, Sherlock Holmes is not dead."

I sat there like a fool, not knowing what to say or even what to feel, anymore. My body and mind were as limp as rag dolls and I felt like I was falling into a bottomless void. Would these shocks never end?

"Dr. Watson, did you hear me? Mr. Holmes is alive. We have him."

"We? Who is 'we'? Where do you have him?"

"Doctor, as I have said, we are from those that first sent you and Mr. Holmes on your task. We have Mr. Holmes, in protective custody, shall we say?"

"What are you talking about? Why would Holmes be in your protective custody? The whole world thinks he is dead."

"Ah, yes. And that is precisely the point. But tomorrow morning, the world shall know that you are alive. That you slipped back into England quietly. Every reporter and newspaper in the world will be camping outside your door for a story."

"But I had nothing to do with Holmes' death."

"Of course you didn't, doctor. But where have you been all this

248

time? Where were you when Holmes was killed? Why were you not with him? What sort of mission were you both engaged upon? These are just some of the questions they will be hurling at you quicker than hand grenades; each one potentially as deadly as the last."

"I still do not understand. Why do you have Holmes? Why have you let the world think him dead?"

"I'm coming to that, Dr. Watson." The man had the manners of a jackal. He was too polite and consequently I was left with the feeling that he would bite at any moment; which was precisely what he was about to do. Compared to this creature, I can honestly say I preferred the company of Clay.

"You see, doctor, the world will expect from you a chronicle of Holmes' last adventure. Everyone will want to know everything about it. The Hun villains: the secrets stolen and retrieved; all the gore. That's where you come in. We want you to write it."

"What do you mean, 'write it'? Write what? You yourself say Holmes is alive. Why should I write such lies?"

"Because, Dr. Watson, if you do not, Mr. Holmes will not be alive for very long."

"What? You threaten to kill Sherlock Holmes?!"

"Dr. Watson, I can assure you of this: If you do not write what we want of you, Mr. Holmes shall disappear like a coin in the hand of a cheap magician."

I was trying to think quickly while I could think at all.

"How do I know you are not lying? How do I know Holmes is not already dead as the world suspects and the British government has stated? How do I know if these things are false?"

"You do not, Dr. Watson; you do not. Furthermore, once the reporters descend upon your house tomorrow, you shall also not have the time or wherewithal to continue that little investigation of yours. Yes, we've been watching you. We know who you've spoken with and we can guess what about."

"Are you threatening them, too?"

"Dr. Watson, may I remind you that you are talking to representatives of your legally elected government? Would we threaten the lives of such important men as Admiral Richard Yardley and Sir Thomas Preston? Come, now, Dr. Watson, do you think we are monsters like your Mr. Clay?"

He was right; with Clay, you always knew he opposed you. Here, you did not know whom to trust. I thought about what Reilly had said: in his line of work, the criminals were the vanguards of society.

I knew that if these two individuals were sent to me in the middle of the night, their master needed something important of me. They would not dare harm one hair on my head. For the time being at least, I decided to play for time and shook my head.

"You will regret your decision doctor and you will change it before long. If not, I promise that your Mr. Holmes will die an agonizing death." With that, the two turned tail and left.

I fell into a chair and just sat there trying to puzzle this out in the semi-consciousness of my mind. In just a few hours the reporters would be hammering at our door and my family would be frightened for me all over again. I had no time to lose. Time and lack of timidity were the key.

I went upstairs and woke Elizabeth. I told her not to fear and to get John ready for a quick journey. I told her I was going out and that I would be back as soon as possible. When she begged to know where I was going, I said to sup with the Devil.

July 11, 1919

It was just after midnight when I stepped outside my front door and saw a man whom I knew to be of Clay's minions. As I had suspected, Clay had my house under observation. I hastened to the man; although, he tried to deny his connection. I explained my urgent circumstance, and he said I should follow him. As we walked, I wondered if were we being followed by those in league with the two blackguards who had so recently left me.

We eventually reached an alleyway some two miles from my home where I was to wait until sent for. Right enough, forty minutes later, a coach stopped in front of me. The door opened and I heard a now-familiar voice say, "Get in, Dr. Watson."

I obeyed and we were off.

"I did not expect your call this quickly" said Clay.

"Nor did I expect to make the call. But I now know for a certainty that you are one of the few people in England I can trust at this moment."

A look of incredulity came over Clay's face.

"I still find our alliance uncomfortable doctor. Yet you appear sincere. Tell me exactly what has happened."

"Those who are sworn to defend all Englishmen and uphold our laws may be at the bottom of deeds more base than you ever laid at Holmes' feet. I am watched, my family is threatened by these people, and I now know what I can give you in return for your succour."

His eyes widened. He still unnerved me, but I knew he would want what I could give; and even the Devil held to his bargains.

"What? What can you give me?"

"Death!" I said.

He grunted. "Death?"

"Yes, and a welcome one at that. Think of how free you shall be if Scotland Yard and the whole of England believe you to be dead. All suspicions of you shall cease. All trails that might have led to you shall now be thought false and the hunt called of. You shall be free, Clay, free to follow your desires without the encumbrance of existence."

"Exactly how do you plan to achieve this?"

"I shall be shortly called upon by the world to give a final account of the death of Sherlock Holmes. To honour his memory I shall write how he foiled insidious espionage plots stretching all the way to the Caribbean and gave his life in doing so. I shall also write

251

that his last adventure in London before he began the service to his country which claimed his life, had claimed yours. I shall detail how your own men had mutinied against you and drowned you in the Channel, weighing you down so your body would never be found.

"Once you are thought dead, the world shall believe it and be thankful for it," I thought I saw an expression of remorse in his eyes at those words. "You shall be set free to spread your black wings. But should you be apprehended because of your mistakes or those of your underlings, you shall attach no blame to me or my family. Is that understood?"

"It is, Dr. Watson." He looked at me, literally from head to toe. "Are you sure you are not Sherlock Holmes in a Dr. Watson disguise? I would have never thought you capable of such subtle brilliance."

"Nor would I. Now, this is what I need of you..."

The government men who were left to watch my house were 'relieved' of their duties by those in the employ of Clay. Then, with John and Elizabeth safely with others of his choosing, on the way to her parents in Yorkshire, the second part of my plan was put into motion.

I was taken by carriage to where Admiral Yardley had been followed by another of Clay's men and I roused him from his slumber. I begged him put his trust in me and get dressed. In a few moments, we were hurtling through the London night to the home of Sir Randolph Newsome.

As our carriage lurched violently and pitched us, it seemed, contrary to the laws of gravity, I told Yardley about my nocturnal callers, and told him the time had come to force Newsome's hand.

Before the carriage even came to a complete halt, Yardley was pounding on Newsome's door. In a few moments, we were let inside.

"Richard. What are you doing here at this hour? Who is this with you?"

"Hurry, Newsome, there isn't time. Is anyone here with you?"

We followed Newsome into his study and he sat at his desk.

"No, not tonight. I'm quite alone. What is this all about, Richard?"

It was at that point that Yardley pulled out a revolver and placed it tightly against the skull of Randolph Newsome.

"Newsome, you may have cost my son his life. Now sit down. I'm going to count back from ten. And if you haven't told me everything you know, your brains are going to be all over your stylish, new wallpaper. Ten!"

"I don't know anything." He calmly lit a cigarette.

"Nine!"

"You must be mad, Richard; I don't even know what you're talking about." It was as if he was sitting on a block of ice.

"Eight!"

"I know nothing. Are you going to shoot an innocent man?" He blew a smoke ring.

"Seven!"

"Innocent of what?" I interjected.

"Six!"

"Innocent of anything. I was only following orders."

"Five!"

"What orders?" I asked.

"Just orders: I was doing my duty!" He jammed the cigarette into the ashtray.

"Four!"

"Speak now, man," said I, "or the admiral will do as he says!"

"Three!"

"What do you want to know?"

"Why was the *Salvator* sunk and who gave the order to sink her?"

"I don't know." I thought I detected a qualm in his voice. "No one gave orders. It just happened."

"Two!"

"Look, Richard, I know you're still upset about William's death, but this is too much."

"But I'm the one with the gun now! One!"

"All right, all right. I'll tell you everything. Just put that infernal toy away." He was more peeved than frightened.

Yardley pulled the revolver directly from touching Newsome's head, but kept it only one inch away.

"It was Balfour. Balfour gave me the order to have Reilly insure the failure of the rescue attempt."

"But what about William?" screamed the admiral.

"I don't know. I don't know what happened there."

Yardley pushed the revolver hard against Newsome's skull again.

"Listen you piece of wretched filth, I stopped at number one." He cocked the trigger. "Now I'll ask you one more time: What about William?"

"It wasn't just William. It was Holmes and Preston, as well. He wanted them all dead." He reached for another cigarette.

"Who wanted them all dead? Who?" he screamed.

"I don't know, but someone had signals sent that led the Germans to believe the ship was a spy ship. They torpedoed it. I had nothing to do with any of it, Richard. You do believe me, don't you?"

Yardley then stepped a few feet away, but with the pistol still aimed right at Newsome's forehead, and said, "The only thing I believe is how much I shall enjoy pulling this trigger!"

Then, before I could stop him, he did.

We ran to the waiting carriage as one of Clay's men asked what happened. I said there was a man dead. He smiled and with the greatest air of nonchalance said, "Don' worry. The place'll be clean and the body'll vanish. It 'appens awl the time."

July 12, 1919

It was now about two A.M. By killing Newsome, Yardley had killed our chances of possibly discovering if Holmes was, in fact, still alive, and the other answers we sought; the most important of which was who was really behind all this. But I understood fully his emotions at that moment.

We still had much to do before the morning's light, based upon what Newsome had told us. But my plan had ended prematurely with his death. I had only wanted the information. Now that we had it, I had no further idea of what to do with it.

The admiral had, however and I concurred completely. We would go to 10 Downing Street. Lloyd George would be told all and he could then move against Balfour immediately. I agreed and when I told the driver our destination, he looked at me with terror in his eyes.

"Don't worry," I said. "The Prime Minister is on our side."

"I 'ope so; he sure ain't on mine!" and he drove on.

We were there no more than twenty minutes later. There were so few motor cars about at this hour that I was thrown back to the days of Queen Victoria; when Holmes and I had been truly young, and he was just beginning his career. I suddenly felt him beside me there in that carriage, as if he was patting me on the back and saying, "That's it, Watson. Now you have it. We shall prevail yet!"

The admiral spoke with the constable on duty at the door, and the officer went in for a few minutes. When he came out, the admiral motioned me to join him.

We were shown to what I imagined was the same room in which Holmes and Lloyd George had met that fateful, first night, and after a few moments, Lloyd George appeared in a dressing gown. He was not happy about being disturbed at this hour.

"This had better be as extremely urgent as you have claimed, Admiral Yardley; I don't think you'd like going up and down the Thames on the bridge of a garbage scow." It was a jest, but the point had been made. "Who is this?"

"Sir, I have the honour to introduce you to none other than Dr. John H. Watson."

"Eh?" For the briefest measure of time, I thought the Prime Minister looked like a rat that had just had a light shined on him; but this grotesque impression quickly evaporated. He stuck out his hand.

"Dr. Watson, this is one of the very few, singular honours I have had during these past years. I congratulate you, sir, and offer my condolences and apologies at the same time. You have been a true hero."

I was so embarrassed I knew not what to say, so I simply thanked him and indicated to Yardley that he had better get on with it.

"Prime Minister, I believe you'd better sit down."

"Sit down? Why should I sit down?

"Well, for starters," said the admiral, "I've just killed Randy Newsome."

"You have what!?!"

The admiral was being so blithe about the thing, I believe he may have been in a mild state of shock, his actions only now beginning to register. I took up the cudgel.

"Prime Minister, if you will permit me, the admiral and I have just discovered that there was an infamous plot afoot in your very own government: a plot to thwart the wishes of yourself and a certain person of royalty who shall remain nameless. This plot called for the death of a particular family which Holmes prevented, but tangentially led to his death and that of the admiral's son, William, and Sir Michael Preston on that ship."

"What are you saying, Dr. Watson? The Germans torpedoed that ship."

"That is true, sir. But it was a member of your own cabinet that supplied the information to the Germans secretly, and who was behind all the evil I have now recounted. Not only that, but this very night I was visited by thugs claiming to be sent by those who had sent Holmes and me into Russia. They claimed that Holmes was alive, and that if I

256

did not comply with their wishes, Holmes would, this time perish for certain."

Lloyd George was enraged. He ran around to me and grabbed me by my shoulders.

"Who is this traitor? I shall have him hanged!"

"Sir, it is Arthur Balfour," said Yardley.

The Prime Minister's head snapped back as if he were slapped in the face. His hands dropped from me. In a whisper, he said, "What? Balfour?"

"Yes, Prime Minister," I said, "and if you pray grant us the time now, you shall have all of it."

He was like a wounded deer, the way he dragged himself back behind his desk and fell into his chair.

"Gentlemen, I cannot believe this. It is too dark and too malevolent. Why should Balfour, of all men, seek to do this? He is no traitor. He was once Prime Minister. He is part of the very fabric of my government. You shall have to be specific and I shall have to fully believe you before I confront such a man."

For the next hour and a half, the admiral and I recounted the entire story directly up to Newsome's demise, with only the fewest of questions from The Prime Minister. Then he finally spoke.

"I cannot even begin to digest all you have just told me. There are layers upon layers here. There may be more behind this 'Black Faction' of yours, Dr. Watson, or others who are the true masterminds."

"There is much here to chew over and if you are correct about your theory, there is no slender problem facing me. England has never had a Prime Minister who was a traitor. We have never had a high member in serving government as such. Even if this were true, I am not sure how I would move against Balfour.

"There is more here than even England itself. There is the very fibre binding the Empire, and our commercial ties with the world to consider. I must think about this and shall have to speak with you again when I have decided how to proceed.

"As for Newsome, of course I cannot condone what has happened, but speaking realistically, you have simplified matters by having him vacate his premises, shall we say.

"Even if he were innocent of all you have claimed and I wanted prosecutions, Admiral Yardley, in all honesty, the scandal of what you have this night told me and your subsequent testimony in court would most certainly bring down my government. Under no circumstances will I permit that. I must, then, perforce, become your umbrella and shield you from any downpour."

He stood, as indication we now were to leave and as we moved towards the door he asked, "You have told no one else about this? You are the only two who know?"

"Yes," I said.

"Good, please let it remain so" said Lloyd George. Then he stopped as he shook my hand one more time and said, "Dr. Watson, when Mr. Holmes and I met on your task, I must say, it was one of the more pleasant duties I had during the entire war. He was so open and honest and willing to serve his King and Country. I shall miss the man greatly."

As the admiral and I left the office, I thought: was the Prime Minister just trying to reinforce fond memories for me, or was there something very wrong here? It seemed too easy.

I told Yardley my feelings on the matter and although he did not concur, he said it would not be ill to heed any hunch at this phase of the game.

By the time my new chauffeur, Clay's man, Bendix, had brought the admiral back to his quarters, and me home, it was after five in the morning. I virtually staggered up my stairs, turned the key in the lock, and the instant I stepped in, I knew there was someone inside. I had no weapon, and even if I had, I was so exhausted I would not have been able to use it properly. So I simply went in to the parlour, and before I could even turn on the light, I heard a vaguely familiar voice say, "Finally, you have returned. I have been waiting hours for you, Dr. Watson."

I turned on the light, and sitting on my sofa was none other than Holmes' and my smaller nanny, the one who had wished us well when he deposited us at Harwich.

"You! What are you doing here?"

"Forgive me, doctor, but there are those of my colleagues who would not take kindly to my presence here. They might be made quite angry."

"I am sorry, but I have not the glimmer of an idea of what you are saying. Just who are you?" And what do you want of me at this hour?"

"Dr. Watson, I am the man who visited your wife and sent her that note."

"You?" I sat in my arm chair.

"Yes, me."

"But why? Why should you do such kindness to my family?"

"Because you and Mr. Holmes had done such kindness for mine."

"I do not understand., we had not met before the trip to Harwich."

"That is true enough. But you and Mr. Holmes did my family a good turn. And I vowed to repay that favour if ever I could."

"But who are you?" How did we help?"

"Eight years ago, you and Mr. Holmes came upon circumstances so distressing and strange that you chose to keep the incident silent rather than throw it open to the throng. Do you remember the identical twin sisters in Wales, the young, English ladies named Lauren and Lisa Larkin?"

I thought hard and then remembered.

"Oh, yes, the twins who had been impregnated by the same man."

"Right you are, Dr. Watson. This fellow then trumpeted his victories to the baser characters of the town. The twins, pushed over the edge by the scandal and grief of finding out what he had done to them both, executed him. You were going to call the case, 'Twin Black Widows', but you let the matter drop. Do you remember why?"

"Let me see now, I have been through much since that time; oh, yes, the girls' mother begged Holmes to permit her to have them committed to St. Eustace Hospital for the Insane, rather than have them put on trial.

"There was the mental condition of the twins to consider and then the problem of the babies they were carrying. I remember the mother pleading that the family's lot had been ill enough. The father had been with Kitchener at Omdurman, and had been killed. There was a brother who had vanished, and now this tragedy."

"Right, again. The elderly woman was so moving in her tears that Mr. Holmes went against all his own rules and let the woman have her way because the girls would be, and were, committed. You saw to that yourself."

"But what have you to do with them?"

"I am the vanished brother."

"You? But where have you been? How came you to be so intricately involved with the unsavoury business of what happened to Holmes and me?"

"I almost don't even know where to begin, Dr. Watson."

"Try the beginning."

"Very well. You see, in a way, I don't even exist. The man who accompanied me that night to fetch Mr. Holmes, he doesn't exist either."

"My good man, I have not the faintest idea of what you mean. You do not exist; you are alive and you are talking to me."

"In *that* sense, correct. But to the government, or certain parts of the government, I do not. They ensure I do not. In other words, there is absolutely no record of my life. I am a non-person. I *never* existed.

260

"Yes, I told you who I really am, but should anything ever go awry where I am concerned, any investigative body, such as the local constabularies or the press, or another government, would find no trace of me anywhere. My identity changes from day to day, or week to week, depending on where I am and what task it is I must perform."

"And you say the government permits this?"

"You still don't comprehend fully, do you, Dr. Watson?"

"I suppose I do not."

"Dr. Watson, it is the government that has created me or rather, uncreated me. It is they, or a particular branch, I should say, that employs me in this manner. I do things which most people would not. I go places where most people would not. I see things most people will never have to see."

"You mean you are a spy?"

"No, doctor, not really; it's difficult to explain. You know what a task force is, I presume?"

"Yes, of course."

"Then consider me a task force. I, and others like me, get specific and extremely delicate tasks to perform. We perform them and go on to the next task."

"All right, I think I understand now. In essence, then, you are also saying that you are above the law; am I correct?"

"You are, doctor; because how can the law extract retribution from one who doesn't exist?"

"I see. But what have you to do with what happened in Russia?"

"Nothing, really, Dr. Watson. My only involvement came at the beginning when my associate and I escorted Mr. Holmes to the Prime Minister, and then you and Mr. Holmes to Harwich. That's when I wished you good luck, if you remember."

"I do. In fact, Holmes and I remarked on your good wishes, coming as they did from one who seemed not overly friendly, shall we say."

261

He laughed, a little. "Well, I was with the other man, you see. But when I was free of his presence, I was able to express my personal sentiments."

"If all this be true, then you are the only one, it seems, who is willing, and able, to tell the truth behind all that has happened. Do this, and I shall forever be in your debt."

"No, Dr. Watson, I'm repaying a debt to you and Mr. Holmes with my information. The slate will then be clean. And as far as you will be concerned, I shan't exist, either. Now perhaps you should have a stiff brandy. In fact, I wouldn't mind one myself, if it's at all possible."

I brought us both large brandies, and left the decanter between us. After a few large sips, 'Mr. Smith' began.

"Take a sip, Dr. Watson. For what I have to tell you, you may not believe. You may call me liar, scoundrel, or worse. But as God is my witness, and on the souls of my dear sisters and mother you have already saved, every word I will speak is truth."

"Then, tell me quickly," I said, "we know it was Lloyd George trying to help us. But who was it trying to kill us?"

'Mr. Smith' took another large sip, and while looking into the glass he answered: "Lloyd George."

Lloyd George

"There are many things a government does to keep itself in power," said 'Mr. Smith'. "Of course, I am only talking about our government, mind you. We have laws. We are free. Without our freedoms, we would be no better than the Kaiser and Krauts we were fighting.

"But, after all, we didn't get the largest empire the world has ever seen by playing pretty with our enemies and turning the other cheek. That's for the Kingdom of Heaven, not the British Empire here on earth.

"Now, this war had confused things. Old enemies had become allies and vice versa. And until the Americans came in, we didn't even know if we could win.

"We were fighting for home and hearth, but we were also fighting to keep the Empire together because without the Empire, there would not be an England. Not the way we know it.

"With the Russians pulling out of the war like they did, the French and the Yanks and Lloyd George and some of his crew saw the blood on the wall. Not only could the Krauts free up a hundred divisions or more for the Western Front, and that's bad enough, mind you; but what's going to happen to all our investments in Russia?

"Now, we're not talking small change, Dr. Watson. We're talking billions of pounds in bullion, and francs and dollars. What's going to happen to all that? Whose blood kin in England, whose fat cat corporate heads in the States, whose French franc millionaires are going to bleed red ink? Although we didn't really give a rat's tail about the French anyway.

"Now, as I said, Lloyd George had a double problem that soon became a triple problem. One, he's got to worry about those new Kraut divisions hitting the Western Front. Two, he's got to worry about all those Lords and Ladies and people so high up you wouldn't believe, who might be losing the money they invested in Russia. Then along

263

comes number three, the King wants him to save his relatives, the Tsar and bleeding Tsarina.

"If I was Lloyd George, I probably would've shoved a pistol in my mouth about that time. But Lloyd George is too cool and cunning a character for that sort of thing. So David, the bleeding Lloyd George, starts thinking. How the bloody hell can he satisfy everyone, with different groups needing different imperatives, and without getting caught at it, without making enemies, or at least as few as possible, and still win the war?"

Mr. Smith was taking his third brandy by this time, but his speech patterns and words were at an even keel and what he was saying was absolutely riveting.

"First things first, Dr. Watson. There are those that are *in* government, and those that *are* government, if you understand what I'm trying to say. Believe me, Lloyd George is not going to confide in those merely *in* government.

"The old school ties, the old blood, that's who he contacted when he figured out what he was going to do. And it was a true, monumental piece of brainwork, it was. You have to give the old sod, that, you do." He lifted his glass in salute.

"So he brings in poor Balfour. Why? Because even though Balfour is the bloody Foreign Secretary, Lloyd George kept him out of his War Cabinet. And for someone like Balfour, he'd do anything to get back in to where the people who really matter settle all matters.

"Now, their first problem, above all others, is to win the war. Win the war! They figure the only way they can do that is if Russia gets back into it. And Lloyd George knows he wouldn't stay Prime Minister for a second if our English boys were getting killed like flies because of all those Germans running around loose.

"So he says to himself, 'Now what will Comrade Lenin want to jump back into this thing? Obviously the blighter needs money. The Americans have plenty of that. Let the Yanks pay the bills. Or give them credit. Without American and British money there isn't going to be any new, bloody, Bolshevik utopia anyway.

"'Acceptability'. The Bolshies need that. The whole goddamned world is heaving its guts at what's going on in Russia from that bloody revolution. But the Bolshies want to be accepted by the world for what they think they are: saviours of the bleeding masses.

"They also have another little problem; it's called the Romanovs. If they let the Romanovs go, the Allies and the Whites will join forces to put them back into power and the Reds can kiss their rumps good-bye. If the Romanovs remain captive, the Allies and Whites continue harassing the Bolshies until they let them go. At which time, the Allies and Whites will join forces and the Reds can kiss their rumps good-bye. If they kill the Romanovs, the whole world will tell them to kiss off. The English, and the Americans especially with Mr. Woodrow 'Morality' Wilson, would be so sickened by a Romanov bloodbath that the Reds would never get another cent and they could kiss their rumps good-bye.

"Whichever way they turned, the Bolshies had a hell of a lot of rumps to kiss or rumps to lose.

"So Davey says to himself, what if I make a deal with Lenin that'll solve both our problems?

"'Lenin,' Davey says, 'listen to this proposition I have for you. The King is breathing down my neck to get his damned cousins out of your country: so I'll arrange to have them rescued and we'll keep the whole thing a big secret. The King'll be happy because his cousins are alive. The Romanovs'll be happy because they're alive. And you'll be happy because you'll get them out of your hair.

"Then Lenin says, 'But I have no hair.' 'Good point,' says Davey." Number four and five brandies had come and gone.

"'How am I to explain their disappearance to my people?' asks Lenin, 'My people want them dead. That's why we made our revolution.'

"'All right, calm down, Len,' says Lloyd George, 'no skin off my nose. We'll kill 'em. What's a few Romanovs, more or less?'

265

"'But what about your King, he wants them alive?' asks Lenny.

"'Oh, yeah, right,' says Davey, 'Okay, I got it. I'll tell Georgie I'm going to rescue his cousins, I'll send in some poor fools to try, then we'll have their boat capsize and they all drown trying to escape, or some such thing. That sort of thing happens all the time. Not your fault, not nobody's fault. And you can claim you were about to turn them over to the British when this horrible thing happened.'"

"'Yes, Davey,' says Len, 'but you have to be sure we Bolshies don't get blamed. Because if we get blamed, everybody will say we're monsters and nobody will give us any money. And I can't stay in power without any money and I certainly won't come back into the war.'

"'Don't worry, Len,' says Davey, "Deal?'

"'Deal.'"

I was beginning to feel violently ill.

"Wait, there's more, doctor. So the deal, again, is this: Lloyd George tells the King he really can't help because of the law, but he and certain parties will help. Wink, wink."

"The invisible others," I interrupted.

"What?"

"Oh, nothing. Though you are leading me into such quicksand as I would never have believed, please, go on."

"Correct and certain parties will help, but it's got to be a big, fat, juicy secret. Now he tells Lenin that he'll have the Romanovs killed and no blame will lay at his door. But he also tells Lenin that the Brits have got to make the rescue attempt look real in order to save face with the King, and to make it look good so the world will buy the story. Lenin says, 'Great.'

"Now Davey tells Balfour exactly what he wants, and Balfour is to make sure everything goes according to plan.

"'But, Artie,' says Lloyd George, 'I do not want to know who or how. And no matter what happens, I shall know nothing.'

"So Balfour goes to people he knows before birth. Blood ties.

266

Money ties. People who have a lot to gain by not losing Russia.

"The fools were easy. You and Mr. Holmes. What naturals. Lloyd George took care of that himself because that was the part he was supposed to control. The whole bloody world knows the two of you are bloody goody-two-shoes. They'd believe it if you were killed trying to enter hell and baptize the bleeding Devil. Yes, that was easy.

"Balfour now passes word of the rescue to Buchanan, and Buchanan buys the fairy tale because it comes from his boss.

"But Buchanan doesn't know what's really going on, so he gets Kolchak involved. If Kolchak helps, the Brits will see to it that Kolchak becomes King Dung in Russia.

"'Yeah,' says Kolchak, 'that's for me, chaps.' So another fool joins the fool's club.

"But Kolchak begins thinking, and he says to himself, 'These British can't really be trusted. I go and help them and then they'll just turn around and put Nicky back on the throne. No, I think I better just kill them off and make sure I'm the only one the British can push. After all, I'm the guy that's leading all these White armies. The Americans love me for that. And the Americans have all the money.'

"So that, Dr. Watson, is why Kolchak attacked you when you weren't expecting it. Neither was Lloyd George. Neither was Buchanan or Balfour. This was one case where we were the double-cross-*ees* instead of the double-cross-*ers*."

"Of course," I said.

"I'll continue. The fools upset the applecart. Well, one fool really, Mr. Holmes. He brought the rescue off. You were all supposed to die, and he works it so you all live.

"Well, that ended the game for Lloyd Georgie boy. All of a sudden Lenin finds out that some local pinheads pulled the plug on the Romanovs and he's left with egg on his face and nothing in his pockets. He thinks that Davey played him for a fool; that the whole phoney rescue story was really not phoney. Now Lenin and his mob are going to hear about the executions good and loud.

267

"Lenny figures the whole world is going to come screaming at him like banshees, which it did, and he and his bleeding Bolshies are going to be pariahs to the decent folk of the world, which they are.

"Now Davey tries to talk his way out of this one to Lenny, but Lenny won't play the fool twice. 'You can't fool Lenny, Comrade Lloyd George; well, not twice, anyway.'

"So Lenny says to Davey, 'If you think we're coming back into this war, you're off your bloody noodle. You're bloody lucky that we don't come in on Germany's side. You lied to me. You cheated me. You made me look bad to the whole friggin' world. You can kiss my Bolshie behind in Harrods' window.' End of conversation.

"So there goes Russia down the tubes for good as far as the war goes. And there goes Russia down the tubes as far as all those lovely pounds and dollars and francs go.

"But Davey is the one that comes out smelling like a rose anyway. Remember, you and Mr. Holmes succeeded. You got the Romanovs out. You saved their bloody hides.

"So Davey takes a secret bow from the King and is secretly rewarded. Balfour is the one who did all the black work and he has to keep his mouth shut which is hard for him since he likes the limelight and hates to lose. He's got our hooks into Palestine and he isn't going to let go. It's part of the British Bleeding Empire now.

"But back over here, he's got people who think they've done what they were supposed to do. Like Buchanan. So Buchanan takes a bow from Balfour."

"Yes," I said, "these other people you speak of, the ones who thought they were doing what they were supposed to. If I give you names, can you give me stories?"

"If you pour another brandy, I'll give you the moon."

I did, and he did.

"What about Sidney Reilly?"

Mr. Smith laughed. "Oh, Reilly. He had more important things going on in Russia."

"Yes, he told me. What happened to Reilly? Is he safe? Do you know?"

"Well, yes and no. If Reilly told you what he was about in Petrograd, you know how dangerous it was. Just before he and his men were set to move against the top Bolshies, and we still don't know by whom or how, they were tipped off. Reilly, true to being Reilly, managed to get out and make his way to Finland.

"That's where he got new orders from his mates at SIS to go back into Russia for some other business. He would be met by men he had worked with before."

"What happened?"

"He went back in, all right, but no one has heard one word from him since. And it's been about a year, now."

"My Lord. Is he dead? What do you make of it?"

"Dr. Watson, knowing the kind of people Reilly and I work for, my guess is that Lloyd George put the kibosh on him. He was set up. He went back in expecting to meet men he trusted, and he was disposed of. Lloyd George had to cover all his tracks. No loose ends could be left."

"Is that what happened to Holmes and young Yardley and Preston?"

"Exactly. Sir Michael happened to be at the wrong place at the wrong time and was disposable anyway. He had also found out some things Newsome didn't like and Newsome told Balfour. I am very sorry about Mr. Holmes. It was Lloyd George. But..." and he shrugged.

I sat there stunned. It was true. It was Lloyd George all the time. He was the true head of the 'Black Faction'. The swine was all the time playing both ends of the game. And that is what Holmes had finally divined.

I just could not believe that my own government could have been playing so low. Every moral precept I believed England stood for was made mockery in mere minutes. But I still had questions, and though wrung of every last ounce of strength and feeling, they had to be asked.

"Please, what about Thomas Preston?"

"Which one? The real one or the fake one?"

"Both, if you could."

"The fake one was SIS. He had been sent in at the direct request of Reilly because Reilly was a man who usually covered every foreseeable eventuality, and he couldn't take a chance on a novice gumming up the rescue attempt. It had to succeed so you all could be killed. If the real Preston was in charge, God knows what would've happened. So Reilly had some of his men kidnap the fool and hold him until he could get home on the ship that brought you all in."

"What about Arthur Thomas?"

"Another true one. He didn't know Preston, so when he got to Ekaterinburg, of course he believed Preston to be Preston. No, Thomas was on the square. Same goes for Admiral Yardley. Newsome played him for a fool as well and didn't even blink an eye when Yardley's son wound up dead. That Newsome should be shot, as well." I looked at him warily.

"Do you know anything about that German, Von Mirbach?"

"Of course, I do. That was Kolchak. He figured that by killing Von Mirbach, the Kaiser would really put the squeeze on the front, and it would make Kolchak even more important to the Allies. Kolchak was going to come back into the war if he was made Supreme Ruler, or whatever the hell he wanted to be.

"Oh, I tell you, Dr. Watson, Lloyd George had this thing figured out a million ways to Monday; or is it Sunday?"

"Another question, if you please?"

"Another brandy, if you please?"

"General Poole, was he in on any of this?"

"Nope, just following orders. Solid army man - thick."

"And please, this is the most important of all, is Holmes alive?"

"What are you talking about? He was killed on that ship,

wasn't he?"

"You are asking *me*?" I then told him about my previous visitors, and I described them to Mr. Smith.

"Yes, I think I know who they are. They are like me. They only work for one person in the end: the Prime Minister. But until this moment, Dr. Watson, I hadn't heard anything of the like you've conveyed."

"Is there no way of finding out?"

"Sure there is. I can kill one of the bastards if they don't talk. But they're like me. They won't."

"All this information you have given me this night, how have you come by it?"

"That's a funny question, doctor. You see, men such as I are always around for the men who employ us. They soon begin to think of us more as pets than people. But the very things we're needed for keeps our eyes sharp and our ears open and there is much to be learned as we stand in the shadows.

"Have you ever noticed that Dr. Watson? How if you stand in the light and look into a shadow, you can't see a thing? But if you are placed in a shadow, you can see all that goes on in the light?

"And," he paused here for a moment, "if you are able to supply succour to certain tastes, at certain levels, there is much to be learned of that which is hidden; if you know what I mean."

That was all; I had run dry. There was nothing left inside me. I looked at my inebriated friend and felt inordinately close to him. Probably because I knew that here was at least one man who held some of the values I held; although, in a twisted sort of way. He was literally risking his life to repay what he felt was a personal debt. A debt Holmes and I knew nothing about. As into his cups as he was, though, I just had to ask him this one last question.

"Please, pray tell me, in your heart of hearts, then, do you think there is absolutely any chance that Reilly or Holmes may still be alive?"

271

'Mr. Smith' put his glass down, used the arms of his chair to aid him in his quaking attempt at setting himself erect, pulled down the sides and rear of his jacket, looked down at me and said, "I really don't know. If either of the two were me or you or most of the men in England, I would say 'no'. But look at who you're asking me about. I just can't say.

"And based upon all else you've told me, Dr. Watson, I should write the trash they want and have done with them. Consider it insurance. If they do have Mr. Holmes, maybe he'll be spared. And if they don't, what have you lost?

"Give them what they want and to hell with them. Somehow, some way, I am absolutely certain you'll think of something to set the record straight without putting you and yours in jeopardy."

July 13, 1919

I then guided him to the door and he zigzagged into the street as the first touch of light competed for dominance with London's lampposts. I wonder if I shall ever see 'Mr. Smith' again. I hope I do not, though, for it would be as he said: his debt will have been paid. And he shall no longer exist for me.

Sleep, now, would be foolish and futile. I walked upstairs as if both my legs were tethered to balls and chains; bathed, which brought some vigour to me, then dressed and went back onto the streets.

The idea of reporters at this time was unconscionable, and I needed time to ponder all that had happened in two sparse days; days that for me had taken on the aspect of epochs.

I knew now that I would give Lloyd George what he wanted. I would write a truly fitting end to Holmes' career. It would satisfy the darkness from above, and with Clay, the darkness below. Although I now began to have my doubts about this man's true character.

After all my years with Holmes, it suddenly occurred to me I had let his every action colour my own. His triumphs and defeats became mine, his prejudices and likes became mine, his fears and exuberances became mine. I had, in an inextricable way, become an appendage of Sherlock Holmes; but had never truly grasped that fact until I sought to come to grips with the true, complex nature of Clay, of all people.

He could not be all bad because he was, at the moment, engaged in aiding one of his life's enemies. Either that required an inordinate amount of forgiveness, or the intellectual intensity to make such a gigantic philosophical adjustment. I suspected the latter, wished for the former, and hoped for a combination of the two. And though I do not know what will happen in the future, as I write this journal, Clay has proved a friend in shielding my Elizabeth and John, and in aiding me further in the way I shall now describe and end the detailed accounting of these past year's events.

As I walked and thought, with absolutely no idea of the direction I was going, and for how long this aimless odyssey continued I am not sure, I was finally accosted by an urchin, not unlike Billy, one of Holmes' 'Baker Street Irregulars', and asked to follow him.

I anticipated my destination, but only in general, as it seemed I was being led through every filth-strewn alleyway in London. Finally, as I had surmised, Clay's carriage awaited me in the pits of one of these alleys, and I climbed into it with antique familiarity.

"Well, Dr. Watson, this has been a busy night for you."

"I have had more tranquil."

"I hope matters have resolved themselves."

"Resolved? Yes. But only in the most perverted of ways."

"You know your family is completely safe?"

"I did not even have to ask it, did I?"

I believe those words brought what amounted to as close to a smile form those lips as one could expect. "No, no, you did not, did you? Doctor, since you have not asked my aid concerning Holmes, should I interpret it to mean you have discovered the truth?"

"I am not sure. But I caution even you to keep your distance

273

from those I have dealt with last night. The air they breathe is noxious and it is of their creation. The alleyways your boy has taken me through this morning are infinitely more fragrant."

"I see that you wrestle with weighty troubles, Dr. Watson. I wish I could be of further assistance, now that the time of my death draws near."

I would not believe it. Humour from Clay. This was indeed incredible. I nearly chuckled.

"The one last act of assistance you could provide is to determine if Sherlock Holmes is alive or dead. I now believe you are the only one to whom I can turn with sufficient means to discover the truth."

"Are you serious about this request, doctor?"

I was now drifting off as we spoke, and I believe I answered in the affirmative.

"Then for now, sleep, Dr. Watson. My carriage may be one of the last sanctuaries in London for you. Sleep and I shall give you in unconsciousness a tour of those parts of the city you would never have fathomed in a state of wakefulness."

And with those words, spoken in such a strangely calming tone, I fell into a much-needed slumber as the carriage rocked like a cradle.

When I awoke, some three hours later, Clay was gone. I was told by the driver he had departed long ago; then he handed me a note from Clay:

Dr. Watson,

Since the removal of my only challenge from my immediate environs, I have felt too listless and uncomfortable. I demand a steady diet of comparable confrontation. Without Holmes, I am not sure where I shall find this again.

To this end, I have decided to honour your last request and am now making arrangements to personally travel to Bermuda to see what I can uncover. Of course, my people here shall do what they can to learn anything that may also help solve our mystery.

Until I contact you again, you have nothing to fear. Should you need anything, you have only to speak with a Mr. Paul Frank of Denholm Street, a solicitor. He shall know who best can serve your needs. I will leave full instructions with him about you.

I anticipate this new challenge with a greater joy than I have known in many a year, doctor, and I thank you for it. Please give my warmest regards to Mrs. Watson, and to your son.

Good fortune, Dr. Watson, to us all.

It was signed, simply, 'Clay'.

I just stared down at his note, completely disbelieving, yet joyful that perhaps I should learn of Holmes' fate; although, I knew it would not be for some time.

I then thought of the odd circumstance if Clay were successful and found Holmes alive. I might make them allies in some way I had no way yet of knowing. What a boon to mankind that would be: Holmes and Clay working together.

I put the note into my pocket and asked to be taken back to my house; but as we came around and I finally saw the boisterous crowds of news hounds at my stoop, I lost heart and asked to be taken to the Diogenes Club, where I knew I would find Mycroft Holmes.

After explaining that I could not, as yet, give him full information about his only brother because the government had requested me not to, he said he would wait, and then asked which of Holmes' possessions I wanted.

I asked for one of his deerstalkers and a few of his pipes. And then I asked for the one item he had always used to destroy my serenity: his infernal fiddle. Why that item, I still do not know. Yet perhaps because of all his possessions, that was the one that married all aspects of his complex character. And discordantly at that, I might add.

Mycroft reminded me that the fiddle was a Stradivarius,

understood my choice was not for the monetary value of the item, and said he'd have them sent 'round presently. We shook hands, and I decided to go home, face the madness that engulfed my street and was sure to make me quite unpopular with my neighbours.

August 12, 1919

It has taken me the better part of a month, now, to complete this journal, and as of yet, I have had absolutely no word from Clay about Holmes. Although I have been in contact with Mr. Frank, there is nothing to report as even Mr. Frank, himself, has had no word about anything. Or so he claims; though I believe him to be telling the truth.

Reilly has not shown himself to be alive, if he is; and, as yet, there is no way I can communicate with the Imperial Family.

Admiral Yardley is on sea duty again, but he and I and Sir Thomas have spent quite a good amount of time together since I introduced them. It is as if the father without a son and the son without a father have replaced the loss with each other. They are such good men.

As for me, Elizabeth and John, we are all well, and the publication of my account of the demise of Clay, entitled "Feet of Clay", has met with success. In fact, the public is now clamouring for more of Holmes' cases as yet not chronicled. Including the account of his secret war effort which, I claim, is still secret. These stories are the only way I have of keeping my friend alive.

Oh, yes, between the last page of this journal and the rear cover, you shall find an envelope sealed by Holmes at the beginning of the Great War and given me for safekeeping. It contains his detailed deductions of what he felt would be the course of the war and, he claimed, its eventual outcome. I would open it myself, but the sight of his fowl-like scratching will only serve to upset me needlessly. And knowing Holmes, it will only be another matter in which, of course, he was correct.

I know not what the world will be like seventy-five years hence, nor even seventy-five days hence, but I pray with all my heart for my son John's sake, and for little Sidney's sake, and for all the world's children, that there is no repeat of the insanity of the Great War.

Use the information I have just given you, wisely. I know that you will.

I wish you health, happiness, prosperity and peace.

Farewell.

The New Day

As I finished my grandfather's journal, I didn't notice how night had, in its stealth, become day. I'd begun the journal at Chris Wyatt's desk and there I still sat, as if Chris had bolted me down while I read.

I closed the journal and fell back against the high, soft leather behind me. I held the envelope up to the light, a mere reflex action, I suppose, because I was afraid to open the thing. Here was a sealed envelope, written by Sherlock Holmes himself, over seventy-five years before. I would now read something lost to the world for all of that time; something even my grandfather knew nothing about.

As I opened the envelope and took out the precisely folded pages, my heart was beating as quickly as it had when I first opened the journal. And there, in Holmes' own hand, was a letter as incredible as my grandfather's words:

"My Dear Watson,

If you are reading this letter, it means I am no longer at your side. Forgive a friendly subterfuge, but as you go to speak with Mrs. Watson, right before you and I are to leave on our journey to Russia, I shall go to where you have secreted my original letter, and I will substitute this.

Upon leaving the Prime Minister's office this night, I am gripped by a feeling I cannot explain. I should like to think it is based upon my judgment of my fellow man's character, and if it is, then I hope I am woefully incorrect in this instance. However, I believe I am not.

My Friend, I believe that I shall not be permitted to live much longer than the successful completion of our task, if, in fact, it shall be successful. I have feelings of dread I have never before experienced, and I do not like the sensation. I am not referring to this ominous

278

oppression as much as I am to the idea that I am writing about a 'feeling' rather than a piece of evidence.

However, I make myself more cheery by using my interview this night with Lloyd George as all the evidence I might need. Whatever this man's true motives may be, I firmly believe he cannot permit those salient to this task's completion to remain as testimony to its very existence; although, I have no such feeling where you are concerned. Indeed, he has done all in his power to convince me not to make you part of this thing. I believe our Prime Minister's animus, at this time, to be directed solely at me. But I cannot resist what I perceive as an ultimate test.

Since I have no idea of knowing when you will be reading this, whether we shall still be at war with Germany or we shall have won it by this time, I do not want you to think I have deprived you of my original prognostications on the war; so rather than the in-detail papers I had first left, I shall make a brief outline for you:

1. The war shall be won by England and France, but only with the help of the United States, which, as of the time I had first written at the outbreak of war, was as far from becoming a belligerent as I was of sprouting wings.
2. It shall last, unfortunately, until 1918 or 1919, because the United States shall not come into the war until a late date, and then only because of overt actions by Germany.
3. By the time the United States enters the war, England and France shall have been virtually exhausted of men and money. Again, it shall be the United States that will supply both.
4. The old order in Europe, and I by no means am

referring to England, will probably be changed irredeemably. I have no true idea of what shall replace monarchy in certain nations, but am hopeful England shall serve as an example.

5.   The United States shall increasingly, after the war, play a major role in world dynamics, for it is a nation now almost free of puberty.

So there you have, albeit in abbreviated form, what I had first left in your care. If I am incorrect about any of the points, I would not mind if you keep it to yourself. Which, I know, you will.

Watson, you have a wife and child and abundant home life most men are not fortunate enough to acquire; although, my life certainly precludes such happiness. Yet I pray you cherish what you possess dearly, and though circumstances may alter what I believe will happen, I shall take this time to say my good-bye to one who has been my true friend and brother."

At the bottom was Holmes' singular scrawl.

This, coming as it did right on top of what I'd just read, left me as exhausted as my grandfather had been that second night back in London. There was too much to digest. Too much of such unbelievable nature that my mind just could not, or would not, take it all in. As my grandfather had warned, it went against everything I'd been taught; against everything everyone has been taught.

I remembered his admonition about the wrath of the world coming down on England's head; but as 'Mr. Smith' ventured, he was sure my grandfather would find some way of getting back at those responsible for the evil they had inaugurated. And now he would, even though it was so many years later. But my grandfather knew that. He didn't mind the world waiting, as long as the world finally knew. And now it does.

There were still so many questions left unanswered. So many trails left unexplored at the time my grandfather completed his journal. Those trails were left for me to explore. With the publication of this information, new facts shall have to be taught to new generations.

Now, I'd like to give you the information on some of the lesser-known figures that were central to my grandfather's journal.

Admiral Yardley continued to serve his King and Country, retired, remained a lifelong friend of my grandfather, and died right after World War II; even having offered his services again at the outset of that war.

Sir Randolph Newsome was reported drowned in an accident on a holiday in Greece. He was declared a hero and given a state funeral.

Sir Thomas Preston and Sir Arthur Thomas served their country well in long and distinguished careers.

A special place must remain for Mr. John Clay for what he did for my grandmother and father. If I was a religious man, I would find my way to a church and say a prayer for his soul. I truly believe that what he did to help my grandfather went a long way in expunging many of his former sins. There is no further record, even by the police, of any subsequent activity by Clay. He, like Holmes, vanished. But of course, my grandfather's story, "Feet of Clay" told of his death.

So the four main mysteries have not been answered by time, and as I finally left Chris' offices that morning, those four questions kept rushing around my mind like race cars out of control.

First, history says that Sidney Reilly did disappear in Russia and that he was never heard from again. But what if that was just the way he wanted it? What if he got out of Russia, found out where Tatiana and the Imperial Family had been brought, and made his way to Eleuthera? What if he contacted my grandfather and they agreed to keep his whereabouts secret?

Secondly, what happened to the Imperial Family? Did they

281

stay on Eleuthera and live out their lives there? Did Alexei and the Grand Duchesses depart after the eventual death of their parents? What happened to Tatiana and Baby Sidney? For all I know, they might have come back to London and lived near my grandfather.

Thirdly, what became of John Clay? Did he succeed in discovering if Holmes was dead or alive? And if he did, why would he not inform my grandfather? And if Clay had returned to his former way of life, why was there no further evidence of it; even as some other entity since my grandfather had told of his death?

And most important of all, what really happened to Sherlock Holmes? From everything my grandfather ever wrote about his best friend, from everything history has taught us about him, we know that his intellect was at the pinnacle of minds joining the last century to this. So, somehow, might not have Holmes, being Holmes, survived? And if he had, what happened to him? Why would he not have contacted by grandfather to make him aware that he still lived?

Judging from the note my grandfather never read, Holmes was more prescient than supposed, and perhaps he knew that his 'resurrection' might bring real death to himself and my grandfather. My ken of Sherlock Holmes is that knowing these things, he let himself be buried by the world so my grandfather could continue to live.

After all the thinking I'd done, one thing was absolutely clear: my grandfather's words had given birth to even more mysteries than the ones they had answered. I was getting a headache from it all. So I closed the journal tight with Holmes' letter back where it had rested those many years, put everything back into its paper wrapping and tucked it under my arm. I had had enough for one night.

As I left Chris' private office, I'd completely forgotten that he'd stayed there with me. He was sound asleep on the sofa in his anteroom, and I left him there. There'd be plenty of time to tell him about the journal when he was fully rested. A dulled mind couldn't even begin to grasp everything to which I'd just been made privy.

So I left my friend's office quietly, and as I stepped out into the blessing of a glorious London summer's day, I happened to notice a magnificent old Rolls Royce parked to the right of the street. I remember thinking what a beautiful old car it was.

As I passed it, though, its rear door opened and an elegant old gentleman, I guess him to be in his seventies, got out as he called my name.

I turned to him. "Yes, I'm Dr. John Watson."

The man came close. "Forgive me, doctor, I didn't mean to startle you so early in the morning and right after all you've just learned."

Now that certainly did give me a start. According to my grandfather, no one knew about what he'd written. No one. Yet here was this elderly man saying otherwise.

"What do you mean, all I've just learned?" I asked.

"Well, if you're anything like your grandfather was supposed to be, by now you should've asked yourself questions for which you have no answers.

"But not only do I know all you've just learned, I have the answers to all the questions you've now just asked."

"But how could you? No one is supposed to know about this. No one! Just who are you?"

"Oh, please forgive the lapse of a weary old man, Dr. Watson. Permit me to properly introduce myself. My name is Sidney. I'm the son of Tatiana and Reilly."

The journal almost fell from my hand, and if I weren't a physician, someone trained to know better, I would swear that my heart ceased beating and my lungs ceased breathing at the impact of those words. All I could manage was a stammer, a stutter, an incoherent attempt at verbal communication. I utterly failed. Sidney helped. He laughed.

"You heard me, doctor. I'm the baby your grandfather delivered on Eleuthera. As you see, I've long since outgrown the nappy stage." He laughed again. I followed suit, but I believe my mouth continued to hang in "O" formation like an open jam jar.

"My boy, my boy. Come, come." For a moment, it seemed as if my grandfather was standing there, comforting me and taking my arm.

"John, if I may call you that, please get into my car. I'll bring you home."

I did as I was told, and still not uttering a decipherable syllable, virtually crawled into Sidney's palace on rubber. He got in after me, bade the chauffeur drive on, shook himself comfortably into his usual seat, turned to me and sweetly said, "I'd prefer not to tell you everything now for a number of reasons. The first, we shan't have the time. The second, you've just been up all night trying to come to grips with the contents of that package you're clutching tighter than a boy would his teddy bear. You're in no state to receive the rest of the information."

I began to protest, but Sidney cut me short.

"John, please calm yourself. I'm simply going to drop you off at your home and let you sleep."

"As if that's possible now," I interjected.

"Quite. Look, I'll ring you later on in the late afternoon and we can meet again. John, while it's true there's much I can impart to you, after you've slept and regained your power of speech, I suspect, there's much that you can impart to me."

"I could run on adrenaline, but you're right," I finally said. As much as I needed to know the answers, I needed to sleep on all this.

"Just tell me this, then: did Holmes live? And if he did, did he ever come in contact with my grandfather again?" I asked.

"All right, then, the answers to those questions only. Yes, Holmes lived. And yes, he did come in contact with your grandfather again; only your grandfather didn't know it. And it was better that he did not."

As he said that, Sidney seemed to give a slight shudder as if he

284

were recalling something horribly painful or frightening. And though I desperately wanted the answers to everything, I kept to my part of our little bargain and I didn't ask any more.

I was also quickly losing energy, and was thankful as we stopped in front of my home. I shakily emerged from the Rolls with the journal still in my hands. And as I turned to say goodbye, Sidney said with a sly smile:

"Until later my boy. As they say in the nightclubs, have I got a story for you."

Phil Growick loves Sherlock Holmes, Dr. Watson, and his family.

But not necessarily in that order.

When not bemoaning the fact that he wasn't born as Holmes, he has the fun of recruiting for the top creative advertising people in the world as the Managing Director of the Howard-Sloan-Koller Group in New York City. And scuba diving.

But not necessarily in that order.

Also From MX Publishing

From one of the world's largest Sherlock Holmes publishers dozens of new novels from the top Holmes authors around the world.

www.mxpublishing.com

Including our bestselling short story collections 'Lost Stories of Sherlock Holmes' and 'The Outstanding Mysteries of Sherlock Holmes'.

New in 2012 [Novels unless stated]:

Sherlock Holmes and the Plague of Dracula
Sherlock Holmes and The Adventure of The Jacobite Rose [Play]
Sherlock Holmes and The Whitechapel Vampire
Holmes Sweet Holmes
The Detective and The Woman: A Novel of Sherlock Holmes
Sherlock Holmes Tales From The Stranger's Room
The Sherlock Holmes Who's Who
Sherlock Holmes and The Dead Boer at Scotney Castle
A Professor Reflects on Sherlock Holmes [Essay Collection]
Sherlock Holmes of The Lyme Regis Legacy
Sherlock Holmes and The Discarded Cigarette [Short Novel]
Sherlock Holmes On The Air [Radio Plays]

www.ingramcontent.com/pod-product-compliance
Lightning Source LLC
Chambersburg PA
CBHW052008020726
47501CB00004B/1051